Praise for

# PATRICIA WILSON

'Full of raw emotion'
**SUNDAY POST**

'**I was engrossed** and hanging on each and every word. This
book will leave a lasting impression . . . [and is] one that
I will find myself recommending to everyone I meet'
**REA BOOK REVIEWS**

'We race to the end with our hearts thumping . . . **Terrific stuff**'
**LOVE READING**

'A **beautiful, heartbreaking story** of sacrifice and
love in the face of evil'
**FOR THE LOVE OF BOOKS**

'Full of raw emotions, family vendettas, hidden secrets
and three very strong women'
**THAT THING SHE READS**

'The **perfect blend** of fiction with historical fact'
**SHAZ'S BOOK BLOG**

'Day by day the story unfolds . . . secrets are revealed, feuds
revisited and three generations of women reunited'
**PEOPLE'S FRIEND**

# Secrets of Santorini

# ABOUT THE AUTHOR

Patricia Wilson was born in Liverpool. She retired early to Greece, where she now lives in the village of Paradissi in Rhodes. Her interest in archaeology began when she discovered an ancient piece of pottery under her olive trees. She was inspired to write this book by seeing the four-thousand-year-old frescoes found on Santorini. Patricia's previous novels are *Island of Secrets* and *Villa of Secrets*.

www.pmwilson.net
@pmwilson_author

# Secrets of Santorini

## Patricia Wilson

ZAFFRE

First published in Great Britain in 2019 by
ZAFFRE
80–81 Wimpole St, London W1G 9RE

This is a work of fiction. Names, places, events and
incidents are either the products of the author's
imagination or used fictitiously. Any resemblance to
actual persons, living or dead, or actual
events is purely coincidental.

A CIP catalogue record for this book is
available from the British Library.

ISBN: 978–1–78576–897–2

*Also available as an ebook*

3 5 7 9 10 8 6 4 2

Typeset by IDSUK (Data Connection) Ltd
Printed and bound by Clays Ltd, Elcograf S.p.A

Zaffre is an imprint of Bonnier Books UK
www.bonnierbooks.co.uk

*For my darling grandchildren:*
*Nathan,*
*Florence,*
*Olivia.*

## Poseidon's Final Destiny

Waves that frighten

Lighthouses

Heave

And

Roll,

Turbulent

As your lovemaking

Quakes our island, Atlantis.

Mermaids' sighs of pleasure echo

Through pearly corridors in pink conch shells.

As your eruption nears, our mountain heaves and boils.

Discharge your fiery brimstone lusty God of tempest and terror

For you and your kingdom may yet drown in the depths of Thira's tears.

Patricia Wilson

A mother, and a mistress, and a friend,
A phoenix, captain, and an enemy,
A guide, a goddess, and a sovereign,
A counsellor, a traitress, and a dear.

*All's Well That Ends Well,* William Shakespeare

# PROLOGUE
# BRIDGET

*Dublin, 52 years ago.*

ODD, THE MEMORIES of a single day that stay with a child. I remember a list of things: the smell of tar filling my head like liquorice cough mixture; the fear of a smack on the legs if I got any on my clothes; the clanking road-roller and tarmac machines that left our street covered with pinkish pebbles; me and my friends poking sticks into the edges to try and get some tar while it was still soft; the dip we found at the kerb.

The day, cold and damp. Boys in home-knitted balaclavas. Girls in stripy bobble-hats and scarves crocheted from oddments of wool. Friday, because Ma would get her first wage-packet and promised a treat. A sherbet fountain, gobstoppers, liquorice wood or coltsfoot rock? Ma wore her Sunday best that morning, and lipstick, and rouge. My friends said how lovely she looked when she kissed me at the school gate. My ma's last kiss, forever on my cheek.

Ma had a job in the new McDonald's. 'Might be late getting home, Bridget. I'm meeting Da outside the factory, after work.'

Three of us – Margret, Harry, and me – played alleys at the kerb, flicking marbles into the dip. Mrs Doyle called me into her house. Told the others to run home, 'Quickly now!' She made me remove my shoes, leave them on her bright-red doorstep, then stared in despair at my greyish socks that were white last Monday. Mrs Doyle had two boys and no notion of how hard it was to keep white socks clean all week when you were eight years old. Saturday was bath, hair-wash, and clean clothes day; my socks were on their last legs.

She told me to sit on the rug in the front room, then turned the TV on. The thrill – they had colour! I watched *Wanderly Wagon*. Wait until I told Ma: posh Mrs Doyle – front room, television! We had moved up in the street hierarchy because Ma had a proper job and dressed like a film star.

Mrs Doyle's doorbell played 'Greensleeves', the button placed so high us kids couldn't reach it. People came, talked in the hall. Hushed voices. Problems, by the sound. I was hurried home. String pulled out of the letterbox with the door key tied on the end. Ma's shopping bag stuffed with my clothes. Me confused, told to wash my hands and face. Hunger gnawing my stomach.

Back at Mrs Doyle's. The six o'clock news was about to start. She rushed in and turned the TV off. In her kitchen, I ate bread and jam, real jam with strawberries in, not the mixed fruit that Ma got from the Co-op. Then Uncle Peter and Aunty Agnes came to collect me.

That night, in the strange bed, Ma didn't make me say my prayers, and Da didn't tell me a funny limerick. A bomb outside the Guinness factory had put an end to everything.

# CHAPTER 1
## BRIDGET

*Santorini, 29 years ago.*

I PLUMPED PILLOWS AND PULLED the mosquito net over our bed's four corners while recalling that magical moment on the threshold of consciousness. The dream, vivid and thrilling, lingered in my thoughts. Uncle Peter had much to answer for. His fantastic tales adapted from the works of Plato used to fill my young mind with the glory of an ancient civilisation. Ever eager to hear more each night, I let his words melt into a continuation of my dreams.

Remembering his nightly introduction to those stories of splendour made me smile.

'Close your eyes and imagine,' he would whisper dramatically. 'You, the amazing Queen Thira, rule over your ten kings and an entire nation. Beloved by your people in a happy, wealthy land where bellies are full, you can sleep in late, and nobody wants for anything. Outside your marble palace, with its roof of silver and floors of intricate mosaics, swallows duck and dive between majestic lilies. The sun shines on a landscape painted with aromatic herbs and drifts of lilac crocus. From a crystal sea, bright-eyed dolphins leap into the warm air, laughing in their clicking, effervescent way. "Hello, my Queen," they cry in rapid Morse-code before diving back into the mysterious deep.'

And me at eight years old, soaking up every word, allowing Uncle Peter's tales to wash away the reality of our humble Dublin home and my poor, dead parents. Those stories kept me alive in my darkest hours, helped me rise above the heartbreaking truth of my young life, and they ignited a passion for the classics, ancient history, and the Greeks.

While my classmates were destined to be shop workers, waitresses, nuns or nurses, *I* imagined digging deep into the Greek soil, unearthing proof of a past worthy of my uncle's chronicles of Atlantis.

I blinked the dream away, turning my attention to the morning's chores and the day ahead.

'Tommy, will you rinse the mugs before we leave?' I called through the front door. 'And close the shutters or we'll roast in here later.'

He lowered his newspaper and raised his greying eyebrows. 'My God, you're a bossy mare, Bridget! Can't a man have a blessed moment to himself?'

'I've things to do. Get a move on.'

Outside, I turned on the hose, splashed water over my bare feet, and saturated a terracotta urn that overflowed with salmon geraniums. When I soaked the warm concrete terrace, the surrounding air cooled – delicious – but I knew it wouldn't last. Enjoying the moment, I stopped and gazed out across Santorini's caldera. My dream returned, a flashback to a time drenched in opulence and drama on this island that had become our home.

The view from the patio took my breath, never ceasing to amaze me. Tommy and I were *living the dream*, as we had for almost twenty years.

A cruise ship slid towards the quaint port of Kato Fira, three hundred metres below the house. Santorini was the fashionable destination for a new breed of tourists. Wealthy cruisers arrived daily, much to the glee of shopkeepers and tradesmen. The sleek white liner left a dissipating fan of ripples in its wake. I imagined excited, middle-aged, middle-class passengers gazing at the

4

tall cliffs topped by a town of church domes, bell towers, and canvas-sailed windmills.

A sudden racket made me turn. The local donkeys, hooves clattering against the cobbles, appeared in the side road and headed for the six hundred steps down to the port. A sight the tourists adored. Many cruise-ship passengers enjoyed the cliff-climbing ride in the saddle of an unfortunate beast. Through the heat of the day, donkeys lugged overweight visitors with their cameras and guidebooks up to the town.

I caught the eye of a young jenny and fancied we shared a second of understanding. Do donkeys dream? I mused. Green pastures, shady trees, and buckets of clean water? A life of toil in the raging sun probably left them too exhausted for flights of fantasy.

The herdsman cried, 'Yah! Yah!' and swiped the animal's rump with a stinging switch. The sound took me back to a day at school when I received three cane strokes. That evening, Uncle Peter caught me crying under my bed.

'Come out from there, me little colleen,' he coaxed. 'Now tell your worried uncle what's causing those terrible tears.'

The reason for my beating was long forgotten, but I still recalled Uncle Peter's solution.

'Straighten your back and stretch your neck, regal as the queen, now. Always remember this.' He tapped the side of my head with two fingers. 'You have the good Queen Thira in there to guide you. Call on her for help whenever you need it, right? Do as she would and you'll be fine, my lovely.'

From that day on, Queen Thira was my soulmate and constant companion.

The memory made me smile.

'All done,' Tommy said, rushing out. 'Look at you standing there, away with the fairies while I slave indoors. Are you ready to go at all, or will I get another chance to read the news while you daydream?'

I grinned, loving the Dublin lilt that had never left his words despite our decades living far from the Emerald Isle. 'You can put the bikes outside the gate while I lock the door.' I gathered my auburn hair, tied it in a knot, then slipped my trainers on.

'I'll catch you up!' I called propping my bike against a lamp-post in the main street. Tommy lifted an arm as he continued down the hill and out of town.

Minutes later, with my rucksack on my back, I freewheeled after him, heading towards the archaeological site. With the breeze in my face and the sun on my back, anticipation gathered in the pit of my stomach. What would we find on this glorious morning? Would this be a day of great discovery when the archaeological site chose to reveal its secrets?

In a flash, my mind went back to the most exciting moment in our kafenio. A local described a decorated terracotta urn, found by a shepherd on the hillside. When that same pot was brought to us and we suspected it was early Minoan, we persuaded – bribed – the shepherd to show us its location. A series of events followed, leading to a carbon-dating result that confirmed our suspicions. The urn was Minoan. Six months later, two weeks after our wedding, we received official permission to dig. On that same day, we paced the barren area with a surveyor and knocked rods into the soil, marking the boundaries.

I recalled grinning stupidly as Tommy and I broke the earth together, each of us with one foot on the spade, my adorable professor staring at the ground expectantly as we lifted the first sod.

\* \* \*

'What took you so long?' Tommy asked when I arrived at the site.

'Post office.' I waved the envelope before opening it. He watched my face, then matched my grin.

'Good news then?'

'That American magazine's publishing my article!' I cried.

'What did you decide to call it in the end?'

'*The Crime of Antiquities Theft*. Look, Tommy, I've got a cheque for sixty dollars. Enough money for a a month's food.'

'Well done you!'

'God bless *Archaeology Now*,' I muttered, glancing through the accompanying letter. 'They've asked if I'll do a regular column on the same topic.' I hope they remember to send me a copy, I'm dying to see it in print. I slid my arms around Tommy's waist. 'I couldn't have done it without you.'

'Of course you could.'

I shook my head. 'Nobody was taking my essays seriously until you recommended me to that magazine editor, Tommy. Thank you for that.' I slipped the cheque into my purse.

'Nothing to do with me or God, darling girl. You've earned your reputation, and I'm proud of you. Anyway, you've freelanced for long enough; it's time someone recognised your expertise. Let's celebrate with a jug of plonk and a chicken *gyro* for supper. My treat.'

'Spoiling me again, Tommy?' I kissed his smiling mouth. 'I should start another article this evening, but one day won't make any difference, so yes, let's celebrate.'

'Right, better get some work done then!' He pecked me on the cheek, then hurried away.

\* \* \*

Later that morning, the July heat shimmered off every flat surface. A cricket chirruped somewhere on the rubble walls, sounding like my bicycle freewheeling downhill. Under a dusty canvas awning that shaded the trestle and tea corner, I pieced together a small pottery jug. An ache in my lower back forced me to stop and stretch. I scratched the prickling sweat from my neck. Clay gunk under my fingernails reminded me of an ancient potter's hands working at the wheel.

Who had thrown the little jug? The exquisite object had a slender handle and delicate spout, a symmetrical body with fine images of birds and flowers painted onto its belly. Had that artisan also roasted under the Santorini sun? Perhaps the vessel had once held milk, olive oil, fruit juice or wine. Or perhaps rich almond oil to massage into the golden skin of aristocracy.

I imagined a bare-breasted maiden with long black hair, kneading the muscular back of a victorious sea captain who had returned from the wars with Libya.

The site lay silent, holding its secrets close. I sensed our dusty, abandoned city had seen so much and was withholding that knowledge from Tommy and I, until the earth felt we were ready for its fantastic revelations.

We had dug deep and sifted hard for years, loving our Santorini adventure as much as each other. Despite uncovering an ancient metropolis buried in thirty metres of volcanic pumice, to date we hadn't found a fragment of what the public would regard as treasure. The prehistoric capital appeared far advanced of anything else in the country. However, we suspected that before the island erupted, the population had left with their treasures.

Shortly before midday, Tommy rushed forward and thrust his cupped hands towards me. 'Look at this!' he cried, making me jump.

My skin tingled to hear such exhilaration in his voice. 'What is it?' I stared at the mound of dust and grit he held out.

'It's broken, but it appears to be jewellery. Dare I hope we've found an adornment from antiquity and not a modern retro trinket.' He lowered the dirt to the table and drew his hands apart. 'We won't know for sure until we've cleaned and analysed it, but I feel hopeful!'

We pulled up chairs, peered and speculated.

'I think it's silver,' Tommy said, poking the pieces of filigree metal towards each other. 'The shapes . . . they appear to be in pairs, see?'

'Wait.' I grabbed the empty envelope from *Archaeology Now* and pulled on a pair of latex gloves. 'Best not touch it.' I picked out the larger pieces of fine tracery and placed them on the white paper.

Tommy nodded, pulling gloves on himself. I tore my gaze from his, concentrated on the bits of metal and fished more fragments out of the dust. Our heads met above the table. Tommy was breathing hard.

'They remind me of seed pods from a maple tree,' he said.

'Me too! The helicopter ones.' I grinned at the pieces, drinking in the delicate artwork. If it wasn't ancient, it was certainly more exquisite than anything else we had discovered. Then I found a different shape. 'What's this? What's this?!'

Surely, he had discovered something of incredible historical value. Could this be the very moment we had dreamed about on that day when we first broke the earth together?

'Holy God, Tommy, I can't believe we might have found something metal after so many urns and animal bones.' My throat tightened, and for some inexplicable reason my tears were rising. 'I love you so much,' I whispered.

He looked up, our faces only inches apart, his clear grey eyes sparkling. 'Don't get too excited, we don't know anything yet. There's a chance it might be nothing at all.' Nevertheless, he beamed with excitement and planted a firm kiss on my lips before returning his attention to the dirt.

I nudged a snaking piece of silver towards two of the wings. 'It's an insect, do you think? Perhaps a butterfly?'

'No, the wings are too narrow. Here's a smaller pair; they graduate. It could be a necklace.'

'I think . . .' I slid the small wings next to the larger ones and added the simple curving piece. 'I've got it, Tommy! It's a dragonfly!'

'Bravo, I believe you're right!' He pressed his hands against his cheeks and stared at the tabletop.

'Where was it?'

'B3, behind the altar. I found it in the broken base of an urn, which is almost definitely early Minoan. There're more shattered pots there too.' He glanced at the cluttered trestle. 'You're going to be busy.'

I flung my arms around his neck as he straightened. 'You're amazing, Doctor McGuire.'

'I've always known it,' he quipped. I sensed his desperation to get back to the trench.

'Yes? Well, return to work, you lazy good-for-nothing,' I ordered. 'You've got half an hour before lunch. Find more jewellery while I put this dirt through the fine sieve.'

With a grin and a nod, he rushed back into the maze of rubble walls.

* * *

Pleased with the morning's work, I straightened and rubbed my back again. Although in pieces, the dragonfly necklace appeared to be complete. I stared at it for a moment before slipping it into the envelope that my cheque had arrived in. After lunch, I would measure, photograph, record, and report the find.

'Tommy! Come and have a sandwich, it's time for a break.' I splashed water over my face and rinsed my arms and hands at the standpipe sink. Although desperate to see what else he'd discovered, I stuck to our policy of not interrupting each other while working. I pulled a plastic lunch box from my holdall and shouted again. 'Egg mayo and crisps – your favourite, Tommy!'

For our lunch break, we always used two folding chairs and a makeshift table, which was once a wooden cable reel, set in the shadiest corner of the site. Bottles of frozen water, packed that morning, had chilled our lunch and almost defrosted. Gulping cool water in the noon-day heat was one of life's simple pleasures, but now all I could think about was the relic Tommy had found.

Our fellow archaeologists – four boisterous Irish students – were away on a trip to the ancient site at Ephesus in Turkey. Tommy and I always enjoyed working alone.

Where was he? Our lunch would soon spoil in the heat. 'Tommy!' I walked around the deserted buildings that were last inhabited four thousand years ago. A city of secrets we had yet to uncover.

'Tommy McGuire, lunch is on the table! What's keeping you?'

The walls absorbed my words. I stopped to listen but the site was silent.

Around the next building, I found my husband.

Tommy lay on his back, slumped in a corner, eyes wide and pleading as he clutched his left arm.

'My heart,' he gasped, barely audible. 'Help me.'

# CHAPTER 2
## IRINI

*Dublin, present day.*

I HAVE TO ESCAPE! My watch stopped at 9.15 a.m. and I feared I was stuck in a time warp with twenty fidgeting six-year-olds. The long morning, exacerbated by a fire drill and Layla's cat being run over before school, had tested my patience.

'Any questions, class?' The lovable munchkins, restless for lunch, need their sugar-fix.

'Is Chairman Meow in heaven, miss?' Layla asked.

I nodded, smiled, and glanced at the clock while trying to block the memory of Jason, last night's yelling, tears, and anger, from my mind. Like Layla's cat, it was all over with no possibility of going back. Layla's lips curled and she stared out of the window. Feeling her sadness, I struggled to bury my own broken heart.

Ryan Flynn shoved his hand in the air. 'My mam says God made the sea and the earth and everything. Is that true, Miss McGuire?'

'Many religions claim God made everything, Ryan.' I reminded myself that 2B were too young to be subversive, yet I sensed a tricky question.

'Please, miss, if God makes all the dogs and cats and cows and people . . . where does He get all the meat? And, miss, you know the trees, where does the wood come from?'

'Ideas, anyone?' Could I stall until the lunch bell?

Tiffany O'Leary, class know-it-all, pistoned her hand. 'Miss, miss, miss!'

'Go on, Tiffany.'

'eBay, miss. My da's a builder and he gets everything off the internet. It's cheaper but delivery can be ... extortionate.' She nodded emphatically, then frowned. 'What does extortionate mean, miss?'

There was a knock on the classroom door and secretary Mrs Cut-Above O'Kelly entered. All eyes fixed on the grey M&S suit, white tailored blouse, and heavy gold jewellery.

My pupils stood and chanted, 'Good morning, Mrs O'Kelly,' and I was proud.

'Good morning, class. Sit down, put your hands on your heads, and no talking.' She turned, glanced disapprovingly over my latest outfit – a retro dress of Laura Ashley fabric, with puff sleeves and a dirndl skirt. The creation had pleased me immensely but, under her glare, my clothes felt shabby and homemade. She seemed to sense my disappointment and her brittleness softened. 'Sorry to interrupt.' She swallowed, squinted around the room, then returned her attention to me. 'Reverend Mother wants to see you. I'll stand in for ten minutes.'

My end of term reports were *almost* finished, it had been a difficult week and I had spent too many evenings crying, sewing to take my mind off things, avoiding anything to do with school, including fellow teacher Jason.

I faced the children. 'I want to hear good things when I come back, class. Don't let me down. Ryan, you can ask your question to Mrs O'Kelly.'

In the corridor, I reached for the office door handle, my nerves tingling like static. After a calming breath, I entered Reverend Mother's office.

Mother Superior looked up from her desk. 'Take a seat, Irini.' Her eyes were also restless, then they settled on me and she sighed. 'I'm sorry, Irini, it's bad news.'

*I'm going to lose my job . . . Redundancy?* Perhaps this was the push I needed to break away from the school. The truth is, I never really wanted to be a teacher. I loved the children, but longed for a greater challenge.

As if reading my mind, she shook her head and said, 'It's about your family.'

'Oh . . . not my father? But the doctor said it was just the flu, he was improving.' I hadn't seen Dad for a couple of days.

'No, they haven't told Mr McGuire yet. The home received a call from Greece yesterday and Matron telephoned me this morning. They couldn't get hold of you.'

'Ah, my phone's turned off. My fiancé . . . we broke up.' I went to twist my engagement ring but it was not on my finger. She glanced at my hands, which I separated, quickly pressing the palms against my knees.

'I see,' she said. 'Sorry to hear it, Irini. Matron thinks *you* should break the news to your father. You see, it's about your mother, God save her soul.' She stared at the desktop while the comment sank in.

*My mother, God save her soul . . . Oh!*

Reverend Mother was talking. Words seemed to float between us and I could not catch what was being said. The room smelled of soap powder, which didn't make sense. Dust motes danced in a shaft of light that splayed through the window. Time hung. I forgot to breathe then gasped suddenly, startling us both.

'Sorry, sorry, can you repeat . . . I didn't . . .'

Reverend Mother blinked at me, then her words rushed out with disrespectful speed. 'A serious accident, Irini, at the archaeological site yesterday. I regret to say that your mother is critical. She's peaceful, in intensive care. I'm terribly sorry, but they don't think she will survive.'

She reached across the desk and took my hand. I stared at it, blinked, almost cringed with awkwardness. Sensing my discomfort, she let go and withdrew. Then she spoke slowly, her words full of concern. 'The incident happened suddenly, Irini. They said she didn't suffer. Our thoughts and prayers are with you both.'

I should have felt something – panic, emotion, tears – but all that came was a great negative void. I hadn't seen my mother since she turned up in Dublin with my father a year ago. She left a week later. He was home for good; silicosis made breathing, and even walking, difficult for him. My mother returned to her precious archaeological site in Santorini, claiming if she stayed in Ireland another day she would go stark staring mad.

For some reason, on hearing that my mother was dying, I had a horrible, *horrible* feeling it was my fault.

Reverend Mother broke the silence. 'I've got a Greek number.' She handed me a fluorescent Post-it note. 'Sign off for today, Irini, and come back in September. There's less than a week to the holidays. Is there anything I can do?'

I shook my head, stuttered, 'Thank you,' as I stood and turned away.

'Oh, while I remember,' she said awkwardly.

I reached for the door handle, eager to leave the room.

'Sorry, Irini, but the end of term reports?'

\* \* \*

After a restless night of weird dreams that lingered like the smell of burned toast in my kitchen, I sat at the breakfast bar with a thumping head and a mug of sweet tea. July had been the worst month ever. My wedding – cancelled; Dad so ill he couldn't stay on his own; and now my mother dying on a Greek island. This was not how life should be. I needed time with my mother; we hardly knew each other.

I must fly to Greece. The Archaeological Association offered to take care of everything in Santorini, and promised to keep me informed of my mother's condition. 'Little hope,' they said, preparing me for the worst news on my arrival. I told them I would get a flight ASAP.

If only we had been closer, Mam and I, but in truth, a normal mother–daughter relationship had never existed. I don't think Bridget McGuire had a maternal bone in her body. My helplessness and regret were not exactly for my mother, but for what might have been. Perhaps her distance was my fault? The room went cold. I glanced around, wondering if she'd gone – perhaps her soul loitered in the corners of my kitchen, listening to my thoughts. I ignored her, as she had done me through most of my childhood. Then, ashamed of thinking such an awful, bitter, thing, I muttered, 'Sorry, Mam.'

Money was a problem. All my savings had gone on driving lessons and non-refundable wedding deposits. Even my credit card was maxed-out because of a new wardrobe and a few home comforts for my Dad when he moved into residential care. Also, I splashed out on a high-tech smartphone for us both. The gifts for my father were not simple generosity, they were driven by guilt, because when I say *moved into residential care,* I mean I actually forced him to go.

I had tried, and I cried, and I begged social services for more help. In the end, I admitted that I couldn't cope with the incontinence, poor health, and dangerous forgetfulness of my father. It wasn't fair on either of us. Dad wasn't getting the care he

17

needed. While I worked, I constantly fretted about him all alone in my little house in Sitric Road.

Yesterday afternoon, I went to the care home and gave my father the awful news about Mam. The recent bout of flu had taken its toll, making him appear more fragile than usual.

'Poor Bridget.' Too upset to say more, he stared out of the window, tears creeping down his deeply lined face. I sat next to him and took his hand. He squeezed tightly before letting go, rather like our relationship.

'Dad, Mam was doing exactly what she loved, what she's done all her life, the very thing that brought you two together,' I told him. 'They say she didn't know anything about it. A wall toppled and knocked her unconscious immediately. She hasn't suffered any pain at all.' I took his hand again. 'They've induced a coma. They say there's a small chance her brain might repair itself, but it's unlikely.'

'Small? How small?'

I stared at the floor. 'Very slight, almost none, but despite her age she's very strong and fit.' Was it cruel to give him hope when they implied there wasn't any? My heart went through the shredder. 'Miracles do happen, and she's a fighter, Daddy. Some people . . . against all odds . . .'

'I know,' he said, patting my hand.

I longed for them to love me, and I wanted to love them, but we had all lived our lives in a kind of mysterious limbo. We were only together for a week after my father came back. Days filled with tension and aggravation. My parents bickered from dawn till dusk. I knew they didn't want to be dependent on me. They both missed the outdoor life, the sunshine of Greece, and their archaeology – and also space from each other.

18

From them, I had wanted explanations, affection, and despite a youth spent coveting the closeness of other families, I found myself desperate for some privacy in my own home. The overcrowding situation eased when my mother returned to Greece, but despite Daddy's continual grumbling, I knew he missed her.

'Perhaps *they* did it,' he muttered. 'She should've let me die, then everyone would be safe.'

His words stung me. 'What? Who did what, Dad? Why should you die? What are you talking about?'

My seventy-five-year-old father shook his head, his face pale and stony. 'Leave it, Irini. I can't talk about it now, not with Bridget at death's door.' His lips trembled. 'Will I ever see her again?' He sucked on his inhaler. 'It should be *me* on my death-bed, not your poor mother.' His damp eyes met mine, then he turned away. 'I miss her.'

My heart rolled over. Why couldn't we be a normal, happy family? Why couldn't we talk things through? They couldn't even talk to each other civilly. There was so much I didn't understand about my parents and, try as I did, I could never get them to open up.

'What do you mean, *it should have been you*? It shouldn't be anybody at all, Dad! You're just feeling a bit rough after the flu. It's knocked you back hard. She'll understand you're not up to travelling yet. Give it another week and you'll feel much better.'

He dragged a crumpled hankie over his face. My father was fifteen years older than my mother. Professor Thomas McGuire was Bridget Gallagher's tutor at university, where they shared an obsession for Minoan archaeology. According to my Uncle Quinlan, it was a real love story. A fascination for ancient history consumed them both, sucking them into the vacuum of over-powering love for each other. I like to believe that in the heat of that fiery romance, they abandoned university and ran away to Santorini on a quest to find Atlantis. In truth, I don't know a lot about my parents' past.

'Don't go, Irini,' Dad said. 'I can't, I'm not well enough to travel right now. Let the Archaeological Association take care of things. Poor Bridget has no clue what's going on. By the sounds of it she probably won't wake up, and there's nothing we can do to change that.' Although I heard a ring of bitterness in his words, his voice was also heavy with sadness. His eyes flicked to mine, then away. 'What if I'm not here when you get back, you know?'

*Oh!*

'I can't not go, Dad. You'll be fine for a week – you're much better already. She's my mother, and if the worst happens, I can't let her die all alone. I'd never forgive myself.' I glanced into his eyes, saw the grief that was suffocating him, and the struggle to hold on to his pride as his tears rose again. Why? They seemed to hate each other a year ago, yet here he was trying to hide so much inner pain.

'She's not alone, not at all. What's his name . . . Aaron, that's it, he'll do what needs to be done. He's like a son to her, been there since before you were born, Irini. We're powerless in the great scheme of things, you have to accept it.' Dad's battle with grief made his voice hard. I felt his devastation and wanted to hug him, take away some of his pain. When his eyes met mine, I sensed he felt the same way towards me, yet still, that big old wall stood between us. The inability to open up isolated us both.

*He's like a son to her? Why couldn't I be like a daughter to her?*

I sighed, still not understanding what happened between them when my mother left us in Dublin and returned to Santorini a year ago.

Quinlan had told me that my parents had married in the Catholic cathedral in Fira, Santorini's capital. Later, I was born there and they named me after the island, Santorini, Saint Irini, due to the miracle of my survival. Reluctant to breathe, they said. Dad claimed I had the luck of the Irish. Mam, a staunch Catholic, said it was down to my guardian angel.

At the age of five, I was brought to Ireland and boarding school at the Dublin convent. I always wondered why they sent me away, and last year, when they returned to Dublin, I asked Mam that very question.

'Look, Santorini's a small island. There's no choice of schools so to speak, you just get the one that's there.' She glanced at Dad who turned his eyes to the ceiling and shrugged.

As usual, I was excluded from their telepathic communication.

'We didn't want *you* missing out on a good education, like some others I could mention, Irini,' Dad said, squinting at Mam.

'*I* had the best, Tommy McGuire,' Mam said quietly.

For a split second, a glint flashed from his eye. I wasn't sure if it was anger or joy; then he scowled and returned to his newspaper.

I hadn't wanted a good education; I wanted a family.

'She should never have gone back to Santorini!' my father cried, breaking my thoughts. 'She's brought this on herself, it's her own fault and we're left to pick up the pieces again!'

'That's a terrible thing to say! You should be ashamed.' What did he mean, *again*? I stood, annoyed, but as I looked down at my father, I saw his tears rise. A deep sob shuddered through his body.

'Why did you do it, Bridget? Why? Now look what's happened. I wasn't worth it, darling girl!' he cried.

'Oh, Dad!' What was this thing that tortured him?

Through my childhood, there was little contact between us. My parents were always strangers to me and I felt nervous and shy in their company. I withdrew into myself whenever they returned to Dublin. Over the years, I had letters from my mother, which I kept but rarely answered. They came to visit at Christmas, and I remember the occasional phone call, stilted and awkward, along with birthday gifts given to me by Uncle Quinlan.

My father calmed down and remained silent with his thoughts.

After a while I kissed his cheek and said, 'I love you, Dad. Try not to worry too much. I'll phone you every day.'

'If you must go, be careful. There are bad people out there.' He paused, then looked straight at me. 'Are you quite sure this was an accident?'

'Of course it was an accident – who would want to hurt her?'

His brow furrowed and he glared at nothing, perhaps recalling a painful memory. After a moment he said, 'I'm not happy about you going through all this on your own. Can't that young man of yours keep you company?'

'Ah, I wanted to tell you.' I sighed. 'We split up. The wedding's off.'

His eyes met mine again, but this time they softened. 'Then it wasn't meant to be, Irini, love. Better to find out now than later.'

I wondered if he referred to his own marriage.

\* \* \*

22

The kitchen phone rang.

'Don't hang up!' Jason, my two-timing fiancé – ex-fiancé. 'I've just heard about your mother, Irini. I'm really sorry. Is there anything I can do? Shall I come by this evening, help with the arrangements?'

I wanted to yell: 'She's not dead yet, you lying, cheating bag of shit!' but my heart shattered. I had an enormous feeling of loss, and loneliness, and abandonment – not for the first time in my life. Grief rushed through me and I broke into tears that seem trivial compared to my painful emotions.

After a moment, I tanked my feelings, steadied my voice and said, 'Thanks, but no thanks,' and hung up. The call was kind of him. Remnants of Jason's love still lingered in the cracks and crevices of my heart.

Hemmed in by four walls, I grabbed my mug and escaped to a garden bench in the backyard. Met by a dull, damp morning, I tugged my dressing gown closer, but the cold seemed to come from inside me rather than the weather. I could hear the build-up of traffic, a pneumatic drill, children going to school, and a cat mewling at my feet. Tinker, from next door, jumped into my lap. I stroked him, wishing the pain in my heart would ease.

A picture of my mother in intensive care gathered in my mind. Tubes and graphs and lights blipping. Stiff white sheets, silence, the smell of disinfectant, and an empty chair waiting for me at her bedside.

When the travel agent's opened, I planned a walk into town to get a flight organised. I had tried to do it online but couldn't concentrate and ended up drinking half a bottle of wine, something I hardly ever do because I suffer more than most after drinking alcohol. I woke at midnight with my head on the kitchen table and my laptop battery flat. Pathetic.

If I sold my beautiful solitaire engagement ring, the money would buy a flight and leave enough cash to deal with my responsibilities. I glanced around, absently searching for direction.

A single bright yellow dandelion poked from between grey cement slabs. The high wall enclosing the yard was a flaking abstract of crumbling brickwork and white paint, topped by broken glass. It was bin day; I needed to haul my wheelie through the terraced house and onto the front pavement.

Storm clouds, as grey as my miserable soul, threatened rain. Uncle Quinlan and my parents were the only family I had. Like many Irish Catholics, the rest of my relations had emigrated to Australia, years ago. I never really knew them.

I still had to tell dear Quinlan the bad news.

Fat raindrops plopped onto the flagstones. As I plucked the dandelion, tossed it into the bin, and returned to my empty kitchen, I recalled last Wednesday evening when my hopes and dreams were smashed.

When I caught Jason kissing one of the bar staff from Donahue's pub, he admitted to an affair. Devastated, I cancelled everything I could for our wedding, which should have taken place next month. Kohl-eyed Calla, all chick-lit and cheap clothes, had won the day and my man.

\* \* \*

I marched into the family jeweller's near Grafton Street and plonked my small blue ring box on their counter. My smile bright, but my heart breaking. I'd worn black, it seemed appropriate.

'Hi, my boyfriend and I bought this a year ago but ... well, I guess you know how it goes. I wondered if you would buy it back?'

Shortly, ringless but rich, and with tears dangerously close, I passed a travel agency. The words 'Crete' and 'Last Minute Bargain' caught my eye. Perhaps they had a late deal for Santorini? I stepped inside. I had been too exhausted to properly look for flights online the night before. They seemed few and far between and horribly expensive.

'Sorry, fully booked for the next two weeks,' the woman said cheerfully. 'Peak season.'

'What? No flights! What am I going to do?'

'We've got the final seats to Crete. It's only sixty-something miles from Santorini and there's a fast ferry that runs every day. You could go on a day trip while you're on holiday in Crete.'

'No, you don't understand. It's not a holiday.' I found myself telling the travel agent about my mother and almost breaking down in the process. Her sunshine smile clouded over.

'Let's see what I can do.' Her long nails clacked on the keyboard, then she spoke to an on-line colleague using words like 'emergency' and 'death in the family'. Back on the keyboard, she worked in silence, her eyes flicking up to meet mine now and again.

Eventually, she nodded. 'Right, here's the best solution. You fly to the island of Crete tomorrow afternoon, arrive at eight in the evening. Transfer to the last internal flight for Santorini, leaving at nine. Your accommodation in Crete's included, so you can go back to it whenever you want in that fortnight. You'll have to collect your luggage at Crete, so with only an hour between flights, it's tight.'

# CHAPTER 3
## BRIDGET

*Santorini, 29 years ago.*

THREE DAYS AFTER FINDING my darling Tommy in the grip of a coronary, I returned to Santorini and the archaeological site. The egg mayo sandwiches had gone – mice and birds, I guess – the bottles lay warm and bloated on the ground. Tommy remained in hospital on the island of Crete, awaiting further tests. For the first time since running away together, we were apart. I glanced at the sky and crossed myself.

*Please God, don't take my Tommy yet. He's a good man and I love the bones of him. He's all I have.*

Defeated, and as low as I'd ever been, I realised the archaeological site was nothing but dust and ruins without the man I loved. We had travelled this adventure together, abandoning work, family, and friends in our search for proof that Santorini was Atlantis. The Atlantis that captured Plato's imagination hundreds of years after its disappearance. The magnificent and wealthy island that the Egyptians traded with and wrote about in their hieroglyphics.

Sniffing and swiping at tears, I stared around at four thousand square metres of light brown pumice and a maze of old stone walls. The magic had gone. Perhaps the site had always been that way, but with Tommy near, the place held the enchanted air of myths and legends.

Awash with tiredness, I up-righted a chair in our lunch corner and fell into it. I had hardly eaten in days. After being flown to the Heraklion hospital, doctors had bombarded me with information about Tommy's heart. His condition was serious.

Staring into the distance, I went cold thinking about what would have happened if I hadn't felt those pangs of hunger and gone looking for my husband. Just as well we hadn't managed to start a family yet. I might not have been at the site if there had been children to care for.

We both longed for the day I could tell Tommy we had a baby on the way, but it never happened. Over time, my monthly disenchantment faded into reluctant acceptance. Pregnancy could still happen, of course, but it seemed unlikely after so long.

We had little in the way of savings. Like my parents, our emergency fund was a gold wristwatch that came from my grandmother. When I was a child, that watch had been in and out of our Dublin pawn shop more times than I cared to remember. Thank goodness Ma had not worn it on the day the bomb went off. That awful day when I became an orphan and moved in with Uncle Peter, Aunty Agnes, and their five freckle-faced sons.

'Hello! Is anyone here?'

The man's voice made me jump. Our four archaeology students appeared from between the ruins.

'Ah, Bridget, why so glum?' Aaron, leader of the student group, lumbered towards me. 'We're back, you'll be pleased to know, and a grand time was had by all. Ephesus is awesome.'

'Hi, guys.' I forced a smile.

'Where's Tommy? Skiving again?' Aaron glanced around excitedly. 'Tell us what's new, Bridget. Did you find remarkable things while we were away?'

Unable to think of anything but Tommy, I shook my head, then dropped it into my hands and wept.

'Oh no, Bridget . . .' Aaron sat in Tommy's chair and put his arm around my shaking shoulders. 'What's the matter? What's happened?'

I shook my head again, then nodded at the youth whose good humour and enthusiasm for ancient history inspired us all. 'It's Tommy – he's had a heart attack. It's serious, Aaron, and I'm completely lost in it all.'

'Poor you. Come on, dry your eyes. Look, I've got a hire car for a couple of days, let's lock your bike in here and I'll take you home.' Even at the age of twenty, Aaron showed the steady dependability that leaders are made of. 'Can I take you for something to eat? You look as though you need a good meal.'

'Very kind, but I need to be near the phone in case there are any changes in Tommy's condition.' I would be glad to have Aaron there when I re-wound the answerphone. I dreaded listening to the messages on my own.

He stared at the ground and nodded. 'Right, then we'll pick something up on the way back.'

*　*　*

Night had fallen by the time I started a third beer on the patio. I found myself telling Aaron things I had never recounted before, and with the telling a weight lifted from me.

'How did you and Tommy meet?' he asked, sensing my need to talk.

I smiled, remembering myself as a love-struck student. 'I got myself lost on my first day at college and wandered into the sports hall. Tommy was playing ping-pong with the wall.' I paused.

It seemed like yesterday. 'He asked if I wanted a game. My God, he was so handsome I blushed like hell and told him I'd never played before.' Recalling the moment made my face heat up again. I placed a hand on my cheek and laughed. '"Good!" Tommy said. "This means you might be my very first win," and with that he handed me a paddle and beat me straight down the line.'

'That's Tommy for you, competitive to the end.'

'Do you think so? I've never thought that. I was a poor orphaned kid, and felt I had no right to be in a grand university with all those wealthy and intelligent people. I was nervous, tired, and oh so lonely. I had a job with a cleaning company, vacuuming banks and offices before dawn, and a weekend job stacking supermarket shelves, all to help pay for books and clothes and a little housekeeping money for Aunty Agnes too.'

'Must have been tough.'

'It was, to be sure, but it didn't occur to me at the time. I was driven by necessity. The next day I started my course, and Dr Tommy McGuire was the tutor. He was the youngest tutor at the university and he had a relaxed aura about him, like he knew he was bordering on genius. I hung on to his every word, but he was a git and picked on me all the time. Like many new, wide-eyed university kids, I had an instant crush on the professor. This made me desperate to impress him with my work. People said that part of my infatuation was because I longed for a father figure. You see, my parents had been killed ten years earlier. The troubles, you know?'

Aaron gave me a sympathetic look. 'Before my time, Bridget, but I vaguely remember them from school, of course.'

I nodded and sipped my beer. 'Tommy avoided me like the plague, but for me, it was love at first sight. Poor Tommy resisted my advances for almost four years.'

'A man of steel, our Tommy, then?' He sat back, grinning at me.

I smiled. 'I guess starry-eyed students were an occupational hazard. Anyway, I persisted, and joined the ping-pong club – so square, hardly any other students joined, but I had to be near him. I couldn't cope. Life without him wasn't worth living. Things got worse when I told my aunt and uncle the reason for my love-sick misery. They were horrified!'

'Because you'd fallen in love with your tutor, or because he was that much older than you?'

'Well, that as well, but mostly because he was a Protestant. You see, it was a Protestant bomb that killed my mother and father.'

'That must have been difficult for them to accept.'

'You're not wrong. Though the seventies was an era of ban the bomb and fight for equality for women in Britain, the fact was, Ireland remained way behind the times. In those days women were not allowed to buy any form of birth control and it was against the law for a woman to refuse to have sex with her husband – can you belive that? We Irish women were second-class citizens and the only thing the seventies did for us was make us realise it.'

Aaron blinked at me, taking it all in and clearly speechless for a moment. 'I didn't realise it was *that* bad.'

I nodded. 'I was expected to put all this archaeology nonsense out of my head and become a history and geography teacher. Everyone would have been proud. Naturally, I was supposed to find a nice Catholic boy, marry, give up work and have lots of nice little Catholic children.'

'Of course you were.' He laughed. 'They didn't know you very well then?'

'They did their best, God love them, but with their five boys I was an oddity that they cherished. They did love me very much, I don't doubt it, but I wanted to spread my wings and fly to my professor. Tommy persuaded me to take a year out. He got me a placement on an archaeological site in England. Now I look back, I suspect he thought I would meet a suitable boy my own age and fall in love.

'For a year, everyone was pacified, apart from me. When I returned to Dublin for my finals, I knew Professor Tommy McGuire was the only man I wanted to share my life with. Three months later, we were secretly seeing each other. Six months later, we were saving for our wedding. But then we were found out. In those days, having a relationship with a student was totally unacceptable. This resulted in Tommy resigning so that I could finish my studies.'

'No way! Wow! What an amazing sacrifice.'

I nodded. 'It was indeed. Tommy sent me a letter telling me to get my degree, then I could join him in Greece if I still wanted.'

'And did you?'

'Sort of, but that's another story.'

*　*　*

Talking to Aaron had helped me come to terms with the situation. When he had gone, I dragged an old suitcase from under the bed and delved beneath musty cable-knits and heavy jeans, stored for ten months of the year. At first, I couldn't find the metal box, but then my fingertips touched the tin that had once contained Oxo cubes. When I lifted the lid, a distinct smell of salt and malt brought back childhood memories. Steaming hot drinks on cold nights, intricate ice patterns on the insides of my Dublin bedroom window, and my mother's voice.

'Are you cold, child? Here, get this drink inside you and I'll put the coats on your bed. Warm you up, it will. Have you said your prayers?'

I had shaken my head. 'The lino's cold on my knees, Ma. It makes them hurt, it does.'

'Now come on, be a good girl.'

Shivering in my pink flannelette nighty, I kneeled at my bedside, joined my hands and said:

*'Gentle Jesus, meek and mild, look upon this little child.*
*Make me humble as thou art, with thy love inflame my heart.*
*God bless Mammy and Daddy and everyone who knows*
    *me. Amen.'*

Then I scrambled back into bed, pulled the covers tight around my neck and waited for Da. I forced my tired eyes open when I heard the stairs creaking.

'Will you tell me a limerick or a jingle, Da?' I preferred his rhymes to Ma's prayers, and there was a kind of mischievous conspiracy between me and my father.

'Close your eyes then.' And I would, knowing he smiled down on me.

*'If I had a penny, do you know what I would do?*
*I'd buy a rope and hang the pope,*
*And let King Billy through.*
*'Cause if the pope were dead, sure everyone does know,*
*Me little Bridget would be spared, the pain of cold lino.'*

We giggled together, then the scrape of his red beard and his good-night kiss on my cheek.

I had loved my father so very much.

From the Oxo tin, I pulled out my mother's pink plastic rosary beads that had come from Lourdes, and an envelope containing my birth, baptism, and wedding certificates. I unfolded a yellowing page from the *Irish Times*, neatly wrapped around my grandmother's gold watch. The inheritance that was sure to give my darling husband more time on this earth.

Exhausted by the day's events, I lay on the bed and thought about my life with Tommy, united in our quest to find Atlantis. I closed my eyes and allowed one memory to lead to another.

Only in my dreams had I seen the place we searched for, and in those visions, it was I myself that ruled utopia. That seed had grown from a variation of Plato's stories, as told to me with grand embellishments by Uncle Peter. Later, crazily in love with my professor, I still imagined myself as ruler of Atlantis. Omnipotent, and loved by the populous, this queen dedicated her life to the peaceful and happy existence of her subjects. As a hobby, I continued to research Greek legends that told of the fearless queen who led her people in war against Libya, and in peace on her island of Atlantis.

Possibly my own desire for a daughter had transferred itself into my dreams of Queen Thira, Goddess of the Marches, Supreme Ruler of Atlantis, and her beautiful red-haired child, Oia.

I drifted in the borderland of sleep, my thoughts leading me back in time to 1500 BC. The worry about Tommy must have carried over into my dream that night because, for the first time, I had a strong feeling of foreboding.

\* \* \*

33

I, Queen Thira, stand alone on the palace terrace, moments before dawn. I pluck a sprig of night-scented jasmine and hold it to my nose, hoping its heady perfume will block the malevolence in the air from entering my mind. If only my anxiety would fade with the night. I touch the sacred necklace at my throat. A row of dragonflies that represent transition, prosperity and justice, and symbolise an understanding of the deepest meanings of life that they say are only realised at the moment of death.

'Gaia, mother of all, help us in our hour of need,' I whisper. 'I am committed to keeping my people safe and I'll do anything, give anything, to ensure that outcome.'

A sliver of dawn light cracks open a divide between the sea and sky as Helios, the Sun God, awakes. What catastrophe will this day bring? We have not experienced an earth tremor since the last moon-cycle, yet every day I fear another shake.

If the earthquakes continue, and the mountain awakes, my people will suffer a terrible end.

I cry over the water, 'Poseidon, Great God of the Sea, leave us in peace!'

The sky pales from grey to pink. Droplets of night rain bead the silver-green olive leaves and purple iris with dawn's jewellery. The earth is quenched after a hot, dusty season. Bamboo stands motionless in the groves. Feathery fronds that sparkle with dew top the sturdy canes like giant candles lit in homage to me, Supreme Ruler of this land.

Perhaps the earthquakes are over and the great mountain will sleep, will not kill every living soul, will not destroy Atlantis.

Poseidon answers my thoughts with a seismic boom that forces me to clasp my hands over my ears. The noise thunders from below the earth and roars across the land. Not a bird in the sky nor a dog barking. I spin around and stare at the distant mountain.

The world holds its breath. Then the earth shivers beneath my feet. Is this the beginning of the end? The ground shifts and shakes. Ripe dates rain down like bronze hail from tall Egyptian palms in the palace garden. Gold leaf and marble dust float on the air as cracks snap open in ornate columns around the terrace. A distant vineyard, lush with grapevines, slides down the hillside like dirt off a shovel. Clouds of earth billow in its wake, leaving a wide, clean scar of pale rock. I turn to the sea. A mountainous swell is heading for shore. Foam roars into the air before waves crash along the coastline in a thunderous round of applause.

I imagine Poseidon's smile as he takes a bow in the fathoms. Everything shifts. The ground ripples and heaves. My heart bangs against my ribs and my heavily embroidered robe swirls around my body like flimsy gauze.

Atlantis undulates, lifting then lowering me as if it changed its mind. I fear the ground will rent apart and take me down to Hades' domain. I see that very thing happen to a row of ancient olive trees. Sturdy limbs snap into splinters, leaves fly in the air, and the grove is swallowed whole as the earth's crust rips open like a grinning, toothless mouth.

Suddenly, the earth stills. Bamboo stands motionless and the sea calms.

My beautiful daughter, Oia, comes running onto the terrace, her red hair flying behind her. The girl flings her arms around my waist.

'My Queen!'

I hold her for a moment before she steps back and bows.

'Forgive me, your highness, I was concerned.'

'It's over now, Oia.' I stroke her silken locks, a constant reminder of her father's unique red hair. 'Go back to your chamber. It's too early and you need your sleep, child.' I watch her leave, then return to my own bed, close my eyes, and contemplate the day ahead.

\* \* \*

The soft light of Santorini filtered through cracks in the shutters as dawn broke. I wandered outside, sat on the patio wall, and stared across the caldera. Perhaps because I was alone, with Tommy in hospital, I recalled every detail of my vivid dream and decided to write it down while it was fresh in my head. Queen Thira was a wonderful leader who always seemed to do the right thing. I drew comfort from that. If I modelled myself on this strong, wise woman, I too could surmount all problems.

# CHAPTER 4
## IRINI

*Seat 11A, somewhere over Europe, present day.*

I stared out of the aeroplane window. White billowing clouds were rimmed with gold, reminding me of my cancelled wedding. My ring was back in the shop, and my wedding dress had pride of place on my Facebook fashion page: *Rags to Riches – exclusive designs by Irini McGuire*. That gorgeous gown was the most beautiful thing I had ever produced.

The slinky, Gatsby-influenced dress of heavy white lace over cross-cut silver satin could have come straight out of a silent movie. A scooped, off-the-shoulder neckline topped the body-hugging front, while a dangerously low-cut back flowed out into a long cathedral-train. As I walked, the dress flowed like liquid mercury. Conscious that the congregation would be looking at the back more than the front, I had fastened the gown with two hundred white pearls that ran from below my shoulder blades to the spill of the train's hemline. I slid my thumb across my fingertips, remembering the blisters and the pain – and with the last few pearls, the blood that I feared would stain my fabulous frock. My wounds had healed, but would my heart? Soon, my wonderful wedding dress would be cherished by another, a bride-to-be with no notion of the blood, sweat and tears that had gone into its creation.

I had a massive price tag on the dress, mostly because I didn't want to sell. An image of Miss Havisham came to mind.

Me, an old woman draped in cobwebs, still in my wedding gown awaiting the man of my dreams.

Mam's last words played on a loop in my mind. We had stood on my doorstep after a week of disgruntlement. Her suitcases were already in the airport cab. Divided by awkwardness, neither of us could find the right things to say.

She reached behind her neck and unclasped her little gold crucifix. 'I'd like you to have this.' She fastened it around my neck. 'It's not worth anything, only nine carat, but it's my confirmation cross from Uncle Peter and Aunty Agnes, and I value it highly.' She smiled sadly, then gave me a hug. I recalled the toilet soap scent of her skin, and how badly I didn't want her to go.

'I'm very proud of you, Irini.' She placed her hand on my cheek for a second. 'I've left that piece of pottery for your father to work on. I'm getting nowhere with the symbols and it'll give him something to do. Make sure he doesn't lose it, will you?'

I nodded. 'I wish you could stay. There're so many things I want to ask you, but we never seem able to talk. I'm sorry I've been . . . well, you know.'

'It's been a difficult week for us all. Let's put it behind us and when I come back, we can start afresh.'

*She was coming back?* My heart lifted. We would have another chance to sort things out. I would be nicer. Before I could stop myself, I took her in my arms and squeezed hard.

'I'm so glad you're coming back. Honestly, I wanted it to work so badly. I'm truly sorry, Mam.'

She stepped out of my embrace, took me by the shoulders and sighed, the tomato soup we had for lunch still fresh on her breath. Her green eyes, sad for a moment, reflected my own heartbreak.

'Nothing to be sorry about; it's not your fault, Irini. I'm the one who should apologise, landing on you the way we did. I wish with all my heart things had been different, but I can't help who I am. It's impossible for me to fall into the devoted wife and parent role after all these years. There are reasons – things I have to put right – and I can't explain them yet, but I will soon.'

She bit her lip, glanced at the sky, and I sensed she was calling on God for guidance. 'I'd tell you, Irini, but part of me's just too ashamed. It's like a penance. I'll put these things right, once and for all, then I'll explain everything. I know it's hard, but I respect you and your father enough not to pretend.' Shivering, she rubbed her arms, her slim figure stiff with tension. 'It's so *cold* here.' She glanced at the sky again and turned her mouth down, yet I sensed her deep excitement at returning to Greece.

'I do love you, Irini. You must always believe that because it's the truth. I know I haven't been much of a mother.' She tilted her head to one side and placed her hand on my cheek again. 'It's as if I've no control over my destiny. I *had* to marry your father, I *had* to save his life, and I *had* to keep you safe, no matter what the cost.'

What was she saying? I found myself lost in the enormity of her words and before I could string a question together Mam shook her head and shrugged, appearing as perplexed as I felt. 'I guess it's God's plan,' she said. 'Though I don't understand where it's leading. It's out of my hands. No threats, or promises, or family ties can keep me away from Greece and the archaeology. It's bigger than me, Irini, and the pull of it grows stronger each day. I simply have to return and sort things out.' She looked over my shoulder and lowered her voice. 'Anyway, Tommy will be happier with me out of the way. Poor man.' She pushed my red hair away and kissed my cheeks. 'I know you'll take good care of your father. Thank you for that.' Her face crumpled, and my heart ached as I realised she was fighting to keep her emotions in check. 'Goodbye, darling,' she managed to whisper.

She took one step back and looked at me, as if taking a mental photo. Shocked to see tears well in her eyes, I had a fierce urge to pull her back inside and lock the door. She seemed so lost and alone.

My mind was screaming: *Stay! Stay and love me and I'll be anything you want me to be!*

We hugged stiffly, our guards up, bottling our emotions. I was reminded of a hug filled with passion and pain from long ago, my very first childhood memory. Mam had snatched me up and held me so tight it hurt. I cried and so did she, kissing my wet face and saying 'sorry' over and over. I can never quite recall what it was about.

After that last embrace on my Dublin doorstep, Bridget McGuire turned swiftly, got into the taxi and waved through the window. Tears spilled down her face, then she was gone from my life.

With that memory came the weirdest feeling that somehow, we both knew we might never meet again.

*Let me be wrong!*

Could I have said or done something to make her stay? To make her want me near her? To make her love me with the unconditional love of a mother? I wanted to fold my arms and stamp my foot with the shallow resentment of a spoiled child. *It's not fair!* Yet I knew if I had found the power to keep her in Dublin, something inside Bridget McGuire would have died. I wouldn't want that because, underneath my regret for all that had happened, I did love my mother very deeply.

\* \* \*

40

I woke with a start. Why was this journey taking so long? A three-hour delay in Dublin and now we appeared to be making no progress. I had to get to my mother, and my constant recollections seemed to slow everything down. The cabin staff wheeled a trolley down the aisle. My chicken salad and a pudding of flaky pastry filled with nuts and honey was passed to me. Why didn't the food smell of anything?

Although I tried to block thoughts of the past, while I ate I recalled Santorini. When I was fourteen, Uncle Quinlan had taken me to visit my parents. That dense cobalt sky, crystal turquoise water and the unbearably hot black-sand beaches. A town of sizzling colours and pristine white walls. Windmills with canvas sails reaching the ground, blue-domed churches, tiered bell towers resembling ornate wedding cakes and, above all, the warm sunlight on my bare shoulders.

That fortnight was a rare occasion, the four of us together. A real family. I wished so hard it could stay that way.

The scene returned with startling clarity. My parents' compact, traditional house slotted into a jigsaw of similar buildings on the high cliff face. A cube of tangerine stucco with arched royal-blue shutters and door. A terracotta urn that overflowed with salmon geraniums on the patio. The terrace looked out over Santorini's caldera, which was almost a complete circle. The inside of the island, a thirty-two-kilometre skirt of steep rock around flat water. From this high waistband, the land flounced down to the sea on the outer perimeter. Centred in the shimmering caldera, the black lava of Burnt Island stared unblinkingly at a sky the colour of glazed Greek pottery.

Only the largest cruise ships had an anchor chain long enough to secure them in the endless depths of the caldera. They appeared toy-like from my high viewpoint. The vessels glided

41

into the circle of calm sea and then the shuttle boats ferried two thousand guests to the quaint fishing port. From my parents' patio, I had watched donkeys plod wearily under the weight of camera-waving passengers, ascending the three-hundred-metre cliff. Then they trotted back down for another fare.

Many tourists were lifted by cable cars, while a surprising number of brave souls decided to walk, bare shoulders burning before they reached the top. The trek up six hundred steps led them to the postcard-picturesque town of Fira, teetering on the edge of the caldera. From a distance, the closely knitted buildings resembled a white towel carelessly flung over a rich-brown balcony rail.

I recalled sitting on my parents' patio, talking to Quinlan while my mother and father were at work.

'You're telling me we're *actually* on the rim of a volcano, Uncle Quinlan?'

'Absolutely. Look around – all you see is an enormous mountain peak that once stood in the centre of a huge and wealthy island.' His eyes twinkled in his pale, effeminate face, and his bow tie twitched as he talked. 'This volcano was easily the largest eruption ever known. Several historians say that before it exploded, this very island was at the centre of Atlantis.'

'Atlantis? Wow! Is that why Mammy and Daddy are so obsessed with the place?'

He nodded, a tendril of sandy hair falling over his forehead. 'It is indeed, Irini. They're looking for clues to prove that very thing.' He raked back a wayward curl and flashed a wide smile, eager to offer snippets of information that thrilled, making me want to know more.

Far below the plane, the sea appeared crumpled and silver in the light of a full moon. I had to face it, I would not get to

42

Santorini and my mother's bedside as planned. The connecting flight had long gone. The captain apologised again for the delay at Dublin. He reminded us of the local time: 11 p.m.

I wanted to knock on the cockpit door and complain. My mother was dying, my journey urgent, yet time stood still.

We descended into Heraklion airport on the island of Crete. What if Mam died before I got to Santorini? In the whole scheme of things, it made no difference when that moment came. Yet it mattered to me, and I knew it would matter to my Dad too. I had to be there.

*Wait for me, Mam! Allow me to hold your hand once more.*

I recalled that flight to Santorini with Uncle Quinlan, excited to re-visit my birthplace and my parents. This time I was alone and tense. Once again, I searched my memory for clues as to why I received that crushing hug from my mother so long ago, and why she packed me off to Dublin. Could the two incidents be connected?

The cabin lights dimmed and the crew strapped themselves in. Thank God we were landing! I closed my eyes and concentrated on my breathing. When I looked out again, the sea was so close I could see every wave. The water drew me, while at the same time repulsing me. I imagined crashing into it. Palpitations hammered at my ribs. I glanced around the cabin and wondered how you got out of a plane under water, wishing I had paid more attention to the emergency drill. At the last moment, runway lights fled past the window and a clunk, bump, screech, and roar told me we were safe on the ground. I unclenched my fists.

Passengers traipsed through passport control. Like a sheep, I followed. My head woolly, and my body light, as if my feet were not quite on the ground. Eventually, I stood by the luggage carousel in my red cotton jersey dress that had been so simple to make. A tube of calf-length fabric that clung to my body and moved with me. I fancied the rolled boat-neck and long, hugging sleeves looked sophisticated, yet the dress was also quite comfy for travelling.

The airport could have been anywhere in the world. It smelled of bleach and coffee, and noises echoed. I found the scrap of paper with the hospital's number, called them, and explained about the flight. I would be there tomorrow, and how was my mother? No change. Such was my relief, I felt my body relax and realised how tense I'd been. My eyes were hot with held-back tears. I closed them for a moment and pinched my nose, but when I looked up, Dad's old suitcase had passed out of reach.

'My bag, the brown one!'

'I've got it,' a manly voice called from crowd ahead.

I rounded the jostling passengers and found a tall, slim, bearded man wearing well-worn clothes that gave him a comfortable look. He had my bag. I didn't know why my heart started racing, perhaps subconsciously, I thought he was going to steal it.

'Thanks. I thought I'd lost it for a moment. Half asleep.' I stiffened my jaw to stifle a yawn.

His eyebrows bunched and his smile, which was slightly mocking, transformed his face into a thing of beauty. 'It would come around again . . . It's your first flight?'

'More or less.' Our eyes met and, bang, my heartrate went into overdrive again.

He laughed. 'Wait, here's mine.' He hefted a bulging rucksack onto his trolley and threw me another grin. 'Just one case?' His accent was heavy and rounded, as if he had chocolate in his mouth. I guessed he was Greek.

'Yes, thanks. You were wonderful, being so quick and all.'

'Where's your trolley?'

I shrugged. 'I've my daft head on today; things on my mind. You know?'

The frown and smile reappeared and I blinked at him stupidly. A 'Jason' spark rose inside me. That flutter of excitement and an instinct to step closer. This man had the most beautiful eyes, accentuated by his hirsute face. Then, recent heartbreak flashed across my mind, vivid as a danger sign. Feeling tired and vulnerable, I looked away.

He lifted my case onto his trolley and we walked towards the exit. 'Someone is meeting you?' he asked, breaking the silence between us.

'No, I've a coach transfer to Agios Nikolaos.' Like the travel agent, I pronounced it, Eye-oss Niko-loss.

'Then I will leave you the trolley.' He slung the rucksack onto his back.

I grabbed the trolley but it swung right. I tugged hard and cringed when a wheel rolled over his foot. We both stared at a grey dust-and-chewing-gum stripe that ran over his blatantly expensive shoe, the only opulent thing about him.

'Oh lord, sorry, I'm such a catastrophe!'

He stared at his shoe, then at me. 'Enjoy your stay,' he said, before heading towards the car park.

I took a few steps towards my coach and then turned to watch the stranger. He stopped, bent slightly to examine his shoe, then looked my way.

I hurried onto the bus.

\* \* \*

I finally arrived at the Cretan hotel too tired to do anything but fall into bed.

The next morning, after phoning the hospital and hearing there was no change, I rushed down the Hotel Mediterranean's black granite staircase and headed for the restaurant. Everything in the hotel was new and shiny, and I thought about my mother and her dusty life in the Santorini dirt.

At a table on the restaurant's balcony, I attacked my breakfast-buffet selection but, after a few mouthfuls, my appetite disappeared. I felt guilty for almost enjoying it, and then guilty for leaving it. My mother was dying. The thought, those words, made the food in my mouth taste stale. I was grieving for her already, and wasn't that stupid? Perhaps there was a chance, the smallest possibility, that she might recover? I held my own hand and imagined it was hers. I could give her strength, and I would. Thank God she hadn't passed away in the night. A great feeling of emptiness and regret filled me. Why didn't I visit her in the last school holidays? Inconvenience, fear of rejection, lack of funds? I couldn't come up with an honest answer. I had the power to heal a rift between us and I did nothing but sulk and feel sorry for myself. It was too late to start beating myself up for never visiting.

I stared across the sea and imagined the coffin lid being closed on my mother. The fear that I wouldn't get there for her – for me – gripped me. An age of regrets, the broken link in life's chain letter, an unfinished dispute that could never be resolved, unspoken words left to hang in the ether for eternity.

I had to get to her bedside and tell her I loved her.

The beautiful view drew me away from my heavy heart. I soaked it up, hoping it would help me understand my mother, and the reason she needed to be in this country. I guessed the travel agent's poster had been over-Photoshopped, but the sky really was saturated blue, the sea an iridescent turquoise with a gloss that defied belief. I turned my back on it and took a selfie for my dad. Some photos to look over later would help us both to talk, because I knew I was not always going to feel as dismal as I did today. It was no good regretting the past, I had to learn from it, move on, and hope it was not too late to take a step closer to my father.

But it was no easy task to get over the hurt of my mother dismissing me from her passion. I understood that Greece and archaeology were her passion, and I understood about having such dedication – I felt that way about designing clothes – but my appetite for *haute couture* would never get in the way of my relationship with the people I loved, and certainly never come between me and my child. I did appreciate she loved me, and in her own way she cared, but knowing that did not lessen the pain or make sense of my past.

So much was lost. But as an adult I should have made an effort to bridge the gap between us. Why didn't I try to understand more in the week she was with me, rather than avoid my parents' strained relationship and dream of having my own space back? I'd been selfish and had no right to lay all the blame for our estrangement on my mother. If I could turn back time . . .

My father and I were never close, but perhaps deep down he yearned for my affection just as desperately as I longed for my mother's. This concept had never occurred to me before. Although I took care of Dad as best I could, it was in an insular way, never allowing my feelings to surface.

The dutiful daughter saying the right words.

I had lost Jason after being together for two years and the hurt was awful. Plagued by sleepless nights, I wondered what was wrong with me. Hating him. Hating myself. Going over precious moments and wondering why they couldn't last. Telling myself he didn't deserve me. Fearing I wasn't good enough. I started to realise how Dad must have felt after Mam's leaving. They had spent decades together.

My father always kept his emotions to himself, seldom laughing, or getting angry. Had he lain on the other side of my bedroom wall at night staring at the ceiling, wondering if it was his fault that Mam left; his poor old heart in bits? The young adventurous man with dreams of finding Atlantis, the crazy professor who ran away with his beautiful student, he was still in there somewhere.

I had to find the Tommy of old and bring his lost soul back to remember that happiness.

# CHAPTER 5
## BRIDGET

*Santorini, 29 years ago.*

TWO DAYS LATER, I was back at Tommy's bedside in Crete. I had a pillow and sheet, and Tommy's shaving things. I planned to sleep in the chair next to his bed.

'You'll have to get yourself better, Tommy McGuire. I can't be doing with all this back and forth!'

He gave me a weak smile. His pallid skin and dull eyes broke my heart. I made a terrible job of shaving him. Thank God he couldn't see the state of his chin. I felt myself blush when the surgeon entered the room, stopped in his tracks and stared disbelievingly at my husband's chewed stubble.

'Mrs McGuire,' he said in English, his eyes wide as he turned to face me. 'I'd like to speak with you . . . when you've finished here.'

I exchanged a glance with Tommy, gave his hand a gentle squeeze, then nodded at the doctor. Brought up to revere the dedication of medical practitioners, priests, and nuns, I had complete faith in the cardiologist's skills.

In his office, I glanced at the surgeon's white, scrubbed hands and imagined them delicately holding a scalpel to slit open human flesh. I could almost feel the slippery internal organs through his thin, latex gloves, and see his mask pulsing like a heartbeat over his mouth with each breath. I sensed his daily determination to drag someone back from the valley of death. A tournament with God for the life of his patient.

Through the lonely, dark hours of night I had pestered Our Lord repeatedly, begging Him to spare the life of my darling husband. Thumping myself in the chest, I promised to give anything, do any penance, but God must *not* take my Tommy. A worrying memory of Rumpelstiltskin stories came to mind, which I dismissed immediately.

I stared across the desk at the specialist, Splotskey. Not a Greek, perhaps Russian. The cold eyes and twitchy mannerisms of this sharp-faced man with collar-length hair made me nervous.

A hundred thousand drachmas, about two hundred Irish pounds, were tucked away in an envelope at the bottom of my handbag. All I had received for selling my grandmother's watch, even though I thought it was worth much more.

'Thank you for seeing me,' I said, shaking his slender, long-fingered hand. Should I simply pass the money over?

Splotskey nodded. 'Your husband needs open-heart surgery, Mrs McGuire. I'm sorry to be indelicate, but the procedure is expensive and I understand you don't have insurance. I need to know that you are able to raise funds for the operation.'

'Please, call me Bridget.' I dived into my bag, retrieved the envelope, and slid it across the desk towards him. 'There's a hundred thousand drachmas to start with.'

Splotskey's eyes never left my face. 'Bridget, even if there are no irregularities, in the end, you may need ten times that amount.'

I stared at the envelope, fear and shame heating my face. 'Don't worry, I'll find it.'

The air seemed to leave the room. Where could I get that sort of money?! Splotskey was talking about the surgery, his face bright, his voice enthusiastic, but all I could think about was the cash. My own heart thumped and a strange buzzing sounded in my ears. I forced myself back to the present and concentrated on the surgeon.

'If all goes well, Mr McGuire will be back on his feet in a week.'

'A week! Goodness. If all goes well . . . ? You mean there might be problems?'

'No, no, but surgery always involves some risk.'

I shivered, cold with fear. Nothing was more important than Tommy's life, but now I realised that his life came with a price-tag.

* * *

Back in Tommy's room, I did my best to draw us both away from the current situation.

'I was telling Aaron how we met. Quite a story, really, now I look back.'

'Not something I'm particularly proud of, enticing a young girl away from her studies.' The words were dragged out, the effort and Tommy's fatigue both apparent. Nevertheless, I rejoiced to hear his caustic sense of humour returning.

'Nonsense! You taught me more than I'd have learned if I'd stayed in Dublin. Besides, I was – and still am – in love with you. Remember when I turned up in Santorini, you were furious and made me continue with my thesis? You said I had to prove the Island of Atlas, Plato's Atlantis, was more than a fictitious place, and that Plato only used the bare bones of the story to make a philosophical point.'

An old twinkle, which brought joy to my heart, returned to Tommy's eyes. 'An impossible task?'

'Perhaps, you old git, but I was determined to see it through. I've still got that dissertation, and you know what? When I have the money, I'm going to do an OU course and submit it.'

'I'm proud of you, darling girl. But talking of money ...' His voice trailed away and he closed his eyes for a moment.

'Don't change the subject. I'm telling you now that three times Plato's cousin, Critias, claimed the stories of Atlantis were true.'

Tommy fell silent, his mouth a familiar determined line, set for battle, but I would not be put off and continued.

'Critias said he heard the story of Atlantis from his great-grandfather, Dropides, who in turn heard them from the remarkable truth-teller and law-maker, Solon.'

Tommy's smile twitched. He opened one eye, shut it again and tested me. 'And where did Solon get this tale from?'

'Solon himself heard it during a trip to Egypt.'

'You're hanging this whole tale on Solon? Very weak, Bridget. I'm disappointed.'

'Wait, I haven't finished. Crator, the scholar, went to Egypt to check Solon's facts and, on his return, claimed the story was based on real events.'

'Rubbish! Plato's timeline and location were complete *bollix*. Explain that, my darling girl.'

'Plato was writing a fable, a lesson to be learned through fiction. He claimed Atlantis existed nine thousand years earlier, but at that time, we were just coming together in the first Neolithic settlements. So, we know the timeline was wrong, probably for dramatic effect. He exaggerated the location too, making it more mysterious. These discrepancies can be attributed to poetic licence on Plato's part.'

Tommy's smile widened, then he straightened his face. 'You haven't convinced me at all. Check your timeline, expand your argument, and come back with something more plausible, miss.'

I laughed. 'My God, just like the old days. You really were hard on me, Tommy.'

'Mm, I guess I was.' Above dark circles, his eyes narrowed mischievously.

* * *

I returned to Santorini that evening, glad to lay on my own bed, but sleep was held back by my memories of Tommy and his teaching in those early days. 'Prove it!' he would yell jubilantly, knowing I couldn't. Then I would research some more, eager to go back at him with my theories. 'Rubbish! Don't quote Plato to me. The man was a liar. He wrote fiction, and fiction is lies from cover to cover. Give me facts, Bridget Gallagher! Give me proof!'

'But my Uncle Peter claimed—'

'Bah to Uncle Peter too. The man clearly thought you were a mushroom. Kept you in the dark and fed you bullshit!'

'What about Solon? He went to Egypt—'

'Don't give me words! Words are misinterpreted and numbers are fudged! Show me evidence of canals that ran in concentric circles. Show me solid evidence of the Queen Goddess that ruled the island. Show me an artefact that binds the story together!' he would yell, smirking with glee, loving the debate, himself believing that one day we *would* find that proof.

The thrill, and the hope, sparked inside us every day that we went down to the site. That very day might be the one when we found a vital link. Something that verified that Plato's Queen Goddess, ruler of Atlantis, really existed. An artefact that connected the story, the mythology, with fact. We dreamed of unearthing the all-important relic, proof positive that Tommy and I dug in the dirt of Atlantis. An artefact that demonstrated beyond doubt that we were right all along. The saffron gatherers, the smelters of orichalcum, the ship builders who invented the anchor and lived in the shadow of a volcano so enormous, it wiped out their island domain. Perhaps with that proof, we would also find clues as to where they went.

Memories of those debates also brought me deep sadness. Tommy had loved the lectern. He ranted at students, fired up debates, bullied and cajoled in a good-humoured way. Teaching was his lifeblood and he missed it terribly. He gave up university so that I could finish my degree, and I hadn't – not yet, anyway.

Uncle Peter, God bless him, knew somebody at the college and managed to send books and papers out so I could continue my studies. I worked hard, eager to prove I wasn't simply an irresponsible runaway.

Despite Tommy's disparaging words about Uncle Peter's stories, I had grown up with the legend of Queen Thira, Supreme Ruler of Atlantis. Without Thira to guide me, I, timid Bridget, would not have developed and had the courage to rule the archaeological site. I learned to speak to the students with authority, and I lost my shyness.

If ever I was unsure of myself, I still closed my eyes for a moment and imagined myself as the noble ruler of Atlantis. Thira would fill me, stiffen my backbone, lift my chin. I stood taller, dealt with authorities head-on, and demanded self-discipline and good timekeeping from the young scholars. In return, I knew I was highly respected.

I turned on my side and pulled Tommy's pillow towards me. The scent of him – dusty, musky, and masculine – reminded me of those early days when I would fall asleep with my head on his chest and his arms around me. He would stare at the ceiling with a lost look on his face and sometimes I wondered if it was regret.

My life was an exciting adventure. Everything thrilled me, and I was completely in love. Now I look back, I suspect Tommy was worried out of his mind.

Eventually, I fell into a sleep filled with dreams of the distant past, Atlantis and its queen. My mind needed a distraction from current problems. The moment I woke, I sat on the patio and wrote in what I had decided to call my *Book of Dreams*, recalling the details of my fascinating flight into antiquity.

I suspected I could learn something important from my night-time fantasies. Pleased that the necklace Tommy had unearthed on the day of his heart attack had once again appeared in my vision, I reminded myself I still had to clean, record, measure, and photograph it, then register the find. However, for the next half an hour, I was content to sit quietly and document the lucid experiences of my sleeping hours.

*　*　*

My attendants bathe me, dress me in silks, wax and coil my raven hair. Then they place the sacred dragonfly necklace around my neck and heavy gold rings through my earlobes. When I am satisfied with my appearance, I enter the great temple of Poseidon.

'Lord God of the Sea, why do you frighten my people? Has your watery kingdom become dull and jaded? Do your nymphs no longer excite you?'

Standing on his gold chariot, drawn by six winged horses, Poseidon is represented by a magnificent bronze. He stares ahead, following the line of his outstretched arm. Balanced in his other hand, the immense golden trident is pulled back in aim. The figure is both awesome and terrifying, this God that holds our destiny, but I am bold in his presence, feeling his disdain for weakness.

'Great Lord of the Seas, stop this aggravation.' With a mixture of awe and fear, I gaze at the gigantic figure about to hurl his three-pronged spear.

I touch the sacred necklace at my throat. Dragonflies, born from the water to fly free as the air, like mankind at the beginning of time; like every baby emerging from the womb. The spirit of life for all things emanates from water.

The towering doors of the council chambers are opened to reveal the assembly. My ten kings await. They stand until I take the throne, then all but one sits. A broad-shouldered man with a silver beard.

Since my husband's death ten years ago, Hero, one of the ten kings who serve me, has taken his place as speaker for the council. He is my closest friend, and like a father to Oia.

'King Hero, you have the damage report?'

He bows slightly. 'Revered Goddess, the canals are breaking. Poseidon destroys our waterways. The pillars in the grand palace have cracked. I'm afraid the next tremor will bring the roof down.'

'Instruct the stonemason to cut new columns of granite.'

Hero bows again. 'How can we appease Poseidon, my Queen?'

Our eyes meet. 'We shall offer fresh virgins' blood on the altar, and decorate his temple with orichalcum and silver.'

I turn to the next king.

'Dear Goddess, the mountain shakes. The earth's hot on the slopes and our vineyards are failing. Without wine, our people will become sick. The beasts are restless and their behaviour strange. I fear Poseidon's turned the animals against us.'

'I agree. My first concern is for the safety of our subjects.'
I stand tall. 'Therefore, I have decided to evacuate Atlantis.'

A sharp intake of breath is followed by silence. The kings
stare at each other.

I address Hero again. 'Send an envoy to Crete. Take a vessel of
gifts to King Minos for his temple at Knossos. Tell him we come
in peace. Ask permission to store our treasures and people on
his island until our homeland is tranquil once more.'

'And if he says no?'

'Then we go to war, sir.'

\* \* \*

As the Santorini sun gained strength, I quickly finished writing and then placed the *Book of Dreams* on my bedside table.
Spurred on by Queen Thira's bold statement – that she would
save her people from certain death – I knew what I had to do
for my Tommy. The day would be dedicated to fundraising for
his surgery.

# CHAPTER 6
## IRINI

*Crete, present day.*

THROUGHOUT TEACHER TRAINING, I had promised myself a proper vacation the moment I earned a suitable wage. Although years had passed since I started at Saint Mary's, the opportunity to flee to warmer climes never arose. Jason's love of motorbike racing meant holidays were spent traipsing across the country from one meet to another. Then I had my father to look after.

\* \* \*

I refused to sit around playing host to misery. A hire car, a drive to the city, and a ferry to Santorini would hopefully get me to my mother's side by the end of the day. My dad's old suitcase lay unopened on the spare hotel bed. I should wear something strong and vibrant for my mother. I dived in and pulled out my latest creation.

A pair of shorts, made from stressed, charity-shop jeans, appliquéd with heavy white lace and a few pearls left over from my wedding dress. The top had also come from the Marie Curie shop. A fluorescent pink (great with my red hair) extra-large tee. I'd cut the neck into an off-the-shoulder boat, chopped off the sleeves, and split the sides to bring them around and tie in front. Love it or leave it! Clothes had the power to lift my spirits, especially my own designs.

At reception, I shoved my wild hair behind my ears and produced my driving licence.

'It's brand new,' I said, determined to dwell on the positive. 'Passed my test first time.'

She glanced up from the forms and smiled. 'Well done, Miss McGuire.'

I wished my mother had said as much, been proud of me.

*Oh, for God's sake!*

Time to face a few facts. The reason my mother never congratulated me was because I never bothered to tell her I was taking lessons. I could have written, emailed, texted, phoned. When I thought about my behaviour, I didn't exactly make her life pleasant while she stayed with me. The truth was, my conduct had been quite unacceptable. I missed my evenings in front of the TV with Jason, objected to cleaning my father's toothpaste out of the washbasin, and was irritated by my mother's underwear drying on the radiators.

Petty stuff. I can't imagine how my parents must have felt giving up their dream in Santorini for such a confined existence with their intolerant daughter. I'm sure they realised I wasn't thrilled about them moving in. But the truth is, at first I *was* ecstatic.

Filled with longing, I desperately wanted us to bond and be loving towards one another. It felt like everything I'd ever wanted at last – the three of us together. I hoped to hear stories of their romantic adventure, of star-filled nights on an exotic island. So often, I dreamed of them sharing their lives with me. Days of wide smiles and hugs, joyful conversation and laughter.

In fact, our lives were a parody of that ideal. My parents barely tolerated each other. They sniped and snarled from morning until night. I wondered why they lived together when they could hardly stand the sight of each other.

A long list of minutiae gathered to aggravate us all. I could have been nice, and I did try, but there was no escape from the atmosphere in the house. The week dragged. Too much time was spent apologising to each other, and trying not to get under each other's feet.

There were mixed feelings – relief and sorrow – when my mother abandoned us for Santorini a week later.

I picked up the Fiat Panda's keys and towered over a good-looking Greek, who led me to the vehicle. Outside the air-conditioned hotel, a warm breeze welcomed me. Yellow umbrellas mushroomed around the pool, and below them tanned bodies soaked up the sun.

I was shown the indicators, reverse gear, and lights. The car smelled of lavender polish, and the scent reminded me of my father stuck in the home. I felt bad about leaving him alone, poor thing, but what was the alternative? I opened the windows and the memory of his misery was replaced by fresh air. This was my first proper break from Dublin, so despite the terrible circumstances, I was not going to carry excess baggage. I needed to leave my problems behind, gather my strength, and focus on my mother. The trip felt more urgent by the minute.

Most women my age would nurse a hangover on a sunbed all day and party all night, but my alabaster skin and low tolerance to alcohol meant that, even in happier times, this would not be an option. Besides, I was not very good at making new friends. As for the pool, an incident that took place when I was seven left me terrified of water.

Uncle Quinlan had taken me for a picnic on the riverbank. I went to paddle on the sandbar while he read. The outgoing tide swept me off a sandbank into the Liffey estuary. In an instant, the memories of those horrible, desperate moments returned. Frantically attempting to doggy-paddle up to the water's surface. The seabed sloping away below me. An outgoing riptide pushing me further and further away from safety. The blurry, sand-speckled water sucking me down again, and again, and again.

I remembered seeing an old bicycle on the seabed and pushing my feet hard against it to launch myself up, but my foot slid between the spokes and I couldn't get free. Trapped, struggling for my life, I stretched my arms over my head, unsure if they broke the surface, desperate to catch hold of something and pull myself up. The need to breathe in hurt. My lungs were bursting. Terrible pressure built in my chest and head.

The water in front of me exploded. Uncle Quinlan lifted the old bike and my head came out of the water. I gulped air, shaking, crying, clinging to his neck while he freed my foot.

Later, Quinlan said a sensation of foreboding made him look up from his library book. Horrified when he couldn't see me, he raced along the bank shouting my name. He spotted my hands, leaped into the sea with all his clothes on, and saved my life.

Despite the passing years, every detail remained clear and terrifying as on that afternoon. The lasting phobia meant I never learned to swim, and I usually avoided any form of boat travel. Now I had to organise the trip to Santorini and, considering hospital bills and funeral costs, another expensive flight was an extravagance I could not afford. I glanced at the fuel gauge: quarter full. First stop – the petrol station.

Blinded by dazzling sunlight, I slid my new sunglasses on. After a kangaroo start, I attempted to familiarise myself with the vehicle. Although I had not driven since my test, two months ago, I hoped it would all come back, like riding a bike. I drove across the hotel's forecourt, remembering my instructor's mantra: 'Mirror, indicate, mirror, manoeuvre.' After a quick glance in the mirror, I flicked a lever and the windscreen wipers came on.

*Idiot!*

I wished I'd had a little driving practice after passing my test. I thought about asking reception for a New Driver sticker for the back window, but then I wondered if they'd refuse me the car on hearing I had never driven on my own before.

Tourists in open 4x4s passed. I lurched ungracefully out of the forecourt, fumbled for the gear stick, which I forgot was on the opposite side, and tagged onto the convoy's tail. When sure of myself, I planned to drive into the city and buy a ticket for Santorini. With no notion of where the convoy was headed, I stayed close. We passed a sign pointing the way to Elounda village. The road climbed and the view became spectacular. Steep bare rock rose to my left, a sheer drop to my right. The jeeps pulled into a viewpoint near the summit.

I stopped and got out of the car. A deliciously warm breeze was perfumed by local herbs, reminding me of Quinlan's Greek salad. I wondered if lunchtime neared. The beach curved, resembling a giant sandy shepherd's crook, dividing an azure sea from a picturesque fringe of villages and towns clinging to the coastline. Squares of grey-green olive groves preceded high mountains of red rock and pine forests, which became sparser as they neared the peaks.

Lost in the beauty of it all, I suddenly flinched with a stab of pain at the thought of losing Mam. I could see her on the doorstep in dull, damp Dublin a year ago.

'I'm sorry,' she said. I caught a sparkle in her eye that contradicted the downturn of her mouth. Yet, it may have been the glint of a tear. I can still hear her voice as she stepped away from me. 'Goodbye, Irini.'

*Don't go, Mam! Wait for me!*

My heart rolled over and tears stung my eyes. This amazing view, the warmth, the scent; these were the things that my mother *had* to come back to. But there must be more because, for her, the pull of Greece was stronger than beautiful scenery and lovely weather. Stronger that the love of her husband and only child. It hurt. Why did she keep so much of her life from me? What damage would it have done to let me in?

Could I discover what captured her soul . . . and would that thing ensnare me too?

I continued behind the 4x4s until Elounda came into view. The village fringed a calm bay. Opposite, a causeway connected a barren island of softly rolling hills to the landmass, and three sail-less windmills stood on the isthmus.

Where the bay met the sea, towering mountains belittled Spinalonga islet, a Venetian stronghold that became a leper colony. I had read the population moved to London's Hospital of Tropical Medicine in the fifties. Brightly coloured trip boats moored along the islet's shore, and more vessels shuttled across from the village. I imagined old ghosts watching the tourists with their smartphones capturing the crumbled remains of so many ill-fated lives.

The travel agent had raved about the area before she knew the reason for my visit.

'You simply have to snorkel there! You can see remains of the Sunken City of Olous. Truly amazing!'

Too horrified to speak, I wondered how a whole city came to sink.

She had continued: 'Thousands of years back, Daedalus and his son Icarus lived in Olous and built a great temple.'

I peered down and imagined ancient walls and columns inhabited by octopuses, sea horses, and brightly coloured fish.

'That was before Daedalus designed the labyrinth at Knossos, of course.' She had caught my blank look. 'You've heard of the Minoans? King Minos and the Minotaur, half man half bull, and the palace of Knossos? You'll love Crete, it's fascinating.'

Perhaps there was a ticket office in Elounda.

Just before the village, a petrol station loomed into view.

Mirror, windscreen-wipers, *damn*, indicator. I pulled into the forecourt.

'Full, please.'

'Open fuel tank, lady.' The Greek had an unlit cigarette hanging from his mouth.

'Uh? Sorry, it's a hire car.'

He yanked the door ajar, reached under my legs, and muttered, 'Very nice.' There was a clunk, then he came up, grinning.

I ask you, why can't they teach these things in driving school and save the likes of me this embarrassment? My phone pinged with a text. The hospital? I pulled away from the pumps, stopped, and checked the message. Relieved to see it was from my fashion page; a woman interested in a gothic net and brocade ball gown I'd put together and offered for sale. I knew someone would love the wickedly strong design.

The skirt came from a yellowing, meringue-type wedding dress, dyed black. This was stitched to a heavy charity-shop, lace-up corset that I had carefully covered in dyed curtain brocade. Replacing the back-fastening lace-up with a string of black glass beads had added to the glamour. The finished creation was powerful and had tons of WOW factor. Valentino with a twist.

With a full tank I drove onto the empty highway. Bright sunlight flashed through the windscreen when the road swung south. Still thinking about the ball gown, I navigated the bend and reached for my sunglasses, but they slid across the passenger seat. I unclipped my seatbelt and stretched over.

Bang! Crash! Blackness . . .

* * *

Out of the dark came confusion. My body was thrown about, my head slammed against something hard. Blinding pain, flashes, lightning, glimpses of folk running. Above all, an acute sense of danger all around me. Real, but not real. A blonde in my ball gown, running; the car hire guy riding a zebra, spinning a lasso, buildings toppling around them. I was in a nightmare, hurled to the ground. Images queued in my head, waiting to be analysed – fact or fantasy? I sifted through my thoughts and discarded the impossible.

Someone was speaking.

I knuckled my eyes, stared at the blood on my hands, realised I was in the hire car. Everything blurred, tinted pink and red. White dust hung in the air. A hand touched my shoulder. I jumped, startled.

'*Mademoiselle?*' A French voice, well spoken.

Reality drifted back, followed by pain. A tightening band around my forehead. The dust made my throat itch. I smelled pear drops, expensive aftershave, burning rubber.

'Dear Jesus, what happened?' I rasped. Beyond the cracked windscreen, an ornate lamppost had crumpled the Fiat Panda's bonnet.

'You're in an accident,' the Frenchman said. 'Your 'ead is bleeding. You were knocked out. We 'ave called the ambulance.'

I tried to rewind the last few minutes: blinding sunlight . . . unclipped seatbelt . . . reached for sunglasses. I blinked slowly, a flash behind my eyelids – nonsensical images, heartbreak and pain.

Suddenly, I felt close to my mother, as if she was in the passenger seat. I blinked at the empty space, wanting to reach out, feel safe in her arms. If only I could be with her, just for a moment, and say all the things I never said. I remembered nights in the convent when I wished she was there. Time had no measure to a young girl: *One day, when my mother comes for me* . . . My childish plan had been to become a great ballet dancer and surprise her with pirouettes in my sequined tutu. I wanted to make her proud, so proud she would never leave me again.

I closed my eyes and tried to invoke her, but she had gone. A dream, back-slapped into my consciousness by the crash. Dizzy and trembling, I held my head; it rattled like rocks in a bucket, leaving me with the reality of the situation.

'What's that?' I asked the Frenchman, clearing my throat and flapping my hand at the dusty air.

'Powder from the airbag. 'Ow do you feel, miss? You banged your 'ead. Can you sit up?'

I moved my legs and arms, fearing the agony of fractured bones, but I seemed to be okay.

'Is anyone hurt?'

'I am afraid yes,' the Frenchman said. 'The cyclist 'as a broken arm.' He stood and peered behind my car. 'My wife is making 'im comfortable. Are you in pain?'

'What happened?' I stared at the blood on my fingertips.

'You pulled out of the petrol station on the wrong side. I tried to beep, but didn't find the 'orn until too late.' He nodded at the white convertible across the way. 'It's an 'ire car. They forgot to say where the 'orn is.'

The information sank in. 'You mean *I* caused the accident?! Me? All this chaos?' I struggled to get out of the vehicle. The world spun, throwing me off balance and I slumped against the bonnet.

# CHAPTER 7
## BRIDGET

*Santorini, 29 years ago.*

MID-MORNING, I HURRIED TOWARDS the cathedral of Saint John, found the priest, and explained Tommy's situation. In turn, the priest had a word with the Bishop of Santorini. The church offered a donation of two hundred thousand drachmas towards the operation.

In the silence of our little house, exhausted by the emotions of the day, I struggled to accept the reality. I hadn't enough money for the operation. Our only surety was the small house, bought for cash when we first arrived on the island. Flush with money from the sale of Tommy's semi in Dublin, we were captivated by the view the moment we saw it. The simplicity of the two-room dwelling, which had a decent front patio overlooking Santorini's caldera, thrilled us both.

I stepped outside and sat on the low wall. The local estate agent would make a valuation after noon. What we actually bought, all those years ago, was little more than a cave with a toilet, a crude shower, and one large room carved out of the soft volcanic rock. How in love we had been, and what an adventure we were on.

Such dwellings, called *hyposkafa* by the locals, were common on the island. We christened our property The Love Nest, and purchased cinderblocks, cement, and a spirit level, which were delivered by donkey. Our only furniture consisted of a bed, a gas burner, a tin table and two chairs. For a whole month, we camped in the cave, making plans by candlelight and reading snippets from archaeology magazines and history books to each other.

Life was harmonious, every day a glorious adventure.

With the help of neighbours, we built a larger room on the front of our *hyposkafa,* into which we placed our table and two chairs, a sofa and a bookcase. Then we built a simple kitchen along one wall. Most of the year we lived outside, on the terrace with an amazing view. We painted the inside white, and the outside sizzling orange, with a Santorini-blue door and window shutters.

Apart from our childlessness, life was wonderful. We had learned Greek together, and cycled around the island talking to locals, searching for the likely location of hidden archaeology.

I put these memories to one side and decided to call on what little family we had left in Ireland.

Tommy's older brother was a drinker who laboured on the Dublin docks, and his wife worked part-time as a sales assistant in the Thomas Brown store on Grafton Street. I doubted they could help.

Tommy's sister had three children and one on the way, and her husband had just lost his job thanks to a spate of redundancies at the Jameson's whiskey plant. I imagined they had financial problems of their own.

His youngest brother, Quinlan, of whom we were both very fond, was the most likely candidate.

The situation did not look promising. Needing a distraction, I glanced at my essay for *Archaeology Now* and wrote: *The Repatriation of Artefacts* across the top. I thought about the Parthenon Marbles in London, and in Paris, the Venus de Milo – or Aphrodite of Milos, which was its proper name. This huge and controversial subject would take my mind away from the niggling problems of money for a while.

One thousand words into the article, the phone rang. A woman's voice spoke in Greek.

'Mrs McGuire, Mr Splotskey would like to speak with you.'

'Yes? My husband . . . is everything all right?'

'Hold for a moment.'

I waited.

'Mrs McGuire? Splotskey here. Nothing to worry about, your husband is stable. I wanted to tell you we'll be operating on Mr McGuire on Monday morning. I've booked the theatre and my team's ready to go.'

'I can't thank you enough!'

'Sorry to be impolite, but I need to know you have the funds to cover costs. You don't have insurance, as I remember.'

'Yes, Doctor, it's in hand. The estate agent's coming to value the house today, then I'll go to the bank for a loan using our property as collateral. The house is paid for, you see, so there shouldn't be a problem.'

After a long pause, Splotskey said, 'Call me after you've talked to the bank. I have to pay for the theatre and anaesthetist. I need to be certain that at least you have the funds to reimburse me for those expenses.'

'Would six o'clock be convenient?'

\* \* \*

If anyone saw me pacing the empty room, muttering to myself, they would think I had gone mad. I searched for the right words to say to Splotskey. The estate agent viewed our little house and purely because of its location – the view, to be precise. They offered a pleasing valuation. I didn't think there could be a problem when I offered the house as security for a bank loan, but I hadn't realised the country was on the brink of a financial crisis. The bank had so many properties, from loan defaults, they would not take any more as collateral.

There had to be another way to raise funds. I phoned Quinlan, the most sensible person I knew, but he had just tied his savings up in a five-year bond. However, he offered to transfer two hundred pounds if it helped. I accepted, promising to pay the money back as soon as possible.

Sick to my stomach, I realised I had nothing else to sell. Even my wedding ring was only nine-carat gold. That thin band, the only lasting thing from my mother, was taken from her finger on the fateful day of the bomb. Tommy had slipped it onto my finger on our wedding day.

Any spare money we had went on archaeology books and magazines. I took stock: I had the money from the church, and another two hundred from Quinlan plus my last two magazine cheques. Nowhere near enough and I'd be living on bread and water, but if that's what it took to fix Tommy, so be it.

Hoping for a miracle, I watched the clock tick around to six, then dialled Splotskey's number.

'Mr Splotskey has been called to a patient. Who can I say has called?'

'Bridget McGuire. My husband's in his care.'

'Mrs McGuire, oh . . . wait a moment, please.'

I heard muffled talking and guessed a hand was over the receiver. I strained to hear but only recognised that the words were sharp and urgent.

A different voice came through the phone. 'Mrs McGuire, Mr Splotskey will call you back shortly.'

'Is my husband all right?' My head was spinning with a sick feeling Splotskey was with Tommy.

'Sorry, I can't answer questions over the phone. Please wait for the cardiologist himself.'

\* \* \*

I paced, and prayed to God. A tumble of magazines on the bedside table caught my eye and for want of something to do, I tidied them into a stack. A heavy envelope slid from between the magazine pages and fell heavily to the floor. I stared at it, questioning what was inside, then I recalled the morning of Tommy's heart attack and the dragonfly necklace. When the ambulance arrived, I must have shoved it into my rucksack without thinking.

The moment had escaped my memory with all that happened later.

Over the years, we had uncovered exquisite pottery bowls, urns, and jugs with delicate paintings of swallows and lilies. Oh, those finger-trembling seconds when an artefact made its first appearance, the slight change in the sound of the trowel as it scraped, or when an uneven surface bulged under the brush. Heart-thumping moments as the roll of a rim or the turn of a handle was uncovered. Breath held, eyes fixed, as more of the relic exposed itself. They were the highlights of the archaeologist's life, the thrill of the dig, when long-buried things from a secret civilisation were brought back into the light of day.

The dragonfly necklace was a whole new adventure, quickly overshadowed by Tommy's heart attack. I hadn't even mentioned the necklace to the students when they returned, such was my distress about Tommy. I sat on the edge of the bed and gazed at it, then I stared at the envelope and remembered the article I had written.

Antiquities theft, the subject of my essay, was an evil we were both passionate about. *There is no excuse that justifies robbing mankind of its historical artefacts.*

The phone rang. I lowered the envelope onto the bed and picked up the receiver.

'Splotskey here. How are you, Mrs McGuire – sorry, Bridget, isn't it?'

'How's Tommy, Doctor?'

'Hum, yes, yes, he had a little relapse. A minor problem considering what he's been through, but serious nevertheless. It's important we proceed with the operation on Monday. How was your meeting with the bank?'

I told him how much I had raised, then, knowing it wasn't enough, I was sobbing so hard I couldn't say more.

'Take your time, Bridget.' For the first time, I heard kindness in his voice, but it only made me more emotional.

'Oh, sir, I'm so sorry. Poor Tommy. What am I going to do? I tried, but the bank . . . the bank said they had problems of their own. I don't know who else to ask. I have nowhere else to turn.'

There was a long silence. I heard him swallow and sigh.

'Please can you help us?' I begged. 'I'll sign part of my house over to you, even pay you double, only you have to save my husband's life.'

'Have you any other assets, Bridget? A car?'

I sniffed hard and shook my head. 'No, I've tried everything I can think of. I receive a cheque each month from an archaeology magazine, but that's all.'

'Archaeology? Ah, yes, yes, your husband mentioned . . . Is there nothing, you know, you could sell?'

Shocked by the suggestion, I stammered, 'No, it's impossible, against the law, against all we stand for. Tommy would go crazy. Please don't suggest such a thing to him. God knows how he would react.'

'Yes, I see. I understand,' he said quietly. 'I'm sorry. Under the circumstances, I'll have to cancel the theatre.'

'But wait . . . What will happen to my husband without the operation?'

'There is always a chance,' he said. 'I've known patients live for several years if they take life slowly. Nature can be unpredictable, and hopefully smaller veins and arteries may compensate and take over the job of damaged ones.'

'But if they don't?' I whispered.

'I'm sorry, Bridget.'

\* \* \*

Broken-hearted, I stood in the doorway and leaned against the solid frame, imagining it was Tommy. With my eyes closed, I recalled how it was when we fitted that door. We mixed a bucket of cement and fixed the frame into the hole. The next day we hung the door and realised our mistake. The frame was askew. How we laughed! For weeks we were shaving a bit off here and a bit off there, until finally we could shut the door.

*Oh, Tommy! Somehow we will get over this too.*

Out on the patio, I watched an old wooden schooner in full sail drift towards the sunset. The early evening light turned the square sails into sheets of gold. Tourists aboard the vessel would be thrilled. From below, the sound of a beautiful melody played on a lyra drifted up, adding to the scene. A clopping on the pebble path that rose from the port made me turn. The donkeys were heading home, heads drooping, eyes dull, step weary.

I rubbed my forehead, trying to erase the headache that had plagued me for a couple of days now. Perhaps I had some aspirin in the bathroom. Tired out, I went indoors and poured a glass of water. If I could get a full eight hours sleep for once, I might be able to think more clearly tomorrow and come up with a solution for Tommy.

Standing before the cabinet, I studied myself in the mirror. I looked as jaded as I felt. When I pulled the cupboard door open, a box of sanitary towels fell into the basin. For a solid minute, I stared at it. When was the last time? It had to be more than two months ago! I turned on the shower, ripped off my clothes, and quickly washed. The chemist closed at 9 p.m.

* * *

At midnight, I swung my legs out of bed and stared into the dark room. I was pregnant. After all this time, and at the worst possible moment, we were going to have the child we yearned for. Fate was cruel; my glorious pregnancy could not have come at a worse time.

I wondered if this miracle was what Tommy needed to set him onto the road to recovery? Exhausted from the stresses of the day, I lay down again, closed my eyes and allowed my mind to wander away from the money, the lifesaving operation, and my desperation. I deliberately took myself back to Queen Thira and her ten kings in the council chamber, wondering how they would deal with their enormous problems. If Thira found a solution and saved her people from impending disaster, then perhaps I could find a parallel that would guide me in the right direction. I could not see how but, left with nothing but hope, I was eager to discover how things would work out for the Atlanteans. Perhaps because of my heightened emotional state, the dream was even more vivid than usual. I flew through the darkness until I found myself on the throne in the council chamber, my ten kings before me.

* * *

King Hero nods. 'Then we will go to war with Crete, my Queen.' He returns to his seat.

I address the overseer of festivals, palaces, and the arts. 'King Dalus, gather your finest artists. I want frescoes painted on the insides of every building. Start with our temples and citadels, and continue down to the factories, potteries, and harvest rooms.'

The kings stare curiously.

'The paintings must be so lifelike, Poseidon thinks our lives go on as normal. If He decides to take Atlantis into his watery domain, I want the record of our lives in full view.' I pause while the nobles digest this information.

'Also, gather all the maidens with their first blood-show in the room of adoration. I intend to prepare a sacrifice and offer it to Poseidon at sunset. Gifts will be showered on their families, land and livestock will be theirs. The populous will rejoice.'

I turn to the ruler of sailors and ship-building. 'King Eildon, increase our labourers twentyfold. Build as many of your magnificent oak ships as possible. Work day and night, for I fear we do not have much time.'

* * *

At dawn, hugging Tommy's pillow, I woke from my dream with a sense of urgency. Thira's words tumbled around in my head: *I fear we do not have much time.* Although no closer to a solution, I was convinced she was sending me a message. Something had to turn up and resolve Tommy's critical situation. We were going to have a baby!

# CHAPTER 8
## IRINI

*Crete, present day.*

'I HAVE TO APOLOGISE to the man on the bike. A broken arm, my God!' I said to the Frenchman.

When I tried to stand, emotions rushed through me – helplessness and confusion, but above all, the horrid realisation I might have killed somebody. My stomach cramped and hurled my breakfast in an embarrassing mess onto the road. My eyes watered, nose ran, everything spun away again. I had to clutch the side of the car.

'Sorry, sorry, very undignified. My head's spinning.' I wiped my mouth with the back of my hand. 'Will you help me get to the poor man?'

'There is nothing you can do.' The Frenchman held onto my shoulder. 'I think you shouldn't speak to 'im. Better to stay still, sit in the car and wait for the ambulance.'

Adrenalin with nowhere to go morphed into anger. 'You're wrong – I have to apologise. What are you, one of those professional accident people? No claim no fee, is it?'

'No, I'm not,' he said quietly.

'Oh! What am I saying?' I pulled away, dizzy with remorse and afraid I couldn't walk without the Frenchman's help. 'God, I'm so sorry, that was unforgivable. I didn't mean to be so rude.' I looked into his eyes and saw kindness. 'I'm really grateful, you being so helpful and all.'

His smile was gentle. 'It's the shock, *mademoiselle*. It affects us all differently. Don't worry.'

'But I'm not like that. Please, I have to see how the poor man is and apologise.'

'Come on then, let's take it slow,' the Frenchman said, slipping an arm around my waist and supporting me.

The bike was a wreck and the man, in a blue Lycra cycling outfit, worse. His face turned towards the road as he gripped his arm. I saw dirt in his shoulder-length hair, and one of his sleek cycling shoes seemed to be missing.

'I'm so sorry. Are you in much pain?' I felt awkward talking to the back of his head. His knees and elbows oozed blood and, from the unnatural angle of his arm, I guessed it hit the car and snapped in two. I felt sick again.

The woman started unfastening the cyclist's helmet.

Her husband spoke to her in French. She stopped and left the helmet where it was. 'They will be 'ere soon, *mon cheri*.'

The Frenchman turned to me. 'I'll see if there's a triangle in the car to place around the bend.'

I sat on the road next to the casualty. 'This is awful. I didn't see you at all. I've only had the car ten minutes. Everything happened so quickly.' I rested my hand on his.

When he turned his head, I recognised the man from the airport. He stared at me. 'Oh, no. Not you again. Are you a crazy woman? You nearly killed me!'

'I don't know what to say. Is there anything I can do?'

'Yes. Go back to England!'

I bit my tongue. I weren't even from England!

He tugged his hand away and went back to gripping his broken arm.

I turned to the woman. 'Where's the ambulance? It's clear the poor man's in agony. Can't we take him to the hospital ourselves?'

The Greek's eyes widened. 'No, no, no! You stay away from me!'

The French woman shook her head. 'Better not to move 'im. Listen, is that them?' The sound of sirens drifted up the mountainside.

Minutes later, a police car and ambulance raced around the bend, nearly killing us all.

\* \* \*

One of the medics helped me into the ambulance, where I sat until they had immobilised the Greek's arm. I avoided his eyes when he sat beside me. The medic fastened our lap straps. I found myself trembling.

'Speak English?' the medic said. I nodded. He took my pulse, then handed me a wad of dressing. 'You hold against your head, okay? You feel cold?'

'I'm fine, really.'

'No, you have shock. We will be at the hospital soon. You no sleep, okay?'

The Greek cradled his arm. 'What's your name?' he said.

'Irini. Yours?'

'I am Angelo Rodakis.' He said it as if I should know the name. Perhaps he was famous. He didn't look familiar to me.

'Look, I really am terribly sorry.' I didn't know what else to say.

\* \* \*

In the hospital, I had two stitches in my head, a blood test, a tetanus jab and an x-ray. The policeman breathalysed me, took details of the accident, and asked for my driving licence and passport, which he photographed with his phone. The form-filling was laborious. He asked for my mother's name, and my mother's maiden name. I wanted to tell him all about my mother, the reason I was there. I wanted him to understand. I was stressed, sad, afraid I might miss the last moments of my mother's life.

He asked for my father's name, my parents' address, my address, my hotel address, the car hire address. He had a problem spelling *McGuire* and, in the end, he copied it from my passport. After a long wait in the overcrowded hospital, the doctor turned into the corridor but, before he reached me, he was stopped by the very old, and the sick, and the lost.

'Madam,' the doctor said, glancing at my name on his clipboard. 'You have mild concussion. Nothing serious. If you feel dizzy or sick, you come back, okay? Not much driving, yes, and you take it easy for a few days.'

I never wanted to drive again. I asked about the cyclist and the nurse told me he had his arm plastered. She pointed to Orthopaedics.

On a bed in a busy corridor, I found Angelo, groggy from painkillers.

'I'm really sorry for what happened. Is there anything I can do at all?'

'Yes, you stay away from me.' He muttered something in Greek and then said, 'You nearly killed me. They said I am lucky not to need surgery. Why were you on the wrong side of the road? You should not be driving a car, you cannot even drive an airport trolley!'

'It was a mistake. I didn't . . .' I wanted to tell him not to be horrible to me, that I have enough problems; but I only lowered my eyes and muttered, 'I'm mortified.'

'I am more mortified than you, that is true. The boss will go crazy. My phone is smashed. I can't even tell her what has happened.'

'Let me help. I'll call and explain it's my fault. Are they keeping you in?'

'They will take me to Euromedica for overnight. I am waiting for the ambulance.'

'You must be starved. I know I am. Shall I get you a coffee and a sandwich?'

His eyes narrowed. 'Am I safe? Will you scald me?'

'No, no, really, I'll be very careful.' I caught a glint in his eye and realised he was being nice – or perhaps simply mocking me. 'I *am* terribly sorry.'

'You must stop saying that. Bring me Greek coffee, sweet, okay?'

'I'll be back.'

Half an hour later, I returned from the chaotic café. 'Sorry, the place is packed.'

He thanked me and took the hot cup. 'Where are you from?'

'Dublin, Ireland. You?'

'From here, of course.'

'Of course,' I almost snapped. Why was I angry with him? This was my fault. Be nice. 'My first trip abroad by myself and I end up on the wrong island. The whole thing's been a disaster.'

He frowned, wrapped a hand around his beard and smoothed it down. 'Crete is the most beautiful Greek island, and the beaches are also better than anywhere else.'

I wanted to explain, unburden myself, feel the freedom of walking out of the confessional with absolution: *My mother had an accident in Santorini a few days ago but I couldn't get a flight, so I'm here, desperate to get to the island. If I'd been nicer, in Dublin, perhaps she would have stayed there. She wouldn't be all alone, dying on a Greek island sixty-something miles away.* I opened my mouth but the words wouldn't come, they grew inside me, heavy in my chest, painful in my heart.

'Do you want to use my phone?' I said instead, forcing kindness into my voice.

He nodded and thanked me. 'You came here to work?'

I tried to swallow rising emotion. 'No, I came to be with my mother.' I dropped into a chair and stared at the floor, misery dragging at my jaw. I'd really let her down.

I looked up at the sound of Angelo's raised voice; he appeared to be having an argument on my Samsung.

I waited impatiently, wanting the phone back. I needed to call the hospital. I was still pushing back tears. The desire to be at my mother's side came from deep inside me and I asked myself: why hadn't my mother experienced this compulsion to be with me when I took my first communion, or my confirmation? If I had drowned that day in my childhood, would she have come to my funeral? Then I was ashamed of myself. What a disgusting thing to think, but I was the only child in class whose parents never showed at those important occasions. I recalled the sensation of abandonment while all my classmates felt special. Now, my mother was in a coma and not expected to survive. A fact I couldn't change, but I *had* to be there for her.

An orderly brought a wheelchair for Angelo.

He handed me the phone and my fingers itched to call my mother's hospital.

83

I glanced into his eyes, remembering his smile at the airport, the connection we almost had. Clearly he was in a lot of pain. I wanted to reach out, but instead I clutched the phone, called the hospital, and listened to the ringtone as an orderly wheeled Angelo away. I was devastated that he had a broken arm, and I felt awful that it was my fault, but it would mend. My mother lay in a hospital bed, dying, and it was too late to get to her bedside.

My bright, happy clothes had lost the power to lift my spirits. I stood like a despondent clown in the hospital's monochrome surroundings and waited for Santorini's intensive care unit to pick up.

'Mrs McGuire is stable and peaceful,' they said.

My anxiety eased a little. After explaining my delay, I promised to see them tomorrow and they agreed to text me if there was any change.

I was sick of speaking to strangers when all I wanted to do was talk to Mam. With all the expensive lifesaving equipment bought by the tax payer and used by the hospitals, you'd hope somebody would think of providing a simple pair of earbuds for those distanced and poorly. I wanted to tell my mother not to give up, I'd be there soon.

We've had the technology to share our lives with friends and relatives for decades. Why is it kept from the dying? Being able to talk to loved ones for a few minutes a day would make all the difference to those left behind – my father, for example. If only he could say a few words to my mother. Old school friends could pop in too – 'Remember that day when . . . ?' – and lift spirits for a moment.

Perhaps I could arrange for my dad to speak to her, but then I wondered if that would make him feel worse about not being there.

Back at the hotel, the receptionist was sympathetic. She organised my ticket to Santorini, and a club sandwich in my room.

That night, in the dark, my white cotton sheet felt like a shroud. I wondered what happened to a person's soul when they were unconscious and near death. Did it hover, waiting to go to God? And the big question: is there really a God? Any God? I was a religious teacher, I should have felt confident in these things, but sometimes I had doubts.

*Mrs McGuire is stable and peaceful.*

Her daughter was torn apart and desperate.

\* \* \*

At the Heraklion port, I discovered there was nothing feline about the FastCat ferry. A monstrous navy-and-white catamaran, angular as origami, waited at the quayside. The glass-enclosed, arrowhead-shaped platform bridged two canoe-shaped vessels that kept the passenger deck clear of the sea. Power roared from the revved engines and a hint of diesel drifted by. Four hundred people hurried on board and searched for their seat number. Once underway, the captain announced we should remain seated and keep our lap-straps fastened. He told us we were travelling at twenty-eight knots – it felt like ninety miles an hour.

The vessel rushed onward, bucking and banging against the swell. We lurched in our seats. Someone was vomiting noisily. The man next to me ate a greasy cheese pie and I found the sour smell nauseating. I stared at a couple of flakes of pastry stuck to my thigh thanks to the blasting overhead air-con, which I feared would give me brain-freeze. Most of the passengers were gaming on their mobiles. A baby cried. The seating arrangement reminded me of class and I tried to distract myself by thinking of the children. I hoped somebody had given Layla a kitten.

A wave slammed against my window, making me duck. *Stupid.* For a second, it seemed we were underwater. My thoughts raced back to the Liffey estuary and I was in a seven-year-old's panic, but the glass cleared like a soapy shower screen. We ploughed headlong over and through the undulating Aegean.

*Breathe. Only one hour and thirty minutes to go. Breathe.*

I closed my eyes against the streaming window and tried to divert my attention by counting backwards from six thousand in threes. Sensing the catamaran had slowed, I looked out again.

Santorini loomed from a flat pond of deep turquoise water – a broken brioche topped by startling white icing. The crescent of red, copper, and black rock surrounded us. The cliff ahead was divided by a dramatically zigzagging path that led from port to summit. With a sense of urgency, the crew moved quickly from bow to stern.

Passengers fell silent as the roaring engine noise faded to a purr. An air of relief and wonderment filled the vessel. Most of the tourists lifted their phones towards the windows.

The scene changed again after docking. We shuffled down the wide gangplank in dazzling sunlight. Noise and chaos surrounded me.

'Donkey! Donkey! Four euro!'

'You want room? Very cheap room, best view on island! This way, madam!'

'Taxi! Taxi! Come, I take you anywhere, beautiful lady!'

Dizzy with the relief of standing on dry land, I surveyed the clamouring tourists. Eager to distance myself from the boat, and desperate for a cold drink, I was jostled by people dragging cases and shushing their children.

Thirty minutes later, I was standing outside the new Santorini hospital in my paisley sundress and wide straw hat, ready to see my mother.

I paid the taxi and rushed past a stone-wall façade and tall white pillars that gave the entrance a Greek historical look. Once through the automatic glass doors, I headed for the desk under a sign that said *Enquiries* in three languages. The receptionist wanted me to sign forms. They were in Greek. I told her I needed a copy of the paperwork in English before I would sign anything.

'I'd like to see my mother now.'

She sighed, annoyed about the paperwork, but then softened and led me to Intensive Care. The building was spotless, modern, and very different from the overcrowded Cretan hospital of yesterday. I followed the overweight nurse along a marble-floored corridor until we arrived at the IC unit. She paused at the door.

'Lady, I want you to be prepared for what you see. Your mother is not in pain, but her injuries are serious. We induced a coma, but she may be able to hear you. It is good to talk. Tell her your news, share your memories, tell her you love her.'

She led me into the room. I was determined to keep my emotions in check, yet a sob escaped and I clasped my hand over my mouth when I saw her.

Mam was alone in the two-bed room. Screens over her bed displayed lights and graphs that spoke a language only the medical staff understood. There was a chair with a well-worn cushion between the beds. The nurse pulled it around to my mother's side. I couldn't take my eyes off my mother's gaunt face.

'The doctor will come and answer your questions as soon as he has a moment,' the nurse said. 'There's an emergency call button here, and a vending machine down the corridor if you want—'

I shook my head. She nodded sympathetically and left.

In the silent room, I gazed at my mother, the famous archaeologist. Her head was heavily bandaged and I wondered if they had shaved off her beautiful auburn hair. A tube was taped to her nose and a wire pegged to her finger. A bag of clear liquid hung above, drip-feeding into a vein. Another bag of yellow liquid hung below the bed.

Her eyes were closed behind lids that appeared translucent. Her sun-bronzed skin had an unnatural yellowish pallor. My heart rushed out to her. I wanted to hold her, feel her body against my chest, hear her breathe in my ear, yet I could not move. In the sterile room, I had never felt so alone, or so ashamed of allowing that giant rift to come between us.

'Mammy,' I whispered. 'It's me, Irini.'

# CHAPTER 9
## BRIDGET

*Santorini, 29 years ago.*

I LONGED TO TELL TOMMY my glorious news. He simply could not die when his child was growing inside me, not after waiting so long and hoping so hard! The ferry to Crete would leave in a few hours. I stood, felt nauseous, and plopped down again. Pregnant . . . It gave a whole new dimension to everything. A child of our own after all this time. Surely that was proof: miracles do happen. Everything would be all right. It had to be.

Distracted from stuffing things into a bag by the ringing phone, I stared at it for a second, and then grabbed the receiver.

'Mrs McGuire, Mr Splotskey would like to speak with you. Please hold.'

My mouth dried again. I stared ahead, seeing nothing but the image of Tommy as I had left him in the Cretan hospital.

'Hello, Bridget. Splotskey. I'm sorry to tell you, your husband had another heart attack in the early hours of this morning.'

*No . . . Another heart attack!*

I held my breath, suspended in the moment. Time seemed to go on hold too. Perhaps the earth had stopped turning.

'Hello, are you there?' Splotskey said.

'Yes, I'm here. Is he . . .' *No! No! No! I can't stand it. Don't give me bad news, not now!* I hardly dared ask. 'How is he?'

'He's resuscitated and sedated – and stable for the moment – but you should come over as soon as you can. Please inform any of Mr McGuire's relatives that his condition is considered serious. They may want to be with him.'

*I refuse to let my Tommy die!*

'Please, Doctor, is there something you can do? I . . . I've just discovered that I'm pregnant. My husband's waited all his life for a child. Please, please help us.'

After a long silence, Splotskey sighed into the phone and said, 'I know somebody who buys Greek antiquities.' Another silence. 'If you have anything that might interest him?'

I started to speak, but then realised my hand was over my mouth. 'I will . . . I do . . . I've an artefact – a silver necklace of a dragonfly. It's in pieces but it's beautiful, priceless. At an educated guess, I'd say it's about four thousand years old.'

'Yes, yes, all right,' he said hurriedly, as if not wanting to hear the details. 'I'll contact him. Bring it over and I'll try and help you.'

'I'll be there before three o'clock. Please, don't cancel the operation!'

After a mad dash to catch the ferry, I arrived at the hospital, sickened to discover I had missed my chance to see Tommy before he went into theatre.

Since Tommy's heart attack, I had worried so much that, although my body eventually fell asleep at night, my mind would not lie down. Fear, hope, and the unknown tormented me until dawn. Each morning, I dragged myself from bed feeling more tired than when I first slid under the sheet. In the hospital room, I curled into the Lloyd Loom-type chair and allowed my mind to relax. Tommy was being taken care of. He *would* recover.

My long-running dream of ancient Santorini drifted in like a loved book, opened to reveal a place I needed to be, the print fixed to the page, unchangeable and safe. I wondered if my dreams were fixed too, or did my actions influence the story that unfolded? I willingly lost myself in the otherworld, escaping from the dreadful possibilities of these hours in the Cretan hospital.

* * *

After feasting and merrymaking, the guests disperse and I am alone with my kings.

'After one full moon, we shall have our River Festival. My daughter shall take her place beside me on the royal dais. This will be our last jubilee before we leave for Crete.' I turn to Hero. 'My noble envoy, have you heard from King Minos?'

Hero stood. 'King Minos thanks my Queen for her generous gifts. He offers two choices for settlement. The first is known as the Pillars of Hercules, on the extreme north-west of Crete.'

'I know of this place: two jagged peninsulas, uninhabited and barren. Not a good area for grazing or cultivating, and the sea between them can be turbulent.'

Hero nods. 'The other is to the north-east, near the municipality of Lato and the coastal city of Olous. The area of Istron is in a bay known as Mirabello. A fine area to build a port.'

'Our ships will be laden and difficult to handle. North-east Crete is where we are likely to meet land. Istron is perfect.' I sense this is too easy. 'What does Minos want?'

Hero smiles. 'You are astute, my Queen. He wants the founding secrets of our much-prized metal.'

I stiffen. 'Orichalcum?'

Hero nods again.

I will never reveal our smelting technique. 'We can discuss that at our next meeting. King Eildon, how is the ship-building?'

'One hundred galleys are in the making, and I plan four hundred more. Wood arrives daily, pitch is in short supply but we can paint the ships later. One thousand looms weave the strongest sailcloth, and artisans carve oak oars as we speak. Our fields of papyrus and hemp are harvested and the rope-smiths toil day and night, twisting warps for the lines and sails. More papyrus is arriving from our brothers in Egypt. The blacksmith has melted every scrap of iron to forge a new type of anchor for the vessels.'

'Excellent!' I turn to the lord of livestock and market gardens. 'King Alpheus, from this day, only the oldest animals will be killed for food. The young stock will go with us to Crete.'

The kings exchange glances and I sense a conspiracy. 'Is there a problem?' I ask Hero.

'No problems . . . no problems . . .' The words drift around the room, becoming louder and clearer.

*　*　*

'No problems. No problems . . .' The voice was Splotskey's. I sucked in the chlorine-scented air as the surgeon touched my shoulder. Still wearing his green bloodstained scrubs, he stood over me, his face paler and more pinched than usual.

'Stay seated, Bridget. Sorry, did I startle you? You'll be pleased to know the operation was a success, as far as we can tell. Mr McGuire is in the recovery room.'

'Oh, thank God . . . Thank you,' I muttered, overwhelmed with relief.

Splotskey's sour face lifted slightly. 'I suggest you get some proper sleep now and return tomorrow. Mr McGuire will be under sedation for some time. Come back in the morning, after we've checked him over.'

I nodded, resisting an urge to hug him.

'Do you have a room?'

I shook my head, biting my lip, unable to speak.

'Do you have a piece of paper?'

I delved into my pockets and pulled out the ferry ticket. He wrote a phone number on it.

'It's a rent-rooms establishment my interns use. Cheap and basic, but clean. Tell them I sent you. Now go, eat, and get a good night's sleep. In your condition, you need to look after yourself.'

* * *

In the small room that overlooked dustbins, I listened to a dog barking and recalled the surgeon's green apron spattered with Tommy's blood. Tomorrow, I had to go to the hospital and give half a litre of my own blood. Aaron and the other archaeologists would do the same, like all our friends in Santorini. They were good people and they knew this action would reduce my hospital bill considerably. With an image in my mind of friends queuing at the hospital's blood-donor room, I fell into a deep sleep, where my dreams, so often connected to real life, continued.

* * *

In the sacrificial hall, a line of young women wait to offer their blood. My handmaidens have shaved the girls' heads, apart from four fat tendrils that have never been cut. Their raven locks are waxed and coiled, and their smooth scalps and ears are painted blue.

When ready, each maiden is covered by a long veil and led, barefoot, to me, the Goddess of the Marches. I prick their heel and catch a few drops of blood in the sacrificial dish, then the veil is turned back and the necklace of womanhood clasped around each girl's neck.

I do not relish this ritual, but the ceremony introduces the girls into the second trimester of life and the pain they will experience in womanhood. The first trimester is childhood and the third, matriarch.

'How many more?' I ask my handmaid, Eurydice.

'This is the last one, your highness.'

Relieved, I smile at the veiled figure led into the sacrificial room. Her foot, white and soft, tells me she is a noble girl. The maiden quickly sits on the stool before me and offers her heel eagerly. I prick through her pale skin with the sacred tool and allow her blood to fall into the sacrificial dish. After a moment, the flow stops and I turn back the young woman's veil. Shocked to recognise the maiden before me, I draw in a sharp breath.

'Oia, my child, when did this happen?'

'This morning, my Queen. I am happy to become a woman today. I promise to do all you bid and make you proud of me.'

'I'll always be proud of you, precious child.'

'Forgive me, dearest Queen, the handmaidens would not shave my head like the others. They say my hair is consecrated.'

'Your hair will never be cut, Oia; it's a symbol of the fire in the mountain.' I stroke the girl's vibrant mane. 'It's also a reminder of your father, our most noble King. Wear your hair with pride, Oia, it is unique in our world. Come, let us offer Poseidon the maidens' blood together.'

We walk in unison, Oia limping slightly. Handmaidens slide back the oak screens that divide the sacrificial room from the antechamber. The young women, their families and the kings wait to observe the offering.

Together we tip the blood over the horns of consecration on the ornately painted altar.

I hold out my arms and call the entreaty:

*'Accept our gift of maidens' blood,*
*Save us now from fire and flood.*
*Rest quiet in your sea of blue,*
*Poseidon, we beseech you!'*

The rooms are silent. After several moments, I bring my hands together with a clap and the crowd celebrates.

\* \* \*

The Cretan dawn gathered strength. In my cheap guestroom, I drifted into the borderland of wakefulness and wanted nothing more than to be at Tommy's side. I hurried to the hospital and crept into my husband's room. My darling slept soundly and there was nothing to do but wait.

Should I tell him about Splotskey and the dragonfly necklace? That it paid for his operation and saved his life? Probably not. Better that he stayed calm and concentrated on getting well again. I would explain everything to him eventually, although I knew he would be furious. We had never kept secrets from each other. The necklace had gone to some nameless person, and they had covered the costs that I could not. Tommy was recovering now; nothing else mattered.

I studied my husband's face as he slept. He appeared old, drawn, and tired. I remembered my own reflection in the bathroom mirror. Years of working under the Mediterranean sun, and the dusty atmosphere of the dig, had weathered us both. With a baby on the way, we needed to take better care of ourselves.

Tommy's lids fluttered, he opened his eyes, and stared at me.

'How are you feeling?' I asked.

'Oh . . . like I've been steamrollered.' He groaned and reached for my hand. 'Can I sit up, do you think?'

I shook my head. 'Best stay still until the nurse comes. They tell me the operation went perfectly. Indeed, you'll be home in a week.' I struggled with my emotions. 'You gave me a right scare, you great fool. Don't ever do that again.'

'Poor thing. Sorry about that, darling girl.' He had a look of total defeat about him and I wanted to gather him up in my arms and give him strength.

'Never mind the sorry, just get yourself mended, Tommy McGuire. You have an enormous task ahead of you and you'll need to be a hundred per cent fit.'

'And what would it be, this enormous thing you've got lined up? If it's decorating, it'll have to wait a while.' Although he winced, and talking was clearly an effort, there was humour in his voice. I slipped the monitor peg off his finger and held his hand against my stomach.

'We're going to have a baby,' I said. 'You're going to be a father, Tommy.'

His eyes widened. He stared at my face, then my belly. His mouth fell open but, clearly, he couldn't speak.

Moments later, a nurse rushed in and stared at us grinning at each other. 'Please, you no take this off your finger. The machine told me your heart is not beating!'

We started laughing, Tommy grimacing at the same time. The nurse was not amused.

'Stop it, Bridget,' Tommy said, placing a hand against his chest. 'It hurts when I laugh!'

# CHAPTER 10
## IRINI

*Santorini, present day.*

I STARED AT MY MOTHER in the hospital bed. Her badly bruised face and the dark circles around her eyes shocked me.

My sadness to see her like this was beyond tears. It weighed deep and heavy, crushing my chest, consuming all thoughts and words, to leave me desolate and alone. Not being able to gather her up and hold her against me was unbearable torture, as if my heart had been ripped out of my body. I don't know how long I remained in that state of utter depression, but eventually the pain lifted enough for me to speak.

'Hello, Mam,' I whispered and touched her cheek. There was no reaction, yet her skin felt normal, neither too hot or cold. 'The nurses said you might be able to hear me, and that it's good to talk.'

Words seemed to abandon me for a while. It was difficult to know what to say but once I got going, I told her about Jason, our broken engagement, my father in the home, my journey to Santorini, and even the car crash. I poured out my soul, and with it came relief. All my life I'd wanted to be able to talk without tension, and explain my feelings, but not at this price. My cheeks itched with the drying salt of tears that I hadn't realised were shed.

I had no notion of how much time had passed when a nurse entered and suggested I return the next day. She gave me my mother's rucksack, telling me one of the workers from the archaeological site brought it in after the accident. Inside the bag, I found a set of keys and wondered if I would be able to find the house as easily.

'Excuse me, I nearly forget,' the nurse said as I was leaving. 'The man that works with Mrs Bridget gave me this and said you must call him.'

I glanced at the number scrawled on a slip of paper and pulled out my phone.

The nurse said, 'Is not allowed to use the mobile in here.'

I went back to my mother and touched her hand. 'I'll say a prayer for you tonight, Mam, and I'll be back in the morning. I love you so much.'

On the hospital forecourt, where the flowerbeds were sparsely planted, I phoned the number.

* * *

Aaron was a chunky guy in his late forties. He gave me a wide, friendly smile and I liked him immediately. He took me to my mother's house, which was situated amongst the higgle-piggle of houses on the edge of town. Childhood memories returned as I caught sight of the low wall around the patio – my mother sweeping me up and then crying. I walked over and looked down. The sheer drop to the rocks on the edge of the caldera made my head spin.

The breathtaking view from the patio was exactly as I re-membered it. Cubist houses, mostly dazzling white, but a few painted pink, yellow, orange, and blue. Urns that overflowed with geraniums, bougainvillea, and lilies provided more star-tling splashes of colour. A windmill had enormous sails that almost reached the ground. A brilliant-blue domed church stood alongside a fairy-tale bell tower with intricate plaster-work. Men hauled trollies stacked high with bottled water towards expensive tavernas. Boutique hotels, stark white with turquoise infinity pools, were moulded into the steep cliff face like melting fondant. Scooters whizzed along narrow streets, and donkeys lugged tourists up endless steps. The sun was so bright, everything shimmered.

Two director's chairs and a tin table painted deep yellow stood on the patio. A terracotta urn, next to the door, held a wilted plant that hung, fawn and forlorn, over the sides. Soil was scattered on the patio around it.

'Damn cats,' Aaron muttered, surveying the mess.

I unlocked the royal-blue door and went inside. The room was smaller than I remembered, but neat and tidy, apart from stacks of books and magazines on almost every flat surface. Aaron followed me in, flicked the light switch, tried the gas burner, and ran the tap.

'Everything seems to be working. Will you be okay? I can stay if you want.' He grinned cheekily.

'I'll be fine, thanks. You've been wonderful and all.' I smiled, but in the back of my mind, I wondered how well my parents really knew him.

'Oh, one more thing.' He rummaged through the cupboards over the sink, found a packet of kebab sticks, and took them out-side. 'This will stop the cats using your urn as a toilet,' he said, poking the sticks into the compost so it resembled a bed of nails. 'That should do it. Good luck then. Keep my phone number in case you need anything. And will you let us know if there's any change with Bridget?' Our eyes met, then he looked away quickly.

'I will indeed. Thank you.' I wanted him to go, needed to be alone in my parents' house. 'Oh, I don't suppose you know the Wi-Fi password, Aaron?'

'Of course: it's your name and date of birth.'

*　*　*

I slept fitfully. The house, quiet on account of it being built into the cliff, had an atmosphere about it – as if waiting for my mother to come home. At dawn, I threw open the front door and let some air into the stuffy room. Hungry, restless, and lost, all at the same time, I looked around and took stock.

In the corner, a desk was piled high with archaeology literature, books, and open mail. I wondered about utility bills. Perhaps a neighbour could help me translate. Only a smattering of Greek remained from my childhood days.

I sat for a while, taking in the small house that had been my parents' home for decades. I tried to imagine them living there, going about their daily lives. Once again, I questioned why they didn't share those lives with me, their only child.

Perhaps my mother had an affair, and Tommy was not my real father. I wondered if he set an ultimatum to my mother: me or him, and she chose him. Or could I have been adopted and then they changed their mind, deciding they didn't want a child? Despite my random thoughts, I felt there was more, something deeper that I longed to understand.

I knew I could settle in the house and would feel comfortable living there. The little house had an air of contentment about it, as if the walls themselves had soaked up decades of my parents' love for each other.

I wondered what happened to that love? Perhaps they had left it behind with the island.

I started sorting paperwork on the desk into three piles – mail, notes, and circulars – but then, restless to get to the hospital, I bunged the mail into my bag along with a pile of notebooks from a shelf above the small TV. Santorini's main hospital was a fifteen-minute walk away.

Once outside the town, the dusty landscape stretched out, desert-like. Low stone walls marked boundaries, and the scattered buildings, mostly tourist accommodation, were painted white. Spindly eucalyptus trees occasionally lined the road, as did an abandoned fridge and a smashed TV. A hill on the horizon towards the south was spattered with white houses and, on the summit, a church dome and bell tower stood stark against the deep-blue sky.

I tugged my baseball cap low and marched past a vineyard. No endless rows of vines supported by trellises here. Dusty basins were hollowed out of the earth, each one containing a vine wrapped around itself like a twiggy bird's nest stuck to the ground. Remarkable that they produced enough grapes for a thriving wine industry.

The easy walk, slightly downhill, took me away from the town. A tiled pavement with great, square holes, which I guessed was for lampposts, appeared nearer the hospital. I passed through automatic glass doors, glad to get out of the sun. Although the air-conditioning was delicious, my heart thudded as I approached the enquiries desk.

The receptionist read my anxiety. 'No change, miss,' she said before I had a chance to speak. 'Just go through.'

* * *

Although I spoke quietly, my voice seemed loud in the silent room.

'Hello, Mam. It's me, Irini. How are you today? I hope you're not in pain.' She lay perfectly still. I took a breath. 'I love you, Mam. I should have told you sooner, but I took it for granted that you knew. Please, please try and get better.'

I sat for a while, watching her face. 'I've brought some things to sort through while I'm here.' My mother was completely motionless. Disappointed to realise the Spielberg Happy Ever After was not about to happen, I dragged the notebooks and letters from my bag.

'No point in looking at the mail – I don't understand a word. Mostly bills, I think. I also found this pile of exercise books and thought they looked interesting.' I opened a blue one that appeared to be the oldest. *Book of Dreams* was scrolled and ornately decorated on the front cover. A handwritten letter and an envelope of photographs slid out and hit the floor.

Suddenly, I was a child again, clumsy and reckless. I scooped everything up before I was told off. After placing most of it on the bedside locker, I sat down and opened the photographer's envelope.

'Oh, Mam, look at these. Pictures of your wedding day!' Each photo had two wallet-size prints attached. 'You looked so pretty, and see Dad – I understand why you fell in love with him. What a handsome man.' I sifted through the pictures. 'There's another couple standing with you, in the next one. They look Greek.' I studied the short and dumpy strangers, who contrasted with my tall, slim parents. 'I guess they were witnesses.'

I wondered if she could hear me. She looked so tired and ill now, yet I could see she had been beautiful in her younger days. Odd that I had never thought of my mother as beautiful before.

'I guess you were in your early twenties when you married, Mam.' I stopped for a moment to think about this, asking myself whether I had been mature enough to marry at that age. 'Quinlan told me you married shortly after you left Dublin for Santorini. Such a shame you didn't continue your education, but I guess marrying your professor meant you never stopped learning.' The thought made me smile. 'You must have loved him with a passion, Mam.'

I wondered what happened. These thoughts led me to think of Jason and my own wedding. Would I have given up everything to marry him? At the time, I thought I would, but discovering cow-faced Calla in his arms had changed everything.

I would never have known about their affair, but I was pulling pints in the Raglan Road after school to earn a little extra cash for my wedding when someone complained about a pong in the loo. I went in and opened the little window without turning the light on. I could hear the pair of them, murmuring and giggling, and making plans around the back of the pub. I swear, if I'd had a brick, I would have hurled it through that window and hoped it split Jason's feckin head open!

I had a horrible feeling I was the last to know, but my broken heart would heal, and although I might be left with scars, the pain was sure to disappear eventually.

My mother's letters were tied together with a length of pink baby ribbon. Suspecting they were love letters from their time at the university, I hesitated. Did I have the right to read my mother's personal correspondence?

'I've got your letters here and I can't decide whether I should read them or not. I don't want to invade your privacy but, on the other hand, if there's a small chance you can hear me it might make your poor old brain wake up.'

I sat for a while, thinking about it. If her brain doesn't wake up, they will turn the machine off. I had watched enough TV hospital dramas to know what the papers were about, the ones the receptionist asked me to sign. I do not want them to shut down the life-support system. Not yet. Not until I am quite positive my mother will never wake again. How can they imply she is brain-dead and, in the next breath, say she might be able to hear me? It didn't make sense.

A heavy silence descended upon the room. I stared at the monitor that bleeped with every heartbeat, and after an unknown length of time I dragged my eyes away. After waiting for my anxiety to settle down, I unfolded the first letter and glanced at the bottom. The signature was my father's.

*Dearest Bridget,*

*This is the most difficult letter I have ever had to write, but I have decided it is better for you to hear my news this way, rather than from student gossip.*

*I'm leaving the university and going to excavate on the Greek island of Santorini. Bridget, I hope when you've finished your studies, you'll come and join me. I know this news will break your heart, and I wish I could be there to kiss the tears from your cheeks. Please forgive me.*

*The terrible thing is: there is no hope for us together when I am your tutor and you are my student. We always knew if our relationship came to the attention of the faculty, I would have no choice but to resign my post immediately.*

*I love you, Bridget, more than I believe you know, and I will love you until the day I die. I don't want to keep that love a secret. My heart is heavy to leave you in this way, but your future is at a critical point. Achieve your degree! When you have, we will be free to explore our theory, search for Atlantis, and spend the rest of our lives together.*

*My darling Bridget, I hope you understand and forgive me for the hurt you will be feeling right at this moment, but please believe me, it's for the best. I will contact you again when I have an address in Greece.*

*All my love, from your soulmate, lover, and fellow archaeologist,*

*Tommy XXX*

By the end of the letter, the pain in my throat was so severe, my voice trembled.

'How sad, Mam. You must have been devastated. What a sacrifice Dad made so that you could stay at university.'

I thought about him, the old man in a care home. Doddery, forgetful, and mostly silent. I could not remember the last time I saw him smile. At that moment, I wanted to be with him, give him a hug, tell him I was proud to be his daughter.

Perhaps I had left it too late with Mam, but I would not make the same mistake twice.

To imagine my father as a young man filled with passion and sacrifice was difficult. Currently, he could easily be described as a grumpy old git, but my heart swelled and I promised myself I would phone him the moment I left the hospital. Poor man, all alone because a year ago his wife returned to Greece without him.

Why did she do that, after all he seemed to have given up for her? Mystified and slightly disappointed, I hoped there was a logical explanation.

I tried to bring the subject up while my mother stayed with us in Sitric Road but she refused to talk about it, insisting she would explain everything when she could.

My throat hurt from holding back a sob; the letter had made me too emotional. 'He must have loved you very much, Mam. In fact, I believe he still does.'

I gazed at her face, trying to understand, when a tear trickled from under her closed eye. *Oh!* I couldn't believe it and, for a moment, I couldn't move either. I bent over, my face close to hers. There was definitely a wet line from the corner of her eye to the bandages above her ear.

'Nurse!' I shouted, panic-driven, emotions exploding in my chest. I raced out into the deserted corridor, then turned back into the room and hit the red call button.

Moments later, the medical staff rushed in.

'She's crying, my mother, she's crying!' And I was crying too. 'She's waking up! She's going to pull out of the coma, I know she is, she has to!' I slapped my hand on my chest. 'I can feel it in my heart. She's going to be all right.'

The nurse touched my arm. 'This happens sometimes. It's not a reaction to you,' she said sympathetically, pulling a bleeper from her pocket.

'No, I was reading to her, something poignant, and she started crying. I saw it myself.'

'Irini, she can't wake up. Your mother's in an *induced* coma.' The doctor came in and strode over to the bed.

The nurse's words tore away the hope that had engulfed me. I gripped her arm. 'Then stop inducing the coma. Let her wake up! I know she heard me. She was emotional! Her brain *is* working!' I was shouting – I couldn't help it. They had to listen. They had to! Then I was sobbing so hard I couldn't speak.

The doctor lifted my mother's lids and shone a little torch into her eyes, then he folded back one sheet and put the stethoscope to her chest. I was drawn to a white spear-shaped scar across her breastbone that I had never seen before. Shocked, I couldn't help thinking that the four-centimetre slash looked like a stab wound, or some kind of ritualistic tribal marking. I was still staring at it when the doctor straighted, shook his head and said, 'I'm sorry.'

The room was spinning. My heart banged at my ribs. 'What? No!' I rushed over to the bedside, hardly daring to ask. 'What do you mean . . .' I choked, gulped, and tried again. 'What do you mean, you're sorry?'

'I mean there is no change,' the doctor said.

The relief was exhausting. 'I thought you meant . . .' I dropped into the chair. 'I'm sorry. I didn't mean to make a fuss. It's hard to deal with, that she might not wake up, I mean.' *Oh!* 'I know I have to come to terms with the likely outcome. You did warn me, but it's difficult, mostly because I haven't seen her for a year.' I looked up into the doctor's eyes, begging the forgiveness I needed from my mother.

I had always blamed her for our distance, but I'm an adult now. There was no excuse for my entrenched bitterness. I could have stepped towards her with my hands out. I badly needed to make things right between us.

The doctor was slim. Greek, I think. He nodded, a soft smile of absolution fluttering across his tired face. 'Why don't you take a break? Get yourself a coffee while we make your mother comfortable. Come back in half an hour.' He spoke to the nurse in Greek.

She also smiled gently. Kind people, and me almost hysterical. 'Come, I'll show you where the café is,' she said.

I bought a coffee, took it outside, and sat in a shady corner while thirty minutes ticked slowly by.

# CHAPTER 11
## BRIDGET

*Santorini, 29 years ago.*

A WEEK LATER, I saw Tommy through the glass doors as I approached the Heraklion hospital. My husband sat in a wheelchair, his few belongings in a bag at his side. I noticed how he had aged: bags under his eyes and lines on his forehead.

'Oh, Tommy!' I cried. 'You look so much better. How do you feel?' I stooped and kissed his cheek.

'Hello, darling girl. It's lovely to see you.' He sighed. 'I feel a bit rough, but I'm really looking forward to sleeping in my own bed.'

'Come on then, there's a taxi waiting. The ferry for Santorini leaves in two hours.'

Splotskey approached. 'A word at the desk, Bridget. Some papers to sign. It won't take a minute.'

I followed him across the lobby and signed everything he put in front of me.

'Mr McGuire will have to report to the Santorini hospital in a week's time, and if all is okay, once a month for a check-up. I want him to have complete rest for a fortnight.'

I nodded. 'We're so grateful, doctor. Without your help, I don't know where we'd be.'

'Yes, yes. I'll be keeping an eye on his progress, but I must remind you, there are still some bills to pay.'

'Bills? You mean I still owe you money?' I said in alarm.

'No, no, not me, Bridget. I just assisted you in your hour of need. I don't usually get involved in such things, but with you having a baby on the way, well, I wanted to help.'

'And I'm eternally grateful, but how much do we owe?' I glanced over at Tommy, who was watching us.

'The trinket covered the operation, but there's intensive care, the room, x-rays, blood tests, various other tests, nursing, meals, and so on. I'm afraid it adds up to a substantial amount.'

*Trinket!* Horrified by his description, I found myself stunned for a moment. 'I see . . . Do I have to pay it immediately?' I stuttered once I'd recovered enough to speak.

'No, no, but as soon as you can, otherwise it puts me in an awkward position, you understand?' He glanced around nervously. 'I have to think of my reputation here. If it got out that I'd done favours for a patient, well . . .'

'I understand, I do. I'll deal with it as soon as I get home,' I said hurriedly. Was there no end to my money worries? The cash from the church had gone on ferry tickets and taxi fares, and I'd sent Quinlan his money back, thinking I didn't need it and not wanting to be in his debt.

\* \* \*

The trip home exhausted us both. Between my concern for Tommy, tiredness caused by my pregnancy, and my financial worries, I just wanted to lie down and sleep. My last dream had looped my mind all day. Like a radio tune, it wheedled into my thoughts and interrupted logic to the point of distraction. I was glad to arrive home and unlock our front door at nine o'clock that night.

Tommy was worn out. I made him a mug of strong, sweet tea, which he claimed to be the best in a week, then I got him into bed. A kindly neighbour brought us a plate of warm cheese pies, and we settled on the bed in our underwear, eating supper and drinking from a bottle of cool water.

I lay awake worrying about my husband, the hospital bills, and my piece for the magazine. I had discovered writer's block – every sentence led into a blind alley. With Tommy's heart attack came the realisation that at any moment, our perfect life could change dramatically. More so now with a baby on the way. For the first time in my life, I felt helpless and afraid for our future. Happiness was such a fragile thing.

\* \* \*

A week later, Aaron came to see Tommy and pass on some amazing news from the site.

'How's your heart now, Tommy?'

I could see more than Aaron's usual good humour radiating from his face. Tommy assured Aaron he was on the mend. After sitting opposite him, the young archaeologist leaned forward and rested his forearms on his knees. Excitement danced in his eyes.

I hovered, sensing an important revelation.

'Right, well, you had better try and keep calm, Tommy,' he said. 'Listen to this. We've discovered the top of a fresco in room three! The colours are wonderful. We think it covers the entire wall. Right now, we are about twelve inches down, but it appears to be intact. Everyone's so excited. We've all worked from dawn to dusk while you've been poorly.'

Tommy's jaw dropped and I felt my own excitement rising. 'What do you see?' I asked, conscious of the tremor in my voice.

'Well, you must understand we're hardly into it, but there's a frieze along the top, and today we uncovered the start of a head – a woman, I think. Looks like coiled black hair, perhaps waxed.'

Tommy took my hand and squeezed. 'Could this be the start of something big?' he whispered.

'It's big, believe me!' Aaron stood and paced. 'Judging by the hair, the image is life-size. We've cleared all the way along on the same level and not found anything else in the picture at that height. This means our figure is above whatever else is in the picture. You know what that suggests?'

Tommy's grip on my hand tightened. 'You're probably revealing a ruler, a king or queen, perhaps even a deity.'

'Exactly. Do you want me to pick you up in the morning, take you down there for an hour or two?'

'Is the pope Catholic? For a well-educated young man, you ask some pretty stupid questions,' Tommy replied, then turning to me, he said, 'Bring some beers out, Bridget. This calls for a celebration!'

'The doctor said no alcohol, Tommy. Are you completely mad?'

'Cobblers! One beer won't hurt now, will it?'

So uplifted by Tommy's mood, I relented and gave them a beer each. 'If you drop dead because of this, Tommy McGuire, I'll kill you myself!' I told him. 'Now I'm going indoors to work on my article. Can I trust the two of you to behave?'

They grinned and nodded.

\* \* \*

I had my head down, still struggling with my piece on antiquities theft when the phone rang. Was this the call I dreaded?

I glanced through the doorway at the men, talking in a shady corner of the patio.

'Hello, Bridget McGuire,' I said.

'Bridget, it's Splotskey. How's your husband after his journey home?'

I turned my back to the patio and spoke quietly. 'He's fine, Doctor. A little tired, but glad to be back in Santorini and sleeping in his own home.'

'Good, good. Sorry to bother you, but I'm under pressure here. Can you tell me when you'll have the funds to cover Mr McGuire's medical costs?'

I gulped. 'Well, it's difficult. I mean, I'll pay, but it's going to take me some time to gather the money together.' There was a long silence. 'Doctor, are you there?'

'Yes, yes, but I've a problem, Bridget.' Another lengthy pause before he continued. 'I thought the dealer had underpaid for that necklace, so I tried to ease your burden. I asked if he could let us have a little more money.' Splotskey's aloof tone had gone. He sounded nervous. No, more than that – afraid. 'Now he's threatening me . . . blackmailing me. If I don't provide another antiquity, he'll not only expose me as a dealer in artefacts, which I'm not, but he'll make sure the authorities know *you* sold an antiquity from the archaeological site.'

My knees gave way and I had to cling onto a chairback, then I jumped when Aaron touched my arm.

'Is everything all right, Bridget?' he asked quietly, nodding to the phone in my hand. 'You look pale.'

'I'm fine. It's one of the archaeology magazines I write for,' I said, waving the receiver.

'What are we going to do, Bridget? I'm out of my league here,' Splotskey was saying when I put the phone back to my ear.

113

Aaron nodded and I watched him continue through to the bathroom before I whispered to the surgeon, 'Look, I'll find something. Give me your private number and I'll contact you from a call box in a couple of days.'

\* \* \*

I fretted all night. What was I going to do? If I came clean, called the police and confessed to selling the dragonfly necklace, both Tommy and I would never be allowed to work in archaeology again. There was also a strong likelihood of a prison sentence. Tommy would never forgive me. Our baby would be born in prison and taken away from me. We would lose everything.

There seemed only one solution. I had to give Splotskey something else. I hated myself for even thinking about it, but what could I do? Once I had made my decision, a weight lifted from me and I fell into a restless sleep, but then my nightmares returned.

In the dream, I had given birth, and my baby – a little girl – lay naked on her back in the cradle, trying to catch her toes. I watched her and laughed.

'Will you get on with the dinner!' Tommy shouted, jealous of the constant attention I gave our child.

Furious with my husband, I continued preparing food. I lifted a sharp knife, plunged it into the chicken's breast, venting my anger by roughly disjointing the poultry, but then realised I was dismembering the baby. I stared at the pink meat and small bones in horror, then scooped them up and threw them in the casserole.

Instantly, I found myself surrounded by a mob of angry people. I tried to run, but my feet wouldn't move. I was herded towards a noose that hung over Santorini's caldera. My arms were pinned down, my eyes blindfolded.

The hangman shouted in my ear, 'Wake up, Bridget! Open your eyes!' I struggled against him. The rope was around my neck and I was forced towards the edge of the caldera, closer and closer . . . I dug my heels in and pushed back, but the weight of people behind me would not budge.

'Thief! Thief! Thief!' they chanted.

'Don't let me go, Tommy! Don't let me go!' I cried, my voice so thick the words hardly formed.

In a moment of confusion, between sleep and wakefulness, I was falling, quite sure my neck would snap in the next second and my life would end.

Tommy shook me. 'You're dreaming, Bridget. You're having a nightmare.'

Then I realised it was the mattress at my back and Tommy's arms enfolding me.

'Oh, dear God, I think I'm going mad,' I whimpered against his chest. 'The dream was so real, so horrible!' Then I remembered his operation and pulled away. 'Sorry, did I hurt you with my thrashing about?'

He shook his head.

I slipped out of bed and lit a candle. 'I'm going to make myself a cup of tea. Do you want one?'

He didn't answer, his eyes closed and his breathing slow and even. While I waited for the kettle, I wrote down the terrible nightmare.

\* \* \*

The next morning, Aaron picked us up. I was frantic about Tommy climbing the steps, and although it was a long process, he eventually reached the road and Aaron's pick-up.

At the archaeological site, Aaron led us to the all-important fresco. Tommy was beside himself with glee, and I should have been too, but all I could think was: *what can I steal?* At the trestle, I studied pieces of pottery. The little jug lay where I had left it.

'Sorry,' Aaron said. 'I haven't had time to do anything at the table. It's all labelled with its provenance, but that's about it.'

I stared at the jug, my insides trembling. Would it settle my debt and get rid of Splotskey?

'Don't worry, Aaron. I'll take some home to work on. I don't want to leave Tommy on his own at home.'

'What about help?' Tommy said. 'Anyone coming from the archaeology schools?'

'Yes, good news, we've got another group starting on Monday: ten students from the Irish Institute of Hellenic Studies in Athens. They're staying for a month.'

'Are you sure you're up to it?' I said, carefully packing the jug pieces. 'Students can be difficult.'

He shifted his weight from one foot to the other, and for a second, I fancied that he was blushing.

'It's my dream, Bridget. To be in charge of a dig at my age, it's remarkable. I'm so grateful to you and Tommy for trusting me with all this.' Aaron came from a bad family in Ireland, who were both violent and involved in various crimes connected to drugs. Over the years, he had sort of adopted us, and we were both very fond of him. The short-tempered kid with a chip on his shoulder had grown into a fine young man eager to take on responsibility. Now he spread his arms and grinned bashfully. 'If I have any problems, I'll come to you straight away. Meanwhile, feel free to concentrate on getting Tommy fit again.'

\* \* \*

The nightmares and headaches were driving me crazy. Half convinced they were God's punishment for the wrongs I had done, I decided to go to confession on Saturday and atone for my sins. The Cathedral of Saint John the Baptist was not far from our house. Despite my worries, the beauty of the building thrilled me.

An ornate clock tower rose above the church itself, both painted yellow with sky-blue reliefs and corners. The typical Santorini church dome was white, as opposed to the royal-blue gloss of Orthodox churches.

I stopped on the narrow approach road and gazed through an arch that framed the building and tower perfectly. To my left, more religious buildings competed for space amongst the jungle of dwellings, boutiques, and tavernas. To my right, a sheer drop down to the caldera, with its cruise ships and the smouldering mass of Burnt Island in the centre.

I knew the Catholic priest very well, as he did me, yet we remained invisible to each other with the confessional screen dividing us.

'My child,' the priest said kindly after I had admitted everything. 'You have to get the dragonfly necklace back and return it to its rightful place.'

'But, Father, I can't. It's impossible.'

'Then you must go to the police and tell them what's happened. Pray to God they'll understand and be lenient with you, then your sins will be forgiven.'

I couldn't go to the police. I had wanted to say a few rosaries and receive absolution. If I went to the authorities, I knew I would go to prison, my baby would be taken from me, while Tommy, whom I constantly fretted about, still needed my special care.

We would both be shamed in the world of archaeology, especially as I was steadily gaining a reputation for standing up against the theft of artefacts. I just couldn't take the risk. I had a baby to think of now. Besides that, I came to realise if Tommy ever found out, he would never forgive me; and worse, the shock – rage – might bring on another heart attack.

*  *  *

The next day, I cycled down to the site while Tommy rested.

'Hi. How's it going, Aaron?'

'Good. We've uncovered more of the fresco. I believe the picture is complete, but there's still a long way to go. I've got some more really exciting news: I think this is the first floor. There's another level below us.'

'You really think we're looking at the top floor of a two-storey building?' I asked excitedly. 'Oh, wow, that's amazing! You know what this means? Anything that was on this level may have fallen down to the lower level over time. That would account for the sparsity of artefacts. I wonder what we'll find hidden down there.' I stared at his feet, thrilled at the prospect, and wishing I could stay and help with the excavation.

*  *  *

One sin always leads to another; I know that for a fact now. The theft of the dragonfly necklace led to the theft of the jug, and I knew I would suffer more sleepless nights because of that treachery, but what else could I do? Despite trying to think of an alternative, I seemed destined to live with the lies and deceit.

Tommy was still sleeping when I returned from the site. The little jug still needed some restoration work and this gave me an idea. Knowing that the artefact would be hidden away and cared for in a private collection, probably only to re-appear when the owner died, was small consolation. However, if the artefact came to light in the future, it would simply be a beautiful old jug from thousands of years ago. In other words, it would have no provenance. Although its age could be proved, its origins would be unknown.

Tommy had a micro pen and a magnifying glass somewhere. I found them in his desk drawer. In the smallest writing possible, I wrote on a paper label the date, longitude and latitude of the site, and B1, which was the find area. Then, for good measure, I wrote the phone number of the archaeological site. I stuck a strip of Sellotape on both sides of my note, and then cut closely around the information.

I mixed a little Polyfilla and stuck the label to a section of webbing, already fixed into the belly of the jug. After filling inside and out, the information was undetectable. We usually left these sections blank, but I copied the pattern and painted in the small missing section. This made the jug seem complete and only an x-ray would reveal the mesh, infill, and the information inside.

The charming little jug was pale cream with almost black calligraphy-like drawings of swallows on the wing, sacred lilies, and crocus flowers around the base. I sketched a copy into my notebook. Using a protractor and a ruler, I wrote down accurate measurements, and then took it outside to photograph.

I hoped the buyer did not use x-ray.

Early that evening, I made an excuse to go to the supermarket. On my way, I phoned Splotskey from a callbox.

'I have something for you,' I said, without preliminary greeting. 'A small jug, Minoan era, from the temple. An offering vessel, quite exquisite, cream, decorated with birds and flowers. Circa two thousand BC.'

'Bring it tomorrow.'

'No, wait! I can't bring it to Crete. Can't you come here to collect it?'

'It's impossible – I have surgery, Bridget. Come on the first ferry and get the same one back.'

'But I don't have the money for ferry tickets, Doctor. We're struggling here.'

After a moment he said, 'Borrow the money. I'll give it back to you when you get here.' He hung up.

\* \* \*

'You seem preoccupied, Bridget,' Tommy said when I arrived home.

'Ah, do I? One of the church ladies is having a get-together lunch, over in Perissa tomorrow. It's her birthday and she asked if I could go. I'm trying to figure a way out of it.'

'You should go, take a break, enjoy yourself for once. Make the most of your freedom before the baby comes.'

'Oh, I don't know. I'd need to buy a present and we hardly have money to spare.'

'I've got some coins in my top pocket. Take them, buy a present and go. Have a nice time.'

'Thank you!'

There I was, deceiving my husband again, the lie growing. Yet I believed this would be the end of it. I fell asleep going through my plans for the next day, and those thoughts must have distorted themselves into a dream-scene that involved Thira and her child, the girl who had just come of age. I felt Thira's pride and joy for her daughter; mine would be the same. I had always secretly hoped for a little girl. I recalled where my dream had left off: Thira's beautiful daughter was proud to stand next to her mother, the great Queen of Atlantis. The queen herself under enormous pressure to keep her subjects safe from the wrath of Poseidon. I thought that if Queen Thira could rise above her problems, then so could I.

# CHAPTER 12
## IRINI

*Santorini, present day.*

MAM'S TEARS WERE FIXED in my mind, and despite taking time over a sweet tea in the hospital café, they were all I could think about. When I returned to the ward, the nurse led me to the doctor's office. He explained the details of an induced coma. His team would keep my mother in that state for a while, to see if her brain started to repair itself. The damage was so intense, he doubted there would be a change and, in that event, they would have no choice but to turn off the life support and allow her to die peacefully. They had the power to do that, but would rather have my permission first, of course.

I made my reluctance clear. Miracles did happen.

Relieved to find a taxi outside the hospital, I slid into the front seat.

'Can you take me into town, please?' I asked the overweight Green in his late fifties.

'Yes, madam!' He grinned. 'I take you anywhere you want. You English?'

'I'm Irish.'

'Hello, Iris, I am Spiro. Welcome to my island!'

'Irish.'

'Yes, Iris. Me, Spiro.' He poked himself in the chest with a thumb. 'Holidays?'

I couldn't be bothered to correct him and shook my head. 'No, my mother lives here. She's unwell so I came to visit.' I nodded towards the hospital.

'Ah, quick recovery to her,' he said. 'Who is your mother? I knows everyone.'

I found that hard to believe. 'Bridget McGuire, the—'

'No! The archaeologist! This is my lucky day, to have Bridget's beautiful daughter in my taxi.' He tapped the side of his nose. 'Later, I will buy a lottery ticket. I am very big friends of Bridget. She comes to my house to eat when there is festival. Mrs Bridget is a good lady.' He was quiet for a moment. 'I am sorry for her. She was buried, yes? I heard this.'

For the first time, I realised I had no notion of what happened at the site. 'I don't have any details yet, Spiro, but she is in a coma. The doctor doesn't think she'll make it.'

'What will she not make?' He put the car into gear, glanced at me, then looked sheepish. 'Oh, I understand. Sorry. Sorry!'

He paused, staring out of the stationary car, clearly upset. 'I hope she has no pain. You must tell Bridget I will light many candles for her.' He sighed and then pulled off without looking, almost hitting a passing scooter. '*Malaka* tourist!' he muttered. 'They hire the bikes but they don't know how to drive!'

His ebullience washed over me and I felt some of the tension fall from my shoulders.

'You must come to my house, Iris. My wife is very good cook! She speak perfect English too, like me. Come, eat, be happy for a while.'

'Aw, thank you, Spiro, but I'm exhausted right now. If you don't mind, I'd like to go home.'

He was driving with one hand, the other hung out of the window. We squeezed down narrow streets and bumped down a step into a pedestrian area. The street was busy with tourists and Spiro honked his horn merrily. He pulled up outside a double-fronted jeweller's shop. Gold necklaces and diamond rings glinted from the windows.

'This is as close as I go. You pass through the shop, out the back door, and down the steps opposite. Otherwise, you walk all the way down the road to the next corner, then all the way back along the road below this one. Is too narrow for my taxi down there.' He stuck his head out of the window and yelled, '*Ela*, Yianni. Is my friend here, see, Bridget's daughter, Iris from England!'

I should have corrected him, but I was simply too tired. 'What do I owe you, Spiro?'

'No! No!' he shouted, flicking his fingers at me. 'I no take your money, Iris. I am happy to have you in my taxi. Here is my card. You want anything, you call me, okay?'

I smiled and nodded. 'Thanks, Spiro. It's wonderful of you to be so kind.'

'Nothing, nothing. Now, I go buy Lotto ticket. My lucky day. The gods smile on me. I will light a candle to the Blessed Virgin for your mother. She likes me a lot, the Blessed Virgin, so she may listen to my prayers. And if she is in a good mood, perhaps she will use her holy finger to poke the right balls out of the Lotto machine. Who knows?'

I was giggling as I got out of the taxi.

Spiro observed my mood change, nodded, and pulled away. He scattered pedestrians with his car horn and boomed his greeting, '*Yiassas!*' to several shopkeepers as he proceeded down the arcade.

Yianni, the jeweller, shook my hand and bowed slightly. 'Welcome, Iris,' he said.

I could not believe the man wore a suit and tie. Heat shimmered off the cobblestones and penetrated the soles of my shoes.

Yianni led me through his shop, which I likened to a gilded and highly polished fridge.

'You want anything, you tell me. My back door is always open, Iris,' he said as he pulled it ajar and ushered me through. 'I am a very good friend of your mother.'

A jeweller's with the back door always open? That had to be unique. The people of Santorini must be incredibly honest.

\* \* \*

The next morning, I pulled on a pair of white linen shorts, a baggy yellow shirt, and my white, wide-brimmed sunhat. I once heard it said: *You can't see yellow and not feel happy.* I hoped it would work on my mother. Would she open her eyes today? Was it futile to hope? To pray? To dream the impossible dream? I was clinging hysterically to myths and legends and miracles, which my logical mind told me where highly improbable.

On my way to the hospital, I stepped into a *fournos* for a fresh loaf and a spinach pie. For a moment, I was lost in the warm, yeasty smell of the bakery. Shelves of cooling bread lined the walls, and before me was a counter covered in trays of donuts, buns, and pies. The woman behind the counter looked exhausted. I handed her a small brown loaf and pointed at a donut-shaped pie made from flaking filo pastry.

'Cheese and spinach,' she said, smiling shyly. 'You English?'

'I'm Irish,' I said. 'I'll take the pie, please.'

'Ah, Iris, Bridget's daughter. Yes, of course, the red hair. Spiro told me you were here.' She seemed oblivious to the elderly locals forming an untidy queue behind me. 'Welcome to Santorini, Iris.' She shoved the bread and pie into a carrier and addressed the people now filling the shop.

125

Unsure of what she said, I caught the words: 'Iris' and 'Bridget', after which everyone surged forward and I was taken back to a game we used to play in the school yard. *We all pat the dog; we all pat the dog; ee, eye, addio, we all pat the dog!* I was heartily slapped on my back, shoulders, and arms. Nodding people with wide smiles surrounded me. 'Welcome! Welcome!' they cried.

'Thank you, thank you very much,' I replied. Some of them spoke to me in Greek and I was bewildered as how to answer, so I smiled and nodded. Someone shook my hand vigorously.

'English! English!' the baker cried, and I guessed I would have to get used to that little irritation.

I tried to give her a five-euro note, but she thumped herself in the chest twice, then held her hand towards me. 'You no pay! Is a gift from me,' she yelled. 'Well wishes for Mrs Bridget!'

And everyone cried, 'Yes! Yes!'

I had a bizarre feeling I was trapped in some kind of farce. After a hurried thank you, I squeezed out of the shop and marched towards the hospital.

There was an air of excitement in the day. School children called, 'Good morning, lady,' and giggled, jostling each other playfully. Older folk nodded and smiled as they passed by. At one of the churches, two men with a step ladder were hanging bunting around the forecourt, and short, rotund women dressed in black appeared with wide baskets of glossy-crusted bread.

The church doors were open and I glanced inside as I passed. The interior was nothing like the sombre misery of Catholic churches in Dublin. The walls were a riot of primary colours, clearly a celebration of life. Frescoes of life-size saints and holy scenes covered every inch of plaster. The ceiling was like a vivid cartoon of the Sistine Chapel. Sunlight blazed through high, stained glass windows, streaming a rainbow of dazzling colour diagonally through the air.

Three of the largest crystal chandeliers I had ever seen hung above the nave. The aisles had easels supporting ornate, gilded frames that surrounded silver or gold etchings of the holy family. The door was flanked by intricate wooden cradles of beeswax candles. In sand-filled troughs above them, thin tapers of many different lengths flickered candlelight into the shady church. I sensed it would be easy to find peace of mind inside that building.

So uplifted by the scene, I was tempted to slip in and say a prayer for my mother, but I hurried on.

Outside town, a car skidded to a halt beside me. Spiro in his taxi.

'Iris! Good morning! Come, I will take you.'

I could *see* the hospital. Ludicrous to get into the taxi, but I did.

'You brought me good luck, Iris!' We veered dangerously close to the kerb as he grinned at me and I was so glad the road was straight with no lampposts yet.

'Mind! Oh!' I slapped my hand to my chest, my own recent accident still vivid in my mind. He jerked the taxi back on course. 'Don't tell me you won something on the Lotto, Spiro?'

'Three numbers I needed, Iris. Just three. But if I got those three and won the millions, I would not be driving my taxi today and you would have fried in the sun. Bridget would not have been happy with me if I let you cook, and you would have been in terrible pain. My wife would have wanted new everything, and my friends would not play poker with me if I was such a winner. So you see, I am very lucky I did not win!'

I was laughing again. 'One day, Spiro, I'm sure you'll win.'

127

My laughter died as I entered the hospital and hurried down the hospital corridor, impatient to see my mother and read more of her letters. Infused by the kindness and joviality of the locals, I felt a little more positive. After all, they did say there was *little* hope for my mother – not, no hope at all.

\* \* \*

No change in my mother's health, but she was stable and, as far as I knew, without pain. I told her about Spiro, and the locals in the bakery who sent their good wishes. I had placed her notebooks in the drawer of her bedside locker. This was to stop me from reading them on my own, at the house. I wanted to share this journey of discovery with her. We had never shared anything before.

In the pink ribbon of letters, I found an envelope with *RETURN TO SENDER* stamped across the Irish address. In smaller letters it said: *The recipient no longer resides at this abode.* I opened the sealed envelope carefully and recognised my mother's handwriting.

*My dearest, darling Tommy,*

*Please don't go to Greece without me! I love you more than life itself! Don't break my heart, Tommy McGuire! I want to be by your side, always. I dream of us discovering great things together. You can't leave me this way.*

*You're all I want, all I wish for. University is a complete waste of time if you are not there, because I cannot concentrate on anything but you. I did well because I wanted to please you and you alone. You are my life.*

*I know you say I am too young for you, but what is age when we have true love? Such a thing must be a once in a lifetime gift from God. We cannot abandon our hearts. I cried all night, and I will cry every night until we are together again.*

*We are destined to be happy together because we belong to each other. You can teach me all I need to know, and I don't just mean about archaeology.*

*Please, please, please, reply immediately. End this torture. Stop the tears of my broken heart. Change your plans to include me and, I swear on my life, I will never let you down.*

*All my love, forever,*

*Your broken-hearted Bridget xxx*

I stared at the page. Daddy had already left for Santorini and never received the mail. They were so in love, and this made me wonder what happened to turn them against each other later. I thought back to my time with both of them in Dublin. This passion was nowhere in sight. It had been replaced with resentment and bitterness.

Why didn't they separate? Better to be apart than together with the animosity I had seen every day in Dublin. Yet underneath that display of discontent, I wondered if it was the memory of their love that kept them together. Although they had lived apart for the past year, I knew my father ached for Mam. Sometimes he would look at me, and I knew he was thinking of her. I decided, whatever happened to my mother, I would take the letter home and read it to my father. I opened the *Book of Dreams* and start reading quietly.

\* \* \*

It happened again last night. How can I go on like this? I know Tommy tells me they are only dreams, but when they happen, they are so real! I had the worst nightmare ever last night. Eventually I woke, drenched in sweat. Terrible dread had turned my body to lead. I couldn't move. Suspended in horror, I had no notion of where I was. That's how tangible the nightmarish experience felt. In those initial moments of waking, I don't know how long it took to gather myself together and realise I was still in bed in our hyposkafa.

Such fear would not be measured by time, only by intensity. My first thought: was it a dream or did it really happen?

I placed my hands on my swollen belly. Thank God! Our baby was still safe inside me. Nothing would harm her there. As if sensing my worry, she kicked and rolled, and I felt a small knee or elbow push again my palm, then slide across to the other side. Was she afraid too? She must be able to hear my heart hammering.

The nightmare left me weak and trembling so violently that I could hardly stand when I slipped out of bed for a glass of water. I turned on the small lamp and stared around, looking for something familiar to anchor reality onto. I am terrified I'm going mad.

In the dream, I killed my little girl again! How many times must I go through this, and why? Is it my punishment for leading a life of deceit? Is this what my life has become – one big lie?

I stole the dragonfly necklace because I was desperate. I truly believe I had no choice. And the jug . . . Now I've only made matters worse by lying to the man I love.

\* \* \*

130

I stared at my mother, horrified by what I had read. What was going on? The words were too much to take in. Why would she dream about killing me? What was the dragonfly necklace, and what was its relevance? Had she started shoplifting?

'Mam, I don't understand what I'm reading here. Who did you steal the dragonfly necklace from? Was it Yianni, the jeweller's near the house? I met him yesterday. I told you, do you remember?'

I studied her face while searching my mind for an answer.

'Did you really think you might kill me? You might actually *kill* me? Is that why you sent me away, Mam, because you feared you would harm me? You were afraid for my life?' *Oh!* 'And I grew up thinking it was because you didn't want me . . . I thought you didn't love me and couldn't stand to share your life with me. I thought I was a pest and you wanted me out of the way.'

One page of writing had changed everything. Destroyed the certainty I had grown up with, that I was not loved, not wanted. The lonely child, confused by the affection I had seen other parents give to my school friends. Feeling different, always wondering: *what was wrong with me?* Ashamed.

I thought about it for a long time, considered what she had written, contemplated the years we were apart, analysed the startling fact that I had suffered all that misery through my childhood because of a dream?! The very idea made me furious.

Then I saw it . . . I couldn't believe what had happened. Her thumb twitched. Just a slight movement, but then it happened again.

I hit the call button.

# CHAPTER 13
## BRIDGET

*Santorini, 29 years ago.*

THE NEXT MORNING, I hurriedly prepared Tommy's breakfast and laid out his numerous pills. 'Are you sure you'll be all right, Tommy? I've ordered you a chicken pitta for lunch and I'll be back around dinner time.'

'Go, woman! Stop fussing. I'm not an invalid. Have a good time with your friends.'

I hurried to the square and caught the bus down to Athinios Port. At the harbour ticket office, I bought a single for the ferry to Heraklion, which I could see approaching the quayside at that very moment. I surveyed the curving clifftop along the landmass to the town of Fira. Tommy would be sitting on the patio, looking down at the ferry with no notion that I was about to board it. He thought I was on the bus to Perissa, on the south coast of Santorini.

I had never deceived him in such a way before. First the dragonfly necklace, and now the ancient jug and the lie about a birthday party. Sure that my problems would be over once Splotskey had this artefact, I boarded the ship. In a few hours I would be in Heraklion. Splotskey was going to meet me at the port with my return ticket. All I had to do was hand over the artefact and return to Santorini.

What could go wrong?

I told myself I was doing this for Tommy and our baby. I didn't want my child born in a prison and growing up without a father, and I would rather die myself than have anything happen to either of them. The jug would hardly make any difference in the world of archaeology, but if Tommy had died, then archaeology would have lost a truly great historian who gave his life to the task of revealing the past in all its complicated layers.

The skyline of Heraklion came into view, a low hill of hotels and blocks of flats. Moored at the quayside, a row of ferry ships destined for other Greek islands. The fortress of Koules, on a mole that elbowed its way out to sea, shimmered golden in the midday sun. Dense shadows accentuated the castellated fortification. In one sandstone block, the relief of a lion was softly rounded by the winds of time. Next to the stronghold lay Heraklion's traditional fishing port with its ubiquitous piles of yellow net and brightly painted boats.

If my mission had not been criminal, I would have enjoyed the moment of arrival in Crete, but my mouth dried and heart raced. From my high position at the back of the ferry, I peered at the cement wharf as we reversed towards it, searching for Splotskey in the mill of people below. After waiting until the articulated wagons, trucks, and cars had disembarked, I hurried down three decks to the ship's exit, which was packed with perspiring tourists and thick with diesel fumes. When the stevedore lifted the barrier, a mad rush headed for fresh air and the quayside.

Where was Splotskey? I didn't have the money to buy my return ticket to Santorini! What if the doctor didn't turn up? I scanned the waiting passengers and then hurried to the ticket booth. This was a disaster! I could not get back on the ship without a ticket. The whole plan was a stupid idea and I feared I should not have come. I raced along the quayside, behind the queue of cars and lorries waiting to board. Where was he?!

'Bridget!'

Was that Splotskey's voice? Confused that I couldn't see him, I peered around wildly. People were already boarding. Stevedores swiped the air with a wide hand, hurrying vehicles over the boarding ramp and onto the ferry. I still had no ticket!

'Bridget, over here!'

I stood on my toes, staring over people's heads. A car flashed its headlights, Splotskey behind the wheel. I hurried over.

'Dear God! I thought you hadn't come!' I cried in distress.

'Have you got it, Bridget?' He looked as though he hadn't slept in a month.

I nodded and passed the box containing the artefact through the car window.

He placed it on the seat beside him and handed me an envelope. 'There's your ticket back to Santorini, and a little extra money to cover your expenses.'

'Never again,' I said. 'You'll never ask me to do this again, okay?!' I spun around and headed straight back onto the ship without waiting for an answer.

\* \* \*

Four hours later, I arrived home, flustered and guilty.

'Did you have a good time?' Tommy asked quietly.

'Yes, yes, of course.' I avoided his eyes but the guilt in me would not go away. I went over and fell into his arms. 'No, to tell the truth. I wish I hadn't gone. I missed you.'

'I love you, Bridget, you know that,' he said. After a moment's silence he stroked my hair and continued. 'I'm so much older than you. There must have been times when you've craved the company of people your own age. It's only natural. You *can* tell me, do you understand? I don't want there to be secrets

134

between us.' He held me away from him, to look into my face. 'Just promise me you'll never leave me – and that you'll always be discreet.'

It took a moment for me to understand what he was saying.

'Tommy! You don't think I've been with another man, do you?'

'Haven't you?' He lowered his eyes.

'What . . . ? I'm speechless!' I stared, recalling the young professor I had fallen in love with. He was a little the worse for wear at the moment, but inside he was that same man and I would never even think of looking at another. 'No, of course I haven't. My God, I can't believe you would think such a thing! You're my world, you *eejit*.'

'Oh, all right, sorry,' he said, looking confused and a little embarrassed. 'Only, I know I'm not as young as I was, you'll never get me dancing, and since the op, I haven't had the urge to . . . you know, be very active between the sheets. So I thought . . .'

'Tommy McGuire, you are mad. Whatever made you think such a thing?'

He stared at the floor for a moment. 'Father Yeorgo came around this afternoon and he didn't seem to know about any birthday party. It got me thinking. I can't tell you how relieved I am. I've fretted all day. Made me feel quite ill, imagining, you know?'

'You really thought I'd gone off with some bloke? Tommy McGuire, don't you ever think that of me. You're my world. I'm shocked. Shame on you!'

'Then what is it? I feel something's wrong, Bridget. You've seemed so distracted lately.'

'Of course I'm distracted, you lummox! You nearly died, Tommy; I'm having a baby; and these crazy dreams are driving me bonkers.' I took his hand. 'Let me expand on that. In the first place, I should have realised you weren't well, and I didn't. If I'd lost you, I'd never have forgiven myself. Secondly, my hormones are all over the place. And last of all, I'm desperate for a good night's sleep without my weird dreams. It would be a miracle if I wasn't distracted. Now, no more of this nonsense. I don't want you worrying about me at all, do you hear?'

After that escapade, I concentrated on getting Tommy fit, and I looked after my own pregnancy until the day my baby was born. To my relief, Tommy never mentioned the incident again, nor did I hear from Splotskey.

* * *

Tommy's recovery was slow but steady. Once he could manage the steps, he took it upon himself to get the bread each morning, but after only three trips, he gave up. News about the baby spread quickly. Beaming men grabbed Tommy in the street and shook his hand vigorously; some even hugged him and kissed his cheeks.

After one such occasion, he returned and cried, 'I thought my scar would unzip and my heart pop right out!'

'Our friends are lovely, aren't they?' I said. 'They share their feelings so openly. I wonder when we north Europeans became uptight about showing affection, thinking it's good to mind our own business? I prefer the Greek way. They were all quite amazing while you were in Crete, Tommy. Each one went to our hospital and gave blood, so we had less to pay for your transfusions, and I found eggs or fruit or vegetables on the table each morning. Also, Anna and Spiro brought me a meal every evening so I didn't have to cook. They're so incredibly kind.'

Tommy smiled, and then appeared sad.

'Are you all right?' I asked.

'I nearly died, Bridget. I keep wondering what would have happened to you, with our baby on the way. How would you have managed? Would you have gone back to Ireland? And darling girl, I've been feeling so ill I haven't asked you – what on earth did you do about the cost of the operation?'

'Look, I have a roof over my head, and a little income from the writing. My life is here, Tommy. Besides, you're not allowed to die, not now after all that palaver. As for the medical bill, it's taken care of, and I don't want to discuss it right now. Just get yourself fit, and go back to work when you're ready, okay?'

'But I can't help worrying about the money, Bridget. Don't shut me out.'

'All right. I sold my grandmother's gold watch, the church donated a lump of cash, and your Quinlan lent us some, which I'm paying back in dribs and drabs. On top of that, the surgeon took pity on us because of the baby, and reduced the cost of the operation. So you see, there is absolutely nothing to fret about.'

'Everything's changed. I feel like a different person. I keep seeing myself as a father with a child looking up to me. We've responsibilities. It's never too early to consider our child's education. Let's think about the future and make plans instead of living day to day, lost in the dig, as we do now. I want to be prepared for our child and give it the best start in life, okay?'

I nodded. 'I love you, Tommy McGuire. You'll be the perfect father.'

* * *

I received another commission to write a regular column, this time for an Australian magazine. Other archaeologists kindly contacted me with information about missing artefacts, which

I passed on to a contact I now had at Interpol. Following these leads, some artefacts were recovered, and although I was not involved directly, a little of the credit landed at my door.

While working on just such an article, Tommy interrupted my thoughts.

'I'm so bored. I can't wait to get back to the site. Bridget, I keep meaning to ask: what happened to that dragonfly necklace we found?'

My skin seemed to shrink over my body. I didn't look up from my writing, ignoring the question while I thought. How could I explain? He wasn't ready for the anger that would explode when he discovered the truth. Tommy would never excuse my actions – they were criminal and I knew it. That I had no other course to take did not make it any less wrong.

'Bridget, are you listening? That dragonfly necklace – what happened to it? Did you find anything else?'

'Oh, sorry, I was miles away. False alarm, Tommy. It was nothing but a modern trinket. *Made in China* was stamped into the back of the last dragonfly.' I kept my head down so he wouldn't see the colour rise in my cheeks. 'It probably belonged to one of the students and snapped while they were working. Sorry to disappoint you, sweetheart.'

My head ached, throbbing so fiercely I had to close my eyes for a moment.

'That's a shame. I hoped upon hope the thing was ancient. Impossible to tell in the first instance, of course. I'm desperate to find something that connects the site to . . . erm . . .'

I knew why he hesitated. Tommy was thinking the word we never used. The word that would be laughed at and make us look like one of the many glory-hunters or sensationalists that had gone before. Archaeologists or historians that were so often purveyed as crack-pots.

'*Atlantis*?' I whispered, looking up. Thank goodness there was nothing to suggest that very thing. It would have killed Tommy if the necklace had made any connection between the site and Plato's Atlantis, and I had lost it.

'Are you all right?' he asked.

'I have a migraine coming. I've had a few lately. Probably the stress, or hormones.'

'Why don't you take yourself away to the chemist, see if she can give you something? Little point in being a martyr to yourself.'

Relieved the subject had changed, I said, 'I'd better not, with the baby and all. Can't be too careful, can we? It'll clear soon.'

'I can't believe that we'll become parents after so long. I'm more thrilled than I can say.'

'You have mentioned that once or twice. Just get yourself a hundred per cent fit, Tommy McGuire!'

'Have you thought about a name at all, Bridget?'

'I have indeed. If it's a boy, Thomas Plato McGuire. What do you think?'

'Poor little bugger! What about Peter, after your uncle?'

I smiled. 'That's kind of you, Tommy. I like it. I was thinking on the same lines. If it's a girl, I'd like to call her Agnes – but it's very old fashioned. I thought about this island that means so much to us. What about Irini?'

*   *   *

I filled out as my pregnancy developed. Thanks to the latest technology, we were thrilled to discover my hoper were correct:

we were having a little girl. Tommy continued to make a steady recovery, and a month after his return from Crete he was back at the site, sifting and sorting every day. The summer students returned to Ireland, but Aaron stayed, deciding to take a year out before his finals. Tommy and I both knew the truth. He didn't want to go home.

He kindly collected Tommy and I at seven-thirty each morning, returning us home in time for our two o'clock siesta. Another magazine – Canadian, this time – asked me to write for them, and I added them to my list of regular earners. I was now referred to as an expert on the subject of antiquities theft. Tommy was so proud of me, but every time I saw my words in print, my heart gave a jolt. If anyone ever found out . . .

Only my dreams changed. The fantasia of regal Atlantis seemed to decompose, leaving awful nightmares from which there was no escape. I will always remember the first vision that brought me complete horror. Until then, my sensory experiences of the past had fascinated me, adding to my archaeological enthusiasm.

That particular day was like any other. We worked hard in the hot sun and returned home for our siesta. Beside Tommy, I closed my eyes and drifted away, recalling my last dream of Atlantis. I returned to the council chamber and my ten kings, yet, as I slid into sleep, pleasure seeped away and I sensed danger. In those seconds before total immersion, I wanted to wake, pull myself away from whatever awaited me, but I sank deeper into the experience, unable to hold on to reality.

\* \* \*

King Hero stands. 'Dear Queen, Supreme Ruler of Atlantis, may I speak with you alone?'

Nine kings leave the chamber and the doors are closed. By myself with Hero, my heart races with foreboding.

'My Queen, this is difficult. The people of Atlantis will not leave the island unless we consider every possible plea to Poseidon. We have no choice but to offer him our highest-ranking maiden on the sacrificial altar.'

Knowing what he means, I can't speak, so turn away, frantic to think of a justifiable response.

'No, this cannot happen, Hero. The highest-ranking maiden is my daughter! How can I consent to such a thing?'

'You are the Goddess of the Marches, blessed by the deities, stronger and more noble than us mere mortals. We fathers give our sons' lives in war for the sake of our country. This is no different. You *will* find the strength to do what is needed, my Queen.'

'They ask too much.' I have to stop this protocol, which has not been invoked since my grandmother ruled the island.

'Why do you think the Gods blessed you with a daughter?' Hero asks. 'Consider she was born to save the populous. Isn't it better for one mother to give her child to Poseidon than all mothers to lose *their* children in the most horrific way? To sacrifice Oia will appease our god, and show the people you are prepared to suffer the greatest loss a mother can, for their sake. The population of Atlantis will follow you to the gates of Hades if you asked them.' He thought for a moment. 'I think it's important that you carry out this task after the River Festival, which is sure to be the most joyous day in Oia's life.'

I am trembling, hardly able to stand as I consider his words. 'So soon? Is there no escape?'

'The River Festival will bring Oia more happiness than she has ever experienced. She will carry that elation to her watery grave, in peace, without grief or agony. We know too well, only the Gods of Olympus have an ageless and deathless existence. Take solace that Oia shall never experience the discomfort of old age. Your daughter is bound to walk the Elysian Fields, admired as the young and beautiful princess that she is, for eternity. Her children will be princes and princesses, blessed by Zeus and fathered by Poseidon.'

* * *

I woke, trembling. Just a dream, yet now I was terrified of the next one. Even to dream such a thing was too horrible to contemplate. What was in my subconscious to make me imagine this obscene thing? Bad enough to be given a leaflet on cot deaths at the clinic, without having the remnants of my nightmare lurking in the back of my mind. This was not how I imagined pregnancy to be.

The headaches and nightmares marred my happiness. The ferocity of the migraines increased to the extent that I had to curl up in a dark corner, holding my head and whimpering until they faded. Then the nightmares continued to take over from the strange and wonderful fantasy of Atlantis.

Before this change in events, I had welcomed the dreams. Since the days of Uncle Peter's bedtime stories, I embraced the drift into this strange era in antiquity, where my knowledge and imagination mingled and ran wild. Now I dreaded going to sleep. Even in my waking hours, I could close my eyes and turn my head, and scenes of Atlantis loomed behind me, vivid and terrifying.

Each night, before sleep, I found myself torn between going back into antiquity and trying to change the end of the dream, or taking myself away from the distressing episode altogether. I longed for the ordinary, jumbled, inexplicable meanderings that most people had, but there was no escape. Dragged by the ear through the rooms of life until I found myself in the body of Queen Thira, Goddess of the Marches. I stood there, regal and omnipotent in my colourful silks, hiding my dread of the future.

My punishment was written. For my theft of the dragonfly necklace, my little girl must die by my own hand.

I fought this awful idea with all my mental strength, yet below the solid and sensible floor of my mind wriggled a slow and carnivorous worm that whispered: *Get it over with, pay the debt, and then you can move on.*

# CHAPTER 14
## IRINI

*Crete, present day.*

THE DOCTOR AND NURSE left and I was alone with my mother again. I could see they were fed up with me. They said all the sympathetic things but the bottom line was: they wanted to turn the machines off. I could not dismiss my mother like she had no value, just because her brain was not fully functional and her body not seen to be working. The injustice of it! I guess I looked calm on the outside, but inside I howled with grief and my pain was almost unbearable.

I had searched online about the right questions to ask, what to expect, and how to deal with the intensive care medical staff. Halfway through our discussion today, I sensed a new respect from the doctor, the outcome of which meant they had agreed to bring my mother out of the coma and see how she'd cope. Clearly, they didn't think she had a chance of surviving, but if any positive signs appeared, they would transfer her to a hospital in Crete for a brain scan.

My hopes rose. I felt my mother *could* hear me, and reading to her helped trigger something that I admit I didn't completely understand myself, but there *was*, finally, a connection between us.

\* \* \*

Back home, I opened a bottle of cheap wine, turned all the lights off, and sat outside. It was a stupid plan because I almost never drank alcohol, but you know what? Life's just too damn short, and I needed a little help to relax. Staring across the caldera, I allowed my thoughts to drift, then quite suddenly, I found myself in total blackness. At the same moment, a unified groan went up from the town behind me.

I turned and watched as, one by one, candles were lit on terrace walls and restaurant tables, giving the town a fairytale appearance. Living in the heart of Dublin, I had grown up under the blazing orange light of a street lamp. I turned my back on candle-lit Santorini and found myself staring into the black velvet night. Tilting my head to look at the sky, I gasped to see a million stars twinkling into infinity. Spellbound, I was still staring at the night sky when the lights came on and a cheer went up.

Although my parents' home was on the slopes of the tightly packed town, I enjoyed a wonderfully isolated corner of the patio, dark and secretive. From somewhere above me, I heard the touristy jangle of Greek music. A woman laughed, happy. Turning my attention away from the town, I noticed a bright light in the darkening sky over the caldera. A star or a satellite? It grew stronger, coming towards me, and I likened it to my mother's mind. Then I realised it was a plane, heading for Santorini's airport on the other side of the island. Three hundred people filled with holiday happiness, about to fly over my head. They had no notion of my misery and that, oddly, gave me hope.

I poured another half of red and walked over to the edge of the patio. The town was both vibrant and romantic. Terraces were occupied by tourists eating their candle-lit dinners. I heard a loud splash and more laughter. Someone had jumped into one of the many infinity pools that shimmered pale turquoise from underlighting. A young couple came down the empty, narrow street and huddled in a doorway. They kissed passionately. I could hear their loving murmurings.

Santorini was as beautiful by night as by day, but my shoulders slumped and I was overcome by wine and weariness. Would my mother really get better? Was I foolish to hope?

'Iris! Iris!' Spiro rushed onto the patio and held out a tinfoil-covered plate. 'Good evening, Iris. How is Bridget? Is she better?'

I smiled, shook my head and brushed away a tear. 'Will you have a glass of wine, Spiro?'

'I can't, my wife would kill me. To drink with a beautiful woman at night is dangerous. It has happened before. My wife, Anna, will beat me black and bruises . . . for my own good, of course . . . so perhaps just a half.' He grinned and bobbed his eyebrows. 'A big half. Some things are worth the bruises, hey?! I am fearless Spiro. I live dangerously on the knife-edge of winning millions. Could you put a good word in to the Blessed Virgin? Here, my wife sends you some food. Village salad and pork casserole.'

'You're too kind. Thank Anna for me, please.'

'Come, I will take you dancing, show you the towns. Let's live it up, Iris. The life is tiny. I know everyone and all the best places, you see.'

I shook my head. 'Your wife wouldn't be happy, Spiro.' I fetched a glass, poured him some wine, and we sat at the tin table.

'My wife is always too tired in the evening. I am a man of love, of passion, and I have needs!' he boomed. 'She never wants me anymore.'

Laughing, I held my hands up. 'Too much information. Don't tell me another thing, okay?'

The music above changed to a slow, heavy rhythm. Spiro held his arms up and clicked his fingers, then leaped into the patio

146

space and spun on his heels. 'Opa!' He leaned forward, waved his arms like a seagrass in a gentle swell, and appeared to be sniffing his armpits. 'Opa!' he cried again, clearly showing off. I was reminded of strutting cock-pigeons under the O'Connell monument back home. When Spiro had finished leaping and spinning, I clapped and he grinned again, thrusting his chest out and swaggering back to the table.

'Spiro!' a woman shouted.

Spiro cowered, then dived into the house. 'Shhh!' he called from behind the door. 'Tell her I left!'

A big woman appeared, her wide hips see-sawing as she stomped determinedly. 'You see my Spiro? I kill him!'

'Ah, he left already. Thank you for the wonderful food. It's very kind of you,' I said nervously.

She ignored me and, to my embarrassment, marched straight into the house. A moment later, she dragged Spiro out by his ear, then whacked the taxi driver around the head with alarming ferocity. He tried to escape, scuttling back the way he had come.

Just before they disappeared behind a building, she glanced back. Our eyes met. She raised her chin, jerked her head upward, and threw me a smile. I recognised a look friendship, then she was gone.

After my initial shock and embarrassment, I started to giggle and, once again, I suspected the entire fiasco was nothing more than a pantomime to lift my spirits.

\* \* \*

The next morning, I slept late, probably because of the wine. I would have welcomed more time at the house to sit on the patio

147

and drink in the view, but my mother was waiting. I sensed urgency in the day as I pulled on yesterday's clothes and rushed to the hospital.

Nothing had changed. My mother lay peacefully oblivious to the world about her.

'Hi, Mam. It's me, Irini. I have a nice cup of tea here and I was thinking about you when I bought it. Milk and one sugar, isn't it? I bet you're longing for a good strong brew. We're alone right now so I'm just going to stick my finger in the tea and wet your lips. Would you like that?'

I moved my tea-covered finger over her dry mouth, afraid she might choke if any dripped past the tube. The childhood scene, when she hugged me so fiercely, came back once again. How distraught she had been, kissing my cheeks and crying. Why couldn't I remember what had caused it?

I wondered if she understood what was happening now. Holding her hand, thinking, time passed in red heartbeat blips on the monitor. After a while, I picked up one of her books.

'This is all new to me, Mam, the stories about your dreams. Some of it's quite frightening; seems like you went through hell in your sleep.'

I started reading.

\* \* \*

Last night, I dreamed I had killed my daughter again. The nightmare was so awful I don't even want to write it down. Then the dream almost came true!

I was busy cleaning the house. Irini played with her dolls on a blanket outside. I made sure the gate was secure and she knew she must not go off the patio. The housework was therapeutic. I enjoy putting everything in its place and polishing the little furniture we have.

Irini was quieter than usual, so I went outside with orange juice and biscuits to play with her for a while. When I stepped out of the house, I froze dead in my tracks. My little girl, with her arms out from her sides, walked along the top of the patio wall while singing a rhyme. She had taken off her shoes, pulled a chair to the wall, and climbed up. I lowered the biscuits and orange juice slowly, afraid of startling her. She sang a nursery rhyme, oblivious to the danger.

'Ring a ring o' roses, a pocket full of posies, a-tishoo, a-tishoo, we all fall . . .'

My feet turned to lead. Everything moved in slow motion. I lunged forward, as if through deep water, but tripped on Irini's sandal and staggered towards her with my arms out. Startled, she unbalanced and started to topple! I screamed. In blind panic I snatched some cloth – her skirt, top, I don't know. I could feel her little body slipping through the fabric. Terrified, I clung on, clutched at a limb, scrabbling, dragging her towards me, over the wall . . . and then it was over. We were both safe on the patio.

'Oh, thank God! Thank God!' I wept, dropping to my knees and holding her tightly to my chest. Tears of fear and relief raged down my face. I'd almost pushed her over the wall. She would have plunged three hundred metres to the rocks below!

Irini cried too, startled by my action. I should have talked to her, gently told her to climb down and come to me. Instead, I'd panicked, acted like a lunatic because of my dreams, and it almost cost my little girl her life.

I can't go on like this. I'm not fit to be a mother! I must talk to Tommy about sending Irini away. I can't imagine life without my gorgeous girl, but she needs to be far from me in order to be safe. I am cursed because of all the wrongs I have done.

*  *  *

I realised what I was reading. This was the memory that kept replaying in my mind: my mother clutching me, crying. I felt so unbelievably sad, for my mother and for myself.

'Oh, how frightened you must have been, Mam. I remember when this happened. It's puzzled me all my life because I never understood why you were so upset.'

I was sitting in silence, overwhelmed by the event, when the doctor came into the room.

'Ah, Irini, I hoped to find you here.' The nurse followed him and watched as he lifted my mother's lids, shining the torch into her eyes. 'We've decided to move Mrs McGuire to the University Hospital of Heraklion. It's the largest hospital facility in Crete and one of the largest hospitals in Greece.' His eyes were still on my mother, and he shook his head as he spoke. 'I must warn you, the air ambulance and the MRI scan will be expensive, but it's in your mother's best interest.'

My emotions soared. There appeared to be some hope.

'The scan results will give us a more accurate picture of your mother's injuries.' He looked into my eyes. 'When they have all the relevant information, the specialists in Crete will decide on the right course of action for Mrs McGuire.'

I spent another hour with my mother, then thanked the staff for their care and paid the bill. Horrified by the expense, I realised almost all my ring money had gone, but at least we appeared to be moving forward. The air ambulance would leave tomorrow, so I packed up the notebooks and then held my mother's hand for a while longer.

The walk back to town was a slog uphill in the midday sun. At the halfway point – the bird's-nest vineyard – Spiro pulled up.

'*Ela*, Iris, where you go? Get in! You should not walk now. The sun is too hot. Tomorrow, you call me and I take you to the hospital to see Bridget.'

I pulled open the passenger door and slid in, enjoying the cool blast of his air-con.

'Thanks, Spiro, but tomorrow I sail to Crete. She's going to the big hospital in Heraklion for more tests.'

'Ah, Bridget will be happy – she likes Crete. She was there just a week ago. The day before her terrible accident.'

'She was? Why did she go?'

'How I know?' He lifted both hands off the wheel, startling me. 'Mrs Bridget went to meet somebody, something to do with her work, she said. She came back the same day. Very excited when I picked her up at the port. She said everything would be good now, good for Tommy, good for you, and she was very happy.' He turned and grinned at me.

We veered towards the kerb again. I pointed at the windscreen. 'Look out!' His driving terrified me.

'Ah, you make me remember, Bridget was worried that evening too. She kept looking out of the back window, afraid someone was following us.'

I frowned. 'What? That's odd. And were you being followed?'

Spiro laughed and pulled his chin in. 'But of course!' he boomed.

I stared, waiting for him to continue. 'Spiro! Who was following you?'

'Well, everyone who came in on the ferry, of course. They all come up the one road!'

I did my best to smile at Spiro's joke but I still felt unnerved. My mother had been worried someone was tailing her, and although I couldn't put my finger on anything in particular, I had a strong feeling she had been afraid.

\* \* \*

Back at the house, I made myself a coffee, sat on the patio, and tried to put Spiro's words out of my mind, but I couldn't. Why would she go to Crete? Who did she meet there? Why would she fear that someone followed her home? My unease grew until Dad's words came back to me. I'd not thought about them since I left Dublin.

*'If you must go, Irini, be careful. There are bad people out there. Are you quite sure this was an accident?'*

His hints of foul play and fear for my safety unnerved me further. Could I be in some kind of danger too? I hadn't taken him seriously. Stupid of me.

\* \* \*

The next morning, I packed my few things, along with my mother's books, and took the slow ferry to Crete. The big ship was much cheaper than the FastCat, and frugality had become a necessity. I climbed to the top deck and clutched the back rail as we pulled away from Santorini. The town of Fira was clear to see, hanging on to the top of the cliff. I fancied I caught sight of a dash of orange that was my parents' house.

I recalled Quinlan ramping up my excitement when I was a girl – 'The biggest volcano!' – and I realised how little of the island I had seen. If only I had visited the archaeological site, perhaps I would have learned more.

The ship slipped out of the caldera's flat water and I wanted to slow it down, hang on to the view, keep a hold on all that had happened there. Feeling helpless, as though I was abandoning a part of my own life, I watched the island withdraw, taking my past and the secrets of my family with it.

We pushed past Burnt Island and other crumbs of land that had once made this place a complete circle, then we sailed out into the open sea. Santorini receded towards the horizon, then disappeared in the heat haze. I wondered when I would return, and under what circumstances.

The sea breeze refreshed me, and I realised I was not so afraid of the water. Nevertheless, I wandered over to the ship's orange and white lifeboats. Their mechanisms were buried under thick layers of white paint. Would they work in an emergency? I read the neighbouring emergency poster: *Take your shoes off with your hands behind your head. Leap onto the escape shoot.*

It seemed all of Greece was trying to make me smile.

In the café-bar, I got myself a glass of water and a burger – the cheapest thing on the menu – and took a table next to the window. The view was nothing but miles of sea, but it was as far as I could get from the blaring TV, where a huddle of Greeks added to the noise by shouting at each other. I wondered if it was a convention for the hard of hearing.

With three hours afloat, I decided to investigate more of my mother's *Book of Dreams*. There was a beautiful sketch of a fresco across the top of the next page. Lots of ancient ships and dolphins. I started reading.

\* \* \*

My handmaid retired to her room next to mine. In my royal bedchamber, light and dark shifted mysteriously in the loose

153

shadows of one guttering candle. I lay on the bed, thinking about the festival tomorrow and the awful event it will lead to.

So much horror filled my mind that sleep was impossible. I longed to hold my child. Not wanting to wake Eurydice, I slipped into a robe and tiptoed out of my bedchamber.

In Oia's room, the bed was empty!

Every moment spent with my daughter had become crushingly precious, so little time left, so much I wanted to say. I rushed along the grand palace corridors, my heart thudding, the sense of urgency growing with each vacant room. Where was Oia? Soon it would be dawn! I entered the West House and pulled up, gasping with relief.

'Oia, I was looking for you. Why are you here in the middle of the night?'

My daughter peered up at the freshly painted frieze depicting the River Festival. The room glowed in the light of oil lamps. I glanced around. The artisans had accomplished a magnificent work, far exceeding my expectation. A complete story of life in Atlantis surrounded us in the magnificent frescoes.

Oia bowed. 'My Queen, forgive me, I could not sleep. I was so excited about the festival tomorrow.' She raised a hand towards the frieze. 'This is beautiful. If you are not too tired, please tell me the story.'

My heart slowed. 'Dearest child, of course.' I slipped my arm around her shoulders and turned her towards a corner. 'We start here with our greatest naval triumph. See the naked men drowning in the sea, and the ship with a broken bowsprit at the bottom of the fresco?' I stroked Oia's hair as I told her the story of the attempted Libyan invasion. How nobly her father, my husband the great king, had fought until a javelin through his heart had ended his life. What cruel fate had pathed our lives to suffer so much?

'You will look amazing tomorrow.'

'I wish my father could see me at the River Festival.'

'His spirit will be here, Oia, of this I am sure. He'll be as proud as a king can be.' I indicated the last fresco. 'Look at this painting – the artisans have already placed us both in the picture. I am on the balcony with the horns of sacrifice, and you are with me.' I stopped, unable to speak for a moment.

Oia peered up at me. 'Are you all right, my Queen?'

I nod, take a breath, and continue. 'See here, the noble women watch from balconies behind us as the finest young men march along the shore. The sea is beautifully painted, blue and yellow dolphins leaping into the air around our great fleet of ships. Oh, and look, Oia, we appear again on the royal flagship with the nobles.' I raise my hand, indicating the most detailed ship with flags strung from bow to stern.

'I am not sure of the protocol for tomorrow, my Queen. Do I bow to the kings as before?'

'My child, now you are a maiden, you are superior to all except me. The kings will bow to you.'

'That will feel strange.'

I smile and raise my hand to the fresco again. 'Look, a griffin with its wings raised, pursuing an antelope through papyri and palms on the edge of the marches. And there, a wild cat hunting a pheasant along the river's edge. The picture explains that the river, which springs from the marches, is our source of life. See how it travels from the beginning of the wall to the end, where it feeds the sea? This also displays the relationship between predator and prey; the strongest always conquer or rule the weak. Through life, we have to remain strong no matter how hard our burden, for in the end we must all reach the sea, our destiny.'

'Poseidon . . . I wonder what he's like? Do you think the statue in the temple is a true likeness? Have you ever seen him, my Queen? Will I?'

I could not take my eyes off her. She was so beautiful and innocent, and she had hardly lived.

'One day, I promise you will see him, but enough questions now, we have a big day tomorrow. Come and sleep with me tonight and then we shall prepare for the festival together at sunrise.'

Oia slipped her arms around me and I found it difficult not to cry out with the pain in my heart.

'I love you so much, my Queen,' she whispered.

Drifting in and out of sleep, I held my precious daughter through the night. I recalled every moment of Oia's life: the unique perfume of the baby in my arms, the young princess with the infectious smile, and now the beautiful girl on the threshold of womanhood. But her life in Atlantis would end soon, replaced by eternity as Poseidon's queen.

The dawn of the day on which I was destined to sacrifice my daughter to Poseidon came too quickly. I woke with tears in my eyes, Oia shaking me gently.

'Don't cry, please. Wake up now,' she said. 'Don't cry . . .'

\* \* \*

I did not want to read any more of my mother's book. They were only accounts of my mother's dreams, but just reading those few lines, I completely understood the queen's love of her daughter. Also, the binding commitment to keep her people safe, and the dread she felt for what the future held. My stomach was so tight I felt sick. I closed the book and slipped it under the others. One day I would open it again, but not while my own mother was so terribly poorly.

156

I wondered why she never explained what she was going through. Perhaps she had trought that I wouldn't have believed her, that I would have dismissed her dreams as madness – but surely when I was old enough, she could have discussed these things with me, at least tried to help me understand why she sent me away.

Did my mother actually think she might kill me? Was I cheated out of a proper family life by some historical nonsense? Angry, and frustrated that she couldn't answer my questions, I wanted to hug her and yell, all at the same time.

Through those lonely years, all that time, she was missing me like I missed her.

In the depths of my mind, the confusion and disappointment of my past life would not budge. I slumped in the chair, lost in the bleakness of it all.

On the horizon, a landmass loomed into view. We were approaching Crete, where Mam was already settled in her hospital bed. The scene through the window seemed symbolic. As the island became clearer, so did my hope. Here they had the power to look inside my mother's head and analyse the extent of her injuries. The experts would realise that Bridget McGuire's brain was starting to repair itself. If only I could look into her mind in that same way, see the past – see the scars – understand everything.

The cost of the air ambulance had wiped out my engagement-ring money and most of my holiday pay, and although I'd managed to raise the limit on my credit card, it wouldn't last long. Just thinking about my financial situation made me feel ill. All my hopes were with the MRI scan. If my mother could be saved, then any debt was worth it.

# CHAPTER 15
## BRIDGET

*Santorini, 29 years ago.*

SWEATING AND SHAKING, I stumbled out of bed and staggered onto the patio. As my pregnancy advanced, so had the intensity of the dreams. They sucked me into another life, another world so real that I feared one day I would not, could not, return. Forever trapped in the body of Queen Thira, living her terrible destiny.

Later that day, when we lay side by side at siesta time I told Tommy, 'I know they're only dreams, but they feel so real.'

'I know, but darling girl, you have to remember that they're not.' He turned onto his side and rested his hand on my belly, hoping to feel our baby move. 'I think she's sleeping,' he whispered propping himself on an elbow and smiling. 'Let's hope she keeps it up later, and we still manage a siesta every day.' He rolled onto his back again. 'Do you think she can hear us talking?'

I hadn't thought about it. 'I don't know. I hope she doesn't share my dreams. Wouldn't that be awful?'

'It depends. Are they always bad?'

'Lately they're all pretty scary. In last night's dream, I knew I was going to kill my daughter, and I even justified it. Although it broke my heart, I was convinced the sacrifice had to take place. Isn't that terrible? Why would I even imagine something like that?'

Inside our mosquito-net wigwam, we stared at the ceiling. His hand took mine as he spoke. 'It sounds too horrible to contemplate. Must be terrifying for you, poor girl.' He turned again and watched me as I answered.

'In the dream, it's because my daughter was born to be the bride of Poseidon. I was simply the vessel that gave birth to her. But from the start, I love her as any mother loves her child. That she ultimately doesn't belong to me makes no difference.

Poseidon is causing earthquakes and threatening the volcano's eruption because my daughter has come of age and he is demanding that she be given to him. There's no doubt in my mind, in the dream, that this is true and the entire population is destined to be destroyed if Poseidon's wishes are not met.'

'Astonishing. Is there anything in Greek mythology to substantiate this story?'

'It's difficult to research. The nearest thing I've come across is the story of Polyxena, daughter of Agamemnon. She was sacrificed and, like many Greek stories, the event is depicted on an ancient vase.

'During the Trojan War, Polyxena and her brother were captured, and he was killed. However, Polyxena, a young virgin, said she would rather die as a sacrifice to Achilles than live as a slave. She refused to beg for her life or be treated in any other way than a princess. She met her fate bravely. Before the son of Achilles slit her throat, she arranged her clothes so that she was modestly covered. But there is nothing about Polyxena's mother, how she felt, or if she tried to save her daughter from this terrible finale.'

Tommy shuddered. 'Perhaps the story played on your mind and influenced your nightmares, Bridget. Do you think?'

I shook my head. 'I only discovered it recently.'

'Then you must talk to the doctor. Go and see Kiriaki. Perhaps she can prescribe something to help you sleep. Don't worry about the money, Bridget, your health is far more important.'

'You're right. Anyway, Kiriaki never charges us and the prescriptions cost next to nothing. It's not the money, Tommy.'

'Then what is it, darling girl? Tell me.'

I sighed, reluctant to voice my fears. 'I know it sounds dramatic, but sometimes I'm afraid I'm going mad. Do you think I'm having a breakdown of some sort?' I turned and looked into his face, knowing I would see the truth, but there was only kindness and concern in his eyes.

'No, of course not. You're worrying too much. In the end, they're only dreams. I'm sure you'll make the perfect mother. I've every confidence in you, Mrs McGuire.' He brushed my hair away from my damp face. 'Now, no more worrying.'

\* \* \*

In the surgery the next morning, Kiriaki listened to my problems. She was a well-respected doctor in her early fifties, slim and dark, with a soothing manner that patients remembered her for. She held surgery in the mornings, worked at the hospital in the afternoons, and visited patients in the early evening. A twelve-hour day, five days per week. She dropped the morning's prescriptions off at the chemist to save the elderly or sick having to wait. Yianni-One-Arm, who had had an unfortunate accident in the olive factory when he was fifteen, delivered the medication to her patients. Grateful, they handed over fifty lepta to Yianni for the service, knowing it was his only form of income.

She examined me, and tried to assure me that everything was normal.

'But the nightmares, Doctor – why are they happening?'

'You're going through a period of uncertainty, Bridget. Expectant mothers often dream that their lives, or the lives of their babies, might be endangered, especially when it's their first child. Increased hormone production is the most probable cause.' She smiled softly. 'Hormones affect our emotions and anxiety, and they may change the way our brain processes information. Sometimes this causes more vivid dreams, even nightmares, especially during the third trimester. They can be very intense and quite frightening, and may continue for a short while after the baby is born. Eight hours sleep is a thing of the past. You'll be getting up to feed the baby and attending to its cries all hours of the day and night. You'll find yourself confused, depressed, even angry on occasion, and have many other emotions and feelings.'

'Is there anything I can do about it?'

'Sleep whenever you can. Relax. Take one day at a time and try not to worry.'

'Sometimes I think I'm going crazy.'

Kiriaki shook her head. 'No, Bridget, you're perfectly normal. Both you and your baby girl are coming on fine. Stop worrying.'

* * *

Despite the doctor's reassurances, I continued to fret about my nightmares.

'Keep writing them down,' Tommy suggested. 'We can analyse them and talk them through.'

Later that afternoon, I walked around to the small supermarket and bought another simple exercise book. Everyone

161

asked about Tommy, how he was. Nobody mentioned the baby, although their smiles said everything. I understood this was Greek superstition. My friends did not want to tempt the devil, or put a jinx on me or the baby by confirming our happiness.

While Tommy proofread my latest article, I closed my eyes and recalled last night's dream, taking myself back to the night before the River Festival. With a start, I had woken from my dream of that other life. Or was this the dream, and my other existence the reality? I lay there, lost in my bed, suspended somewhere between past and future.

\* \* \*

On the fateful morning of the River Festival I wake again, still holding my daughter. I shake her gently and beckon, 'Arise, my child. Today you will take your place beside me. You are Princess of Atlantis now and all the land will see your beauty, know your wisdom, and pay homage. First, we meet with the kings, and after, we dress for the jubilee and enjoy the day.

'You will join me in council and help to secure the future of our land. And as Princess of Atlantis, you will learn all there is to know of Poseidon's great power when you are inaugurated with the title of Poseidon's Empress.'

Oia gasps, and although she maintains her regal composure, I sense my daughter is ecstatic.

'My Queen, our country means as much to me as your love, and not even the great lord Poseidon can know how honoured I am to take my place beside you. I hope to learn from your wisdom and sense of justice.'

'You can dismiss your handmaidens today, Oia. I shall prepare you for the River Festival myself.'

162

'My Queen, such protocol is unheard of!'

'Until now, Oia. That's the beauty of being Goddess of the Marches: I make the rules. Come, let us prepare.' I lead Oia to her own chambers, where Eurydice pumps water from the hot springs into the stone bath. I bathe my daughter using my bare hands and the softest sea sponges, knowing I will never have the opportunity again.

'You know that I love you more than anyone in this world or the next, Oia, don't you? You are the greatest gift your father ever gave me and I've always been proud of you.'

Oia ran her hand down my cheek. 'You seem sad today, dear Queen.'

'My child has gone, Oia. Every mother feels the same when her daughter becomes a woman.'

I reach behind my neck and unclasp the sacred dragonfly necklace, only ever worn by the Goddess of the Marches. 'With this sacred necklace, I consecrate you Princess of Atlantis and bride of Poseidon.' I fasten the necklace around Oia's neck, allowing my fingers to follow the line of the filigree insects until they rest on her breastbone, beneath which I can feel the beat of her heart. The very heart that I was bound to pierce with the sacrificial knife.

Oia sighed. 'I think this is the greatest day of my life. I can't imagine anything better, except for the day when I hold my own daughter.'

Her words pierce me so violently, I fall to my knees and break into tears.

Alarmed, Oia rushes to my side and flings her arms around my neck. 'My Queen, please don't cry!'

\* \* \*

163

I woke with a terrible shock. The dragonfly necklace! I tried to remember if I had seen it in my dreams before. Had it really hung around the neck of Queen Thira? Was the jewellery that Tommy pulled out of the earth an artefact of unimaginable importance? What had I done? I had to tell Tommy, confess that I had let it go in order to save his life. He would never forgive me, I knew that. Perhaps the news would not only destroy our marriage – it could also bring on another heart attack. I would not let that happen.

After slipping out of bed, I realised I was unable write down the dream. Tommy would read it, recall the day he found the necklace and later collapsed. I had to remember every detail of the dream, store it in my head in case it contained information that I needed to know. My body and mind seemed full of turbulence. I could neither sit or stand. Hastily, I pulled my clothes on, let myself out of the house, and marched through the empty town as dawn broke. I stormed along street after street, going nowhere. Foraging cats froze on the top of the green garbage-bins and stared at me. Donkeys, in the red livery of the town council, clattered to a halt on the cobbled steps and nodded, their backs loaded with rubbish bags. I marched with such vigour I was soon breathless, and my anxiety abated a little.

Shopkeepers appeared as the light gathered, unlocking their doors and preparing for the tourists. I caught sight of my reflection in a window. Hair, sleep tangled; face, white as death. I returned home.

Later that morning, the dream still nagging at the back of my mind, I worked in the ruins next to Poseidon's temple. After brushing pumice dust away from the fresco, I gazed upon its fine artwork.

For over a decade, Tommy and I had excavated thirty metres into the volcanic ash of Santorini. The fruit of our work lay exposed to daylight for the first time in almost four thousand years.

The life-size painting filled a wall. Muted tones of ochre, wine-red, and cobalt depicted a regal woman on a throne with handmaidens and monkeys in attendance. Several pieces were missing – a hand, a foot, one shoulder and the neck of the woman on the throne – nevertheless, the fresco was almost complete and a fine example of Minoan art. It would remain in place while we searched for the missing pieces, which we believed lay in the dirt below the painting.

The scene in the fresco seemed familiar. It drew me, and for a second I was in my dream again. Surely this was my mind playing tricks. Lack of sleep, confused hormones, worry about Tommy, and my pregnancy, all played a part in my strong sense of déjà vu.

Tommy had mixed feelings about the missing pieces of fresco, desperately wanting to see the painting complete, yet knowing that when it was, it would be taken away and eventually displayed in a museum. The students had already started digging a trench and sifting through the dirt below the wall. If the missing pieces had fallen though to a lower level, it would be years before we found them.

It seemed appropriate to discover the mural now, in spring, when the landscape of Santorini became an impressionist painting of yellow and blue wildflowers daubed over hill and vale.

I stepped back to admire the fresco, but my foot twisted on uneven ground. A piece of broken pot – the bottom of a plate or dish – had unbalanced me. I lifted it out of the dirt and stared at the enigmatic symbols in the centre of the base. Some were vaguely recognisable ancient scripts, other shapes were more

165

mysterious, perhaps the Phoenician alphabet, but I had never seen the different alphabets mixed in this way before.

'What have you got there?' Tommy asked.

'Not sure. A base, symbols, mixed alphabets, perhaps.'

'Hardly likely.'

'Maybe it was written in a transition period, when all three alphabets were being used to some extent somewhere, or perhaps inscribed by several potters who were new to the area and didn't use the same system,' I suggested, while pushing down on my expanded belly.

Tommy studied me, his concern clear. 'Are you all right, Bridget?'

'Heartburn. It feels like your daughter has an elbow in my ribs. Little minx. I'll be glad when she's in my arms.'

He smiled and placed his hand below mine. 'Is she kicking?'

'Not so much these days. No room, I guess.'

'You should take it easy,' he said. 'Anyway, about your theory, as we've no record of the Minoan language, we can't possibly understand what the strange letters say, can we? You're heading for disappointment if you think you can decipher it.'

'Nevertheless, do you mind if I try?'

'Go ahead, make it your project; give me a bit of peace, won't it?'

'Cheeky devil!' I laughed, watching his back as he returned to a trench across the site. I studied the symbols again, excitement racing through me. Perspiration trickled between my breasts, and the hairs on my arms lifted as if a cocoon of static enfolded me.

*Who had last held this piece of pot? Could it be an offering dish? What might the cyphers tell us?*

I closed my eyes and tried to imagine the scene on that very spot when the bowl broke into pieces. Was the act of smashing it deliberate? Could it be a sacrificial artefact, after all, I was standing in the temple? We knew very little about their religion. What other clues to this ancient civilisation lay hidden in the dirt beneath my feet?

Music drifted over the archaeological site from a festival taking place in the distant forecourt. I recognised the *syrtaki*, Zorba's dance. Young men and women wearing national costume entertained tourists with a display of Santorini's culture. Visitors would taste the local food, partake of the island's fine wine, and hopefully buy replicas of the antiquities. I, and my fellow archaeologists, were desperate for funds.

Hot, tired, and dusty, I placed a hand on my swollen belly once again. The dull ache in my back had started on my frantic walk through town at dawn. Now the pain intensified and fresh perspiration beaded my brow. Only one month to go, then I'd give birth to my child, our wonderful daughter.

As if invited by thoughts of childbirth, a pain, fierce beyond measure, ripped through me. I fell to my knees, clutching the jagged dish to my chest as my waters broke.

'Tommy!'

# CHAPTER 16
## IRINI

*Crete, present day.*

I HURRIED ALONG A MAZE of corridors in the University Hospital of Heraklion. Corridors filled with bustling people. When the door of my mother's room closed behind me, I stood for a moment in the oasis of silence, then pulled a chair to her bedside.

'Hi, Mam. It's me, Irini. We're in Heraklion now, on the island of Crete. You've been here before, when Dad had his heart surgery. Do you remember?' I sat next to the bed and took her hand. 'I phoned him last night and he told me about it.' I sat there, silent for a while, wondering how long it took for her damaged brain to absorb information. Wondering if it could. Hoping against hope.

'I wasn't going to read your books on my own, but the ferry was such a long journey – nearly four hours – so I finished the first *Book of Dreams.*'

She had written that book almost thirty years ago, and now I wondered if she remembered what was in it. 'I want to tell you that—'

Before I could say more, the doctor and three interns came in and asked me to leave. My mother was about to have the various tests necessary before tomorrow's scan. I worried about her, and the costs, and wondered again whether she could really hear me.

Defeated by everything, I realised that I had to make a plan, concentrate on the logistics. I had to get a job, even though I had no idea how long I'd be in Greece. Perhaps there was a temp agency on the island. I should register, though heaven only knew what for. Teaching English might be an option. Could I give private lessons? Or work as a care person? I could honestly say I'd done jobs before. If push came to shove, I would wait on tables or clean hotel rooms, anything that might help fund my mother's recovery.

I had arrived in Greece expecting nothing more than to hold her hand as she slipped peacefully away, but now everything had changed. We had grown closer. I understood things. And, more than anything in the world, I wanted her to get better.

My grief was so intense, I stood in the corridor and prayed for a miracle.

Desperate for a cup of tea, I made my way to the hospital café, which was packed. I spotted an empty chair, the table occupied by a slim woman about my own age.

'Hi. Do you mind if I sit here?' I said, hoping she spoke English.

The woman nodded her raven bob. 'Feel free. On holiday?' she asked. I detected a north-west English accent.

'Not really, my mother's poorly. They brought her over from Santorini for an MRI.' I glanced around the café. 'This place is manic, isn't it?'

'You're not kidding. I slept on a gurney in a corridor last night. Unbelievable.' She pointed below the table. 'Broken tibia. Idiot tourist knocked me off my scooter last night. Hurts like hell. What happened to your mum, then?'

'There was an accident, a wall fell . . .' I stopped, frowning, still uneasy about my father's words and Spiro's story of my mother believing she was followed off the ferry. 'At least, they say it was an accident, but the more I think about it, I'm starting to wonder.' Surprised I had said those words aloud, and to a stranger, I studied her face for a reaction, but she didn't seem fazed at all.

169

'God, sorry about your mum. That's a pretty crap thing to happen. You know they've got vendetta here?' I shook my head. 'There was this bus driver last year, in Agios Nikolaos, whose mother was run over and killed. The old girl doddered across the national road at night, wearing all black. I mean?! Nevertheless, the son went out and ploughed his bus into the culprit's car. Killed him stone dead, like.'

'Good grief! You're kidding?'

She shook her head. 'According to the Cretans, justice was done.'

I winced, remembering that I was an idiot tourist that ran over a Greek cyclist. Would he come after me intending revenge?

'Where're you from?' I asked.

'Liverpool. I work here through the summer, though I'll probably lose my job now. My bloody phone's in the scooter too, so I can't even call my boss. I'm Jane, by the way. Where you from?'

'Dublin. I'm Irini. Is it hard to find work? I was just thinking . . .' Her brow furrowed and I realised she wasn't listening. Too many problems of her own. 'Do you want to call work?' I held my phone out, glanced at her leg, and wondered how the Greek was coping with his broken arm.

'Brilliant, thanks! He'll go ape-shit when I tell him I can't work tonight, but what can I do?'

I thought about my finances again. I needed a roof over my head. I had the hotel room for a few more days, but then I was on my own. Suddenly it dawned on me: I couldn't go back to Dublin if my mother was still in a coma by the end of August. What would I do? How much would an air ambulance to Dublin cost?

Was anyone interested in my fantastic wedding dress yet?

When I looked up, Jane was pleading into the phone, then she ended the call.

'That's the best paid job I've ever had, and now I'll lose it if I don't find a replacement. How can I, stuck in here with a gammy leg?'

'What do you do?'

'I'm a barmaid in the Shamrock, in Malia. It's an Irish bar, plays rock.'

'Hard work, behind a bar. I worked in the Raglan Road for three years, pulled pints all through uni.'

Jane's eyes lit up. 'You're kidding me?'

'No, it's true. I still help out now, saving for my wedding ... or at least I was.'

We stared at each other for a second, both seeing a solution to our individual problems.

She grabbed my hand, her eyes pleading. 'Stand in for me for a couple of nights, please, I'm begging! Just while I find a replacement.'

I wanted to say yes. *But what about my mother? What if something happens and I'm not there?* I needed the money, but my mother needed me too. I hesitated, buying time to think.

Jane took my hesitation as a yes. 'Let me tell Jack I might have somebody. Quick, give me your phone,' she said, and after a moment, I handed it over. While talking to her boss, she looked up and asked, 'What do you do now?'

'I teach religious studies in a Catholic school.'

Jane blinked at me for a moment, then said into the phone, 'She does PR work for a consortium based in Rome.' After a couple of beats, she rolled her eyes. 'No, Jack, not for the mafia! Nine o'clock then.' She returned the phone.

For a second, I felt manipulated, and her grin made me angry, but then I realised Jane had just solved a great chunk of my problems.

'You've got the job!' she said triumphantly.

'I don't know what to say. This is all so sudden, Jane. I'll do it for a week, then we'll see, okay?'

\* \* \*

The drive to Malia after my last motoring experience was scary. To make things worse, I had never driven in the dark before. The roads were busy, but I told myself: if all these people can drive at night, then so can I. Hunched over the steering wheel, constantly dazzled by oncoming lights, I eventually lurched into the 18-30s resort.

The town was buzzing. Jane's advice – to pull into the first car park I came to and walk – was simple enough. I got out of the car and took a moment to catch my breath and calm down.

A group of women ahead wore bikini tops, bunny ears, and black stretch shorts with fluorescent pink letters across their bottoms: Bride, Bridesmaid, Sister, Friend, and so on. A handful of guys, bar-hopping, invited the hen party into a club. Music thumped into the street. Outside another bar, a mechanical bull bucked and turned under a frantic guy while his beer-swilling mates laughed raucously.

I had never seen so many tattoos and piercings, or so many people in so few clothes. The air smelled of pizza and burgers, and reminded me of Dublin on a Saturday night.

I walked quickly, reminding myself I was only twenty-nine, yet I felt horribly out-of-place and overdressed.

The Shamrock was just off the main drag, opposite a closed-down supermarket with a small car park in front. The stylised Irish pub had an ornate green and gold fascia, with beer-barrel tables and high stools on the cobbled forecourt. An A-frame billboard in the shape of a leprechaun advertised: *Happy Hour 9–10.30 p.m.* on one side and: *Draft Guinness & Poteen* on the other.

From a speaker over the Shamrock door, Annie Lennox blasted: *I Need a Man*.

She was not the only one!

I hugged myself, warming to the place that was an escape from the misery of hospitals. The pub's front, quarter oak-panelled, had stained glass windows that depicted two emerald-green shamrocks. I took a breath and pushed through the swing doors.

Inside the dimly lit pub, it was extraordinarily quiet.

An elderly man sat in the corner with the dregs of a pint. 'Happy hour doesn't start 'til nine, love.'

'Yes, I read the billboard. I've come in place of Jane. She's had an accident. Are you Jack?'

'Ah, no, Jack's changing a barrel.' He pointed at the floor. 'What's your name?'

'Irini McGuire. Yours?'

'Fergus McFadden. You can make yourself useful and get me another half a Guinness while you wait, Irini, me love.'

I laughed and it felt good. 'Thrown in at the deep end, am I?'

Behind the bar, I orientated myself and then pulled Fergus a half. I wiped his table and gave him a clean beermat before setting his drink down.

'Proper job,' he said. 'I'm impressed. Nice to have another authentic Irish accent in the place. Where're you from?'

'Dublin itself, Mr McFadden.'

'Well, isn't it just a small world we live in? I'm from the fair city myself, and Ma and Pa before me.' He lifted his glass.

'*Sláinte*. Will you tell me about Jane's accident? Is she fine now? I guess not or you wouldn't be here at all, now, would you?'

'I'm afraid she has a broken leg and some bad scrapes and grazes.'

'What do you do in Dublin, if you don't mind me asking?'

I remembered Jane's job description and smiled. 'I teach religious studies at Saint Mary's.'

'Well, God bless us, isn't that the very school Jack went to?! He's me nephew. I comes out here for three weeks every year, I do. The warmth helps me rheumatics. I've had a knee and two hip replacements.' He chuckled, clearly happy to talk. 'They calls me the bionic man at the infirmary. Ah, look now, here's the very person himself.' A trapdoor in the bare wooden floor opened and a portly man in a green apron climbed out. 'Jack, here's yer new barmaid. A lovely colleen all the way from Dublin's fair city.'

Jack wiped his hand down his apron, then offered it to me. 'Jack McFadden. You must be Irini. Thanks for helping out.'

I shook his hand. 'Pleased to meet you, Mr McFadden.'

'Jack, please. Can I get you a half while we go through the ropes?'

'Very kind, I'm sure, but I'm driving later.'

'Time for me to go,' Fergus said. 'Will I open the doors, Jack?'

\* \* \*

After a hectic night behind the bar, I stood outside the Shamrock while Jack locked up. I rubbed my forehead and inhaled the cool night air. Odd flashbacks of my mother's dreams had returned through the evening, accompanied by my father's warning and Spiro's words.

174

I should follow my mother's example and write everything down. See if I could make any sense of my father's concern for my safety.

Longing to be back in my hotel room, I closed my eyes for a moment. Jack's hand on my shoulder made me jump.

'You all right to drive, Irini?'

'Sure, just having a mental moment, don't worry about it.' My brain was muzzy and my skin tingled. Music and laughter drifted down the street, but at three in the morning, I was tired of revellers and needed my sleep.

'You did a good job, Irini. Thanks. I can see you're truly knackered. It's been a long night.'

'Never worked so hard behind the bar in Dublin, Jack, but it was fun. I don't get out much back home.'

'How come?'

'Too many commitments. For the past year, I took care of my father. He's just moved into the residential home. With homework to check, and a little online fashion business I started last year, there aren't enough hours in the day, really.'

'That reminds me. Tomorrow, I know it's short notice, but could you do the two-to-nine shift?'

'Sure, no problem.' Hopefully the work would take my mind away from the MRI scan.

'Thanks. I've an appointment and I'd rather not leave my father in charge. We've a fashion company doing a photo shoot in the forecourt, so you might find that interesting. They'll need soft drinks, perhaps tea and coffee, and use of the loo. Apart from that, it won't be busy.'

\* \* \*

After a sleep filled with more jumbled dreams of my parents, the collapsing archaeology site, my mother's MRI, Jason in bed with Calla, and the bank manager snapping my Visa in two, I pull the sheet over my head. Held by the beautiful fresh bedlinen, with the sun streaming through white muslin curtains, I felt painfully lonely.

I had no real friends, that was my problem. Never had much time for a social life, but I missed my fellow teachers. To be honest, I missed Jason. Apart from being lovers, we were great mates, always laughing together. I didn't remember laughing much since we broke up.

*Enough!* I was on a Greek island in an amazing beach hotel. I *would* make the most of it!

After throwing myself at the bathroom, I raced into the hotel restaurant moments before the ten o'clock deadline.

'Sorry, sorry!' I apologised to the waiter.

He grinned. 'Don't worry, be happy.'

*I want to be happy* . . . The words formed in my mind, but before they reached my lips he had turned away and I was alone again.

The English breakfast was somehow not quite authentic, but nevertheless delicious. Once the first pangs of hunger abated, my thoughts returned to the past.

Although I was practically brought up by nuns, through university years I lived with Uncle Quinlan, whom my parents had made my legal guardian. Quinlan was a man I loved dearly. We were both solitary people, and we both shared a great passion for fabric and design. Which reminded me – the fashion shoot outside the Shamrock should be interesting. I might pick up some tips on how to market my own creations online.

Breaking into my thoughts, the waiter asked, 'You want anything? I finish now.' His eyes narrowed sexily and the corners of his mouth twitched.

'Another pot of tea would be grand,' I said, ignoring the come-on.

He sighed, and I turned to gaze out over the sea.

I thought about my mother and her dreams. Instead of trying to block them out, it seemed she was always trying to reverse time and change the end. How very alike we were, because that was what I longed to do: change the outcome of this difficult relationship with my parents.

If *I* could turn back time, I would have gone to Santorini years ago and tried to understand my mother, instead of just resenting the way she abandoned me.

Now, as the truth crept up on me, I realised her actions were out of love, not coldness. She believed it was the only way to keep me safe. I had always hoped that when I understood everything, when things were explained, I would feel cleansed in some way. Reborn. That moment when a light is turned on in a dark room and you see everything clearly. When you realise you are exactly where you want to be. That was how it should have felt learning the reasons behind my distanced childhood.

I had read that page again, and knew I would go on reading it over and over until something changed in me. For now, it was too much to grasp, too many wrong beliefs to change into this new version of life.

Suddenly, I was yearning to visit her. If only I *had* gone to see the archaeological site, explored my exact birthplace and the area that captured my parents' hopes and dreams. Aaron also seemed interesting. He could have painted in many details of my parents' lives. I wanted to know exactly what happened to cause my mother's injuries. I recalled my father's words: *She should've let me die, then everyone would be safe.* What was he talking about? Why wouldn't he tell me?

I decided to call the home and ask how he was.

He didn't answer for ages, then a voice said, 'There you are, Tommy.'

My father's voice came next. 'Where do I speak into?'

'Nowhere, just hold it to your ear and speak normally.'

'Hello?!' he shouted.

'Hi Dad. It's me, Irini. How are you?'

'I just forgot how this new-fangled contraption works. What's the matter? How's Bridget?'

'There's no change, Dad, she's still in a coma. I just called to see if you're feeling better?'

'I am indeed, but they told me to get a flu jab before the winter.'

'Good plan!'

'That young man of yours came around here yesterday, brought me a bag of toffees. He apologised about the wedding and was asking about you. Said he'd made a mistake and was sorry.'

'Jason? That was nice of him.' I bit my lip to stop myself saying something nasty.

'No it wasn't, he's trying to wheedle his way back in. Don't you listen to him. He's a knob!'

'Dad!' Shocked at my father's choice of words, I started to laugh. 'That's not very kind.'

'There's plenty more fish, Irini, and you deserve better than that one.'

'Aw, what a kind thing to say, but you don't have to shout, I can hear you.'

'When are you coming home?'

'I . . . erm, soon, I think. Mam's having an MRI this afternoon. I'll call you again tomorrow, okay?'

'Remind me, what's an MRI?

'A head x-ray, so they can see the extent of her injuries.'

After a short silence, he sniffed and said gruffly, 'Yes, all right then. Be careful, Irini. Bye.' And before I had a chance to tell him I loved him, he ended the call.

\* \* \*

Shortly after midday the road to Malia was quiet. Most tourists were sunning themselves on the beach, or dining in all-inclusive hotels. The locals took their siesta. I looked forward to a chat with Fergus and a peaceful afternoon in the Shamrock while my mother had her scan. I wondered what they would find. After a lot of soul-searching, I decided that if there was any chance of her brain repairing itself, I'd dedicate my life to getting her better.

I had misjudged her all along.

# CHAPTER 17
## BRIDGET

*Crete, 29 years ago.*

TOMMY BOBBED UP FROM the other side of a rubble wall. 'Bridget, did you shout? What is it?'

I dropped the pottery and, seeing blood on my hands, realised I had cut across my breastbone with the shard of terracotta. 'The baby's coming, Tommy! Oh God, get help!'

Another pain, fiercer than the first, forced me to cry out again. Sweat ran into my eyes, stinging and blurring my vision.

Tommy raced to my side, the colour leaving his face as he fell to his knees. 'Your chest's bleeding. What happened?!' Then, without waiting for an answer, 'There's a phone in the giftshop. I'll call an ambulance.'

But I sensed this was far from a normal birthing. 'Don't leave me,' I cried. My head swam, reality pushing back into darkness. I screwed my eyes shut, fighting to stay conscious as the contraction climaxed with debilitating force. A vice-like grip crushed me tightly around the middle. I tried to pant, rebelled fiercely against the urge to push, but my control was shattered by another explosion of pain. Overbearing forces were wringing the life out of me. If our baby wasn't expelled from my body at that moment, I sensed we would both die.

Tommy attempted to get me to my feet, but my bulging eyes and knuckle-breaking clasp of his hands told him the effort was futile.

'Help! Somebody, we need help, the baby's coming!' he yelled in the direction of the site entrance. Jangling bouzouki music and loud applause drowned his words.

Another contraction rushed through me, every muscle and nerve in my body concentrating on my womb. The life inside me was forced towards the waiting world. Vaguely aware of Tommy tugging at my underwear, I swung a fist at him and swore like a sailor. Sanity and reason had gone. I pulled my knees to my shoulders, lifted my head and bore down with all I had.

Although just as intense, the pain of the contraction changed and I felt our beloved baby inch down the birth canal. If the earth had exploded around me, it would not have dammed the urge to shift my daughter towards daylight. I pushed again and again, draining every ounce of effort from the contraction. Minutes passed, everything a blur. Panting and gasping each time, I wondered where I would find the energy for the next urge to push, but it came with glorious agony.

Tommy glanced around wildly. Seeing no prospect of help, he ripped off his shirt.

'Jesus, Mary and Joseph, I can see the top of her head!' he cried, sounding both jubilant and afraid.

I took a deep breath, knowing it was nearly over. Desperate for part of my own body to become an individual human being that I would love more than life itself. I gathered all my energy to deal with the looming contraction, far more intense than the last, yet somehow less painful. Filled with euphoria, the urge to push came upon me and then I was lost in the overwhelming need to bear down.

Tommy gave a yelp. 'Her head's out! Bridget, Holy God and all the saints, she's turning around all by herself. Shall I pull her out? I don't know what to do. Bridget – tell me what to do!'

And then it was over, pain subsiding, Tommy's face awash with awe.

'Oh, Bridget, look, our little girl, Irini.' Tommy wiped the baby with his shirt and lifted her. 'But she doesn't seem to be breathing' he said, terror in his voice. 'Come on, baby! Take a breath!' He placed her on my chest. 'Why isn't she breathing?' He trembled violently, tears brimming as he swiped the sweat from his forehead. 'I don't know what to do!' he said again. Overcome by emotion, he sobbed. 'Stay here, I'll get help.'

Our tiny baby, unnaturally dark in colour, appeared limp and lifeless. This couldn't be happening! I lifted her and shook her gently.

'Wait! Make her breathe, Tommy! Jesus Christ, she has to take her first breath.' I exclaimed. 'Please! Clear her mouth and nose, hold her upside down, and smack her bottom to make her cry. Quickly, do it now!' Another gripping contraction stopped me from saying more.

Tommy struggled with the slippery little body, which seemed to be turning darker by the second. Despite his efforts, he failed to get a reaction. 'It's not working. I'll get help!' he cried. He placed the baby in my arms, climbed out of the deep excavation, and raced towards the exit.

I tapped Irini's cheek. 'Come on, baby, breathe.' Overcome by exhaustion and fear, I shook her again and called on God for help.

Out of the gloom, a woman approached. Clearly someone taking part in the culture exhibition outside the archaeological site. She wore the same clothes as the figure on the throne in the fresco, and likewise her raven hair was waxed and elaborately coiled.

She lay the baby on my stomach and gently pressed her chest before breathing into her mouth. After repeating the action for a few moments, the infant shuddered into life and then cried.

I cried too. Tears of joy. Irini, my beautiful child!

The strange woman used the terracotta shard to cut the umbilical, and then she placed our baby girl in my arms. I stared at the tiny body, which turned a healthier shade of pink with each breath. I wiped Irini's head and noticed the abundance of copper hair.

My impromptu midwife smiled and nodded, then stepped back into the dim distance as Tommy appeared with help.

\* \* \*

A week passed before I returned to the archaeological site with baby Irini in a carrycot. My neighbours disapproved. 'You must keep the infant indoors for three weeks!' they cried. 'And you too, you are unclean until you stop bleeding. It's not right. You'll bring bad luck!' But I feared I would go stir-crazy if I stayed home any longer. The pull of the archaeological site was irresistible.

We wanted to send flowers to the strange woman who had saved Irini's life, but neither the Department of Culture nor the dance troupe performing in the forecourt knew who she was.

I lifted my baby and stood before the mural. 'Where did you come from?' I whispered, staring at the regal figure on the throne. 'We owe you so much.'

I felt myself drawn into the picture.

\* \* \*

Baby Irini slept soundly after her first feed of the day. I placed her in the carrycot and returned to the patio. The mysterious piece of pottery lay on the table. I picked it up, recalling how my blood ran into the centre and settled in the indent of the star and the mysteriously embellished spear shapes, outlining them in red. The red star ... the red star of morning ... Where had I read that before? Perhaps the information came from a long-forgotten book?

I peered at the sky, which graduated from periwinkle to ultramarine, then my eyes followed the crescent-shaped clifftop to the very end of the island, where the last town hung onto the point. A place of white cubist houses, windmills, vermilion bougainvillea, churches, and artists' shops. The town of Oia. Then I recalled there was another Oia on the island, close to the remains of an archaeology site, Ancient Thira. This dig stood on the ridge of a four-hundred-metre-high mountain, Messavouno.

Ancient Thira was discovered when they excavated volcanic rock for the Suez Canal construction. Below the ancient town, on the outer edge of Santorini, lay the Ancient Port of Oia, where ship-building had taken place and sailors lodged over a thousand years before Christ. Apart from a sprinkling of tourists, the site hardly interested anyone.

Bits of information whirled around in my mind. The answer was close, teasing me, although I wasn't even sure about the question. Then it exploded in my head. Oia ... Oia, the red star of morning. Yes, years ago I had heard of that ... I rushed indoors with the pot still in my hand.

'Tommy! I have all these bits of ideas that are not making any sense at all, but I keep getting a weird feeling they're connected.'

'Do you want toast?' Tommy mumbled, dropping four slices of yesterday's bread into the toaster, ignoring my excitement.

'No. Are you listening? Why is Oia called Oia? What does it mean?'

He frowned. 'No idea; it's too early. Will you let me wake up, darling girl?'

'Sorry. But what about a ritual concerning the red star of morning?'

He raised his heavy eyelids and sighed. 'No peace, is it? Wait, that rings a bell, let me think.'

The smell of toast was making me hungry.

'I did a paper once on human sacrifice,' he said.

My dreams rushed back and I slapped my hand over my heart. 'Human sacrifice!'

'Yes, but hang on. Ah, I've got it now: Oia means red morning star in one of the Pakistani languages.'

'Pakistani?!'

He grinned. 'Not what you wanted to hear?' The toast popped up.

'And what made you connect it with human sacrifice, Tommy?' I started buttering.

'You won't want to hear this either. The Pawnee tribes in Nebraska and Kansas are said to have sacrificed a pubescent girl to the red morning star every few years.'

'Holy God!' I crossed myself. 'How?'

'They strung her up, naked. One shot an arrow through her heart, then all the men fired arrows into her. The ritual was a fertility thing. Bound to bring generous crops and lots of babies, don't you think?'

I grimaced. 'Not funny. When did this happen?'

'Until quite recently – the early nineteenth century.' He sat opposite me at the patio table. 'Why all the questions, and why are you eating my toast?'

'Hungry now. I'll put some more in. That broken dish is driving me mad. Wait, I'll get it.' Moments later, I placed it on the table between us. 'I wondered if it was connected to some kind of ritual. I'm trying not to get excited, but I keep finding connections.'

'How do you mean? Connections to what?' He spread marmalade.

I swallowed hard and stared at Tommy, hardly daring to say what I was thinking.

'Come on, Bridget, spit it out.'

'Plato said there were ten kings of Atlantis, am I right?'

Tommy's butter knife clattered to the plate. 'What . . . you're not thinking . . . Plato?!'

I nodded. 'I know Plato was only a storyteller, many hundreds of years after this very island erupted. And like any author, he would have taken a few facts and distorted them into a romping good tale.'

Tommy nodded, the toast poised halfway to his mouth.

'Let me throw some ideas your way. Plato tells of ten kings, each with different responsibilities, and a goddess queen who rules above them, right? On this plate, there are ten arrowheads pointing to the star in the centre, and each has different markings on it. Then, between the circle of arrowheads, there's one lily. I'm sure it's a lily because it's exactly the same as the lilies in the throne room frescoes at Knossos, the Cretan site. I'm thinking the lily represents the goddess – sacred flower and all.'

Tommy pointed at the plate. 'What's this – another small lily?'

'Indeed. I've thought hard about that. The small lily puzzled me for a while, but then I remembered my dreams and I wondered if the flower represented the goddess's daughter. Perhaps she had a child. In my dreams, her daughter is Oia. You notice the two lilies are either side of the only complete arrowhead, a diamond shape. Perhaps that king was the girl's father.'

We both stared at the dish in silence.

'So you think the diamond represents one of the kings, the lily is the Queen Goddess, and the small lily is their child? What makes you think it is some kind of religious vessel?'

'I think it's a blood sacrifice vessel, because on all the other pots we've found, the decoration is in relief, standing out. They often used a crudely indented stamp. But this has the pattern cut into it, quite deeply too. The symbols were not very clear at first, but after I cut myself on it, they seemed to be etched in blood . . . my blood, and later Irini's blood when that strange woman used it to cut the cord.'

'Mmm, interesting hypothesis.'

*   *   *

The next morning, I curled around Tommy's back. After all our years together, I still loved to wake up with my body pressed against his. Recalling the tipsy ambience of him when we tumbled into bed brought forth a smile. We made love for the first time since before Irini's birth and I recalled penetration being a little painful. Tommy was gentle, reining in his excitement. He caressed me, kissed my face and mouth, asking if he should stop.

'By the mother of God, I believe I have my virginity back,' I said.

'It's a miracle, it is,' Tommy quipped. 'I'll be on my knees for a month.'

I giggled. 'I'm not sure I have the right picture in my mind. Would you care to be a little more descriptive?'

'Teasing wench,' he whispered.

In the stuffy bedroom, I found myself grinning at my adventurous archaeology professor. Aware that Irini was awake, I

187

turned away from him and lifted her from the cradle. Before venturing outside, I pulled a large veil of fine muslin over us both to protect us from mosquitoes. Barefoot, I stepped out into the cool dawn air.

Above, stars faded in an insipid sky. On the horizon, a band of peach light silhouetted Burnt Island, which was nothing but a tower of black lava in the centre of the sea-filled crater. The magical light of Santorini gained strength by the second. I stood for a moment, rocking Irini as I gazed over the peaceful scene.

# CHAPTER 18
## IRINI

*Crete, present day.*

FERGUS, IT TURNED OUT, was friends with my father through his childhood and early teens. The old man abandoned his seat in the corner, hooked his walking stick on the end of the bar, and struggled onto a stool. I suspected I was about to learn things about my family.

'Yer ma was a pretty young thing,' he said, gazing into the distance. 'There wasn't a lad in the city that didn't set his cap at Bridget when she left school, but she wasn't interested. 'Course, nobody knew why. Then she disappeared off the face of the earth. All sorts of rumours, there were. 'Twas a while before the truth came out. Yer da was a lucky man, everyone said so. Where are they now, Irini, me love?'

'Dad's not too good, Mr McFadden. He's got silicosis and moved into a home a few weeks ago.' I took a breath and stared at the floor. 'I'm sorry to say, my mother had a terrible accident in Santorini. That's how I came to be here. Dad's lost all interest in archaeology . . . and everything else too. He seems to be fading to dust himself. Sometimes, when he's half asleep, he has his confused head on and thinks I'm my mother. He calls me Bridget and says the most loving things. It breaks my heart. He lived for her, you know.'

This was an odd truth, because that week they were together in my house, all they did was snarl at each other. Would I ever find out what caused such an odd relationship?

Although I was talking to Fergus, I felt I was testing my own emotions towards my father. 'I wish I'd known them both more than I did, but they were away during most of my childhood. Now my father's not too good, and half the time he's no notion of what's happening.' I sighed and blew my cheeks out. 'To be honest, I really needed this break, although I wish it was under different circumstances. It's been a difficult year for us all.'

'Poor old bugger. I'll go visit him when I gets home.' He studied his drink, lost in thought for a moment. 'Me and Tommy was good mates, years back. We had some rare old times.' He grinned and stared into the past. 'Once, me and Tommy made poteen in our backyard. The grand plan was to sell it and make a fortune, but we were scuppered when the still exploded. It blew the shed window out, ruined Ma's line of washing, and scalded our neighbour's cat.' He chuckled. 'I felt Pa's belt for that one.'

I smiled, seeing a new side to my father. 'I notice you advertise poteen on the billboard.'

'We do indeed, but it's just raki. They look and taste similar, and by the time the boys and girls come in 'ere, they're half-cut and wouldn't know poteen from dandelion and burdock. There's a huge number of similarities between the Irish and the Cretans – you'd be surprised. What were your parents doing in Santorini?'

'To be honest, Mr McFadden, I'm not sure. They had discovered an archaeological site buried deep under the volcanic ash, years before I was born. I stayed in Dublin, boarding at the convent for most of my schooling but, when I was fifteen, I went to stay with my uncle until after college.' I smiled to myself. 'He's a fine man, my uncle Quinlan. I love him to bits. I did go to Santorini once, but I wasn't interested in the old ruins. Boring, I thought. I was drawn to the beach and the sea – but with my skin I suffered with terrible sunburn.'

'Ah, I remember Quinlan – your pa's younger brother, wasn't he? Is he still messing with frocks and the like?'

I laughed. 'He is indeed. He makes all the costumes for Abbey Theatre and I'd like nothing better than to do that job myself – design clothes full time, I mean. I sort of fell into teaching with the nuns looking after me and all, but I really enjoy fashion and sewing more than anything. I've started a little online business, selling my own designs.'

'Well, you could start by repairing those trousers you're wearing, Irini, me love. There's a great rip right below your arse.'

I laughed again and rubbed my aching forehead, then my attention was drawn to a ruckus outside. The pub doors were flung open and a petite blonde, late forties, wearing stiletto boots, tight jeans, and a crimson crop-top, barged into the pub. She had to be one of the fashion team.

'Can you turn the outside lights on?' she asked as she approached.

I glanced at Fergus. 'Sure, no problem.'

Fergus said, 'The panel's in the first cupboard under the bar.'

I ducked down and threw on all the switches. The Shamrock's interior lit up in a blaze of neon.

'Oh, for God's sake,' the blonde cried. 'Just the outside coach-lamps, if it's not too difficult!'

'Top left corner,' Fergus called.

I dived under the bar again and turned everything off apart from the one they wanted. The bar was plunged into gloom.

The woman sighed, tension falling from her face. 'Any chance of a coffee, black, strong, no sugar?'

'Sure, I'll bring it out.' I turned to Fergus. 'How do I turn the bar lights on? I can hardly see a thing.'

Fergus struggled off his stool. ''Ere, I'll do it.'

The woman interrupted. 'Proper coffee, not that iced stuff, okay? Ask for Paula if you don't see me.' She ran her ruby nails through her hair and sighed so hard her body seemed to deflate a little. She turned to the door, but before reaching it a scruffy-bearded man, with panic on his face and his arm in plaster, rushed in.

The man ushered what I thought must be a model straight through to the toilets, then turned and strode towards me. My heart leaped into the back of my throat. It was the guy from the airport, the cyclist that I hit with the car. Angelo.

In the gloom of the Shamrock, Angelo didn't recognise me immediately, so I ducked behind the bar and watched them in the mirror.

Paula raked through her hair again. 'Another day wasted. Hell! Two models with the trots already, and now this. What else can go wrong? How is she?'

Angelo shook his head. 'She cannot continue. We have three more outfits to shoot today. This is crazy. What can we do? We're supposed to go to print on Monday! It's impossible to get anyone else here before we lose the light. *Malaka!*' he swore loudly. His voice came closer, above my head, and I realised he had leaned over the bar. 'Excuse me! Could you take a glass of water into the Ladies? Thank you.'

I bobbed up. Our faces were only inches apart as Fergus flicked the bar lights on. Angelo's eyes widened and he took a step back, his hands raised.

He cried something in Greek, followed by, 'It's you! You are a jinx on me! Shoe-wrecker, bone-breaker, and reckless driver. Why are you here?' He hugged the plaster cast to his chest, as if to save it from further damage, and turned back to Paula. 'This is all her fault!'

Paula raised her eyebrows. 'Don't be ridiculous!' Then she turned to me. 'Was it you who ran him over?'

I'm not sure if I caught a glint of glee in her eyes. 'It was an accident. I'm truly sorry.'

She nodded and squinted at me. 'Under the circumstances, I think perhaps you can help us out. After all, this chaos is partly your fault.'

'My fault?'

'Absolutely. We're a day behind with the shoot because he was in hospital. Now the models have food poisoning or a virus, who knows? Anyway, the fact is, we need a model right now.' She eyeballed me again, and despite her small size, I could see she wasn't a person you'd mess with. 'Come around the bar, let me take a look at you,' she ordered.

I glanced at Fergus, hoping for an ally.

'Go on, girl. What are you waiting for?' he said.

'No!' Angelo shouted. 'I don't want this woman anywhere near me, or the shoot! She has the evil eye on her. Besides, she's too old!'

'I'm twenty-nine!'

'See!' Angelo retorted.

'Don't be ridiculous!' Paula yelled back. 'The range is aimed at thirty-five to fifty, and what woman in that age group doesn't want to look twenty-nine? It's about time we used a mature model.'

*Mature model!*

Paula continued, 'Anyway, you told me yourself, if you hadn't been calling me – *checking up on me* – you'd have seen her and it wouldn't have happened.'

*What?!* I could hardly believe what I heard. 'You were on the phone . . . while riding your bike? You sod! You let me believe it was all my fault!' I turned to Paula. 'I'll do it!'

Angelo was protesting when a terrific din stopped us all. Fergus was ringing the brass 'time' bell that hung over the bar.

'Now, now, children. This poor girl's mother is dying in hospital, that's why she's working here. She needs the money really badly for hospital costs. So, stop the fighting, hire her for your modelling job, and I'll look after the bar.'

Angelo bit on his unkempt moustache and then turned to me. 'Sorry, I didn't realise your mother was so ill. How is she?'

My blood was still boiling. I shook my head and lowered my eyes. 'There's not much hope. She's having a brain scan this afternoon. I haven't had a chance to speak with the hospital yet.'

Paula interrupted. 'Let your hair free and come out so we can see you.'

I dragged the elastic from my ponytail, allowing my crazy red hair free rein as I emerged from behind the bar.

'Amazing,' she muttered. 'Turn around.'

I turned, feeling Angelo's eyes on me. Heat rose in my face.

'Okay, we've established you've got the body for the job,' Paula said. 'But let's see how you get on with the modelling. If we like your work, five hundred a day, plus full board at Elounda Paradise if you want it. That's the deal we give all our models.'

'What?' Angelo cried. 'Paula, we should discuss these things!'

Stepping up to him, Paula tried to make herself taller. 'I'm managing this shoot – it's my call.'

'Remember, I can still fire you,' he said quietly.

She stretched her neck and responded, 'Don't forget, I can walk away from this.'

They eyeballed each other, then Paula turned her back on him. They were like the man and woman on a Bavarian weather clock, I thought – destined to spend their time together, but never actually meeting in the middle.

'Okay, you win,' Angelo said quietly. 'Take her to the trailer. Tell Sofia we want a fast makeover, but don't blame me if this doesn't work. I'm telling you, she's bad luck!'

Paula gave him a *don't tell me what to do* look.

If it was the last thing I did, I would prove Angelo wrong. Modelling couldn't be that difficult – especially for a *mature* model.

Paula led me to a Portakabin, which stood in the super-market forecourt across the road. When I entered, I saw it was divided into four parts. To the left, a dress rail stuffed with clothes ran to a square window at the end of the room. Against the opposite wall sat a well-worn sofa and a small fridge. To the right of the door, one complete wall was taken by shoe- and hatboxes, a couple of packs of bottled water, and a door into a small boxed-off area.

The fourth quarter of the trailer was the domain of the beautician. I had never seen such a confusion of lotions and potions. Narrow shelves of lipsticks and coloured pencils were reflected in the large mirror they surrounded. There was a small table, also cluttered with cosmetics.

Sofia, a classic Greek beauty with dark, waist-length hair, was small, curvy, and probably in her mid-forties. She lifted my chin, peered into my face, and then muttered something in Greek.

'Sorry, I don't understand.'

'Ah, I Sofia. I no good speak English. Sit.' She manoeuvred me into a chair before the bulb-framed mirror. 'You is easy woman, I thinks.' Her dark eyes danced merrily beneath sweeping lashes.

'Excuse me?'

'You English women, you all easy.'

'I'm Irish.' I glared at her reflection.

'Is same.' She dragged my hair back. 'No 'airs on lip. Skin goods. And eyes, green like bowels of salad.'

Was that supposed to be a compliment? I imagined the chat-up line: *Darling, your eyes are like bowels of salad.* They'd be talking shite, of course. I giggled at my own joke.

'What?' Sofia stiffened. 'You laugh at my English? Is no nice. You's in my country. How much Greek *you* speak?' She put her fists on her hips.

'No, sorry, I wasn't laughing at you, Sofia. I'm nervous, that's all. I've never done this before.'

The make-up artist considered my words. 'Okays, let's start. You have beautiful hairs.'

'Thank you. How do I say *thank you* in Greek?'

She grinned again, her mouth wide and her olive face suddenly jolly. '*Efharisto.*'

'A fairy's toe?'

'Very good, you say like a Cretan. No talks now. I fix hairs, nails, and face of yours.'

While my hands were in a contraption that dried my scarlet acrylic nails quickly, I watched her apply a range of colours to my skin, starting with pale cream right through to brown. My eyelids and cheekbones and the bridge of my nose were highlighted, then my face was sculptured with various tones of brown and beige. My brows were darkened and shaped, false lashes glued on and mascaraed. Then my lips were highlighted, outlined, and painted with three shades of red, making them appear almost twice their size.

I kept fretting about my mother, the MRI scan, and the prognosis. I longed to phone the hospital but I could just imagine Sofia's agitation if I held a phone against her masterpiece.

Sofia worked something through my hair, making me yelp when she touched my stitches.

'Ah, you have problem. No worries, I be careful,' she said, as she transformed the frizz into an avalanche of auburn curls that cascaded over my shoulders. I studied myself in the mirror, unable to believe the result of her work. I screwed my nose up; so did my reflection. Amazing – the beauty in the mirror really was me. I felt like a fraud, but I wished my mother could see me. Another selfish thought. I sighed deeply.

'You no like?' Sofia scowled.

'I can't believe it's me, Sofia. You've done a fantastic job. *Efharisto!*'

Paula came in, huffed, and dragged an outfit swathed in a plastic bag from the rail. She thrust it towards me. 'Put this on. What size shoes do you take?' She frowned at my feet.

'Seven.'

'Just my luck. An amateur with big feet.'

I bit back a retort and smiled apologetically.

'Don't smile, you'll crease the make-up,' Paula snapped before she headed for the door. 'I'll be back in a minute.'

I put on a long, wraparound white linen skirt and a matching top that fell in soft folds over my breasts. The outfit was beautiful, but my knickers, dark blue, showed right through the skirt.

My underwear hadn't always been that colour; they started life as brilliant white. After a brief affair with a navy T-shirt in the washing machine, they were destined to spend the rest of their lives like Billie Holiday – seriously affected by the blues.

What to do? I scrunched the back between my cheeks and twisted around to study myself in the mirrored door. I was just deciding what to do about the front when Paula entered. I got such a fright when the mirror on the door swung around, my gluteus maximus let go of the fabric, which immediately sprang back into a dark triangle beneath the skirt.

'Oh, for God's sake!' Paula wailed. 'You can get those off right now!'

'What? I'm not going out there with no underwear! What do you think I am?'

'Well, obviously Angelo was right, you're not a bloody model, and the way you're shaping up you never will be! Don't talk, you'll ruin the make-up.'

I thought Paula was my ally, but she blew hot and cold. It couldn't be easy working with Angelo. Nevertheless, I refused to exit the trailer in a skirt you could practically see through and no undies. People were in the street, watching the shoot. Angelo was out there. That thought alone brought heat to my cheeks. I'd be humiliated.

Was this the end of it all? Me letting everyone down at the first hurdle? I had made a fool of myself thinking I could do the job. I cursed myself. Should I give up now, when this could be the beginning of an adventure, a dream?

Sofia rummaged through a hatbox marked *Swimwear* and held out a pair of white bikini bottoms. I nodded gratefully and caught a sympathetic glance.

Paula stared at the ceiling and tapped her foot while I changed. 'The biggest shoes we've got are sixes,' she said. 'You'll have to hold one and have the other hanging off your foot.'

I nodded, afraid to speak or smile. It was difficult to know how to make her like me. Her complaints seemed routine, not personal, and in an odd way I admired her for that.

'Angelo will help you pose. He knows what he's doing.'

That thought alone ramped up the tension. I had to loosen up, enjoy the experience. After all, this was a once-in-a-lifetime opportunity.

Paula examined me. 'I suppose you'll have to do. Breathe, drop your shoulders, stretch your neck, relax.' She opened the door. 'Off you go.'

Relax? Easy for her to say. But what else could go wrong? I would simply obey orders and get on with the job.

Sofia led me out of the trailer. Holding my breath, unsure of myself, I stepped out of the Portakabin. Everyone turned and, for a moment, I felt like a star, but then I was reminded of my cancelled wedding. This is how I would have felt in my beautiful dress, stepping into the church, walking down the aisle towards Jason, everyone admiring me. A shallow bit of vanity, but I had wanted it so badly.

Angelo seemed relieved. He reached for my hand and an odd collection of feelings raced through me as we touched. A hint of annoyance was quickly followed by excitement.

He uncurled my clenched fist. 'Don't be nervous, lady,' he said, his tone cold and businesslike.

The crew and onlookers fell silent. They watched as he led me to a stepping-stool in front of a huge barrel, as if it were the centre of a ballroom.

'It's quite safe,' he said, and for a moment I was Cinderella and he was Prince Charming.

Once I was perched on the vat, he told me to lean back and cross my legs, then he tried to slip a shoe onto my foot. Again, it could have been a Prince Charming moment, but it wasn't.

'They're too small,' I said, looking down at the casually-dressed guy in expensive shoes, who jangled my nerves every time we met.

'Don't talk; keep your face still. You don't have to stand in them, so let's try to squeeze your feet in.' I grabbed his shoulders to steady myself, willing my feet into the shoes. While he struggled with the footwear, the wraparound skirt fell open and I thanked God for Sofia and the swimwear.

'Okay, they're on,' he said, stepping back, suddenly noticing how much leg was on show. 'Mmm, nice, but not what we want. Keep still.' He delved into his jeans pocket and pulled out a roll of double-sided tape, ran a length of it along my thigh and halfway down my shin, then pressed the skirt against it.

*Holy God!*

'What's the hold-up? We'll lose the light,' Paula yelled. 'Oh, for God's sake, look at the colour of that woman's face. Get Sofia back, quickly!'

The make-up artist brought powder and, with a large brush, applied it to my face.

Angelo came in so close, his beard brushed my jaw. 'Relax. Don't worry about the dog-ess, she just arf-arfs a lot.'

I murdered a grin, then was engulfed by guilt that I was having such an adventure when my mother was critical.

Angelo told me to keep absolutely still. He spoke softly to Sofia, slipping an arm around her shoulders and saying something, which sounded kindly, in Greek. Adoration shone from the make-up artist's eyes.

He turned to me. 'We are ready. Do not think about anyone but me, understand?'

He tilted my head and arranged my hair over one shoulder, his fingertips brushing the side of my neck. A shiver ran through me. I watched his face, which was tense with concentration. I glanced at the trailer for Sofia's approval. The beautician stood in the Portakabin doorway, phone in hand. She glared at Angelo,

200

her dark eyes glinting with tears. I wondered what had caused such a dramatic change of mood but before I could analyse the situation, the photographer started shooting.

Angelo called out instructions: 'Drop your right shoulder; look into the lens; lower your chin; twist your shoulders to the left – the other left!'

'Okay, let's move on to the cover shots,' the photographer shouted. 'Bring the fan and get me a cold beer, I'm sweltering.'

Paula stuck her hand in the air. 'Sofia, bring iced drinks for everyone. Irini, come and change for the next shots.' In the trailer she gave me a retro black dress with little cap sleeves and a plunging, sweetheart neckline. My narrow waist was extenuated by a wide red patent belt and a voluminous organza calf-length skirt, which reminded me of Quinlan's creations for a local *Swan Lake* production.

* * *

'I've just seen the first photos,' Angelo said when I joined him in the forecourt. 'They're good. You did well. Now we will take the most important shots.'

I caught the scent of him – lemon shampoo, and on his breath, peppermint. I shivered again.

'You are cold?' He sounded surprised, and, for the first time, concerned about my wellbeing.

I shook my head. 'Nerves.'

'Okay. The photographer wants you to sit on the edge of the barrel and face him.'

He helped me onto the barrel, then squeezed my feet into another pair of size sixes. The full skirt tangled around my legs, and the more I struggled, the worse it got.

'Wait.' He placed his hand on my shoulder and shouted: 'Manoli, Stefano!' Two men appeared beside him. He spoke to them in Greek while keeping his eyes on me.

'When they lift you, open your legs wide as you can, then hold the position as they put you down, okay?'

I bit my lip, not wanting to think about two strange men touching my skin.

'Don't do that.' He scowled and then called over his shoulder, 'Get Sofia – again!'

Another mistake. Desperate to get this right, I cursed myself.

The men moved behind and lifted me by my armpits. Feeling glaringly conspicuous under the bright stare of onlookers, and conscious of the warm-handed men, I was determined not to frown or blush. I opened my legs, feeling exposed and vulnerable for a moment, but I told myself to woman-up and get on with the job.

Angelo leaned forward, his head almost on my shoulder, his mouth next to my face. Perhaps because at that moment I deliberately willed myself to drop the nerves, I became aware of his breathing in my ear. In a thrilling instant, I imagined him in bed. Unaware of my wicked daydream, he pulled the surplus fabric from under me and then nodded at the crew. They lowered me onto the cask and moved away.

A new, and oddly conflicting magnetism drew me towards the Greek. 'Now, grip the edge of the barrel between your legs and hold the skirt there,' he ordered.

I felt the heat of the day and the onset of a headache that had periodically plagued me since the crash. Being this close to Angelo was not helping the situation, because suddenly I realised how much I wanted to please him.

While Sofia stood on a step-stool and worked on my lipstick, I scrutinised her face. Beautiful large brown eyes with lashes to die for, and her lips were full and well defined. A look that models suffered to achieve, but her mouth turned down miserably at the corners. I sensed this woman had suffered pain for her glamorous looks. A victim of the personification of a beautiful woman. Was I on the threshold of falling into that trap?

Angelo spoke to Sofia in Greek again, rubbing the woman's back as if to console her when she stepped down.

Sofia smiled at him and then took the stool away. I was intrigued by her mannerisms, she seemed so heartbreakingly sad. Perhaps she was lonely. I decided that if anything came of this job, I would try to befriend her. She could teach me Greek, and I would be the shoulder I sensed she needed.

'Now, let's see if you can do this without another catastrophe,' Angelo said, looking straight into my eyes.

Of course I could, if only my heart would stop hammering every time Angelo touched me.

# CHAPTER 19
## BRIDGET

*Santorini, 28 years ago.*

I COULDN'T REMEMBER FEELING such happiness and contentment before. Sitting on an old sea chest, with my back against the wall, I nursed my baby at sunrise. Her little fists opened and closed, and her gaze fixed on my face while she suckled.

The previous day, Tommy had found the start of another fresco. Dare we hope our dreams of twenty years ago were coming to fruition? That evening, he had splashed out on a bottle of local red to celebrate but, because I was breastfeeding, I only had one glass. Tommy took care of the rest.

Irini fell asleep in my lap. I gazed upon her perfect little face and my heart exploded with love. How amazing to have a baby of our own after all this time. The greatest gift on earth must be to bring up your child. I felt complete, content with life. We were a family. I stroked Irini's cheek to wake her and changed sides, catching the buttery-vanilla scent of breast milk. Once again, I was filled with wonder at this perfect little person in my arms.

My thoughts went to my own mother. Had she sat in the brick-walled backyard in Dublin, nursing me and feeling this amazing pleasure? I remembered my mother as a subservient woman, a good Catholic, they said, cleaning the church and keeping a spotless house. A highly intelligent woman, who 'knew her place' and shrugged off her dreams in order to fit into the scheme of things in a male-dominated world.

Ma wrote poems and prayers in a little book, which was hidden away in her handbag. She said her rosary every night, mass on Sunday and the first Friday of the month. She also went to confession every Saturday, although I often wondered what sins she had to confess.

'Vanity, for one thing,' she said, her hair wrapped in bits of tissue and pink perming rollers, the kitchen ripe with the smell of ammonia. 'I can't go without my Twink every six months, or a dab of scent for church.'

My parents had never eaten in a restaurant, never stayed in a hotel, never been out of Ireland.

The day was fully light now, and with less chance of a mosquito bite, I pulled away the muslin veil. In a flash, I recalled my dream-daughter, Oia, pulling the veil back in the ritual of the maidens.

A brightly coloured swallowtail butterfly flitted about the patio table, drawing my attention towards the broken dish. My notes were there too, held down by a grapefruit-size stone. What could the markings mean, the circle of symbols cut into the terracotta base? Minoan, almost certainly, but as there was no actual record of the Minoan language, how could I find out what the engravings said? Ten arrowhead shapes, each one made unique by a different pattern, pointed towards a circle of letters that surrounded a simple star.

The cracks and crevices of the shapes were still dark, stained by my blood and Irini's, and I wondered whose blood had run into the pattern before ours? Was the vessel really connected to the religious rights of ancient people? Irini looked up, holding my gaze, her innocent eyes wide and questioning, as if she kept a deep secret too.

The only glitches in my life were the headaches and the dreams. The previous night, I suffered another dream of Thira when I fell asleep with Irini in my arms. As always, the scenes were clear in my mind, and as I rocked Irini and watched her eyelids become heavy, I recalled the events leading up to the River Festival.

\* \* \*

Oia curtsies before me. 'My festival clothes are exquisite! Do I look beautiful, my Queen?'

'You shall see for yourself.' I lead her into my antechamber, where we stand before a long rectangle of highly polished silver.

Oia gasps, turning this way and that, staring at herself. 'What magic! I can see myself so clearly.' She twirls again. 'If I had one of these I would never leave the dressing room.'

'Now you are prepared. Go and wait in my private garden, Oia. I shall join you shortly.'

Oia spins around once more, moving closer to the mirror, clearly pleased with her appearance.

Eurydice comes into my dressing room and bows. 'Dear Queen, the time has come for the festival.'

My heart races. The day is passing too quickly. 'Help me change my gown, and then we shall lead the procession of kings to the ships.'

The River Festival has started and I am filled with dread for the end of the day. The palace doors are opened. I see the populous of the city waving flags. A deafening roar rises from the crowd as I descend the palace steps with Princess Oia at my side. The ten kings, in full regalia, follow. The throng parts for us, cheering and throwing rose petals as our procession passes.

Warriors in battledress, complete with polished breastplates and boar-tusk helmets, line the way, holding back enthusiastic people. The crowd chants: 'Long live Princess Oia!' The ecstatic girl squeezes my hand.

On reaching the royal galley, young Prince Dardanus steps before us and places a wreath of orchids on Oia's head. He draws his sword from its sheath and lays it flat across his hands, the sun flashing from the polished blade. Before he offers it to her, he goes down on one knee and bows his head.

The crowd roars 'Bravo!' at this formal request for betrothal. Oia, her eyes sparkling, turns to me.

'What shall I do, my Queen?'

'You may accept the sword and, after five crocus harvests, become his wife, or you may walk past him.'

The crowd falls silent; the earth shivers slightly. I hold my breath, begging Poseidon to stop his tremors. Everyone waits. Oia seems rooted to the procession-way. She stares at the bowed prince, then reaches out and takes the sword. The populous explode into fits of jubilation. Prince Dardanus straightens, and for a moment the young couple gaze into each other's eyes. Neither smiles, as nobility never shows emotion in public, but I sense their delight and rejoice that Oia has experienced this special moment.

Dardanus lowers his eyes and steps aside. The nobles and their entourage board the royal galley. At the prow of the ship, opposite my ten kings, I sit on the raised dais with Oia at my side. We glance around at the cheering crowd, my people, the people that Oia is destined to save.

I turn to my daughter, about to ask if she is enjoying herself, but her face is tense and her eyes troubled.

'Are you all right, Oia? Is something wrong?'

'Everything is wonderful, my Queen, except . . . you're crushing my hand.'

* * *

'Wake up, Bridget, you're dreaming! Give the baby to me. You're squeezing her hand too tightly.' He lifted Irini from my arms and laid her back in the cot. 'Come on, I'll make a pot of tea while you write it all down. Do it while it's still in your head, then we'll analyse it together. Lay the ghost, so to speak.'

Confused for a moment, my mind was tugged between fantasy and reality, I blinked stupidly and tried to organise my thoughts.

He fetched my notebook. How did I come to deserve such a caring, understanding husband? Despite our problems over the past twelve months, everything was all right now.

* * *

The years passed quickly. Aaron went back to Ireland, graduated, and returned to work at the archaeology site full-time, taking care of all the heavy work. Tommy continued to get better, and it was not until Irini was four years old that everything changed.

We had excavated to the next layer. Tommy went down to the site every day, returning home breathless with excitement as more frescoes were uncovered.

'They seem to have painted their entire lives on the walls before they left,' he said over breakfast. 'The frescoes are almost complete and perfectly preserved behind the pumice. We can learn so much about how they existed.'

Neither of us mentioned Atlantis. If we voiced our dream, that we hoped to expose such a place of myth and legend, somehow our finds would be cheapened, sensationalised, and in a way, we would discredit ourselves. Yet it was always there, in the back of our minds.

One evening in November, we turned the lights out and sat on the patio under a star-spangled sky. The tourists had gone and the island had settled into its sleepy form of winter tranquillity. Tommy opened a bottle of wine and we contemplated the archaeological site.

'You're very quiet tonight, Tommy.'

'A lot to think about,' he said. 'I received an analysis back from a sample I sent away last month. As I suspected, it's dried grass growing from the top of a ruined dwelling. It confirms my suspicions and adds another piece to the puzzle.'

'What do you mean?'

'Something caused many of the buildings to collapse and, looking at the damage, I believe it had to be an enormous tremor. However, we can see that those buildings didn't have frescoes, but they did have tufts of grass growing from the tops of the broken walls. This tells us there must have been at least one season with rain, after a substantial earthquake, for the grass to grow on the ruins. I'm guessing at least a year passed before the volcano erupted and the entire city was buried in volcanic ash.'

'So you think they painted their life stories inside the remaining buildings after that earthquake?'

'Obviously. It's as if they deliberately left a message, telling us how they lived.' He stood and paced. 'What forethought! To imagine their towns being uncovered thousands of years into the future. This ancient civilisation left the equivalent of a modern-day time capsule. Quite remarkable, even for a highly advanced civilisation. And then they departed.' He stared at the stars. 'I wonder where they went?'

'It's difficult to understand how organised they were, to evacuate the entire island and all their valuables. I wonder how big the island was before the eruption?'

'Who can tell? Of course, we know it was much larger before the volcano blew its top. Perhaps they all went to the other end of the island, which sank. Or perhaps they packed the entire populous into their wooden ships and left, taking their livestock and valuables with them, but were drowned by the volcano's tsunami. As we uncover the frescoes, we will learn more about them. Undoubtedly, they would think the earthquake was an act of god. They would believe they had angered Poseidon in some way, as he was the deity they worshipped.'

'That bowl I'm trying to decipher, if it *is* a liable blood vessel, do you think they made human sacrifices?' I hugged myself, then sipped the wine. 'My dreams . . . you know? They make me wonder all kinds of things.'

Tommy shook his head. 'I don't see anything in the frescoes to suggest they made human sacrifices, except there was something at Knossos, in Crete. I'll look it up. Although we've uncovered many animal bones, perfectly preserved, we haven't uncovered any human remains. In extreme circumstances, they may have tried to appease Poseidon by offering a life on the altar. The sacred bull's horns in the temple are stained, I guess by blood. I've sent scrapings away for analysis but haven't had the results back yet.'

'But you think that blood is from the ceremony of the maidens, that we see in room three's frescoes? Pricking the girls' heels, catching the blood in a dish, then pouring it over the horns?'

Tommy nodded. 'There's so much more to the puzzle. It's exciting and irritating, like an itch that's just out of reach. Every bit of plaster, every dish, every fragment, has the potential to reveal so much. Just one more clue and everything might fall into place.' He sighed, smiled, and took my hand.

'It's been an amazing journey, hasn't it?' I said.

'We've been lucky to have found the site. How's the writing going?' he asked, changing the subject.

'Good. My source at Interpol can't give me any information about current cases, but he's helped me with some facts about smuggling artefacts across countries.'

'That's interesting. So how do they get antiquities shipped halfway around the world without being detected?'

'The most common way is to have literally thousands of copies made, and then hide the one original artefact among them when they're shipped to America.'

'I guess they can't be sniffed out by the dogs of custom officials – like exotic animals or drugs. It must be difficult to catch the bastards.'

'Yes, it is.' My own treachery surfaced and my mind went to Splotskey, the little jug, and the dragonfly necklace. The shame had never left me, but when I looked at Tommy, and remembered how close I had come to losing him, my guilt lifted a little. That terrible time in my life was over. I could put the incident behind me, and pretend it had never happened.

# CHAPTER 20
## IRINI

*Crete, present day.*

ANGELO STOOD IN FRONT OF ME. 'Now, prove me wrong. Show us you can do this. Give me a long neck with your shoulders down and chin in,' he said.

I did, still gripping the edge of the barrel. The metal rim dug into the backs of my thighs.

'Lean forward, half close your eyes and make your mouth like you're going to kiss me.'

I swivelled a glance at the watching crowd.

Angelo glared. 'Concentrate! Forget them!' he said sharply, nodding sideway at the onlookers. 'Focus on the shot. Let your body soak up the glamour of the dress, how it makes you feel. Take a deep breath and let it out slowly. Imagine we are alone, and you're a very sexy woman. Anyway, you *are* a very sexy woman. You are beautiful, desirable – women want to wear this dress because they dream of looking like you. Show them how it feels to wear this gorgeous creation right now. This isn't about you looking nice. The dress costs one-and-a-half grand and the shoot is all about showing how this amazing ensemble of exquisite fabric and ultimately flattering design makes a woman feel. Now own it!'

No man had called me beautiful before. Well, that's not quite true, Jason did once, but he was asleep in my bed at the time. *You're so beautiful, I want you all the time*, he had whispered. But when I reached for him, he turned over, away from me.

For a vicious second, I imagined dragging my fabulous acrylic nails down Calla's face. I could feel her skin collecting beneath them, smell the oozing blood, hear her scream. My jaw stiffened, my back arched, and I gave Angelo a little nod.

The dress cost more than the MRI scan, which made it feel obscene. I shook off the feeling and concentrated. With my eyes closed for a moment, I felt the rich, delicate fabric against my skin, the softness, the voluptuousness, and I sensed myself become one with the garment.

He placed his hands on my knees and moved closer. 'Now lean in and keep your eyes lowered until Nick tells you to do otherwise, then flirt with the camera, but do not blink.'

I leaned forward as far as I dared and pouted a kiss towards him.

'Good,' he said, before shouting, 'Start the fan!'

A massive gust of wind blew the skirt fabric all over the place, but I clung on, determined to get the shot. My hair was whipped back and I feared my eyes would start watering when I opened them.

'Look in the lens, Irini,' Nick, the photographer, called, while ducking and diving around me. 'Lovely. More neck. Chin out. Shoulders down. Wide eyes, chest out, jaw forward. Give me arrogance. Over here. Look at the sky. Down into the lens again. Relax those feet. Stretch your neck!'

My skin prickled with excitement. Angelo stood behind the photographer, mimicking the actions Nick wanted.

Suddenly Nick stopped, turned, and shook hands with Angelo. He nodded at Paula, who gave orders for the fan and lights to go off.

Paula shouted, 'That's in the bag! Great work, everybody!'

A spontaneous round of applause drove away the day's tension and smiles were exchanged between the crew.

'You did good,' Angelo said matter-of-factly. 'It's not easy when it is so hot.'

*You're hot,* I thought, then gave myself a mental kicking for being unprofessional.

In the excitement I'd hardly noticed the heat, but suddenly I was sweltering and desperate for an iced drink.

'What's tomorrow's weather?' Paula yelled.

'Is that a joke?' Angelo replied as he gripped my waist and lifted me down.

My legs, pressed against the barrel rim for an hour, were dead and folded beneath me. I stumbled and staggered forward in the tight stilettos. Angelo caught me and guided me to a nearby director's chair. He went down on one knee.

'Let's get these shoes off, shall we?'

'Bloody hell,' Paula cried. 'Not another model problem? There's been a jinx on this shoot right from the start. What now?'

'Just give us a moment,' Angelo said, before calling over his shoulder, 'Sofia, bring a cold drink and Irini's shoes.' He crouched on his haunches and peered into my face. 'Are you okay?'

Again, I felt genuine concern come from him. 'Sure, just my legs have gone numb from the edge of the barrel.' I rubbed them vigorously and wiggled my toes. 'I'll be fine. They're coming back now – pins and needles.'

'Pins and needles? What is this? You mean you have the tingles?'

I had to smile. 'I do indeed.' Blood rushed into my dead legs, making me wince. 'Ouch, don't you hate it when that happens?'

'Here, let me help.' He rubbed his hands up and down my calves. 'It's getting better?'

'It is, it is. Please . . .' Embarrassment, and something electric brought on by his touch, warmed my face.

214

He saw it, withdrew, averted his eyes and stood. Sofia appeared with a wonderfully cold bottle of water.

'I have to speak to the driver,' Angelo said. 'Don't move until everything is working, okay?'

'I'll be grand in a moment.'

The bustle of packing up continued around me. I studied Angelo's back as he walked away. Waves of dark hair met the shoulders of a pale blue sweatshirt, and well-worn jeans sculpted themselves to his thighs. Just before he reached the driver, he turned and made a little bow. His eyes flicked down before returning to mine, as if he knew I would be watching him. Then he focused his attention on the wagon driver.

Paula clapped for everyone's attention. 'Heads up, people. Eight o'clock start at the port.' She interrupted Angelo's conversation with the van man. 'Could you work with the barmaid this evening? She needs some idea of tomorrow's procedure. The last thing we want is another bloody hold-up.'

Angelo glanced my way and nodded.

I stood and tested my legs. They were fine.

As I headed for the trailer, Angelo caught my arm. 'Nine o'clock in the Ferryman Taverna?' He lifted his chin towards the port. 'We'll go over tomorrow's shoot, okay?'

'Sorry, I can't. I'm desperate to get to the hospital and learn the result of my mother's MRI.'

His brow furrowed. 'Ah, yes, of course, your mother. Then be at the port at seven o'clock in the morning.' He paused. '*Περαστικά*,' he said, and when I frowned, he translated: '*Perastika*. I hope she gets well soon.'

\* \* \*

I rushed into the trailer and changed into my own clothes. Sofia barely acknowledged me when I thanked her and said goodbye. Her face was sullen, her eyes red-rimmed. I should be on my way back to the hospital, but I'd made a commitment to Jack so I dashed back into the pub.

'Oh, Jack! I'm *so* sorry I abandoned the bar. I wouldn't have done it, but your father insisted. Not that I'm blaming him. It was just . . .'

'Don't worry, he explained. Look at you.' He had a mug of tea ready for me. 'Stay on that side of the counter; it seems you've worked hard enough for one day. I've been watching you. You looked amazing. Still do, in fact.'

Relieved that he wasn't angry, I took a sip of tea. 'What a disaster for the models, Jack. Sofia, the make-up woman, says they've been taken to hospital. They think it's food poisoning or the norovirus.' I spread my fingers on the bar top and stared at my glossy nails. 'I've never done anything like this before, Jack. Today was one of the most exciting days of my life, and now I have to go and see how my mother is doing. I have such a strong feeling it will be good news.'

He dropped his head to one side and smiled.

'They say they might want me for another two or three days, but I should be finished in time for the evening shifts. What a day, Jack!'

'No worries.' His grin lifted me. People were so nice. All these strangers seemed to have no notion of how much they were help- ing me at this critical time. 'We've never had a top model working behind the bar before – it should pull in some extra punters.'

'Top model? I don't think so.' I rolled my eyes. 'Look, Jack, I'm frantic to find out how my mother is. Could you pass my bag over?'

'Ah, yes. My father told me why you're in Crete. Under the circumstances, it's very good of you to stand in for Jane. We both appreciate it.'

'To be honest, I really need the money. If you'll excuse me, I'm desperate to call the hospital.'

\* \* \*

On the way into town, I wondered why the hospital insisted that I came in straight away, despite the late hour. I convinced myself it could only be one of two reasons. Either the brain damage was so extensive that Mam had no chance of regaining consciousness, even if they brought her out of the coma. The thought squeezed my heart. In that case, the life support must be turned off and my mother allowed to die peacefully. Or there was a slight chance that she might recover, and live a life without the machines and drugs. I had never hoped for anything as much.

I found the specialist waiting for me. We shook hands and he led me to his office.

'Take a seat, Irini. Can I get you a drink – coffee, water?'

I shook my head. We sat at his desk, silent for a moment.

'I'm eager to know the result of the scan,' I said.

He nodded slowly, placing his scrubbed hands on a report sheet in front of him. 'I'm sorry, it's not good news, Irini.' He gave me a moment to come to terms. 'We discovered your mother has had a slow-growing brain tumour for many years. I see from her medical reports she suffered from headaches, vivid dreams, and hallucinations ever since she was pregnant with you. In hindsight, we now understand that these were caused by the tumour pressing on her brain.'

*Hope! Faith and hope. Don't tell me it's all useless. Don't!*

217

'Can you operate to remove the tumour?' My voice seemed unreal, calm, as if it didn't belong to me, while my heart was torn apart by every conceivable emotion.

*It can't end like this, please.*

He placed the tips of his fingers together, stared at them and sighed. After a moment, he looked up and shook his head. 'Patients with a high-grade malignant brain tumour have a poor prognosis and cannot be cured. Despite aggressive treatment, surgery, radiation therapy, and chemotherapy, there is no real chance of recovery.

'We can remove the tumour, but the head trauma has disturbed it, and cancer cells, released into her bloodstream, will probably set up home in her spinal cord and every available organ. Yes, we can keep her alive, in an induced coma, but even that will not stop her demise.' He paused to allow the information time to sink in. 'Another problem is that we'll have to handle her pain by administering even greater doses of barbiturates as she becomes more tolerant. This in itself can cause unpleasant reactions, and we can't know what your mother is experiencing mentally. We may be inadvertently extending her suffering rather than relieving it. The morphine alone could ultimately cause her death.'

I had to take a few deep breaths before I could speak. I was aware that my tears welled, but it no longer mattered. All I cared about was Mam. Already, it felt as though she was slipping away from me.

'What can I do for her?'

His eyes were sympathetic. 'Although your mother's body is shutting down, she might well hold on, longing to have the family she loves around her. Hearing you talk, feeling you close, will be comforting for her. Knowing her family are together and that your lives will go on without her is important for her peace of mind. I understand it will be hard for you, but this, I think, is the kindest and most loving thing you can do for your mother.'

'Will I have time to bring my father over from Ireland? He wasn't well enough to travel with me when this happened.'

'Yes, bring him. Let Bridget know that you're both here for her. Share your memories and feelings with her. It's important to reassure your mother that it's all right to let go, whenever she's ready. I know that's difficult, but sometimes people hold on until they've heard this from the ones they love. Trust me, it's the best thing you can do, Irini.'

My throat ached. I nodded, unable to speak for a minute. I wanted to change what was happening, shake off this misery, but I couldn't.

'There's something else you should know, Irini. The specific type of brain tumour that your mother has, there's a very slight chance it's genetic, a gene that may've been passed on from her mother or grandmother. If we'd caught the tumour way back, when it was small, she'd have lived a normal life. However, we didn't have the technology then. You should have some tests, just to make sure you're clear.'

\* \* \*

Outside the hospital, I phoned Dublin and listened to the ring-tone, determined not to cry when it was answered.

'Uncle Quinlan, it's Irini. I'm in Crete.'

'Poor girl. How's Bridget?'

I had to take a very deep breath before I could speak. 'She's dying, Quinlan. She's dying but she needs my dad to come and make peace with her before she will let go. There's no hope.'

I paused, struggling to push my voice past the pain that constricted my throat. 'I know it's a lot to ask, but can you bring him over, even if it's only for one day? She needs to hear that he loves her. Please, Quinlan, please.'

'Of course I will. We'll try and be there tomorrow. Crete, you say?'

'Yes. Heraklion. Let me know your arrival time and I'll pick you up at the airport. I have to work tomorrow, to pay the hospital bills, but I'll find a way to get to the airport when you arrive. I can take care of everything else . . . it's just that one thing.'

'Don't worry, Irini, we'll be there and get to a hotel.'

'Thank you.' I hung up and cried.

* * *

The next morning, I was miserable beyond belief, but I had the shoot to contend with. I needed the money. I made sure I was wearing my best white undies, and stuffed a set of black lace bra and pants into my holdall. They were new, still on their little hangers. I'd bought them for my honeymoon. Now, the thought of being sexy with Jason made me feel sick. At least the new underwear meant I wouldn't have a repeat of yesterday's embarrassing performance. I was literally covered for all eventualities.

After a hurried hotel breakfast, I arrived at the harbour just before seven-thirty. The Portakabin was there already, as were Sofia and the London photographer, Nick. At first, I didn't recognise Angelo. His beard was neatly trimmed back to little more than designer stubble, and his mop of unruly hair was smooth and shiny, and just touching his collar. He wore an immaculate white shirt, instead of the well-worn blue tee of yesterday. He glanced at his watch as I approached.

'Sorry I'm late, the traffic—'

'Go straight in to Sofia,' he said without formality.

Paula and the crew arrived at eight. Clearly, Paula was not a morning person either. The photographer hurried everyone. The light, I came to learn, is perfect early on and deteriorates as the sun gets higher.

By eight-fifteen, I was thrilled with my appearance. Sofia had excelled again. I was dressed in a flouncy floral frock. Angelo glanced over me and nodded approvingly. He went to tug his beard, a habit I'd noticed, but for a second the shortness of it appeared to confuse him. His eyes met mine and for some stupid reason I blushed.

I was told to sit on a great pile of yellow fishing net, which was not easy.

'My sandal buckle's tangled in the stuff,' I cried as everything slid beneath me and I ended up rather like the morning's catch. Angelo and one of the crew sorted me out and we tried again.

The sun gathered strength, and although someone was holding a huge white diffuser to soften the glare and keep me in semi-shade, I found it hard not to squint.

'Lower your eyes until Nick says: "lens"!' Angelo shouted.

'She's doing all right,' Nick said. 'You can leave her to me.'

When Angelo backed off, I found Nick was easier to work with. The town woke and I became aware of what was going on in my peripheral vision. The harbour came to life as local fishermen returned with their night's catch. Chunky traditional boats – red, blue, yellow, and white – fringed the quayside. Sparkles flashed from the turquoise water, which I could hear lapping at the wooden hulls. Across the little port, shopkeepers dragged racks of sun hats and postcards onto the pavement. Taverna owners opened their doors and enthusiastically hurled starched gingham cloths over pavement tables. A street cleaner swept the gutters with a giant brush and a dustpan made from half a plastic barrel nailed to a broom-pole.

Stout women in black dresses and grey headscarves waddled out of the bakery with carrier bags of fresh bread. Everyone grinned. Everyone shouted: '*Kalimera!*' – which I knew meant 'Good day!' but I realised this was not a greeting, it was a statement.

Half a dozen cats gathered on the quayside, motionless apart from a slight flick of their tail-tips, eyes fixed on the men sorting their catch. There was a flash of silver, a small fish thrown onto the cement. The felines pounced and the victor raced away, tearing under table legs, around postcard racks, and up an alley. The losers returned to the wharf like vigilantes. They stared, twitching, waiting for another chance.

'Next outfit!' Paula cried. 'Quick as you can, Irini.'

Ten minutes later, I was back out. I had to drape myself around a huge anchor and pose on the harbour wall.

'Try not to get fish shit on the frock, will you?' Paula shouted.

As the air warmed, patience melted, and by eleven, everyone was irritable. Then the shoot was over and I quickly changed into my own clothes. When I left the Portakabin, Paula called my name, but I was eager to get to my mother and pretended I hadn't heard. She called again, and this time I couldn't ignore her.

'Irini, here!' She thrust a baguette wrapped in clingfilm towards me. 'I guess you're going straight to the hospital?'

I nodded, eager to get away.

'Be back by three, okay?'

'Thanks for this. Really kind.' I lifted the bread roll.

She peered over my shoulder, rolled her eyes and muttered, 'What now?'

Angelo appeared from behind me. 'Do not be late. We only have four hours and there's a lot to get through.' He exchanged a tense glance with Paula, before turning back to me. 'We don't want to work tomorrow.' I wondered what was going on. Then his expression softened and his unique smile and frown appeared, transforming his face. 'You did good. I thank you.' He held my gaze for a moment and then marched away.

Paula narrowed her eyes and watched him. I was reminded of the cats.

I drove straight to the hospital, which was half an hour away, pleased to realise my driving skills were rapidly improving, but then disappointed to learn my mother was not.

'There's no change,' the nurse told me. 'Just go through.'

At the bedside, I took her cool, limp hand.

'Hi, Mam. Uncle Quinlan and Dad are coming over to see you. Isn't that nice?'

I watched her eyelids for the slightest twitch, hoping against hope, but there was nothing. Nevertheless, I felt a kind of togetherness and peace. As if she always knew I would be with her at the end, and even if I hadn't read her notebooks, I'm sure I would have come to realise that, above all else, she loved me.

'I'm not going to read your journal today. Instead, I'll tell you about bits of my life that you missed. It's not fair that you lost part of my growing up because of a shocking growth in your head, so I'll fill you in on the best bits.'

I had to swallow hard, because I knew by sharing my memories with her, I was helping her to let go. And the heartbreaking thing was, I didn't want her to go anywhere. I wanted her to fight! I wanted a miracle. What was the point of serving God all my life if He couldn't do me one little favour now?

So angry and emotional, I sobbed, and as I tried to calm myself down, I felt the slightest tremor beneath my fingers. Movement so light that at first, I thought a hair had fallen on my hand. Staring at her fingers, which rested on my thumb, I whispered, 'Did you hear me, Mam?'

I held my breath, my senses electric. Did I imagine it?

# CHAPTER 21
## BRIDGET

*Santorini, 24 years ago.*

IN THE DARK, lying beside Tommy, I gradually emptied my head of thoughts and memories. My grand plan was to relax into physical inertia and mental receptiveness. I had to go back to Atlantis, save Oia and her mother from the terrible finale that awaited them at the end of the River Festival. After all, these were only dreams, the seeds of which were planted in my mind by Uncle Peter, decades ago, when my childish mind was most amenable to fantasy.

With that knowledge, I clearly had the power to wake, yet I decided to stay in my dream to try and change it. Aware that the mind is a slippery fish, and getting a grip was unlikely to happen on my first attempt, I was determined to keep at it until I had control and could change the end.

In my dream, Oia was in my arms, but for all the love and emotion that I felt, it may well have been my own child, Irini. With that thought, I realised the danger and knew I had to dissimilate. Irini had no place in this dream. I drifted on the threshold of sleep.

The nightmare was happening again and, in the dream, I was crying. In that lucid state, I had to stay with the nightmare and control it, reach a time of tranquillity and happiness, because then I believed I would not be troubled again. Despite my fear, I drifted back, allowing myself to hear the jubilant crowds, see the shimmering festival, feel Oia's hand in mine.

I, Queen Thira, took long, steady breaths, opened my eyes, and saw the flamboyant flotilla parading towards the sea.

* * *

Decorated with flags and garlands of lilies, the royal galley heads downriver. A procession of our finest ships follows. I wish we were on our way to Crete, leading the exodus, my daughter beside me.

The kings are sure that when Oia has gone to Poseidon, the island's troubles will be over and we need not leave. Slowly as candles burn down, I also begin to accept their gospel. Could Hero be right? Oia was born to reach this day and save us all. Perhaps it was not my king that I slept with on the night of Oia's conception, but a personification, the shapeshifting spirit of Poseidon, there to sire his future bride.

My head feels hollow from lack of sleep. My world undulates like the surface of the river, nothing solid, nothing as it seems, everything slightly off-kilter.

Oia has forgotten herself and is smiling at Dardanus in the second row. The young man grins back, pulling faces and trying to make her laugh.

'Oia, decorum, please,' I say quietly.

'Sorry, my Queen. I'm so happy, it's difficult not to show it.' She removes the smile, lifts her chin a little, and adopts an aloof expression.

'Dardanus appears pleased with himself too,' I said.

The river narrows and passes under a crowded bridge. The barge is showered with petals. Oia's smile escapes again, her eyes sparkling and her face radiating pleasure. The populous cheer and whistle. At the head of the galley, musicians play their reedpipes as the bosun beats a rhythm for the oarsmen. I want to hold on to these last precious moments of my daughter's life. Minute by minute, as the grand day passes, I seem to hollow out. I never take my eyes off Oia, and smile whenever the girl looks my way.

I glance at the time candle. This tall beeswax cylinder, with twenty-four sparkling stones pressed into the side, is lit in the middle of the night. Another pebble falls to the marble floor, the sound almost inaudible, except to me. I recall the day of Oia's birth, and the exploding joy when I first held my daughter. Three more pebbles, then I *must* take away the life I had given.

There is no escape from the inevitable. I reach out and take my daughter's hand.

'Dearest Mother, my Queen, this is the best day of my life,' she says.

*     *     *

Then the dream and reality became horribly confused. My plan fell apart. Irini was the beautiful princess. She appeared to be sleeping, her long, red hair flowing over her shoulders, her pale skin luminescent.

'I have to sacrifice you, Irini, for the sake of everyone on this island.' Then I saw myself raise the knife and lunge down at my daughter's chest. Everything changed into slow motion, apart from my heartbeat.

*Stop the dream! Stop the dream before it's too late!*

I could not change the dream! My scream seemed trapped inside my chest, coming out as hardly a grunt and my body so heavy, I could hardly move. In my heart, I knew the world depended on me to perform this vile act. Finally, in the moment between sleep and wakefulness, my scream broke free, alarming Tommy and terrifying three-year-old Irini.

When I had calmed, and both Irini and Tommy were asleep again, I wrote down the nightmare, hoping by doing so I could exorcise the terrifying image and would never experience it again.

\* \* \*

Time flew by. Irini, crawling, walking, constantly talking. An inquisitive child, she kept me busy from dawn until dusk. I seldom went to the site with Tommy, and although I loved Irini with all my heart, I did miss the archaeology. It seemed Tommy and I had nothing to talk about when we were together at home.

Things got worse when Irini was almost four. I started sleep-walking. The problem came to a head one morning when I found the door locked. The big old key was in the pocket of Tommy's shorts.

'I was afraid you'd go outside and step off the patio in your sleep,' he explained.

'You mean . . . jump?'

'No, of course not, but I couldn't sleep for the worry,' he said when I slipped back into bed. 'So I locked the door.'

He made light of it, but I realised how deeply concerned he was.

'Go back to the doctor, Bridget. You look worn out. Ask her for sleeping pills, or perhaps there's some kind of therapy.'

'I'll go, I swear,' I said. 'We can't sleep with the door closed all through the summer.'

'Good. I don't want to handcuff you to the bed either,' he quipped, trying to make light of the situation.

I rested my head against his body and listened to his heartbeat. This awful situation was my punishment for stealing the dragonfly necklace, yet that steady rhythm in his chest reminded me that my husband was alive because of my action.

I wasn't fooled by Tommy. He camouflaged his concern with humour, and I matched it.

'You're a devil, Tommy McGuire.'

The pretence fell away. 'Promise me you'll go, Bridget. See if she can help. We can't go on like this.'

* * *

Tommy was right, I had to find a way to stop the nightmares, put an end to the situation before I hurt Irini. Before I did something irreversible. I went in search of medical help.

'There doesn't seem to be anything physically wrong, Bridget,' Kiriaki said as she ripped the blood pressure cuff from my arm.

'What do you think's causing the nightmares, Doctor? They're truly awful.'

Kiriaki glanced through my notes. 'They started when you were pregnant, yes?' I nodded. 'A number of things can trigger nightmares: pregnancy, as I said, anxiety, post-traumatic stress, or depression. Is anything worrying you?'

'Not at all. Apart from the nightmares, I'm very happy.'

'Perhaps there's been an incident in your life that caused deep distress. Something you've not acknowledged, or that you're trying to deny or forget. Perhaps you've buried an unfortunate occurrence so deeply you don't even remember it. You were disturbed to the extent that you refuse to admit it ever happened. Does any of that sound familiar? Is there anything in your childhood so appalling you were never able to talk about it, Bridget?'

'No, I had a happy childhood. I was brought up by my aunt and uncle, and I know they loved me dearly.'

'What happened to your parents? Why didn't you live with them?'

'There was a bomb . . . Ireland, you know?'

She shook her head. 'Tell me about it.'

'Ma had gone to meet Da after work. She'd just got her first week's wages and she wanted to go shopping with him.' As the memory of Ma returned, I realised I was smiling. 'She was really proud of herself that morning. She wore lipstick and powder, and appeared more beautiful than I'd ever seen her before. I told her she looked like a film star and she laughed, dismissed it, but I knew the comment really pleased her.'

'So, you remember it clearly?' Kiriaki dropped her head to one side, sadness and sympathy in her eyes.

I nodded. 'A neighbour was keeping an eye on me after school. Some of us played marbles in the gutter.' I stared at the desktop. 'Mrs Doyle called me, told me to wash my hands and face, and sit in her best room. I remember feeling important. Whatever was going on, I liked it.'

Kiriaki nodded. 'Then they said your parents had been killed?'

* * *

Kiriaki prescribed sedatives, and from that day, I took them before bed. The pills helped, although my early mornings on the patio were spoiled by a groggy head and dull view of life. Irini started at the local school at Easter and soon she was home for the statutory three-month summer holidays. My daughter either came to the site with her dolls and colouring books, or she spent the day with the neighbour's children. She was a pretty child and the locals regarded her as special because of her mass of tightly curled red hair.

230

On one occasion, Yianni-One-Arm brought my repeat prescription as usual. I thanked the boy, gave him fifty lepta and a bag of homemade biscuits for his mother. That evening, I realised I had somebody else's medicine. I called the surgery and left a message explaining I would return on Monday morning to collect the correct prescription.

That night, I slept well and woke bright and full of life, and the following night the same. I considered giving up the pills, but then the worst nightmare struck, with more horror and violence than anything I had experienced before.

In the lucid dream, I was Thira again, and even as I was dreaming, I knew I had been in this situation before, and I would be again and again, until I completed my destiny. My beautiful daughter Oia lay supine before me.

'I have to do this!' I cried, raising the sacrificial knife in both fists. 'It's the only way I can save our people from certain death! Forgive me! Forgive me!' and I plunged the knife downward.

A slap across my face woke me. The first thing I saw was the blood on Irini's sheets and on my own hands. I dropped the knife and tried to pull the front door open, but it was locked. Overcome by the horror of my nightmare, I pushed myself into the corner of the room, trying to get away from the awful scene. My throat closed. Blackness rushed in from the corners of my eyes. I could not breathe for the terror that crushed me.

'It's a nightmare! It's not real, Bridget!' Tommy was shouting.

Embracing the reality, I gasped and fell sobbing into his arms.

'Oh my God! What have I done? Tommy, I'm going mad! I can't take this anymore!' I stared at the blood, my legs folding, my head spinning so wildly it unbalanced me.

'It's all right, you're safe,' Tommy said. 'You were having a nightmare. Let me see your hand. You've cut yourself.'

'Where's Irini? Oh Tommy, Tommy! I was going to kill her . . . I was really going to stick that knife in her chest. It was all so real. In my mind, I had no choice. Why is this happening to me . . . to us?'

'Irini's on a sleepover, remember, with Maria and Nefeli? Perhaps that was a trigger – that you were concerned for her when you went to sleep.'

'But what if she'd been here? What if you hadn't woken up? Even if you had, imagine how terrified she'd have been to see her mother coming at her with a carving knife!'

Tommy made me a mug of sweet tea and poured a little brandy into it. We sat at the table until dawn. He watched me write down the dream, encouraging me each time I stopped, and passing me tissues when I couldn't see for the tears.

'I was the woman in the fresco, Tommy. I was that woman who saved Irini's life on the day she was born. I understand none of this makes sense, but I'm telling you, *I was her*.'

\* \* \*

When I had recorded every detail, Tommy read through it and asked me questions until I broke down in tears again.

'Let's face it,' I said. 'There's only one solution, Tommy. We have to send Irini back to Ireland for her schooling. She can go to the convent. She'll be safe with the nuns. And I'll have to find a psychiatrist and see if I can be cured of these awful hallucinations. We can't continue like this. It's impossible. Nobody's safe.'

I didn't want to look into his eyes, to see his helplessness, that lingering despair. I buried my face in his chest and he wrapped his protective arms around me. The action was only role-playing

232

on his part. I knew he felt as helpless as me, yet the strength of his hug helped me regather.

'Look, first we'll go and see Kiriaki together,' Tommy said. 'Get your hand seen to. It's a deep cut and might need a stitch. While we're there, I think you should have a tetanus, just in case. And let's have another talk with her about the nightmares.'

# CHAPTER 22
## IRINI

*Crete, present day.*

A YOUNG NURSE RUSHED in and made me jump. I was still staring at my mother's hand, sure that it twitched.

The nurse caught my startled expression. 'Ah, sorry. I'm late with the medication,' she said breathlessly. 'I need to . . . do the . . .' She wrote on the clipboard at the bottom of the bed, then injected something into a capsule that was taped to my mother's wrist. 'I am sorry,' she repeated with urgency, as if saying it louder conveyed her regret more clearly.

I blinked at the nurse. There was an uncomfortable moment. She stared at my mother, then at me, then she left in a flurry before I had composed the question I wanted to ask. Even when she had gone, the words escaped me.

\*    \*    \*

That afternoon, back on the quayside, I had to pose on a little blue and white boat. The *caïque* bobbed about violently whenever another vessel came in, or left the harbour. I clung to its stubby mast, hoping my alarm didn't show.

For the first time in my life, I noticed how light changes through the day. At three o'clock, the sun was squintingly harsh, by four it had softened and at five, there was a golden tint rimming everything that wasn't in the shade. Shadows themselves were longer, and the grey cement wharf turned the colour of pale toffee. I realised that people, too, seemed to change with the light. They became mellow and more relaxed in mood than before.

I sat on the edge of the boat, my bare feet in the water and my head thrown back, terrified I would slip off, fall in and drown.

'I can't swim!' I called out, just in case, imagining the newspaper headline: *Dream come true turns into tragic death for Dublin religious teacher.*

'Keep your eyes closed and look as though you're enjoying the sun on your face,' Nick shouted over the water. 'Soft smile, Irini!'

I wanted to get this right, prove I could do the job. My desire to have a quiet life in Dublin, teach children, get married, and have a family had gone out of the window. Wearing beautiful, expensive clothes and being the centre of attention was so contrary to my former lifestyle it seemed deliciously naughty. But I was still terrified of the water that gently lapped at my feet.

Recalling the Liffey, I wondered what was below me. How deep was the harbour? I swore I would get over this stupid fear and learn to swim. My holdall lay on the quayside and in a quiet moment, I heard my phone ringing. I guessed it was Quinlan calling from the airport.

'Can somebody answer my phone, please? It's important!'

Angelo delved into my bag and pulled out the black Victoria's Secret briefs, much to the amusement of the crew. Then came the matching bra. He draped both garments over his white plaster cast. His eyebrows went up, eyes half closed. The crew whistled and whooped, and I wanted to kill them all.

'The phone!' I yelled, my face burning. 'It's urgent!'

Paula stomped up to Angelo and whacked him on his good arm. 'Now look what you've done. Lobster-face isn't exactly the fashion this year!' She spun around and yelled at the crew, 'Cut it out! Get the boat pulled in and fetch Sofia, somebody.'

Angelo was still grinning at my smalls when he picked up. After talking for a couple of minutes, he replaced my underwear and the phone. The men tugged on mooring ropes, and the boat slid towards the quayside.

'It was a man,' Angelo said. 'He is boarding a flight with your father and he will phone again later.'

The hull hit the wharf and I toppled back. My head, which was still tender after the car accident, whacked against the cabin. I yelped, touched my scalp, fearing my stitches had split. Before I could get my bearings, two men hauled me onto the cement and Sofia attacked me with the powder and brush. I found it hard to stand still and swayed slightly, my sea-legs not immediately adjusting to dry land.

Angelo's smile rapidly lost its charm. I wanted to give him a slap. The cheek of the man, waving my underwear about for all to see. When Sofia had finished, he came over.

'This man with your father, he said they will arrive at nine o'clock. He's your boyfriend?' He peered questioningly, then glanced at his plaster cast. He was remembering my underwear and I longed to say something smart. However, it seemed I had lost the power of sarcasm, so I kept my mouth shut and shook my head.

By seven, the shoot was over and I headed for the Portaka-bin. Angelo passed me a bottle of water. 'Come with me. I have something to show you.'

From the corner of my eye, I saw Paula slam her fists to her hips as she watched us.

Angelo led me out of the harbour and onto a concrete wall that reached out to sea, protecting the marina. The scruffy anchorage contained a rusting dredger and long-abandoned, half-submerged boats. Huge concrete blocks were scattered like thrown dice.

'This way,' he said, leading me along the top until he stopped at an elbow where the wall changed direction. 'Here, sit.'

I did, wondering what this was about. Perhaps they didn't need me any longer. Working for Retro Emporio had been a great adventure, but if my modelling career was over, so be it. Anyway, it seemed rough justice. With my mother critical, I shouldn't be having such a great time. But then, I fretted about the money.

I glanced down to the detritus of washed-up plastic. A pretty white church stood on the flat rocks to my left, the sort of chapel you see on Greek posters. The immediate coastline stretched away with a length of empty, sandy beach. Further along the shoreline, a giant Ferris wheel loomed from the condensed tourist area of Malia, and offshore, kite-surfers sped back and forth. The dazzling colours of their kit glinted in the low sunlight like jewels scattered over the sea. A small island supported another little white church, a destination for tourists in their pedalos and canoes.

Angelo took my water, opened it, and handed it back. 'Is he your boyfriend, this Quinlan?'

*None of your business.* 'No, he's my uncle.'

'Ah.' He gave a small smile. 'You seemed distracted today. You did a good job, but I think your mind was elsewhere.' He stared at the horizon. 'Tell me your problems. How is your mother?'

A seagull sailed through the air close to the water, its white reflection undulating on the turquoise sea. I followed the lonely, searching bird with my eyes. 'I'm worried about her.' I couldn't speak for a moment, not sure if my emotions would allow it.

'Tell me.'

I took a deep breath, glanced into Angelo's face for a second, and then absently returned my attention to the gull. 'My father and uncle have come to say goodbye to my mother. She may, you know, let go . . .' I had to stop, take another calming breath. 'My mother's condition is hard enough to deal with, but if my father wants her to be buried in Ireland, then I need her passport, and I've stupidly left her papers in the house in Santorini. Then there's money. I have to be out of my hotel tomorrow. I'm working for you through the day – thank you for that – and the pub in the evening, but it's still not enough to cover the hospital bills. And most of all . . . most of all . . . I don't want my mother to die. I don't. I can't even stand the thought.'

Everything welled up, and then I was sobbing against his chest. His arms held me, lightly, as if hovering on a boundary.

'Sorry, sorry,' I said after a moment, pulling away and swiping my eyes, horribly aware that we were in clear view of Paula and the crew. 'I don't know what came over me.'

'Look,' he said, pointing his chin towards the skyline.

The sun was a huge fiery ball just touching the horizon. A shimmering path of red was reflected on the wavetops reaching all the way across the sea, ending below our feet. Overawed by the scene, I stared in silence. I was watching my mother's light go out, her life slipping below the horizon, her echo dancing across the waters to touch me one last time.

In my mind, I was saying goodbye, trying to be brave and let her go. Like the sun, she was going anyway.

With just a sliver of red remaining above the horizon, I could not look away. Those last precious moments. When the sun had gone, the sky became rich burned orange. I turned to Angelo, but the sun had fixed its ghost to my retina and I saw a smudge of red wherever I looked.

'Irini, we all have to watch our parents grow old and die. It's the way things are, but I am sad for you. My own mother died when I was a boy and it hurt me deeply, so I understand.' His big brown eyes stared into the distance and I wondered what he was thinking. My ringing phone broke the silence between us.

I answered, and after a short conversation, ended the call.

'The hospital?' Angelo asked.

'No, someone's interested in my wedding dress.'

'Your wedding dress? You are married?!' He seemed alarmed, so I elaborated.

'No, I make clothes and sell them on social media.'

'Ah, we have competition?'

'Hardly. I haven't even got a proper website. In fact, I've only just acquired my own labels.' I found myself sitting up, proud of the achievement, reminding myself to tell my mother all this. '*Rags to Riches*. My designs are mostly made from upcycled clothes.'

'Upcycled clothes?' His mocking smile was in place, but behind it, I sensed genuine interest and it uplifted me. 'What is this? Tell me more.'

'I'd love to, but I'm already running late. I have to get changed, collect my family at the airport, visit my mother, and then go to work at the Shamrock.'

'Keep the dress,' he said. 'It looks good on you. Visit your mother, then go straight to work. I will send my driver for your father and uncle, and take them to my hotel.'

*His hotel?*

For a moment, words escaped me. 'You're too kind, but . . . your hotel?' I stuttered.

'Well, my father's hotel, in Elounda. Five stars,' he said with pride. 'The models always stay there when we work in Crete. You will too. I think Paula has booked you in from tomorrow night. So no more worries, Irini. No more tears.'

'Thank you. Thank you so much . . .'

'Nothing,' he said with a shrug.

Horrified, I noticed the state of his shirtfront. 'Oh my God! I'm sorry, you've got mascara all over your shirt.'

He glanced down. 'My new shirt. You *are* a catastrophe!' He looked at my face and touched his nose. 'You have snot.'

The embarrassment! I swiped under my nose and sniffed hard.

He laughed and then after a moment's thought said, 'Tomorrow we don't work. I will take you to Santorini to get your mother's papers. I haven't been there for a long time. Your father and uncle will be at the hospital all day I think, so no worries, okay?'

Speechless and overwhelmed by his kindness, I nodded.

'Now, you must go and see Sofia. Your face is a little mess.'

In the Portakabin, I stared at my reflection. I had panda eyes on my tear-streaked face.

'What yous cry for, lady?' Sofia asked with a resigned sign. 'Yous make much works for mees.'

'Sorry, Sofia. How do I say sorry?'

'Συγνωμη.'

'Sig-no-me?'

'Goods.'

She cleaned my face and then I set out for the pub.

*　　*　　*

At dawn the next morning, I packed my case, checked out of my holiday hotel, and drove to Elounda. Quinlan and my father were

240

waiting in their hotel lobby, and our reunion was an emotional struggle. Poor Dad was still tired after the journey. He hadn't slept well and seemed disorientated. I told them all my news and why I would not be with them. Quinlan approved, explaining that perhaps Dad could not talk freely in front of me.

'Why not?' I asked. 'What does he have to hide?'

But my uncle would not elaborate.

As I waited in the car park for Angelo, one tragic scene after another arrived at A&E. People with broken limbs and bloody wounds. I would be glad to get away from the place for a while.

Angelo arrived in a shiny grey 4x4. 'Lock your car and leave it here,' he called out of the window. I had done that already, and given the keys to Quinlan. Despite wearing a white linen shift and a straw hat, I sweltered in the sun. Angelo arrived in a silver, chauffeur-driven Mercedes. 'Lock your car and leave it here,' he said as he got out.

'I have, Quinlan needs it to get back to the hotel.'

Despite wearing a white linen shift and a straw hat, I sweltered in the sun. Angelo held the door open for me. I welcomed the vehicle's cool interior. Greek music played softly from hidden speakers. 'Everything okay?' Angelo asked, once he was sitting beside me.

'Yes. Thanks for this, it's really kind of you.'

'No worries. We'll go to the port and take the FastCat.'

After a length of silence, I tried to make conversation. 'Your hotel's beautiful. How come you don't work there too?'

'That life is not for me. My father and my brother, Damian, do the job very well. I like more the art and fashion, so I have this business.'

'I'm confused, you mean it *really* is your business? In the hospital, you referred to "the boss". Then later, when I met Paula, I brought . . .'

He laughed. 'Sometimes she thinks so too, and one day she will become my partner – but that is the future. Now it is my business.'

'I love fashion too. I have a passion for fabric and design. My uncle, the one who's here now, he makes costumes for the main theatre in Dublin and sometimes I help. I wanted to take art and fashion at college, but the nuns persuaded me I'd be better off as a teacher. It's a secure job.' I thought of all the pleasure I got from making and selling my designs. 'I started taking a college course in the evening, but then my parents came home and I had to give it up to look after my father. I have a fashion portfolio that I still work on, but it's only a hobby, really.'

'You must submit it to my company office in London. We're always looking for fresh talent.'

I knew he was only being nice, but the gesture was kind. I was suddenly overwhelmed by this man's thoughtfulness. Even with his frowning smile he somehow managed to cheer me up.

I turned and said, 'Look, the accident, it wasn't your fault because you were on your phone. I'm the one who drove on the wrong side of the road. We both got away lightly.'

He was silent for a moment. 'You think I am doing this because I feel guilty?' He stared at the traffic ahead, but I saw the furrowed smile in place and it made me feel better.

\* \* \*

At the port, I took in the scene as Angelo went to buy our tickets. Golden sunlight poured from a deep azure sky, refracting with blinding flashes on the gently undulating seawater. A wooden *caïque*, painted in primary colours and piled with yellow fishing net, rounded the harbour wall, interrupting the tranquil scene.

An entourage of gulls dipped and soared over its foamy wake, screaming and jostling for tossed fish guts.

The little boat chugged towards the fishing harbour, next to a sandstone fort. Waiting on the quayside, a line of stooped old women, head-to-toe in black, stood like vultures, greedy eyes set on the approaching *trata* boat and its fresh fish. A traditional village scene in a big city. Although I didn't know the place very well, I got the feeling a lot of ethnicity still lingered in modern, bustling Heraklion.

Further along the port, coaches, taxis, and lorries seemed ant-like in the shadow of a majestic cruise ship, several ferries, and a container ship. The vessels loomed like giants over the quayside.

Suddenly, Angelo was beside me. 'Look, here she comes.' He nodded towards the approaching FastCat. The ship appeared like a floating bridge and had an aura of immense power. Dockworkers secured the vessel to the quayside, and then there was bedlam. The tickets had seat numbers, so why was everyone pushing and shoving to get on?

'Have you been to Heraklion before?' Angelo asked, once we were strapped in.

I shook my head. 'Never even heard of it before.'

'Ah, but you have, you just don't know it.'

Puzzled, I glanced at his way and once again I saw pride shining from his face.

'Candy, candied peel, sweets – they all originated from here, from the city's old name, Candia.'

I had a feeling I would learn a lot on this trip to Santorini.

'You must understand, the Cretan people are your first upcyclers. They waste nothing, never have. But they had a problem with one thing. They grew much citrus fruit, but even the goats and chickens would not eat the peel, so they soaked it in honey and strung it up to dry. It became very popular, this peel from Candia, so they did it with other fruit, and the stems of umbellifers like angelica, finding that it stored for a long time. These sweetmeats soon gained popularity and were exported as far as America. "The sweet that came from Candia" was eventually shortened to "candied-peel". Because of this, most sweet things in America were later referred to as "candy".'

He went on to tell me many surprising things about his homeland, until two hours later, we slowed and entered the caldera of Santorini.

Selfie-sticks were raised all around us, like a unified salute to the island. As we approached the small port, I looked up to the main town of Fira and thought about my mother's house. With sadness, I realised she would probably never see it again.

'Irini! Irini!' I recognised Aaron's voice on the bustling quayside. He lumbered towards us. 'You father called me. Asked me to meet you.'

I introduced him to Angelo. 'Aaron's an archaeologist, and a fellow countryman.' There was an odd moment as the two men weighed each other up, then they shook hands. We squeezed into the front of Aaron's battered pick-up and zigzagged our way up the cliff.

Aaron dropped us close to the house. He promised to collect us after lunch and take us to the archaeological site, which Angelo was also eager to see. When Aaron had gone, Angelo and I stood on the patio and took in the view. I imagined my mother in Angelo's place, and wished with all my heart that she could return to her little house one day. Perhaps in her mind, she did.

'This is amazing,' he said after a moment, breaking my thoughts. 'Can you imagine living here? To see this every day?'

'I know. It's beautiful. My parents loved it here.' The urge to beat myself up for never visiting rose in my chest. Distracting myself, I unlocked the front door and handed him a bundle of official-looking letters that lay on the table. 'Would you mind going through these and telling me if there's anything I need to deal with? I can't read Greek.'

He settled on the wall, and for a second I watched him flipping through the letters. Despite the unfortunate circumstances of our first few meetings, I was beginning to enjoy his company. And I couldn't deny that the haircut and shave had certainly done wonders for his appearance . . . Telling myself to stop it, I returned to the lounge. The air was warm and musty. I searched for my mother's passport and any other documents I might need.

Just when I thought I had everything, I heard, 'Iris! Iris! You came back!'

Spiro rushed onto the terrace and practically swept me up in a hug as I came out of the door. He had not noticed Angelo in the shade.

'Let go of me, Spiro, or I'll tell your wife!' I cried.

'Tonight, I take you dancing, Iris. We will live like there is no tomorrow. Don't worry about my wife. She can beat me, but you are worth the black and bruises!'

Angelo cleared his throat and Spiro recoiled, before swinging around.

Angelo held out a hand. 'Angelo Rodakis.'

Spiro's eyes widened. 'Boyfriend . . . Iris no tell me she have boyfriend! I am Spiro, the best taxi on Santorini. You want taxi, you call me, okay? I make very good trip around the island. Special price for you, my friend.'

Angelo spoke to him in Greek and the panic left Spiro's face.

'I'd like to do that next time, Spiro,' I said. 'But we are only here for today. We're taking the evening FastCat back to Crete.'

'How is Bridget?' he asked quietly.

I looked at the ground and shook my head, not wanting to break this news to him. 'They can't do anything for her, Spiro. My dad has come over to say goodbye.'

Spiro laid his hand on his chest. 'May God forgive her sins. Sorry for you, Iris. I thinks your heart is breaking. Bridget, she talks about you all the time while you were away, when you grow up, but you know that, yes? She shows me pictures of when you have birthdays, when you do things in your church, when you get your university papers. She is very proud to be the mother of you, Iris.'

I turned away, stared over the caldera, fighting back tears.

'But tell me this, Iris, I am confused,' Spiro said. 'Bridget, she never calls you Iris, she always calls you: "My Irini". My Irini this, my Irini that. Why she calls you Irini?'

'It's my name, Spiro. I am called Irini.'

'Then why you tell me Iris?'

'No, I said I am Irish.'

'So you are Iris, not Irini?'

Angelo was grinning. He said something in Greek to Spiro and the taxi driver's eyes widened.

'Ah, you make big mistake, Iris. You should say you are from Ireland, not that you are Iris, you understand.'

'Spiro!'

The taxi driver cowered. 'My wife! I must go. Give my regards to Tommy. He is very good man, like a brother to me. I will see you next time you come, Iris.' He nodded at Angelo. 'You no have to worry about me, sport. Me and Iris, we are just good friends,' he said earnestly, before scurrying away.

Angelo was still grinning at me.

'I'm sure he just does it to cheer me up. He's a kind man,' I said.

'Ah, you understand the Greek mentality already . . . Iris?'

'Stop it,' I said, but it made me laugh.

# CHAPTER 23
## BRIDGET

*Santorini, 24 years ago.*

I COULDN'T STAND THINKING of Irini going to the convent. I imagined her looking out of the aeroplane window, excited, with no notion that we were about to abandon her. How would her tender young mind deal with the situation? I could not explain the reason for our action; she was too young to understand her mother's madness. That she was safe was all that mattered, but I still had time to change the dream.

Emotionally drained and longing for a good night's sleep, I sat on the patio and wrote down my last nightmare. My heart thudded, and my eyes were raw from tears. I told myself the incident I dreamed about had not really happened, yet that knowledge made it nonetheless real. Fell asleep with complete determination to change the outcome of my fiendish nightmares. If I could do that, then Irini need not go to Dublin. I was sure of it.

How many times had I tried and failed? How many times did I have to go through this before I found a way to stop it? The dreams were driving me mad with worry. Was I destined to continue on this hellish, pointless errand like a hamster in a wheel? The pen trembled as I started logging the account of my darkest hours.

Before I went to sleep, I wondered if my torment was some kind of hex connected to the archaeological site. Such curses were common myth, but I had never believed in them. However, if anything was jinxed, it had to be the dish or the necklace. I drew my finger along the scar over my heart and recalled the day Irini was born. I still suspected the pottery was the base of a vessel used to catch the blood of young virgins when they had their heels pricked, as depicted in the frescoes. The other thought terrified me. Was it the dish used to catch Oia's blood when I . . . no . . . when Queen Thira sacrificed her?

If only I could make sense of it all, or at least change the end of the dream. In one last, desperate measure, the day before our flight, I asked Tommy to take Irini to the beach so I could catch up on my sleep. I made them a picnic and, once they had gone, I lay on the bed and tried to take my mind back to the day of the River Festival.

I willed myself to the dawn of that day, the awful day that would end with the sacrifice of my daughter. The outcome of that chilling finale had to change. After all, it was only happening in my imagination – wasn't it?

The scenario that tormented me was *not* a vision of the past. Those events did not *actually* take place. So if they were only in my mind and I was in control, I *could* change them. I emptied my head and relaxed into my pillow, waiting for sleep.

My mind slid back four millennia to a place in history long forgotten where snippets, distorted over time, became romanticised and glorified for the sake of entertainment and gaming. Atlantis. My return to that era deposited me before the altar. Oia, almost unconscious, was held in the last minutes of her young life.

* * *

Looking more beautiful than ever before in her glorious festival gown, Oia swoons. The opiates in her drink were so strong that now my girl's heart is barely beating. Her glazed eyes close and her long red hair flows over the edge of the altar.

Perspiration runs down my back. I am forced by protocol to keep my emotions hidden, but my heart is exploding with grief. I gaze down at my only daughter, taking in the loveliness of her. Our time together has been wondrous with never a cross word. I, Queen Thira, have been blessed to have such a child. Oia's destiny was written before her conception and I accept that this day has been her sole purpose on earth.

I raise the sacrificial knife and call to the Gods of Olympus: 'May Oia's spirit be reborn far into the future. May her heart be pierced, not by the sacrificial blade, but by the force of love. May her destiny be as a life *saver*, not a life taker. And when the time is right, may she join me in the Elysian Fields.'

I close my eyes and plunge the sacrificial knife downward with such force it snaps in two when the point meets the stone altar beneath. I must have swooned at that moment, my spirit racing through the ether, arms outstretched to gather and hold the essence of Oia and pull her to my breast one last time, before she goes to Poseidon.

*Oia, my darling child, I love you more than my own life. Be happy. Come to me if you need me, but if you don't, then forget this earthly existence and rule the seas at the side of Poseidon forever. Permit me to hold you for a moment, sweet child of mine, and then I will let you go, until one day your spirit will be reborn, here on earth. I will wait for that day, no matter how long, even until the stars fade. For now, goodbye sweet bride of Poseidon. Take my love with you and keep it safe in your heart, until we meet again.*

\* \* \*

The next day, Tommy and I took Irini to Dublin. Like Thira, I had lost my daughter, albeit to the nuns. Leaving Irini at the convent was the hardest thing I had ever done. Quinlan agreed to become Irini's legal guardian, and indeed, he loved her like she was his own child. Everyone agreed that when I stopped having the bad dreams Irini could come home.

My little girl had cried, then screeched over her shoulder, 'Mammy! Don't let them take me away!' as the sisters took her to meet her new friends. Her cuddly toy, Rabbs, lay on the floor at my feet. I picked him up, rubbed the satin-lined ear between my fingers as my daughter did when she was tired, and then I pressed it against my face. The little pink rabbit smelled of Irini. I cried. Tommy sat next to me, his hands limp over his knees, his head hanging. Two minutes later one of the nuns came rushing back.

'Rabbs?' she asked, staring at the threadbare toy held to my cheek.

I nodded and handed it over.

I was losing everything.

How could I even up the balance of things? If I found the dragonfly necklace and gave it to the museum, would this terrible punishment leave me? But where would I start? Perhaps if I could find Splotskey.

Back in Santorini, I remembered that our early years as a family had been almost perfect. Both Tommy and I loved our beautiful daughter, but everything changed when we returned to the Greek island without her.

At first, although my heart was broken, the knowledge that Irini was safe consoled me a little. I had done the right thing. I no longer went to bed with the horrible fear I would wake to a bigger nightmare. However, with the absence of our daughter, something changed between Tommy and me. Irini had become the foundation of our love and, without our little girl, the very fabric of our marriage crumbled.

I constantly reminded myself of the amazing love we had felt for each other when we came to Santorini; the excitement of finding the archaeological site; Tommy brought back from the brink of death; the birth of Irini – all those things kept me sane and for that I was grateful. No matter what happened, I would keep the memory of that time safe in my heart.

Over the next four years, I felt Tommy's love slipping away, and although I still invested my time and energy into making his life as comfortable as possible, and he continued to be *nice*, it was all an act. Then, one fateful day, our love reached rock bottom. That moment will stay with me until the day I die.

Tommy found hate and didn't try to hide it. My fault, I can't deny that. I should never have deceived him. The only thing we agreed on was that we were not fit parents for Irini.

The day started like any other. The bluest sky, a shimmering caldera, Santorini, postcard-picturesque.

\* \* \*

I thrust a bag of sandwiches and a couple of bottles of frozen water into Tommy's bag and took it out to the patio. 'Aaron not here yet?'

Tommy shook his head. 'He worked late last night, probably overslept. I can't wait to see what he's so excited about.' He took a breath and smiled. 'Something to do with the frescoes, I'll bet.'

Aaron had been right: we discovered another floor below the one we were working on. Over the years, many frescoes were revealed. Each discovery was important in its own way, painting a greater picture of the ancient city and helping us to understand more about the Bronze Age.

'How's your paper on the Minoan Crete–Santorini link going?' I asked Tommy.

He rubbed his forehead and sighed. 'Just when I think I understand, something else comes along and everything's up in the air again. The frescoes tell us so much, and yes, they could be mistaken for pictures relating to Plato's stories of Atlantis, right? But the carbon dating tells us they were painted many hundreds of years before Plato was even born.'

'What if Plato saw the frescoes and made up a story to go with them?'

What would have been a smile in his eyes long ago was now a glint of irritation. 'You're not thinking it through, darling girl. How could Plato see them? Since the eruption of Santorini, they've been buried under pumice.' He glanced around as if he'd mislaid something.

'And we were the next people to see them! Hell, that's exciting, don't you think?' I said, trying to lift his mood.

His head snapped up and the smile I longed for broke through.

Desperate for a conversation, even if it was about archaeology, I continued, 'Then have you thought: perhaps they were mapped out on some kind of media before being painted into the wet plaster? If the initial drawings were records of the way people lived, and they found their way to Athens, say, couldn't they have fallen into the hands of other philosophers? Then at a later date, perhaps, become the inspiration for Plato's stories about Atlantis.'

'It's an idea, but to prove it's a record and not just artistic decoration, we need to find an actual artefact that is reproduced in one of the frescoes, and so far we've had no luck at all, have we? All the hundreds of pots and urns, each with their individual patterns that you have recorded so carefully, not one is seen in the frescoes. But every day I go down to the site full of hope. Every artefact, every inch of fresco uncovered, I wonder: *is this it*, that vital link?'

His words triggered my guilt. I should have told him about the necklace, I know it, but I never could find the words, so I tried to forget the past and erase the memory of my wrongdoing.

With nothing left to say, Tommy walked to the patio wall and stared across the caldera. 'It's wonderful living here, Bridget. Just look out at the view; it never ceases to amaze me.'

I recognised his attempt to cheer me, yet it was as if a sheet of glass separated us. Our special closeness had gone, and although we both tried to be one again, we had become two separate people.

'We're so lucky, you know, to have all this,' Tommy continued, stretching out his arm towards the sea, then he pulled me towards him. We both clung to the good things, overly bright in our conversation, humour forced, optimistic that our unique relationship would return.

A cloak of bright happiness hid the bare bones of our grief.

'To think I nearly lost it all, and also you and Irini.' He thought for a moment and in a rare moment of honesty said, 'I know you miss her terribly, Bridget. Me too. I'm heartbroken, but things will work out in the end. Irini hasn't gone forever.' His sad smile turned to a grin as he grabbed my bottom and pulled me against his hips. 'I'll see you this evening, you gorgeous creature. I do love you.'

Life had become a cover-up. Both of us trying to hide our pain while simultaneously easing the other's broken heart.

'I love you too, but I'm crushing your butties, you great lump!' My laughter sounded brittle and false, and I wished I could do better. I wriggled from his grasp. 'I hope I can trust you not to work too hard, Tommy McGuire, or I'll have to keep you home for a week.'

'I'll take it easy, promise.' His grin fell. 'I know it's difficult, Bridget, and I appreciate you putting on a brave face.'

The pretence abandoned us.

'Why can't I be a normal mother, Tommy? I miss her so much. Do you think we could go back to Dublin for Christmas again?' My heart cracked open. Tears and sobs threatened to break free. I could hardly bear his kindness and struggled to replace my armour before I hurt him with my unbridled emotion.

'Of course we can.' The concern was clear on his face, then he seemed to throw the switch. Grinning, he made a grab for me again. The performance continued, his way of dealing with the loss of Irini.

'Behave!' I cried. 'Aaron will be here any minute! You're very frisky this morning.' Suddenly, I wished he could stay home. We never spent time together like the tourists that surrounded us. I was at home three days a week, writing for magazines. Tommy was at the site six days a week.

'Can we go down to the beach on Sunday, after mass? Have a picnic and a paddle?' I asked.

'Sure we can. Nice idea.'

Our eyes met and there was no further need for words. He took me gently into his arms, and we stood motionless for a moment, thinking about our daughter and silently sharing our sadness.

Arron arrived and took Tommy down to the site in his old pick-up.

Feeling groggy from the sleeping pills, I walked up to the main road. I had tried going without the medication once Irini had gone, but the nightmares had returned, stronger and more vivid than ever. I came to suspect my visions were connected to the site and was glad of an excuse to stay away from the place. My bad dreams were always of the same theme. Either I was going to kill little Irini here and now, or I was a queen in antiquity, in the city we were excavating, and was destined to kill my daughter on the sacrificial altar.

On the day that changed our lives forever, I was not going to the site. For me it was just a normal day, but when Tommy, a man of routine, had not returned home by four o'clock, I started to worry. At five, I phoned Aaron.

'Hi, I'm looking for Tommy. He hasn't come home yet.'

'That's odd. He left early today. Have you checked the kafenio?'

Tommy was not a big drinker and seldom went to the local kafenio, but nevertheless, I went in search of him. Tommy was drunk, more drunk than I had ever seen him. I found him slumped in a corner of the dim kafenio. His mood was clearly morose and, as he stood, I realised he could not even walk without help.

'Tommy! What's brought this on? Come on home,' I said kindly.

He lifted his eyes and stared at me with a look of utter defeat. A couple of the men hooked their arms through his and walked him back. I had never seen him in such a state.

Late in the night, through the fog of my medication, I heard Tommy throw up in the bathroom. Later, when I was able to drag myself out of bed, I found he had missed the toilet and left a sour mess all over the floor. Although revolted, I cleaned up the vomit and wondered if I should persuade him to visit the doctor.

'Are you feeling better now, Tommy?' I asked when he eventually woke. 'Can I get you some breakfast, or some aspirin? How's your head?'

'I don't want anything from you,' he said bitterly, and for the first time in my life, I saw real anger in his eyes. His behaviour was so out of character, I racked my brains to think what had caused his terrible mood. Years ago, I remembered he had wrongly suspected me of an affair, but I couldn't believe he was thinking along those lines again. The problem with Tommy was his inability to discuss his personal feelings. He always clammed up; whatever he worried about would fester and grow in his head. Anyway, that episode was long ago, and surely forgotten.

'Will you tell me what's the matter, Tommy? I'm worried about you. Don't keep it bottled up, please.'

He glared at me for a moment, then showered, dressed, and left without a word.

\* \* \*

By midday, I could not stand the worry, and despite the blazing sun, I cycled down to the archaeological site.

'Hi, Aaron, where's Tommy working?' I asked when I saw no sign of him.

'Tommy? He didn't come to work today. I dropped him in town this morning. He told me he had things to do.'

'I wonder what's going on?' I tried to keep the alarm out of my voice but my concern was building.

Aaron appeared excited and bright-eyed.

'You look pleased with yourself,' I said, glancing around the site, looking for clues that made sense of Tommy's behaviour.

'Didn't Tommy tell you? That surprises me.'

'Tell me what?'

'Ha! Come with me. You're going to love this.' He led me through a maze of rubble walls until we reached the place where Irini was born. 'Look at that!' He raised his hand towards the fresco of the goddess on her throne. 'I've recovered all the missing pieces. It's complete.'

I stared, my hand over my mouth, darkness creeping in, breath leaving my body. The missing pieces of fresco were in place and the reason for Tommy's behaviour became startlingly clear. Around the goddess's neck hung the dragonfly necklace.

The vital link that proved the frescoes were actual portraits, not fantasy. I had to find Tommy, explain, and ask his forgiveness.

\*　\*　\*

Aaron threw my bike into the back of the pick-up and gave me a lift home. Tommy was waiting, staring out over the caldera. He hardly acknowledged Aaron or me.

'Are you wanting a lift back to the site, Tommy?' I could hear the concern in Aaron's voice.

'No, I'm just fine here,' Tommy replied sullenly.

'Look, I can explain,' I said when Aaron had gone.

'I don't want your explanations! There's no excuse. Twenty-five years I've been searching, every day hoping. Every day desperate to find that elusive link. Every bloody day, Bridget! How many things have you secreted away behind my back? Stolen . . . or . . . sold?! I feel sick!'

'No, Tommy, listen—'

258

'I'm not going to listen to excuses. You lied to me. You *lied*. After all these years. No wonder you can't sleep at night. You're no more fit to call yourself an archaeologist than a mother!'

He knew how that piercing shard of viciousness would hurt. Deliberately wounding me in my most vulnerable spot. Aiming for the heart.

At that moment, I felt a spark of hate. His spiteful words knocked the wind out of me, but then my anger gathered, swift and dark as storm clouds. *Hurt me and I'll hurt you more!*

'I had to pay for your operation! How was I supposed to do that? Do you know . . . have you any idea how much open-heart surgery costs? Never mind the air ambulance, the anaesthetist, blood transfusions, nursing, medication, travel back and forth. You never even bothered to ask how I'd managed, not really. A few polite words, quickly accepting that I'd managed to raise enough money, that was all. You never even asked how much it cost. And to be honest, I'd have given my very soul to save your life, Tommy! In fact, I was prepared to go to prison for it. I was pregnant, don't you understand?!'

'Don't you dare try and pin this on me! How many things have you sold? I can't believe it. You had my complete trust. And you, writing about the crime of antiquity theft, and making money from that too, gaining everyone's confidence and respect – and now I find you're nothing but a despicable thief yourself!'

*Oh!*

Unable to move, I stared at him. *I wish you were dead. I wish I'd let you die, you nasty, cruel man!* I couldn't see or feel anything, nor understand what I was about; all I knew was rage, pure, undiluted rage. It filled every crack and crevice of my body, oozed from my pores, stiffened my bones and vented as a scream.

259

Oddly enough, that very same rage saved me. I wore it like armour around my broken heart. I lived off the constant supply of fury that grew like ice crystals between us; it made me stronger and hardened me to the pain that was always gnawing away inside.

If it hadn't been for my anger, I would have felt nothing but despair, and the sleeping pills would have been too tempting a solution.

# CHAPTER 24
## IRINI

*Santorini, present day.*

ANGELO AND I WALKED INTO TOWN. I had my mother's electricity bills to pay. 'What about rates – you know, council tax?' I ask.

'It is included in your electricity bill. The higher your electricity bill, the more tax you pay. It's a very good system, yes?'

People greeted me like a long-lost friend. Everyone called me Iris, much to Angelo's amusement, and I guessed I would have to get used to it. The smell of roast pork wafted into the street and made me realise I was hungry.

'Come, we'll pay this quickly and then stop for some food,' Angelo said.

In the crowded office, I expected a long wait. Angelo advised me to stand in the corner. He knocked on an office door, entered, then reappeared and called me. Less than five minutes later we passed the queue on our way out, bills all paid.

'I don't know how you did that, but thank you,' I said, wondering if money changed hands in the name of queue-jumping.

'Nothing,' he said smugly.

We ate souvlaki in the street, silently watching the tourists and occasionally exchanging a nod or a smile.

'Thanks for coming with me,' I said, feeling comfortable in his company.

Angelo turned to face me, his eyes searching mine for a moment, the hint of a smile on his lips. He nodded and shrugged, and instead of my infuriating blush, a warm feeling rose from the pit of my stomach.

'I wonder if my mother and father ever sat at this table, enjoying the day,' I said. 'They married in the cathedral here, forty years ago.'

'Forty years?' He made the Greek down-sideways nod. 'Your parents must be very much in love, yes?'

'I guess so.'

'Then they are lucky.' He frowned at the tabletop. 'Some people—'

Spiro screeched to the kerb. 'Iris! Come, I take you to the archaeology. Get in quick, is not allowed for cars in this street!'

After fifteen minutes of Spiro's hair-raising driving, we pulled up at the site. Along the way, I had admired the amazing view. At some points, I could see all the caldera, and at others, I gazed down the gentle slope towards the black beaches on the outskirts of the island. Blue-domed churches, vineyards, and donkeys were everywhere. Nevertheless, I was relieved to get out of the cab.

Apart from a couple of tourists, the archaeological site was empty. We found Aaron using a trowel to scrape the bottom of a trench.

'Hi, welcome to the site!' he cried, pulling himself out of the straight-sided channel.

The trenches and half walls seemed to go on forever. Reaching high above the excavation, hefty steel columns supported an elaborate louvred roof of glass, steel, and wood, which flooded the area in natural light. I reminded myself that my mother and father laboured here for decades, starting from scratch in a bare field.

I was surrounded by streets lined by roofless houses – an entire town. 'They must have worked hard to uncover all this,'

I whispered to myself from a low-slung gantry, which I guessed was in place for the benefit of tourists.

'There's some steps behind you,' Aaron called, his voice tinny and echoing. 'Come down and walk through the streets. I'll show you where you were born, Irini.'

Filled with curiosity and having little memory of the place, I proceeded. Every noise was amplified and seemed disrespectful. Once we were standing on the dirt, the place fell into silence again. I glanced down alleys and sideroads, not sure what I expected to see. Soon, I realised there was nothing but walls and dust. No frescoes, no statues, no artefacts apart from pots of every shape and size – some so large they would conceal a man.

Over time, I had built a picture of something so amazing that it drew my mother away from her husband and child. When I saw the site was hardly different from my childhood memories, I felt deceived and cheated.

'What was it about this place that captured my mother's soul? I can't believe she left us for dust and stones.'

The smile fell from Aaron's face and he blinked at me, then looked around again. 'Ah,' he said slowly. 'I see what you mean. Follow me back to the entrance.'

We returned the way we had come, then he turned to Angelo and said, 'May I?' Angelo seemed to understand and made a down-sideways nod. Aaron took my hand and said, 'Close your eyes and empty your head. Now you are going to see this place as it was. The town is full of people going about their daily tasks. I will walk you through and describe everything.'

His hand felt huge, fleshy and strong, but the grip of this gentle giant was almost tender.

'Use your imagination, Irini. Open your eyes and see for yourself.' I could hear the excitement in his voice.

He held out a hand, indicating the left side of the street. 'Here is area three; this building is two storeys high, with fourteen rooms on each floor. Inside, on both floors, the walls of the main rooms are decorated with magnificent life-size frescoes depicting the lifestyle of those who used these rooms.'

I felt the air around us was charged, and the strange feeling grew stronger with each breath. My mother's *Book of Dreams* came to mind, and with that, the hope that I would soon come closer to understanding them.

I stared around. 'Twenty-eight rooms? A huge building, even by today's standards. Can you describe the frescoes, Aaron?'

He nodded, stood taller, clearly enthralled. After leading me through a stone doorway, he said, 'In this, the largest room on the ground floor, one entire wall was filled with the mystical cult of the crocus gatherers. Three young women, life-size, are splendidly dressed but bare-breasted. The central figure is sitting on a bank of crocuses; she's holding her foot and drops of blood are falling from her heel. The woman to her right has her head partly shaved, and she's covered in a long veil. The woman to her left's holding a necklace out to the wounded one.' He paused while I conjured up the image.

'My mother dreamed about all this.' I closed my eyes and saw her drawings. 'She seemed obsessed by the frescoes and made many sketches of them.'

Aaron smiled. 'I know. Look up, that's the room above. The floor has gone, of course. Above the fresco of the cult was the fresco of Queen Thira, the Goddess of the Marches. She sits on her throne, attended by exotic animals, a griffin and a monkey. Her dress is magnificent, her hair is waxed and coiled, and she too wears necklaces. One is a circle of drakes, the other of dragonflies. Both are creatures of the wetlands. On the adjacent

wall, the scene continues with young women gathering crocuses. Several have their heads partly shaved and painted blue.'

Again, my mother's dreams and sketches came to mind.
'Where are they, the frescoes?'

'Ah, they're in Athens, but photographs of all the frescoes,
with their descriptions, are in my book, Irini. It was published
just before Bridget's accident. There are many frescoes, and so
much to say about each one. I'm sure you'll find them as fascinating as Bridget did.'

I tried to imagine the streets thronging with people. Beautiful
women with elaborately styled hair. Boys with part of their heads
shaved and painted bright blue. I imagined them playing jack-
stones outside one of the houses. My thoughts carried me away.
I saw a bearded man in a toga sitting on the street corner and
strumming a lute; tremulous notes drifted and danced lyrically
about me. Families wandered through doorways and along the
streets, going about their business. Gracious, elegant people.

Aaron touched my shoulder, making me jump. 'Sorry, did I
startle you?'

'I was trying to imagine how it looked and a moment from
my childhood returned. Mam would hold my hand and walk
me through these streets when I was very young. I recalled
hearing her say: "Look, Irini, they turn our way and bow as we
pass." I'd peer inside the rooms and she would describe things.
She made me see, for example, an aged woman at a heavy weav-
ing frame. "She racks down the warp of a blue and yellow rug.
Look, the old dear catches sight of us as she throws the shuttle between tight weft threads on the loom. She's dropped the
bobbin. Now she places both hands on her chest and lowers
her head reverently." Wow! I had forgotten all that. I loved her
stories.'

I returned my attention to the street but darkness invaded the scene, as if someone turned a dimmer switch, and then everything rushed away in a faint. I was falling . . . falling . . .

\* \* \*

Conscious of an arm around my back and a man's concerned voice in my ear, I returned to reality. Flustered and light-headed, I rubbed my eyes and stared around at the empty, dusty archaeological site.

'Are you all right?' Angelo asked.

I was on the ground. He helped me into a sitting position.

'My God, I came over all dizzy. I might need to sit for a moment.' I recalled what I had seen. 'That was the strangest thing, remembering my mother's words and how vividly I imagined what she described.'

Aaron brought me a beaker of water and then Angelo steered me towards a great block of granite.

'Rest here. Look, you lost your shoe.' He picked it up and slipped it back on, reminding me of that first day modelling for him.

'Where did you say the frescoes are now?' he asked Aaron.

'The National Archaeological Museum in Athens, though they're not all on show.' He frowned disapprovingly. 'There's a few in our museum, here in town, but they took the majority away.'

I had the oddest feeling that I needed to call my father. I dialled his number and when I got through, Quinlan answered. When he told me there was no change with Mam, and my father was sleeping, I wanted to hug him.

'I'll see you this evening, Quinlan,' I said into the phone.

Angelo tapped his watch and shook his head. 'Tomorrow morning, Irini. We will not get to the ferry in time now.'

I remembered the specialist talking about my mother's tumour and several questions hit me in a horrible rush. Perhaps I had that same tumour gene. I wondered if the crash, the bump on the head, had woken it up. Headaches had troubled me on and off ever since, and now I'd fainted. I felt sick and short of breath with the idea that an alien growth might be gaining strength, growing, sending out its sproggish spores on a mission to divide and conquer both my body and mind.

'Irini, what is it?' Angelo asked, breaking my thoughts.

I saw no point in discussing my fears with him. Speculating on what might simply be the result of my recent stress and lack of sleep would not help.

'No, nothing. I need to go back to the doctor after fainting like that. He warned me I might suffer from concussion after the crash. He mentioned the symptoms to look out for, that's all. Nothing to fret about.'

While Angelo phoned for a taxi, I continued to wonder if I had the problematic gene like my mother.

Ten minutes later, we said goodbye to Aaron and met Spiro outside the gate.

'Where you go now, Iris?' Spiro asked.

'We missed the ferry, Spiro, so perhaps we'll get something to eat and go back to the house.'

'No, no! You come with me. My cousin baptise his first boy this afternoon. Now we have big party. You come, celebrate with my family.'

As we sped towards the town, I looked out across the caldera and saw the FastCat motoring out into the open sea.

\* \* \*

By one o'clock in the morning I was full of food, and after a glass of wine, perhaps a little drunk too. I phoned the hospital and the night staff told me my mother was stable and peaceful. I still wished I could be there.

'You had a good time, I think,' Angelo said as we wandered through town.

'What amazing people, Angelo. Did you ever see such a thing before?'

He laughed and looped my arm into his as we walked. 'Of course. Every Greek person you see has had such a night.'

'I can't believe those old ladies, and such young children, could dance all night long. And the food would have fed half of Dublin for a month!' I glanced sideways at him. He added a head-waggle to his frowning smile and it made me laugh. 'You're very proud of your people, aren't you?'

'But of course. Aren't you?' He looked at me as if I'd asked a stupid question.

'Never thought about it. I suppose so. I wish we Irish had kept more of our customs, like you Greeks.'

'Tradition is important – it gives our country a strong sense of identity and draws us together.'

We had reached the house. He opened the gate, and then bolted it while I searched for the house key. I pulled a bottle of wine out of my bag.

'What's this? I thought my bag was heavy.'

'Ah, I thought a nightcap would help us sleep.' He had a naughty-boy grin. 'What are you looking for?'

'The key. I dropped it into my bag but I think there's a hole in the lining and it's gone under. It'll be here somewhere.'

'Why you don't leave it under a plant pot or over the door? That's what everyone does.' He nudged the big terracotta urn and smiled when it rocked slightly. 'Here, I will tilt it and then you hold it, okay? My arm is not so good, you know? Do not let it go, Irini.'

Obviously I was still a catastrophe in his eyes. I hung onto the pot while he slid his hand under.

'Here you are – the spare key.'

Inside, he opened the wine and poured two glasses, while I considered the sleeping arrangements. Eventually, I found a sheet, threw it over the sofa, and returned to the patio with a bottle of cold water. The air was deliciously cool too, and a new moon glowed like a thin smile in a sky ablaze with stars. Music drifted over us from one of the small hotels.

'I'm still shocked by what I saw at the site today, and that most of the frescoes have been taken to Athens. I agree with Aaron – it doesn't make sense to do that. Also, fancy me fainting. I must get my head checked out.' We sat next to each other at the tin table, gazing out over the caldera.

'The best is to forget about it. Sometimes things need to, how you say, melon?'

It was my turn to frown. 'Ah, mellow.'

'Yes, mellow, before we see them for what they are. You have too much stress and so you can't think straight. Put your troubles out of your mind for a while and relax.'

'You've been very kind, thank you, but I can't forget my mother. Every time I forget her for a while, I feel guilty. I panic and wonder if . . . you know.'

He nodded. 'Tell me about your life in England.'

'I'm from Ireland.'

'Ah, yes, Iris, I forget.'

I smiled, guessing what he wanted to know.

'I'm an only child, I live alone, and I teach religion to six-year-olds. I've just broken off my engagement.'

He faced me and turned his mouth down, the mask of Greek tragedy. 'Sorry . . . Well, not really.' He rolled his eyes. 'He must be a very stupid guy.'

'I hope you're not going to give me any trouble, Angelo. I'm not ready for . . . you know, and with all that's going on, I'm exhausted.' I glanced into his eyes, then turned away, feeling the need to explain. 'I was supposed to get married in two weeks' time but I found him with somebody else.' I shrugged. 'That's it, really. Same old story, not very exciting at all. How about you?'

He ignored my question. 'Ah, the man, he broke your heart. I am sorry. This is the most painful thing we suffer.' He casually reached for my hands, but I quickly folded them in my lap, confused for a moment. I wasn't ready; didn't want to give the wrong signals.

'No, Angelo. *I* broke off our engagement. *I* broke *his* heart, not the other way around. Don't feel sorry for me.' Although in truth I had suffered, suddenly I realised I hadn't thought of Jason for days.

# CHAPTER 25
## BRIDGET

*Santorini, 20 years ago.*

TOMMY AND I COULD HARDLY tolerate looking at each other. We slept back to back with a space between us. My heart was breaking, and I'm sure his was too. Is it possible to love somebody and hate them at the same time? I wanted his arms around me so badly it crucified me, yet I looked upon him with the utmost scorn. I hardened to him, as he did to me. Something huge died between us. It wasn't our love but, almost worse, it was our trust and friendship, our amazing kindred spirit. The opposite of everything we felt for each other took root. Disdain settled alongside affection like a malevolent bully. I had never felt so alone.

Irini was nine years old, and I missed her more than ever. We went back to Dublin and stayed at the convent with her every Christmas, and I tried to stay close to her through the year by writing every week. In my letters, I told her stories and snippets of life on the island that I thought she would enjoy.

*Dear Darling Irini,*

*Manno's donkey had a baby last night. It's light brown with a black cross on its back. It also has very big ears and thin, wobbly legs. They have asked if you would like to choose a name for her.*

*Anna's turkey ate too many rotting apricots from under their tree and got so completely drunk it was falling over. Then it picked a fight with her pink moped and kept running at it with its wings out. Everyone came to watch and we all laughed a lot.*

*Kiki has lost her two front teeth, like you, but the tooth fairy forgot to leave her some money, so her daddy took her out on his boat instead.*

*Daddy sends you all his love.*

*And lots of hugs and kisses from me too,*

*Mammy XXX*

I longed for her to come back to Santorini, but I was still afraid for her wellbeing. Every Sunday, Quinlan collected Irini from the convent and took her out, and at teatime I would telephone her at his house, but although Quinlan did his best to get her to talk to me, Irini was withdrawn and hardly spoke.

'Perhaps it's better if you don't phone, Bridget,' he said one Sunday. 'I know that seems harsh, but Irini gets a bit upset. She's too young to understand, and I think the calls unsettle her.'

Next to our telephone stood a school photo that Quinlan had sent me. Irini's pale, freckled face stared blankly out, her fiery red hair a flounce of curls about her shoulders. I wanted to hold her so badly that I broke into tears after putting the phone down. Tommy relented and took me into his arms.

'Now then, what's the matter?'

'Oh, Tommy! My life's not worth living. What's life without love? It's empty, worthless, pointless. I can't go on.'

'That's not the way to talk, Bridget. Irini loves you . . . I love you.'

'It doesn't feel like it.' I leaned into his body, savouring the sudden closeness after so long. I wanted to stay in his arms forever, my head against his cheek, his body against mine.

'I can't help how I am,' he said over my shoulder. 'I can't pretend, not with you.'

'Will you ever forgive me, Tommy?' I craved for him to utter words of absolution.

He was silent for a long time, then after a long sigh he said, 'I don't know, Bridget. Even now, the wound is too raw. Perhaps it will heal, but I just don't know.'

* * *

I lay in bed that night thinking about the past. If I could change it, would I? Could I have let Tommy die? Even if he hated me for the rest of his life, that life of his was worth saving. So, in the end, I concluded that I would not have changed a thing.

Although, over the years, we slowly grew back together, a part of our love had died. We were changed. Like one of my broken pots, although all the pieces were there and everything cemented back in place, the cracks that destroyed its perfection were permanent.

I continued to have vivid dreams, though not as frequently. Now that Irini was safe from harm, I stopped trying to change them. Once again, I developed a kind of empathy with Queen Thira. She had lost her husband and her daughter, and although mine were still alive, I felt their love for me was growing more distant by the day and I was helpless to do anything about it.

This broke my heart and dulled my spirit.

As in my childhood, Thira was my ally, my secret friend. I sensed that she understood my pain and sympathised when nobody else could. The dreams moved on. They took me past the horrors of Oia's sacrifice to a time when Thira, like me, grieved for her daughter. Companions in misery.

One night, I gave myself up to the desolation of losing a beloved daughter and a caring husband. Perhaps it was this acceptance that freed my mind, because the next morning, I woke with the conviction that what I had seen in my sleep, was not a dream at all. I had experienced an actual *vision* of what really happened to Thira, her ten kings, and the people of Atlantis.

*  *  *

My darling Oia has gone to Poseidon. I speak to no one, hardly eat, and drink only water. My misery is intense. The dragonfly necklace has not left my hand since it fell from my daughter's neck when the kings carried her away.

If only I could sleep through the night – but this is impossible. Once my guard is down and my mind relaxes, I find myself back at the altar, reliving the sacrifice. My spirit is broken.

Eurydice tells me that Hero requests an audience, but I instruct her to send him off. Hero can take charge; rule the kingdom in my absence. Overcome by my grief once more, I throw myself onto the palace floor and sob, my body shaking with anguish. Then I realise the movement is not coming from me, but from deep below the ground.

'No! Poseidon, you fiend of the deep, don't you dare betray my trust!'

I can hear Hero shouting outside my chambers. He bursts through the doorway and pulls me to my feet. 'Forgive me, my Queen! You must get ready quickly – the people need you. Great trouble is upon us.'

He orders Eurydice: 'Bathe and prepare your queen immediately. We have a council meeting. The kings await.' Then back
to me: 'This is extremely urgent!'

Once in my regal refinery, I grudgingly enter the council
chambers. The kings are downcast. Hero speaks for them.

'Queen Thira, Goddess of the Marches and Supreme Ruler,
we all agree you were right. We must evacuate the island with
great haste.'

'I never doubted it, Hero, but what brought this change of
mind?' My voice is dull and tired. I don't care if I was right or not.
I only care that my darling daughter has gone to Poseidon.

'The shepherds have a cave on the side of the mountain
where they ripen cheeses. It has become so hot, their produce
is ruined. Also, a strange, dirty air is seeping through cracks
in the rocks. Several lambs, kept in the cave overnight, were
all dead by dawn. Now smoke rises from fissures near the top
and the earth is hot underfoot. The oracle warns the massif will
soon explode like an olive pip in the embers.'

'My daughter has gone because of your misgivings. The sacrifice of Oia is irreversible, and we still have to surrender our island
to Poseidon.' I stare each in the face until they lower their eyes.
'Start the evacuation. We leave for Crete immediately.'

\* \* \*

I felt Thira's pain so intensely. Sending Irini to board with the
nuns was hard enough, but the memory of that first Christmas
was almost unbearable. Tommy and I stayed at the convent. Irini
had grown so much in six months, and that alone broke my
heart. I stupidly expected to see the little girl I had left digging

her heels in and crying my name. Her last words had played in my head over and over: *Don't leave me, Mammy!*

When they brought her to us, she was quiet and, for a terrible moment, she didn't recognise me. Shy, withdrawn, good as gold, but her unselfconscious affection had disappeared.

She was already slipping away from me.

After mass, we took Irini and Rabbs to the park. She fixated on the slide. Up the ladder and down the slide, with Rabbs clutched between her knees. I wanted her to smile, squeal, show some emotion, but she simply repeated the circuit over and over, her serious little face never showing pleasure.

We bought ice cream from a van, and then went to feed the ducks. I couldn't take my eyes off her as she solemnly made sure each duck got a little bread.

'Can we go home now?' Irini asked when we were done with the ducks, and for a moment I was startled. 'I want to play with my friends,' she explained parents.

The next day, when we returned to the park, Irini asked if her friends could come too. Tommy and I sat on a bench and watched them play, running and laughing together. We were shut out, redundant parents.

Clearly, Irini was happy in her new home. Later, we looked at her school work and were proud to see she was near top in her class. I hoped to return to the convent at Easter, and the summer holidays, but after our Christmas visit, Irini had withdrawn, her schoolwork had fallen off and she had started bed-wetting. The convent advised us to give her more time before we came again.

# CHAPTER 26
## IRINI

*Crete, present day.*

'IT'S YOUR TURN TO TELL me about yourself,' I said to Angelo.

'I have an apartment in London. It's where my business is based. My father and brother run the family hotel, in Crete, and they are busy building another very lux hotel not far away.'

I found my eyes drawn to him. He wore smart jeans with a scruffy, dog-eared leather belt, and a white shirt with the sleeves rolled to his elbows. A dangling strand of cotton told me he'd cut the cuff of one sleeve in order to get his cast through.

I stiffened my jaw to stifle a yawn.

'You are tired now. Come, let's go to bed.' He grinned and bobbed his eyebrows.

'Look, I . . .'

'I sleep on the sofa, you sleep in the bedroom.' An understanding smile appeared. 'You don't have to worry, you have my word I will behave like a gentleman. But with such a beautiful woman in the next room, it will be hard, Irini.'

He grinned and lifted his eyebrows again, making me laugh, and I remembered his arms around me on the quayside. 'You've been very kind. Thank you. Good night then.' For a second, I struggled with the notion I should kiss his cheek, but I didn't want to send out the wrong signals, so I left for the bedroom and closed the door.

\* \* \*

I wondered if Angelo was awake. The windowless back room was unbearably stuffy and I feared I would suffocate if I didn't let some air in. My parents must have slept with the adjoining door open. I turned on a side light and saw it was four o'clock in the morning. Angelo would be asleep.

I dragged my damp hair away from my face. The door was closed by a simple latch, similar to the one on my back gate at home. Soundlessly, and holding my breath, I eased the bar out of the hook.

Concerned that my light might wake him, I turned it off before slipping through the door. The living room was pitch black. The open front door, hung with a mosquito net, appeared like a rectangle of grey back-lit by the night sky. I remembered the small table in the centre of the room and stepped blindly around it. In a moment, I was outside in the pleasant night air. Such bliss!

The bottle of water from the fridge stood on the table and I couldn't resist making use of it. After taking a few gulps, I poured it over my head, allowing the water to run down my face and soak my damp T-shirt. I wiped the sweat from my face, and felt the cool liquid run down my bare legs. The pleasure was immeasurable.

'You're hot.' The voice came from behind me. I spun around and saw him sitting on the low wall with his back against the house. 'Me too,' he said with a smile in his voice.

I stood there, gawping like an idiot.

'I hope you don't mind me saying: it's been difficult working with you this week. You are incredibly beautiful, Irini.'

'Don't talk nonsense.' I waved his words away. 'I thought you were sleeping. You did promise you wouldn't give me any trouble,' I said, trying not to sound as breathless as I felt.

'But then I didn't know you would stand before me in a wet T-shirt and little else.'

I looked down, mortified to realise what he meant. I crossed my arms over my chest.

'No worries, you are safe – I gave you my word. But you make it hard for me again.'

I wondered if he understood the double meaning of his words. 'It's too stuffy in that back room. I'm really hot.'

'I see it.'

I rolled my eyes. 'Behave, Angelo!'

He laughed softly and came to sit at the table, so I took the other chair and we both looked up at the night sky. 'I don't want you to go back to Ireland. I would like to get to know you better, Irini, without the stress of work or the worries you have with your mother.'

I shook my head and, unable to think of anything to say, I found myself staring at him. The scant moonlight silhouetted his profile, which appeared perfect. When he turned to me, his face fell into darkness, yet I knew he was still smiling. I loved that smile. The half-closed eyes and sweeping lashes – they were both affectionate and mischievous, and made me happy for no other reason. Heat returned to my face as I found myself gazing at him again, glad he couldn't see my blush.

My eyes became accustomed to the dark. The night was clear and beautiful. I stood, moved towards the wall, and stared out over the empty caldera. What sadness brought me here, what emotions I had suffered these past two weeks. Yet these things fell away and, in this uncomplicated moment, I felt I could breathe again.

Then he was standing in front of me. We were an inch apart, two at the most. As if attending an overcrowded party, I could not move away from him, yet the patio was empty. I felt his breath on my mouth, soft as the beat of butterfly wings, and I caught the scent of cinnamon, canned pears, Christmas, and summer. Overwhelmed by many feelings, the jangled, tangled emotions of recent times, I had an urge to cry . . . and why? Why? I didn't know.

Then his body was against mine, and I wanted to resist, honestly . . . God knows how my arms came to be around his neck, and his around my back, holding me against him. Everything left me except for the desire to stay in that safe place forever. His lips touched mine and I lost myself in his embrace. Offering myself up, melting into him, drawing him into me, for the rest of my life. Or at least for that night. I needed to love, to be loved, to lose myself in the ecstasy of erotica, fly on the wings of Aphrodite. Forget everything. A reprieve from the pain and anguish and my soul-eating loneliness.

He eased away, trembling slightly. 'Irini, I . . .'

So I made it clear. I pressed myself against him, and interrupted his words with a kiss that left no doubt. I was both euphoric and exhausted. Too tired to play games. I wanted to stay in his arms. I needed his kisses, and yes, I admit it, I wanted so much more. In a moment, we were back in the house. After a frantic struggle with buttons and wet T-shirts, our clothes abandoned us. In the glorious sensation of flesh against flesh, I lost myself in an overwhelming sense of desire.

\* \* \*

I woke a few hours later, feeling the effect of too much wine, the bleariness of morning, and damp and tangled sheets. Angelo flung the door open, then returned to the bed.

'Good morning, Goddess of the Night,' he whispered. 'Come, let us watch the sunrise, forget our worries, and be happy for what little time we have left.'

An alarm fired off at his words. What 'little time'? Surely, if we chose, we could have more occasions like this? Why was our time together limited? I peered into his sleepy eyes, searching for an answer, but before I could speak, he kissed me gently on the mouth and pulled me into his arms. Our limbs tangled around each other in a prelude to love. His lips danced on my lips, on my breasts, on my belly.

'Oh my holy God! I've gone to heaven.'

He grasped my buttocks with such masculine strength that I melted against him. Time slipped by, or stood still, I had no notion, until I found myself whispering, 'Make love to me, Angelo, I want you so badly.'

Lost in this intense physical pleasure, my worry and fear disappeared. He was an oasis in my troubled life. I wanted to stay locked in the safe haven of his arms, our bodies heaving and rolling in a glorious and sensual dance. The words he whispered with such urgency became passionate demands and my desire exploded, again and again, until I was calling out his name.

Then he was holding me tenderly, whispering endearments, kissing unexpected tears away and telling me he loved me. My infinite longing was satiated as I cried out in ecstasy.

We lay together, drifting in and out of sleep. I could shower and dress, or lie in his arms and enjoy the last moments of our time together in Santorini. The power was mine.

I arched my back, kissed him softly, whispered, 'Angelo,' and in my thoughts he was already mine once again. I slipped my hands behind his back and traced the triangle at the base of his spine. His soft groan was a surrender, the sexiest sound of his weakness and my strength. He caught me and held me against his body, and again I was filled with the need for self-absorbing love. His mouth became wet on my neck; he tasted my flesh with a hunger that sent shivers through me.

I would shower later; there would be other sunrises.

* * *

Not only did we miss the sunrise, but we had missed the damned ferry again!

At nine o'clock, Angelo paced outside, yelling into his phone. 'We'll be there for the afternoon shoot. No worries, Paula!' Definitely not a morning person.

I phoned the hospital, desperate to get there. After a quick shower, I dressed, left my wet hair loose, and stuffed all the things I needed into my holdall. Angelo continued on his phone, then barged into the house.

'We take the ten-thirty flight to Athens, and the two-thirty to Crete, okay? The shoot starts at four. I'll call Spiro. Are you ready?'

I nodded and called Quinlan. 'I'll be at the hospital at eight this evening,' I told him. I didn't want to go there. The situation was too horrible to think about. With my father, my uncle, and myself by my mother's bedside, everything was set up for my mother to die. Like we were orchestrating the end of her life, giving her permission to go. I placed my hands over my face, trying to accept the inevitable.

Angelo's arms slipped around my shoulders. He pulled me to his chest.

'I don't want her to die, Angelo. Why couldn't I have found the time and money and the need to be with her before she was in this

282

state? I could have bridged our fractured relationship if I'd made the effort but I didn't. Too busy with my own life. And the tragedy is, now it's too late. There's so much I want to say, too many things we never did together. I'm her daughter, yet I hardly know her.'

'I know.' He rocked me gently.

I wanted to say, '*How can you possibly know!*' but I bit my tongue, cursing my overactive emotions.

'Irini, your mother knows you love her. Don't let the complications of life get in the way. There's nothing stronger than the way a mother feels for her children. She will take your love with her, and leave her love with you. Nothing else matters in the end.' He stroked my hair and a little of my anguish melted.

Perhaps he was right – I should stop dwelling on regrets. Safe in his arms, I turned my face up. 'I want to thank you for coming with me. It's made such a difference not being alone.'

He peered into my eyes. 'Irini, I want to tell you—'

'Iris! Iris!'

Angelo groaned as I pulled away from his embrace.

Spiro appeared. 'You had good times last night, Iris, yes? Now we go to the airport!'

\* \* \*

At eleven-fifteen we were in Athens arrivals.

'Look, we have some free time,' Angelo said. 'Let's go to the National Archaeological Museum and see the frescoes of Santorini, yes?' His eyes sparkled like a kid at the fairground, lifting me out of my misery. He grabbed my hand, kissed the back of it, and led me to the taxi rank.

Outside the city, the taxi raced through areas of closed-down businesses, empty shops, and half-built houses. A sad sight to see.

'Difficult times,' Angelo explained.

In the vibrant city centre, I was thrilled to catch a glimpse of the Acropolis, with the Parthenon on top. I thought of Mam and her love of ancient history. Reminded that she would never come here again, I tried to see it with her eyes and feel her pleasure.

We pulled up in a No Parking area and Angelo had a huge argument with the taxi driver. I stepped back and let him deal with it. I wondered if my parents had visited the museum. I would take pictures to share with my father, knowing how much he would enjoy looking at the frescoes of Santorini again.

The National Archaeological Museum was a magnificent building, everything I imagined a Greek museum would look like. Granite steps the width of the front led to a wide, open, rectangular façade that was supported by four tall, white-marble columns with ornate capitals. The impressive frontage had wings of similar proportions and style, set slightly back to the left and right. The building was boldly painted in ochre, burgundy, and white. Above, taking centre stage under the sun's spotlight, the blue and white Greek flag waved at the breeze.

In front of the building, a long green lawn was dotted with students and tourists.

After the bright sunlight, the foyer seemed gloomy, disorganised, and noisy. A gaggle of teenage girls on a school trip preened and giggled, their hormones sitting up and waving at boys. Nearby, a gang of adolescent with fuzzy chins and croaky voices cried '*malaka*' every few words. Their teacher, in charge of the group, had the twitchy look of someone dangerously close to losing control. This all reminded me that school in Dublin started soon and my time in Greece was limited.

Marble sculptures lined the walls. Then we came upon a life-size bronze of a boy on a horse, which I could have stared at for hours.

'What do you think?' Angelo asked.

'It's the most magnificent thing. So much movement and drama, and detail. Unbelievably beautiful, apart from the tail. It doesn't quite look as though it belongs to the horse.'

'Very good! You are more observant than most.' He lifted his hand towards the bronze. 'The original tail was lost at sea and this was added recently.'

Ridiculously pleased with myself, I slipped my hand into Angelo's. His eyes narrowed as he glanced my way.

'Three times – phew!' he whispered.

I blushed like crazy and lowered my eyelids. 'Behave!'

'We must hurry,' he said, grinning.

In the next hall, I stopped and stared. There stood Poseidon, as sketched in my mother's *Book of Dreams*. The larger-than-life bronze, muscular and magnificent, about to hurl his trident. The other statues were cold, pale marble, but this had the warmth of burnished bronze. Light played over the curves, giving the impression he was about to move, about to breathe. I stared at the perfectly sculpted feet and recalled my mother's notebooks. The figure was so life-like! It seemed to put meat on the bones of her dreams . . . such a weird thought.

'Speak to me,' Angelo said. 'What are you thinking?'

'Poseidon, about to throw his trident,' I whispered, over-awed. 'Look, he's perfect.' My gaze travelled down the bronze, and avoiding a comment on the smallness of the god's man-hood, my attention came to rest, once again, on his feet. 'Look at that – so perfect you get the impression he's about to wiggle his toes.'

'Some say it's Zeus, about to hurl a thunderbolt.'

'No.' I shook my head. 'It's Poseidon, Lord of the Seas, God of Tempest and Terror.'

Angelo nodded, looked at his watch and said, 'Come on, the frescoes.'

We hurried on to the Santorini section.

The first fresco that took my breath away was of two gazelles. Beautiful life-size creatures painted with grace. A black calligraphy outline on cream plaster, lines flowing to suggest movement, although they had all four hooves on the ground. We stared at it in silence, taking in the artistry.

Next, we looked at the fresco of the boxing boys.

'See how each child only wears one boxing glove,' Angelo said. 'And the boy with the paler face wears jewellery – earrings, and bracelets on his arm and ankle. The other has none. Why is that? And think about this, Irini: there is nothing to say they are boys, they might well be girls. How's that for equality?'

'Look at the shaved heads, painted blue. My mother talked about that in her *Book of Dreams*.'

Angelo glanced at his watch. 'We'll come back, sometime in the future. I don't want to miss the plane.'

*  *  *

On the flight, he held my hand, occasionally stroking the back, or giving it a little squeeze. I guessed, like me, he was remembering our night together. I longed to be in his arms again, taste his kisses, his body against mine, whispered words of love in my ear.

Back in Crete, Angelo and I rushed from the airport to the photography shoot, and when we arrived, the relief shone from Paula's face. I was hurried through make-up and dressed in record time. I didn't think anybody noticed the surreptitious glances that passed between Angelo and I. All through the shoot, I tried not to look his way, but his presence was undeniable, always there behind Nick. To be honest, I tried a little harder because of it.

The afternoon ran smoothly and we were finished by seven o'clock.

Angelo wanted me to eat with him, and once again I longed to feel his embrace, but these were my mother's last days and I was desperate to get to her side.

# CHAPTER 27
## BRIDGET

*Crete, present day.*

WHERE AM I?! What's happening?! I know this is not one of my Atlantis dreams. Time and space are lost to me, yet I experience a floating sensation and recognise that I am surfacing from the darkest black. Oh my God, perhaps I have died? I can feel myself rise through a fog of emotional glue. I want to cry out, but can't. Anguish is surrounding me without shape or form. I am floating towards a spark of consciousness and sense that something important awaits.

That 'something' is pain. A fiery pinprick between my eyes is gathering strength, like an explosion in slow motion. Without the relief of a scream or the ability to flinch away, this agony quickly becomes intolerable. I find myself descending back towards the sanctuary of deep unconsciousness. Yet on that slippery return, I can hear a voice – distant, but recognisable.

'Hello Mam. It's me, Irini. You're in hospital, in Crete. You've had an accident.'

Oh, Irini! Are you really near me? Hospital? An accident? Are you holding my hand, Irini? There is so much I want to say, but if I can't, will you understand the clues I've left you?

In those few lucid moments, I soar above the pain. I can hear and think, but my body seems dead. Crete? I'm in Crete? Can I feel my daughter's hand in mine? I try and try to concentrate. I have to tell her about the dragonfly necklace, that I know where it is! That if she thinks hard enough, she will know where it is too. She must find it and do the right thing. Give it to Tommy, then he'll forgive me. He will never find peace until he does. I've lived with his scorn for such a long time, I can't bear it any longer. I wish I could tell him. I wish . . .

If only I could open my eyes! I want to clutch the presence of Irini to me and hear her speak kindly. How I have yearned for that over the years. I longed to take the place of one of her little friends in the convent; have her smile at *me*; whisper secrets in *my* ear; hug *me* if I tripped and hurt myself. All I have is her voice, flitting like a butterfly in the darkness of my brain. I am desperate to grasp hold of her words and reply.

My chemically induced slide into oblivion has no handrails. Helpless, and incapable of holding on to reality, I am falling back into that blank space where time has no meaning, and then I am descending into another era.

Falling, falling, back through the stars, the sun reverses its orbit, time and space suck me down, eons fly by, until that ancient time grows stronger and more real on each return. I arrive at the place that holds my spirit, when my destiny was written. I transform into Thira, ruler of Atlantis.

\* \* \*

I, Queen Thira, Goddess of the Marches, stand on the palace terrace and survey the scene below. From my viewpoint, I observe the Sacred City of Istron in our new homeland of Crete. I can see all the way down to the port and out over the rolling, turquoise sea beyond. Our great wooden ships, the envy of King Minos and the Cretans, stand in a magnificent row the length of the harbour. We have the finest vessels of

289

all nations. The city flourishes, and the new temple is almost complete.

I turn and gaze over the fields, inland of the city. They stretch away to the mountains, a rich patchwork of leafy vineyards, citrus-fruit orchards, olive groves, and vegetable plots. The livestock flourishes, and with that, so do my people. They are happy and safe.

I think of Oia and my heart is heavy. She went to Poseidon one harvest back. Although her sacrifice was ultimate, we Atlanteans still had to leave our homeland, but at least we now live in peace. Every full moon, I send a ship back to check on the situation at home. My sailors report that the mountain grows hotter by the day.

My people have settled here at Istron. Clearly, they enjoy the stability of their new homeland. Hero comes and stands by my side.

'We have a council meeting later, my Queen,' he says quietly.

'I wish Oia was here to see this.' I lift my chin and look over the town.

'We must thank her for our peace, and you, my Queen, for your sacrifice.'

'Do you think she's happy, Hero? She was so young and had so much to look forward to. I am left alone and broken-hearted.'

He sighs. 'One day, when we reach the Elysian Fields, we will know everything. Until that time, we must put our faith in the Great Gods of Olympus. I believe Oia is happy in her new domain.'

We gaze out at the distant sea, at peace, silent for a moment. A fishing boat is heading for shore. Seagulls bump and squabble in the air behind it, their plaintive calls reaching us through the warm summer air. The boat is low in the water, telling of a bountiful catch.

'Poseidon feeds us,' Hero says. 'The populous will eat well tonight.'

Women, with woven baskets on their heads, walk down to the harbour, hips swinging, infants on their backs. Others hold the hands of skipping children; they gossip and laugh as they walk. The town is filled with contentment and I am happy and proud to see my people living this way. Someone is strumming a laouto. They pluck the strings and a melody that fits the scene perfectly drifts over us.

A distant sonic boom vibrates the air and fear thumps through my body, aching in my neck and pulling my mouth down. My tranquillity turns to fear.

'Look, Hero.' I point at the horizon. 'What is that?'

We stare, mesmerised by a thin black line dividing the brilliant sky and the sea.

People rush from their houses, climb onto their flat roofs, and watch the strip of darkness grow thicker with every heartbeat. Dogs bark, as if they know something we don't.

'It's our homeland, Hero!' I know in an instant that the mountain has exploded. 'The God of Tempest and Terror has finally claimed Atlantis. Praise Zeus we are safe here in Crete.'

Hero stands behind me and takes me into his arms. 'So you did the right thing to persuade us to leave. The people, all of us, owe you our lives.'

I watch a crowd gather around the palace. The dark line grows, thickening, slowly rising from the horizon, while at the same time it seems to float over the water towards us. A tower of black smoke reaches for the sun and the people of Istron find themselves in semi-darkness. My concern grows; foreboding engulfs me.

'Hero, it took the ships one day and one night to reach Crete. How long will it take the poisonous black air of Atlantis to reach this island and smother us all? Tell the people to gather in the warehouses immediately! We need to protect ourselves in case the inferno's evil reaches Crete! Remember, the bad air inside the mountain – it killed the lambs. If it reaches here, it will kill us too!'

'Immediately, my Queen.' Hero bows and rushes away.

The urgency of the situation strikes everyone at the same time. Word spreads quickly. Mothers gather their children and workers come in from the fields. They take water, food, and blankets into the great stone warehouses and hunker down between the icons and treasures.

'Eurydice!' She is at my side instantly. 'Call the kings to council, immediately. The meeting will be here on the terrace, so we can observe the situation as we talk.' She rushes away and, as I wait, I watch the sailors batten-down ships and secure vessels to the quayside with extra ropes, before they join their loved ones in the warehouses.

* * *

Tommy is here. I can hear the worry in his voice. There's so much I want to say, but all I can do is listen. If only I could tell him how much I love him, how I have always loved him, and that I always will. I want to say I'm sorry but I simply could not allow him to die all those years ago. Instead, I turned him into the grumpy and bitter man he is today.

Tommy's voice reaches me through the darkness and my mind soars. You're near, my darling, Tommy. Do you know what that means to me? I long to be in your arms again, but just that you are

292

close is wonderful. You've always been enough. Whatever crumb you throw my way satisfies my hunger.

It's the truth. From the very beginning, I never wanted more than you. Remember our song, *It Started With a Kiss?* But no, the corny thing was, it started with a ping-pong game. I've loved you since that first moment. My heart fluttered so wildly I could hardly hold the bat on that day that changed my life.

'Bridget, I don't know if you can hear me. The doctor told me that you might, but I'm not even sure you understand what's happened.'

He sniffs and I wonder if he's become emotional.

'I should have gone to the police, Bridget, but I couldn't stand to get you into trouble, especially as I knew you'd done it for me. And now you're dying, Bridget, and I want to die with you. How can I live without your life in my thoughts every day; thinking about you in Santorini and wondering what you're doing? I've always loved you, though sometimes I've almost hated you, but in an odd way, even that was an honour. Oh, my darling girl . . . my darling girl . . . I'm sorry for every unkindness.'

He's sobbing, and I'm grateful to Uncle Peter and his definition of crying. 'Tears, they are God's way of washing out the soul.'

So, I'm dying. There is some relief in hearing that, and understanding what's going on. It's all right. We all die, and I'm glad to have these moments with you, Tommy, before I go. You're an old man now, and not in good health. I can see you clearly in my mind, and you're always in my heart. I remember the first time I walked into the lecture room and there you were, the man I'd played ping-pong with.

'Decided to join us, have you?' you said. I cringed, late for the lesson, embarrassed and self-conscious.

'Sorry, I got lost.'

'There's a place in the front row. Can you find that, miss . . . what's your name?'

'Bridget Gallagher, sir,' I said, blushing.

'Right, Bridget Gallagher, do you know what your surname means?'

'Yes, sir.' There was a moment of silence between us and I caught the glint in your eye, you devil. 'Foreign helper, or lover of foreigners, sir.'

'Very good. Sit!'

Your lecture was Sir Arthur Evans and Minoan art at Knossos, in Crete. You gave me an A+ for my paper with no knowledge that I had already fallen in love with you. You took every opportunity to pick on me. You're a git, Tommy McGuire. What are you talking about now?

'Bridget, I don't believe what happened in Santorini was an accident. I think you were knocked unconscious and then the wall pushed over you. I've got no proof, it's just a feeling. I get befuddled sometimes so I may be wrong, but there are too many coincidences.'

You're holding my hand, Tommy, or am I imagining it? I'm trying to move my fingers. I want you to know I can hear you. I want to tell you you're right. There was somebody at the site that day. They found out what I had done and came after me.

Aaron had gone to get petrol for the generator when I heard a noise. I didn't see who it was, but the sun was behind him, and I saw his shadow along the ground coming out from behind a wall. I was staring at it when I saw the shadow of the scaffolding bar as it swung towards me.

I think it was the man who had threatened me earlier.

I don't know what happened after that. It wasn't Splotskey, I'm sure. I never heard from him again, and they told me at the hospital he had died. This was a big, strong man with wide shoulders. Next thing I knew, I was surfacing from a fog in a hospital bed. I feel I've been sleeping for a long, long time and just can't open my eyes. You know how it goes, that pleasant, safe feeling just before you wake up fully, except that this feeling is always followed with pain so intense I can't stand it. Then I think they drug me again.

But I'm frightened, Tommy. The villains might come after you, or Irini if they think you have the artefacts. I'm helpless here. Wait now, you're speaking and it seems only part of my brain is working. I can't think and listen at the same time.

'We have to get the dragonfly necklace back, Bridget. Reverse the damage that's been done. I've decided to tell Irini everything. She's an adult now – she has a right to know what happened and why we took the actions that we did. Then she can choose for herself what she wants to do about it. We can't keep the truth in the dark. We've hurt her enough, sending her away. It's broken her heart, all this subterfuge. She's grown up thinking we don't love her.'

Another voice reaches me and I realise the nurse has come into my room, the one with the very young voice. I don't know how she does it, but she puts me to sleep for a long time, and I know Tommy will have gone when my mind comes back.

Tommy is talking again. 'They're just going to give you your morphine, Bridget, to keep the pain away. I've come to realise that your dreams were always wonderful, until you took the dragonfly necklace, then they were torture. I think, subconsciously, you were punishing yourself. You've suffered enough;

we both have.' I hear him gulp, sniff, and blow his nose. His voice drops to a whisper. 'My anger was never really at you, Bridget, but at myself. Can you forgive me, darling girl? It breaks my heart to say this, but it's time to let go, Bridget.'

*No!* Don't put me to sleep! I have to think, find a way to tell you what you should do. The pain is building, becoming close to unbearable, but I must speak. Tommy, you have to help Irini find the dragonfly necklace! I got it back. I have it! But how can you know that? Why didn't I tell you everything? I could have phoned you and explained, but I wanted to make the grand gesture, didn't I? Put everything right in one great flurry. Wipe out the past. I wanted you to love me like you used to. Oh, how much I wanted that.

'You'll be off into dreamland shortly, Bridget, so I'll leave you in peace, but I'll be back in a few hours. I also need to sleep, otherwise my head gets confused and I forget things.'

Don't go, Tommy! Don't let them put me to sleep. I can stand the pain. I need to wake up. It's important!

Tommy is silent for a moment, and I can feel myself slipping away. I try to resist, but it's like I'm being pulled under a heavy blanket, dragged away from the sound of his voice. He's speaking again but it's difficult to concentrate on his words as they float through the darkness; they get fainter, but I must try to grasp them, listen, hold on.

'I know what you did was wrong, Bridget, and over the years I've made it clear that I've never quite forgiven you. Heartless of me. Terribly cruel. But, when this happened, when I heard you had little hope of surviving, I could not come over with Irini, and do you know why that was? Because in truth, I would have sold my heart, or Tutankhamun's death mask, or anything, in exchange for your life. I was wrong to judge you, my darling girl. I'm ashamed of the way I've treated you. You see, I'd do the same as you, right now, if it would save your life. Please forgive me, Bridget. I'm sorry beyond words for treating you the way I did. Now I must go . . .

His voice has gone. I am alone again. If only I could make things right! I tried so hard. My journey was difficult, but I'm almost there. Will they find the dragonfly necklace? They don't even know I managed to get it back. What would Thira do? I allow my mind to slip, fall back to times long gone, when a great queen wore that very same necklace. I concentrate on her, feel her take over my body and mind . . .

*   *   *

In the gathering darkness, I, Queen Thira, stay where I am on the palace terrace, giving my people a sense of calm. They bow hurriedly as they pass. Coughing and spluttering, they rush to the safety of the great sandstone warehouses.

Another distant boom, and through the darkest smoke, a distant red glow roars upward, as if the sun itself has fallen into the mountain and exploded. Impenetrable smoke spews into the atmosphere, spreading rapidly towards us in Crete. Then, in the engulfing darkness, the black sky is lit by a storm of burning pumice. Like a billion miniature meteorites, it hails down on us. Eucalyptus, olive, and pine trees, volatile even when green, burst into flames.

People are running along the burning streets, towards the warehouses – screaming – hair or clothes on fire.

I retreat under the white marble canopy of the terrace and peer between the tall red columns. My eyes are streaming from sulphur and smoke. I hold my sleeve over my mouth to make breathing easier, but even so, it seems my chest is on fire. I stand firm, waving the stream of frightened people towards our strongest buildings.

'Go, you will be safe in there. Zeus will protect us,' I call out.

Burning lava fires out of the distant mountain. Hungry for oxygen, the massive inferno causes offshore winds so strong, I see people pulled to the ground, dragged through the burning ash, along the roads, on their backs or bellies. Screaming, tumbling and rolling like autumn leaves in a fierce storm. Skin and flesh flayed to the bone as they are dragged across or over rough walls. Eventually, those still in the streets are sucked into the sea, their charred bodies floating like blackened corks along the waterline.

Fires that rage through pine forests and orchards on the mountainsides are vacuumed towards the shore. Our majestic fleet bursts into flames. I retreat, pressing my back against the palace wall as the inferno races past, over the marble canopy. The air is unbearably hot, searing my lungs as I breathe.

In the dark sulphur-stinking inferno, the wind suddenly changes direction, coming towards us, so strong it extinguishes the fire. As it does, the smoke is blown away and the air clears for a second. Horror fills me when I glimpse the cause of what, at first, seems like a reprieve.

Now I know, I understand, this is the end for us all.

A wall of water, higher than the mountains behind me and infinitely wide, races towards the north coast of Crete. For a moment, I think of King Minos. I will thank him for his hospitality shortly, when we meet in the Elysian Fields. As the tsunami nears, it lifts the great harbour walls clean out of the water and pushes them up against the warehouses, sealing my people inside.

Knowing it's over for me and my subjects, I throw my head back and watch the giant wave loom and curl high above me, ever closer. The tsunami races forward, the air drenched and howling louder than all the tortured souls in Hades. I am surely one with the sea. Poseidon has claimed us all. He is about to drag my battered body into his depths, when the stone floor collapses beneath my feet. I am falling. Columns snap and the marble canopy crashes down on my head.

When I open my eyes, I am on a riverbank. Chaos has gone. Dusk shrouds everything in mystery and the air is still. I turn and see the hooded ferryman emerge out of the darkness. I am not afraid. Silently, he beckons that I step into his boat. The Elysian Fields await me on the distant shore, and I, Queen Thira, Goddess of the Marches, know I have reached the end of my mortal toil.

* * *

I believe time has passed, but how can I know? I'm surfacing as if from a deep sleep and pain is gathering once again. Tommy's words come back to me. I wonder if he is still with me. So, I'm dying, and I guess these dips into semiconsciousness happen when my medication is wearing off. I remember the shadow, the man who swung a scaffolding pole at my head. My next recollection was Irini's voice. Sometimes, I heard her read my notebooks, and with her words came terrible memories.

Does she know how much I love her? It's important that she does, not just for my peace of mind, but for hers too.

We tried to protect her from my appalling nightmares, but it was a mistake not to explain everything when she became old enough to appreciate that our actions were in her interest. I was ashamed, ashamed of my illegal activities, yet still, I couldn't think of another solution. I could not let Tommy die, especially when his child was growing inside me. Then, I remember that Tommy is here. He promised to tell Irini everything, or did I imagine that? I don't know. I'm confused.

The problem is, Tommy does not *know* everything. He doesn't know the danger he and Irini are in. Irini must find the dragonfly necklace and the jug, and hand them over to the museum immediately. Only then will they be out of danger.

Fire gathers between my eyes and spreads until it is so intense I want to scream. I can hear people talking again, a nurse, perhaps, but who is she speaking to?

Now the pain is easing and I'm sinking into the euphoria of painless sleep.

\* \* \*

Time has passed. I can hear Quinlan's voice. Such a wonderful, kind man. I owe him so much for being the one stability in Irini's life. Now he's talking in his steady, humorous way. Quinlan has the quality that, after you've been in his company, you somehow feel uplifted. I know Irini adores him. I fear, deep down, he's very lonely. Is he holding my hand? I don't think so. He would feel it an imposition. He'll be sitting in his freshly ironed pastel shirt and a bow tie, and loose linen pants held up by wide braces. Knees together, hand between them.

I hope one day he finds love, the kind that Tommy and I had . . . have. Because despite everything, I know Tommy still loves me.

Quinlan is speaking again. 'You don't have to worry your poor battered head about Irini and Tommy, Bridget. I promise to keep an eye on them both. Rest assured about that, lovey. They'll be all right. Irini has grown into a fine young woman – you should be proud. Irini told me that after reading your notebooks, she understands the sacrifice you made in order to keep her safe. And Tommy, well, we both know Tommy well enough. He's mortified that he hurt you with his hard-heartedness. You may have heard him ask for your forgiveness, but if you didn't, he's truly sorry for the way he behaved. He said he'd have done the same as you, or far more if needs be, in order to save your life.'

There is someone else in the room. Oh yes, it's the nurse. Quiet, concerned talking, then Quinlan speaks again.

'The nurse is back, Bridget. She's given you your medication, so you'll be feeling more comfortable shortly. I'll stay a while longer, then Tommy will take my place. We won't leave you by yourself, there'll always be one of us by your side.'

I feel a weight taken from me and I am lifted above worry and discomfort.

I'm so tired. If everything was resolved I could sleep forever. The goddess who takes over my mind feels the same way. I have experienced her pain in my dreams and know her torment is almost unbearable too. Queen Thira wants to rest, find harmony, be forgiven for her sins. More than anything, she longs to be pardoned for sacrificing her daughter.

I am only a vessel for her spirit in its restless search for peace, and I no longer fear her taking over my mind. I sink into darkness, drifting away, back in time, back to Thira's reign. After feeling her pain for so long, I want to help her. Did she save her people? I can't remember. I long to go to the Sacred City of Istron and excavate, but with Tommy at my side. Poor Tommy, an old man who never quite reached his ambition of proving Santorini was a mountain in the centre of Atlantis. I wonder if anyone ever will.

Tommy and I always suspected the island's populous set-tled on the north coast of Crete. I've visited the island and talked to other archaeologists, never admitting the true reason for my investigation. There are several possible sites in the vicinity of Istron that also lend themselves to the theory: the magnificent excavation at Malia, or Gornia, or there is the little island of Mochlos, now a hundred metres offshore. Before the eruption of Santorini, Mochlos was much larger and part of Crete's mainland. However, my dreams indicated Istron, and I have no reason to doubt the location of Queen Thira's city.

\* \* \*

## The Elysian Fields, present day.

I CAN SEE HER, Queen Thira. She waits for me on the oppo-site bank of the River Styx. She regards me as the mortal who was responsible for the re-birth of her daughter. I stand at the prow of the ferry, knowing the Goddess of the Marches looks forward to welcoming me into a peaceful afterlife. I am not afraid, or sorry. Life will go on without me. Thira has suffered her own pain, turmoil, and heartbreak too. She stretches out her arms, eager to reassure me, as she did on the day I gave birth to Irini.

The reason for my dreams becomes clear in a blinding flash. Thira regards Irini as her own child! I refuse to give my daughter away. My serenity gives way to anguish. I have suffered enough because of Queen Thira and now I am angry that she came between me and my child all our lives.

'I must go back! My husband, my daughter . . .' I call over the black water. 'I am not finished with my life!'

The hooded ferryman dips his paddle, holds it in the water and the boat turns, veers away, returning to the mortal shore.

Thira lowers her arms and I hear her thoughts: *You are not ready, sister, but I will wait. Do not fear, you will be happy here, at peace, with only good memories. Don't be sad, there is nothing to be sorry about now. Can you hear me? Can you hear me, Bridget?*

The voice deepens and I realise it's Tommy saying those words: 'Can you hear me, Bridget?' His voice is quiet and full of remorse. 'Darling girl, I'm sorry I drove your love away with my bitterness.'

You didn't drive my love away at all, Tommy. You were hurt, and who could blame you?

'You risked so much to save my life, darling girl, and me with my self-righteousness condemned you for it. I've been a nasty bastard for so long, I don't know how you stuck it. Then, in Dublin, I drove you away again and let Irini think you'd simply abandoned us.'

\* \* \*

They're at my bedside again. How can I tell Tommy and Irini the things they need to know? I came so close to putting everything right, but now it's down to them.

I discovered Splotskey had died. I don't think he was a bad man, not a hardened dealer in antiquities. He simply knew somebody who'd pay for your operation, Tommy. I wish I could say these things to you, but the truth is I hardly have the strength to think, and even that only comes in short stretches before the pain returns. Then the medication numbs my mind.

'Irini's going back to Santorini today to get your things from the house, Bridget,' Tommy says. 'She'll be back this evening to tell you about it. I wish we could go with her, to our little *hyposkafa* overlooking the caldera. We were so happy, remember? Our little cave was so filled with love we seemed to be grinning at each other all the time.'

Irini's in danger at the house! The dragonfly necklace – they don't know – how can I tell them what's happened? I try to speak, move something, make contact, but the effort drains me and I'm helpless.

'I was uneasy about her going alone, but you'll be pleased to hear she's with her new boss.'

I feel I'm slipping back into that twilight place of dreams. I can imagine Irini sleeping in our bed, as she did sometimes when she was a little girl, cuddling up to me and Tommy and Rabbs while the effect of my sleeping pills faded with the dawn. Memories of those happy times drift in.

I recall our attempt to live frugally. We did crazy things, didn't we, Tommy? Remember when, instead of paying for electricity, we invented a way to warm our water using the heat of the sun. You bought fifty metres of black pipe and we coiled it neatly on the flat roof, connected one end to the mains water, and the other end to our tank. This was a brilliant idea, Tommy, but with only one water supply into the house, we hadn't thought it through.

We had boiling water all through the day, and it lasted all the night long too. Water that was so hot we could not even wash our hands without the risk of scalding. Too hot for the shower, and the disgusting stink when we flushed the toilet with boiling water meant we had to sit outside until the pong dispersed.

How we laughed!

After that, we invested in a proper solar water-heater, and the black pipe was given to Spiro for irrigating his olive grove. We never had to buy olive oil from that day on.

Recalling these things makes me smile inside.

Spiro removed the pipe from our roof, forbidding us to try and roll it up in case it kinked.

He came down the steps with a length of rope, tied it to the pipe, and attached the other end to the towing hitch on his taxi, parked in the street above. When he drove away, we were nearly knocked off the roof by the coil flipping over as it unravelled. We raced up the steps. Followed the snaking black hose. Watched it slithering along the main street long after the taxi had disappeared out of town.

Little Irini sat on your shoulders, her arms wrapped around your head as she squealed with laughter. Children chased the pipe, jumping over the end. What a good job it was out of season and the pavements were free of postcard stands and menu boards. I could imagine the chaos.

The uplifting memory floods me.

Then there were the bad times. It took a long time for us to grow back together after you discovered the truth about the necklace. Things were never quite the same between us, were they? At the site, I felt you were watching me, Tommy, afraid I'd be tempted to secret away another artefact.

Our age difference became more apparent as the years passed. Me in my late forties, still fretting about Irini, longing to be a proper mother taking care of our daughter. You in your early sixties, resigned to the situation. You seemed to forget about Irini. I thought about her every day.

Quinlan and Irini became very close and that consoled me a little. He kept us informed of her development, and sent photos when she had an important occasion, like her first communion. When she was fourteen, Quinlan brought her over in the summer holidays. Irini was disgusted that I couldn't buy her tampons when she had her period, but they weren't available on the island.

Sadly, I realised her childhood was gone. She'd grown into a beautiful young woman. While she was in Santorini, every boy in town had his eye on her. Her long red hair fell in coils to her waist, and her fair skin was lightly sprayed with freckles. I adored having her near me, but sunburn and a tummy-bug ruined the holiday. She missed her friends and wanted to go home.

I sat on the patio and cried as her plane flew over.

Then you started getting chest pains and shortness of breath. I feared for your heart, but the doctor said the problem was your lungs. They were caked with dust from years of working at the site.

The inhaler helped, but your health deteriorated, and eventually you couldn't walk more than a few metres without having to stop and hold on to something. I could see myself having to push a wheelchair in the not too distant future, and such a thing would be impossible in the steep and uneven streets of Santorini. I knew we had to return to Ireland and the National Health Service.

By this time, Irini was a teacher and had made the little house in Sitric Road her home. There was no question about where we would stay when we returned to Dublin.

My mind's drifting. I must concentrate. What did you say, Tommy? Irini's gone back to Santorini, to our house?

I'm afraid she's in danger!

# CHAPTER 28
## IRINI

*Crete, present day.*

AT THE HOSPITAL, I found my uncle and father were still with Mam.

Uncle Quinlan had a heart of gold and I loved him dearly. He rose from his seat and gave me a stiff hug. His bow tie bobbed as he swallowed hard. 'Chin up, lovey,' he said.

I kissed his cheek and turned to my father, knowing this was going to be difficult. 'Are you all right, Dad?'

He nodded, gave my hand a squeeze, then pressed the tips of his fingers against his eyes. After a big breath, he tried to speak. 'I . . .' Then he shook his head, unable to say more.

'Do you really think she can hear us?' he said after a moment.

'I believe she can, at least some of the time.'

He took her hand in both of his and lifted it to his mouth. 'I've been a bastard. Poor girl.' He turned to me. 'Where've you been? We waited all day.'

Quinlan cut in. 'I told you, Tommy, Irini went back to your house in Santorini to get Bridget's papers, she phoned us, remember? Missed the ferry. Then she had to go to work, to pay the hospital bills.'

Dad sighed. 'That was how it all started – my hospital bills. Is there much to pay?'

'A few thousand. Don't worry, I'm getting there. I was lucky to get an amazing job, modelling.' I wanted to tell him about it, but it seemed indecent to voice my pleasure when he looked so defeated. I glanced at Quinlan and saw he understood.

My phone pinged with a message. 'Speak of the devil, it's Paula, my boss,' I said, reading it out. '"Can you work for two hours tomorrow morning? There's a problem with one of the shots."'

'Go,' Quinlan said. 'It'll do you good to have something else to think about. Take your mind away from all this.' He rested his hand on my father's shoulder. 'I can take care of your father, lovey, and he needs to be alone with Bridget for a little longer.'

\* \* \*

That night, I lay in bed thinking about my parents, and Angelo. Since I'd had a call from someone interested in my wedding dress, I'd started to wonder if I should keep it. A mad idea. Yet my mind was uplifted every time I thought about Angelo and our time together. I had hopes, dreams, and crazy heart-melting imaginings.

At six-thirty the next morning, I drove to Malia for the shoot. I needed to see Angelo, look into his eyes, and feel the strength of his arms around me. I desperately hoped we would get a moment alone, and perhaps that night . . . Oh, to be back in his arms. I wouldn't tell him I thought I was falling in love, but I wondered how he felt about me? He had said such passionate things in the heat of the moment, but were they true?

Paula, stressed to the hilt, made everyone jumpy. 'Quickly! Get ready. Tell Sofia to make my coffee the second she's finished with you. The tech's gone for a new gas bottle.'

I hurried to the trailer.

While I stared at myself in the mirror, my thoughts went back to Mam. What would happen when they turned the machines off? My tears came dangerously close so I tried to put the hospital out of my mind by thinking about Angelo. Hardly difficult; I seemed to be obsessed. Just recalling his arms around me made my toes curl up. He excited me, yet at the same time calmed me. I wondered what it would be like to live with him. A ridiculous thought. I hardly knew him and we lived in different countries. At the same time, I felt as if I'd waited for him all my life. Were we meant for each other?

Sofia's small hands twisted my hair around dozens of bendy rollers. Had she known such love?

'I like much the red hairs,' she said, and it reminded me of the *Book of Dreams*. The fiery-haired princess Oia and her troubled queen. I wondered what happened to them. The notebooks lay in the bottom of my suitcase, to read when I got home.

With so much on my mind, I hardly listened to Sofia rabbiting on. Mam's accident, the glamour of modelling, the prospect of assembling a portfolio, and the love I had shared with Angelo in my parents' house. My life had changed dramatically in a few short days. Once Angelo and I returned to Crete, I had wanted him to stay the night but in the small suite I shared with my father and Quinlan, there was no real privacy.

Paula's voice winged in from the trailer door, snapping me from my daydream. 'Twenty minutes! Make sure you're ready, everyone!'

Where was Angelo? I hoped he would turn up any second, wearing the smile of a shared secret. Sofia chattered away, her Greek accent so heavy I gave up trying to understand. She finished my make-up, then undid the curlers. My frizz was transformed into cascades of glossy waves that tumbled over my shoulders.

'. . . and so Angelo say I come works with hims, together. I no have choice, lady.'

Jolted from my musings, I paid attention.

'He is big, charming, my husband . . .'

*Husband? Sofia's husband?*

'. . . no ones know what *malákas*, bastards, he is. Angelo know 'e's bastards but say 'e can't change nothing. 'E say is my mistake. I should no to marry 'im. But I 'ave boy mine. I 'ave big love for Michalis mine. I wants much more childrens, but nows insides kaput after my Michalis borns.'

The air seemed to rush out of my lungs. Images of Sofia's misery on the first shoot, when Angelo was giving me all his attention, rushed into my head.

Sofia continued. 'So many girlfriends, there in front me. *Maláka.* What I do, lady? If I goes, husband mine takes my boy. I much love boy mine. Bastards husband!'

*He had a son? Was married with a child? What have I done?*

Sofia paused and, as the echo of her words faded, I could hear nothing but the blood pumping from my broken heart.

'Once, I complains for his *poutanas*, whores, and 'e's threatens divorce,' Sofia said. 'Fathers-in-laws, he takes boy mine to stay London schools. I much sad, lady.'

*Why didn't I think Angelo might be married?!*

'Look, is *photographea* of sons mine, is ten years befores.' Sofia moved the bottles aside and there, taped to the mirror, a faded snapshot of a much younger, but just as glamorous, Sofia holding a baby. Standing behind her, Angelo, clean-shaven, smartly dressed and a few pounds heavier, but those eyes, yes, it was Angelo.

Nothing remained inside me but despair. Wasn't I a fool not to think of it before? That the only two Greeks working together in a London company, and showing a certain affection for each other, might be man and wife? I touched my eyes.

'Eeh, why you look so sad, lady?' Sofia said. 'Ah, you have problems with love, yous, yes? I no ask. Love is much difficult. Befores, I 'ad much love for husbands mine. No now. Is bastards now. And . . .' Sofia went on.

I wanted to scream: *Shut up, just shut up, I don't want to hear any more*, but Sofia didn't shut up.

'Fathers-in-laws sick now, they fly him Athens. Angelo go Athens for be with father his. I not know when Angelo come back. He like you much, he says so when you works with hims.'

*He even told his wife he fancied me? No wonder she looked so upset when she saw us working together. And all the shouting and arm-waving on the set . . .*

The make-up artist continued: 'I don't cares for husbands, I no cares what he do, who he with. I go sees sons soon as. You understands?'

Paula stuck her head through the doorway. 'Are you ready? Quickly now!'

'Okay!' Sofia answered.

'Lady, how I make yous eyes nice when yous is cry.' She handed me a bunch of tissues. 'Ah, you remembers, love makes you cry. Dry eyes, lady. I never make talks of bastards husbands again.'

A knock sounded on the door and a young man's voice shouted: 'Mrs Rodakis, the new gas bottle's on!'

*Mrs Rodakis* – that confirmed it then: Sofia was Angelo's wife.

\* \* \*

How could I have let it happen? Poor Sofia must never find out. Angelo's behaviour had lifted me from my gloom, a spark of hope for the future in the darkness of my mother's death.

312

Something wonderful to cling to, to look forward to. Something short-lived.

Without Angelo's help, work got behind and Paula's mood worsened. 'Irini!' Her voice cut through my thoughts like a rusty razor. 'Listen to the photographer, will you? Christ, I'll kill that bloody Angelo. Drops me a novice then buggers off to Athens.'

There I had it, double confirmation – Angelo had gone to Athens. A few hours ago, I'd lain in his arms. He told me he loved me, said all the things I wanted to hear, then he ran off without a word. Those whispered endearments had meant so much, stolen my heart, and just as quickly abandoned it. I'd given him everything and he hadn't even bothered to say good-bye. A gullible fool I'd been.

\* \* \*

I agreed to meet my father and Quinlan in the Shamrock after work. Trying to hide my pain, I walked into the bar. Quinlan recognised my distress immediately. 'Stiff upper lip, lovey. Do you want a drink?'

'No, thanks. Can we go next door for something to eat? Then I'd like to visit Mam for an hour or two.'

Jack came over. 'Sorry about your mother, Irini. Your uncle's just told me there's not much hope. Under the circumstances, I can't expect you to work tonight.'

His kindness made me feel worse. 'Thanks, Jack, but I can work, don't worry. I'll be here at nine.'

Quinlan took a last sip of his Campari and turned to my father. 'Drink up, Tommy. We'll get a bite to eat, I'll drop Irini at the hospital, then I'll take you to the hotel for a rest.'

'Irini, me love,' Fergus chortled as he hobbled across the lounge and struggled onto a bar stool. His mischievous twinkle changed to concern when he saw my face. 'You all right? How's your ma?'

'There's no change, Mr McFadden.'

'Poor woman, God bless her.' He stared at the ceiling for a moment and I had the impression he said a little prayer, then he returned his attention to me. 'Me and your pa had a good old natter, but this place is miserable-quiet without you, Irini. I hope you're going to work here when you've finished the fancy modelling stuff.' The twinkle returned and I understood he was trying to lift my spirits. 'I hope those fashion people are paying you pots of money. And where's the Greek that couldn't take his eyes off you the other day?'

Before I could think of an answer, Quinlan cut in. 'Sorry to interrupt, Fergus, but I need to get some food inside these two before Irini comes back at nine.' He ushered me outside and Dad followed. 'Are you all right, lovey?' His eyes were soft and his mouth a rare straight line.

'Oh dear, Quinlan . . .'

He pulled out a chair at the neighbouring taverna. 'Come on, let's get some food. Boys, beer, and banter – that's what you need right now.'

I managed a smile.

'That's better,' Quinlan said. 'It's a difficult time for us all, but I'll tell you something, your mother would not want you to be so unhappy.'

'You don't understand, Quinlan. It's not just Mam. I was . . .'

Quinlan raised his hand to a waiter. 'Three of tonight's specials, a jug of dry red and a bottle of water, please. We're in a hurry.'

'What have you ordered, Quinlan?' my father asked.

'No idea, Tommy. Let's live dangerously, on the knife edge, see what turns up.'

'I hope it's not snails,' Dad muttered.

Quinlan made a mischievous pout at my father, then turned to me. 'I suspect love's let you down again, Irini. We've all been there lovey, even me. Everyone in that bar's had their heart broken, probably more than once. Unfortunately, it's happened now, just when you need a shoulder, but it's not such a catastrophe.'

'I'm a catastrophe,' I said, remembering.

He shook his head. 'We're your family – trust us, you're not alone. Affairs of the heart sort themselves out. *Que sera sera*. Let's stick to our plan, do what we can to support Bridget, and when we get home, we'll put a portfolio together. Even if this thing with Retro Emporio doesn't materialise, you should be submitting your work to other fashion houses. You've talent, Irini – too much to be spending your time teaching six-year-olds and working behind a bar.'

The waiter appeared with pastítsio, Greek salad, and drinks. The delicious aroma of mince, cinnamon, and cheese made me realise how hungry I was. I looked up to see my father frown.

'Nobody bakes a pastítsio like my Bridget,' he said.

\* \* \*

That evening, the Shamrock was mad busy, but at ten o'clock the place emptied.

'Where's everyone gone?' I asked.

'Beach party,' Jack said. 'Goes on till sun-up. You can finish early if you want, Irini.'

315

I was just thinking of calling Quinlan when Paula, wearing a tight red shift that was barely decent, sauntered into the Shamrock.

'Ah, here you are. I was hoping to catch you,' she said, pulling herself onto a barstool. 'Get me a large G&T, would you? Ice and a slice. I've brought your wages.' She pushed a brown envelope over the counter. 'Cash.'

'Thanks, I'm really grateful. That's going straight off the hospital bill.'

'Thank God it's in the bag, darling,' Paula said, her scarlet fingernail tracing the glass rim. 'You saved the day, Irini. Did you enjoy it?'

'I did indeed, and the money, I mean . . . things were getting behind – travel, medical costs, you know.'

'Yah, sure.' She poked the slice of lemon in her drink. 'That's what I want to talk to you about. Angelo suggested that you submit a collection of designs to us.' She crossed her legs and appraised the few men left in the room.

Angelo? My heart skipped. *He's married with a child.*

'Yes, I plan to work on it as soon as I get home.' This was a lot to think about. Would he still want the portfolio when he discovered that I was not the sort to have an affair with a married man? But then again, as I recall, it was me that threw myself at him. Did I regret it? Oh, God, no! Not really. The big question was: could I resist doing it again when this terrible hurt I was feeling faded?

Paula finished her assessment of the opposite sex and returned to me.

'Quinlan, my uncle, designs costumes for the Abbey Theatre in Dublin. He's helping me put the portfolio together.'

'We're looking for fresh talent. Angelo's away for a while, but he's asked me to look after you.' She met my eyes with a knowing look. 'I'll give you my number. Call me when the portfolio's ready. Okay?'

Jack slid a mug of tea in front of me.

'Meanwhile, I want to discuss our next promo shoot. The location's undecided yet.' She narrowed her eyes. 'I want you to work for us again, Irini. You know the ropes, so it will be easier next time. Also, using the same models keeps continuity on the website, helps with our image. In the trade, it's called *branding*.

'I've been scouting for a mature model for some time. Those already in the business are botoxed and lip-plumped. Not what we want. You've a very natural look about you – just the job. If you agree to work for Retro Emporio again, it's all expenses paid and an eight-hundred-euro retainer. When's half-term?'

'Mid-October.' *Eight hundred euro!*

'Perfect.' Paula uncrossed her legs and sipped her drink.

I stared at a crescent of scarlet lipstick on the glass while she wrote a cheque and passed it over. I had never held a cheque before. 'It's all so sudden . . .'

'Bank it and don't forget to call me when the portfolio's ready. Make sure your passport's up to date too.' Paula stood and smoothed her dress. 'Oh, and sorry to hear about your mother.'

Jack rolled his eyes. 'A bucket of sympathy, that one,' he said as she left.

# CHAPTER 29
## BRIDGET

*Dublin, 1 year ago.*

WE DID NOT LIVE HARMONIOUSLY. Tommy resented the return to Dublin and blamed it on me. He said I should have let him die with the heart attack. We bickered from dawn till dusk, and this made Irini's life hell, not that we saw much of her. She worked at the school all day, and behind a bar in the evenings. When home, she was sewing, had books to mark, food to cook, or rushed around cleaning the house.

I did my best to ease her workload, but nobody was happy.

After only a week at Sitric Road, everything changed again. I received a call from the member of Interpol that I corresponded with occasionally in relation to my articles. I helped Harry Edwards by writing about missing artefacts, and he reciprocated whenever he had information to share. He even took me out to lunch when he had business in Santorini, and I enjoyed his company.

With the arrival of the computer, I continued to communicate with him on the subject of antiquity theft. The Athens archaeologists passed on information too, keeping me up to speed with the latest finds.

'Some Minoan artefacts have come onto the market,' Harry said. 'We suspect they're from Crete and we're looking for information that might lead us to an excavator, broker, or collector. Have you heard anything?'

'Nothing. What are they?'

'Mostly jewellery. Our team's only three men, so it's an impossible task. That's why I'm calling all archaeologists to help us out.'

'Jewellery?' My heart skipped a beat. 'And you think the dealer's in Crete?'

*Pure coincidence, or could this be my lead at last?*

'Everything points that way, but so far we've drawn a blank.'

* * *

I could hardly sleep for the questions tumbling around in my head. Was this a connection to the dragonfly necklace? When I gave in to tiredness, I took myself back to dreams of Thira and her buried city on the island of Crete. My restless mind searched for clues that may lead me to a dealer and the dragonfly necklace. Clearly, Thira left the necklace in the temple at Santorini, where Tommy found it. But almost all their other treasures had gone, according to my dreams, to the Sacred City of Istron.

Never having been to Istron, I longed to investigate. If someone had discovered the site, then I suspected they found a wealth of artefacts, everything of value that the Atlanteans removed from Santorini.

I *had* to return to Greece and find the necklace. Undo the wrong I did. Then Tommy would find peace. The biggest disappointment in his life was that I betrayed his trust.

* * *

After breakfast, Irini attempted to mark homework books, despite Tommy having the TV volume on high and the rugby commentary blasting out. I was concentrating on my next article when Aaron phoned from Santorini.

'A guy came looking for you, Bridget. He wanted your address but I wouldn't give it. I said I'd contact you on his behalf.'

'A man? What did he look like?'

'A big guy, in his forties, Greek, good-looking, I guess. He said to send regards from someone called Splotskey.'

'Splotskey! Are you sure?' I cried.

Tommy's head snapped up. 'The cardiologist?' he muttered. I saw him put two and two together – making five.

The man Aaron described was not Splotskey, but what was the connection? Thirty years had passed since I last saw Splotskey, but was this my lead?

'I'm sure. Splotskey. I wrote it down,' Aaron said. 'He gave me his number and insists you call him.'

I jotted down the digits as Aaron recited them. If this was a dealer, which I suspected, then I *had* to meet him. He was too young to be Splotskey, or the man he dealt with, but obviously he knew something about what had happened all those years earlier.

'Actually, I'm coming back over, Aaron,' I said, making a snap decision. 'I need some photos for my next article. Will you pick me up from the airport?'

Tommy and Irini were staring at me when I ended the call. I avoided their gaze, my mind searching for an explanation I could offer for my upcoming departure.

'So it was Splotskey. I always wondered. And now you're going back by yourself,' Tommy said, glaring at me.

I nodded. 'You would never let me explain, remember?'

'Can I ask why now?' he said, his tone brusque now and his eyes hard.

'Something's come up.' I wanted to go over to him and explain, but the small room was filled with tension and we were like magnets on the same poles, so alike we were forced away from each other.

'That's all you're going to tell us? I hope it's not more of the same, Bridget!' He glanced at Irini, as if to say: *See what I have to put up with?*

'No, of course it's not! Can't you ever ... Oh! Look, I don't have a choice, Tommy.'

Irini stared down at her homework books, clearly not wanting to get involved, but she didn't turn a page. After a few minutes of our bickering, she looked up.

'Why can't you stay, Mam?' There was so much sadness in her voice. Then her eyes met mine. 'I know it hasn't been easy for us this last week, we're set in our ways and it's hard to change, but that doesn't mean you have to leave. I'm involved with somebody. I might end up moving in with him soon, then you'll have the place to yourselves.'

Momentarily side-tracked, Tommy turned his attention to Irini. 'Who?'

Jason, one of my fellow teachers. I haven't had a chance to tell you about him yet. We planned to take you out to dinner next week and break the news, you know, have a bit of a celebration. It would have been so nice. We got engaged just before you and Dad arrived here. He loves me.'

'Don't we all?' Tommy said.

Irini looked glumly from him to me, and back again.

'You're not wearing a ring,' I said.

'Jason was going to do the formal thing: ask Dad's permission in the restaurant, go down on one knee, propose, and slip the ring on. We had it all planned, even bought gifts for you and Dad. The perfect surprise. Silly, really.' She sighed and stared at the floor. I felt her utter disappointment. 'Anyway,

Jason thinks it's better if we keep quiet about it until he gets a position at the comprehensive. It's frowned upon for anyone to get romantically involved at school.'

'Oh, that old rule still going, is it?' Tommy said, glancing at me.

'I see,' I said, ignoring Tommy's quip. 'I'm so sorry, sweetheart, I just have something to sort out in Santorini, then I'll be back,' I said.

'Of course you will,' Tommy mumbled with a tinge of sarcasm. 'And you're not going to tell us why, no explanation, just pack your bags and leave, is it?'

'It's about some antiquities that went missing,' I said quietly.

'Oh, that old chestnut,' he snapped.

Irini was following our conversation. 'What? I don't know what you're talking about,' she said.

Tommy thrust his jaw forward and I realised he was going to share my darkest secret.

'Nothing, Irini,' I said quickly. 'Just something that disappeared a long time ago.'

Tommy snorted. 'That's one way to put it.'

'Why do you have to be so horrible all the while?' My anger rose. 'You're a bitter and twisted old man, Tommy McGuire.'

'Honestly!' Irini shouted. 'I don't know why you two can't talk to each other like normal, civilised human beings. If you hate each other so much, why have you stayed together all these years? All you do is snarl and snipe all day long. It's been hell this past week!'

'We stay together because of you, Irini, love,' Tommy said, squinting at me. 'We always hoped you would come back to live with us.'

'If all this nastiness is because of me, I wish I'd never been born!' She gathered up her exercise books and stomped upstairs.

'Satisfied, Tommy?' I said, pulling my magazine research into a pile and following her.

I tapped on Irini's door, and when she didn't answer, I stuck my head inside and said, 'Can I come in?' I sat on the bed next to her. 'I'm sorry, Irini. I know how difficult it's been for you.'

'I don't understand why you two are always fighting.'

I sighed. 'It's a long story.'

'It might help if you shared it with me.'

'I will, I promise. I'll tell you everything as soon as I come back from Santorini. When I've put everything right.' We sat in silence for a minute. 'It will be easier all around if I'm out of the way.'

'Do you really think that, Mam?'

'I do. For now, at least. There are things I need to put right, in Greece. Do you understand? It's something I *have* to do.'

'I wish we could have been a normal family.'

'Me too. Were you terribly unhappy at the convent?'

She took a moment to answer. 'Not really. I loved getting your letters. Remember the donkey . . . the name I chose?'

I smiled sadly. 'Ring-a-ding Rosie. She's a grandmother now, and trots up and down to the port with her offspring every day. I always wondered if you got the letters, with you not replying.'

'I tried, but I never knew what to say. If I won the lottery, I'd open a donkey sanctuary on Santorini.'

I smiled. 'Will you come and visit me if this takes longer than I expect?'

'Do you want me to?'

'Nothing would please me more.' I pushed her hair back and kissed her cheek. 'You have no idea how much I love you, Irini. But one day you'll understand.'

Her sad eyes looked into mine, and although she didn't speak, I knew exactly what she was thinking: *Then why did you dump me in the convent when I was a little girl?*

'Like I said, I'll tell you everything when I'm sorted.'

Again, I got that questioning look, and felt my heart breaking.

Three days later, I left for Santorini.

* * *

After landing at Athens, I boarded the small prop-engine island hopper. The Olympic plane was packed, but I had a window seat. My neighbour poked around the armrest for a phone charger.

'My battery's flat,' he said, as if running out of oxygen.

'I doubt you can charge it on here.'

Like most youths, he couldn't travel without his personal noise. He had noticed me at Dublin airport and introduced himself as Nathan Scott. We buckled up and he chatted throughout the forty-minute flight. As we started descending for the airport, he leaned across to peer out of my window.

'Look, that's Santorini. Can you believe you might be looking at all that remains of Atlantis?'

'Do you really think so, Nathan?' I smiled to myself, playing along. What were the chances of sitting next to another person who shared my love of that myth?

'Quite possibly, and a lot of very learned people seem to think so too.'

'I thought Atlantis lay in the Atlantic and that's how it got its name?'

'A slip-up by old Plato. He might have been a great story-teller and poet, but he would have flunked maths. One nought too many had generations of archaeologists, scientists, and historians way off-track. Unless he had a great sense of humour and did it on purpose. You know the sort of thing?'

I shook my head, glad to have my thoughts distracted from Tommy and Irini.

'Come on. You arrive in a strange city, you ask where the bank is. Some local sends you half a mile in the wrong direction and laughs all the way home.' Nathan grinned again. 'A bit of a wag, our Plato, don't you think?'

'From up here, it's a bit hard to imagine that scrap of an island as Atlantis,' I said over my shoulder as we peered out of the window.

'Ah, well, that's just the tip of the mountain. Before, an entire country surrounded the bit you see now; a huge island it was before it fell into the sea. The largest volcano in all of man's existence. Changed the Nile Delta. And you know the ten plagues of Egypt, from the Bible?'

'You're not saying they were caused by that scrap of land?' I loved the passion in his voice, and it reminded me of Aaron when he was a student.

'Exactly that. The pollution, darkness, strange wildlife behaviour. The whole eruption would have played havoc with the environment.'

I thought I talked too much, but Nathan never shut up. I smiled at his effervescent enthusiasm.

'And think about this: old Moses must have laughed his holy socks off when the Red Sea was drawn back by the tsunami. He and the Israelites picked up their robes, legged it across the seabed and, just when Pharaoh's mob almost caught them, along came the big wave and wiped them off the face of the earth.' He laughed at the thought. 'Moses one, Pharaoh nil – match declared a wash-out.'

'A tsunami, like the one in Japan?'

'More like the one in Greenland, twenty-seventeen. That was three hundred feet high, but this one, the biggest wave man ever saw, was perhaps around six hundred feet high. Some scientists say, when it hit Crete, it could still have been over three hundred feet tall. Imagine that!'

'Amazing,' I said, wanting to challenge him. 'But going back to the ten plagues of Egypt, what about the death of the firstborn? Impossible to put that down to a volcano, miles away.'

'Not at all. Traditionally, the first male Egyptian child slept on the floor, next to the door of the dwelling, growing up as protector of the family. Poisonous gases are heavier than air, so he would have been overcome first.'

'You have an answer for everything.'

'I'm an archaeologist.'

I blinked at him. He looked about eighteen. He lowered his eyes. 'At least, I will be in three years' time. I'm on a student exchange: three months at the archaeological site here, and some poor sucker gets three months peat-prodding in damp old Dublin.'

'Ah, I see,' I said as we taxied to the terminal. 'Then I'll see you at work in a day or two.'

He blinked at me. 'You work there too?'

I offered my hand. 'Bridget McGuire. It's been lovely listening to you, Nathan Scott.'

'You . . . you're Bridget McGuire . . . the archaeologist?' His mouth fell open, which rendered him silent for a precious moment, then in a rush he said, 'I'm a great admirer, honestly. I've read all your articles. Holy shite, I can't believe it – Bridget McGuire. Wait till I tell my tutor!'

\* \* \*

I stepped off the plane at Santorini airport and, despite the daunting task ahead of me, a huge weight lifted from my shoulders. Instantly, I felt ten years younger, fitter, and energised. The sun blazed down. Tourists chatted excitedly, colours zinged with life, and the air made me feel clean as peppermint toothpaste.

I had arrived home.

Aaron was waiting outside the terminal. 'Ready?' he cried through the pick-up window.

'Do you think we could just sit here and have an ice-cold frappé for five minutes? I'd like to savour the moment.'

'Sure!' He laughed and clambered out of the vehicle.

We sat in the shade with our iced coffees and exchanged pleasantries, until he said, 'How's Tommy really?'

'It's been difficult, to be honest.' Aaron looked away, making it easier. 'Things have been strained between us. There's some stuff you don't know, Aaron. I've come back to sort it out.'

'I realised something was wrong. I love the pair of you, but it became clear you were both a bit tense. Tell me about it when you're ready, okay?'

I nodded. 'What about this guy that came looking for me?'

'He was obviously wealthy. Not your usual touristy historian or archaeology hobbyist. I don't know, I felt a little suspicious, uneasy, like. He asked about the site, and my book, and wanted to know when you would be back. Who's this Splotskey? I've never heard the name before.'

I shrugged and shook my head, but I think he suspected I was hiding something.

'Right, I'm done,' I said, putting my glass down. 'Can't wait to get home!'

'Pick up a couple of *gyros* on the way?'

'Sounds perfect!'

\* \* \*

Oh, the joy of our little house. Although I'd only been away a week, it felt like much longer. All my memories came rushing back. Ten ecstatic years before Irini was born, and even the five years after, apart from my nightmares. Our lovely neighbours, the amazing view, and the archaeology site to look forward to. Aaron had been that morning and put a few supplies in the fridge.

I pulled the table near to the edge of the patio and enjoyed my food and wine while watching the sunset scene unfold. The donkeys wearily clopped up the steps. I thought of Irini and looked out for Ring-a-ding Rosie's offspring, sadly wondering if my daughter would ever come back to Santorini. That would be one of the greatest days of my life. I longed to stand on this patio and hold her in my arms. Just the thought made me emotional.

Once I had told her everything, we could embark on a normal mother-daughter relationship.

Everything was going to change with Tommy too, once I had the dragonfly necklace back. He would forgive me, and our old love would replace his corrosive bitterness.

The trip boats sailed out into the caldera, their sails turning gold as the sun descended. Nothing had changed.

'Bridget! Bridget!' Spiro and Anna came rushing to my side, hugging me, patting me, beaming widely. Anna brought a pan of egg-lemon soup and fresh bread that would feed me for a week. The aroma of succulent chicken and fresh lemons filled the house.

I poured them both a wine while Spiro told me his cousin, also a taxi driver, had seen Aaron pick me up at the airport. They told me all the local news.

Later, I lay in bed and wondered why I couldn't be this happy with my husband and daughter. I longed to share my pleasure with them.

* * *

Harry came to Santorini and, over lunch, he told me of Interpol's latest developments in their fight to stop antiquities theft. He suspected the man who came looking for me was part of a smuggling ring, or a dealer. We both knew that although this was highly organised crime, it wasn't down to one group of people with a 'Godfather'-type head.

'So, if something was looted from, say, my site in Santorini, and passed on to somebody in Crete, how would I get it back?' I asked.

He looked at me curiously. 'Was it?'

'It's better if we talk hypothetically.'

Harry eyed me for a moment, I guess analysing the situation. 'You have some chance if it was bought "legally" by a big, distant museum. USA, UK, or Australia. If you have records of its provenance, and photographs, then it's a lengthy process, but we usually manage to get these things repatriated, and sometimes we succeed in several prosecutions too.'

'But you'd think the great museums of the world would demand proof of legality; after all, their reputation depends on it.'

'They do, but it's not that simple. A series of people will each profit from an artefact as they handle it, but they don't usually know where it came from, or where it's going when it passes through their hands. They only specialise in one small part of the artefact's journey.'

'But would a reputable museum be fooled by forged legal documents?'

'The import-export papers are usually genuine. Antiquities gain documents, which aid in making the object seem legitimate on the open market. These antiquities follow convoluted smuggling paths. For example, a looted statue from Syria might be trafficked to Hong Kong, then London, then the USA, before it is bought by a museum in Sydney. The criminals know what they're doing. Each country has different import and export regulations, and, along the way, the right documents are gradually compiled – sometimes through bribery – to make the antiquity appear perfectly legal.'

'What if my hypothetical artefact was destined for a private collection?'

'Then it's unlikely to see the light of day in our lifetime.'

My heart sank. 'Surely you can catch the looters?'

'But they're not the real problem. Ultimately, it's the collectors with their obsession for artefacts that pay big bucks – and I'm talking millions. They're the ones driving the market. The looters can be forgiven. They are usually very poor, desperate for money, often for life or death reasons.'

I thought about Tommy and his operation. We sat in silence for a minute, staring over the caldera.

'Harry, I think there's somebody in Crete, dealing.' There, I'd said it.

He nodded. 'I'm sure there's more than one. You're hoping I can help you get this hypothetical artefact back?'

I nod. 'I can't tell you everything. It's difficult.'

'Then tell me as much as you can.'

I poured us both a glass of red, and then fetched my sketch-book from the house. Harry watched me open it on a detailed drawing that showed the Goddess of the Marches fresco.

'You see this necklace the queen's wearing?' He nodded. 'The actual necklace was found here, at our site. It went to Crete, almost thirty years ago. I want to – have to – get it back. Has too much time passed? Do you think it's impossible?'

Harry bunched his fist and held it over his mouth, the true scale of the discovery hitting home. After a long silence, he asked, 'Do you know the name of the person it went to?'

'I do, but I'm sure he was only trying to help someone in a desperate situation. He saved that person's life. I couldn't give his name if I thought he would get into trouble. I believe he simply passed it on without profit.'

'I see why it's difficult for you, but without a name, what can I do? The trail is dead.'

I stared at my feet for a long time. Who was more important to me – Tommy or Splotskey? Well, Tommy, of course, but without Splotskey, Tommy would be dead. How could I repay the doctor for saving Tommy's life by giving him up to the authorities?

'I can't tell you.'

He shook his head. 'Then there's nothing I can do.'

'I was thinking . . . Couldn't we chip something, and then sell it to a dealer?'

'Ah, you're fond of crime fiction, are you?' He laughed.

'What do you mean?'

'These days, it's the first thing dealers scan for, a chip. They're always one step ahead.'

'While I was in Ireland recently, someone came here to the site looking for me. They mentioned this Crete person's name. But

331

the Crete person disappeared many years ago, I know, because I tried to find him myself. I believe the dragonfly necklace is in a private collection in Crete. I can't explain why, it's just a gut feeling.'

'Without a name, what can I do? Is there anything else you can tell me?'

'I have to get it back, Harry. All this deceit . . . My family . . . they . . . oh!' And then it was all too much and I was unable to speak for a moment. He fidgeted uncomfortably. 'You see, it was me. *Me. I* took the dragonfly necklace to Crete. I'd just discovered I was pregnant and my husband was dying in hospital because we couldn't afford the surgery that would save his life. I was desperate beyond measure. It was wrong of me and I've never forgiven myself, but Tommy's life depended on it. What am I going to do? I have to get it back. Right the wrong.'

He took the napkin I'd put under his glass and passed it to me. 'Dry your eyes and tell me everything, and I promise I'll do all I can to protect you and your family.'

I told Harry the whole sorry story. My life was in his hands now, and there was relief in that.

# CHAPTER 30
## IRINI

*Crete, present day.*

Mr Mavro came into the hospital room. 'Can I have a word with you in the corridor?' he said quietly.

We followed him out.

'I understand this is a very difficult time for you all. Bridget is due her medication. I can reduce it and see what happens, but she may feel some considerable pain.' He looked at each of us in turn. 'It may be more than she can tolerate.'

'You mean it might kill her?' The ache in my throat made me whisper.

He nodded. 'We don't know if she'll be able to see you, but there is a good chance she can hear you. Her kidneys are shutting down, and her lungs are becoming too stiff to function on their own. I'm sorry we can't do more for your mother, Irini. Her death is inevitable, but there's a slight chance she may regain consciousness for a moment or two. I can perform a simple procedure that may allow her to say a few words.'

I stare through the hospital window, afraid of making the wrong decision. 'I don't want my mother to suffer, not just so I can tell her I love her, but this is a decision I can't make alone.' My heart was twisting and breaking as I peered into my father's pleading eyes.

Quinlan looked as sad as a person could.

'I'll leave you to think about it,' the doctor said, returning to my mother.

We stood in silence, holding hands in a circle until Dad spoke. 'There are things I need to say.' His lips trembled as he pulled his hands from ours and touched his eyes. I wondered if he would be able to say anything at all. He walked over to the window and turned his back on us. His shoulders jerked as he tried to control his tears.

Quinlan slipped his arm around me. 'I know you can't bear to think of causing your mother pain, but perhaps you should put yourself in her situation. What would you want if you were dying and your family were around you? How much pain could you tolerate in order to see, hear, or speak to your daughter one last time? Or would you rather slip away peacefully?'

At first there was no doubt in my mind – I would walk through fire to say goodbye to my child and my husband. But then I wondered if I was being naive and selfish. I had never experienced unbearable pain, nor could I imagine it. The worst I had ever suffered was a really bad toothache! Even my head injury in the crash was hardly debilitating. I wanted to change everything, and not being able to made me feel hopeless and helpless.

I nodded at Quinlan, then went to my father's side. He ignored me and continued to stare out the window, so I stepped in front of him and leaned into his chest. After a moment, he took me into his arms and we cried together. Deep, unrestricted sobs. His hug became tighter, until he was rocking me.

'Oh, Daddy . . .'

'Bridget,' he whispered. 'My Bridget . . . I can't bear to lose her, Irini.'

# CHAPTER 31
## BRIDGET

*Crete, one year ago.*

I WENT TO CRETE with Harry Edwards. At the hospital, we discovered Splotskey had died in a car accident. The current head of cardiology had worked under Splotskey as an intern thirty years ago. He told us Splotskey had driven over a cliff on the coast road, outside Heraklion. His blood alcohol was four times above the legal limit.

'Four times! Gosh,' I said. 'Seems like a lot.'

'Not really. Greece's limit is half our UK limit – not sure about Ireland,' Harry said. 'But still, I'll look into it. So that leaves us with the guy that tried to contact you. The phone number is pay-as-you-go, so even if we had the resources, we couldn't trace it.'

'Why don't I call him?'

'Because we might be dealing with a dangerous person who has a lot to lose. If he's trying to wipe out a trail, he'd then have your number and that could put you at considerable risk.'

'But sooner or later he's going to know I'm back in Santorini. I'm at risk already.' The thought made me nervous. 'The sooner he's caught, the sooner I'll be safe. You said there are Minoan artefacts coming onto the market, and you suspected they came from Crete.'

He nodded. 'Customs found a crate heading for Turkey. Mostly souvenirs imported to Crete from China, but among them were three small Minoan bronzes. The Chinese have a huge distribution network in Greece; you'll find their shops on almost every island, selling cheap clothes and bric-a-brac. Perfect for smuggling artefacts.'

'Can't you find out which archaeology site they came from?'

He shook his head. 'Firstly, they were cleaned up and polished, so there were no soil samples to work with, and we simply don't have the manpower to watch every archaeology dig on the island. Even if we did, they probably came from an undisclosed site.'

'An undisclosed site?'

'A building company excavating the foundations for a house or hotel. Or perhaps a guy owning a digger-for-hire, prepping for a swimming pool, came across them. Those people are always on the lookout for antiquities. They simply hold up the build a few days and pull as much stuff out of the ground as possible.'

I winced, thinking of all the lost provenance.

Harry continued: 'The government pays well for artefacts handed in, but the black market pays ten times more. If it's a big find, the looter opens a hotel or some such business in his wife's or mother's name to account for his family's sudden affluence, and everyone's happy. Anyway, it's a fact that nobody wants their house-build held up for seven years while you lot go in and excavate, so they tell the builder to keep quiet about the find.'

'You're on a losing battle,' I said, feeling hopeless.

'Isn't that the truth? But we plod on.'

\* \* \*

I was so content to be in Santorini, I didn't want to return to Ireland. I didn't want to go *back*. That was how it felt, to take a step back – into the unhappiness that had been Sitric Road. Sometimes,

336

after a blissful day at the site, I would wake in the night, startled, confused, reaching out to see if Tommy was beside me, fearing my return to Santorini had only been a dream.

Drenched in night-sweat, I would take a bottle of water from the fridge and then sit outside. The cool air was all I needed. Depending on the phase of the moon, the star-spangled sky or moonlit view added to my reverie.

I still fretted about Irini. Although she was a grown woman now, I thought about her every day. I had imaginary conversations with her, saved magazine articles that might interest her, planned meals for the day she would come over. I marked every festival on the calendar, so that whenever she turned up, I would have interesting places for her to visit. The behaviour of an obsessive mother, perhaps, but I didn't care.

I had gone back to working with Aaron at the site and loved every moment, but this in turn left me feeling guilty to have left Tommy in Dublin.

'I miss Irini and Tommy, Aaron. I long to share my contentment with them. But I don't want to go back to Dublin. All we do is fight when I'm there.'

'Why don't you Skype them, say once a month? Make it a regular time and date. I'm sure Irini will have a laptop or a smart phone.'

'That's a great idea!'

So it began. On the first Sunday of every month I called them at three o'clock. It eased my guilt, and after the awkwardness of the first few calls, the plan suited us all.

Irini announced her engagement once Jason moved to another school. She introduced me to him one Sunday afternoon on Skype. A boring-looking young man with nice manners. I was convinced it wouldn't last, but hoped I was wrong. I had

337

always imagined her with someone more exciting, more challenging. She kept me up to date with her wedding plans and I promised I would come back for the occasion.

Tommy was the same as always. Clearly, he felt as uncomfortable talking on Skype as he did on the telephone. There was nothing I could do about it. I was just pleased to be able to see them both.

The man who was looking for me did not come back. Afraid at first, I went to bed with a can of oven cleaner under my pillow. A stupid plan, perhaps – I could have blinded myself if the lid had come off in the night. But as time went on, my fear took a backseat.

The odd thing was, without Tommy or Irini to worry about, my nightmares stopped. I still had the occasional dream about Thira and Atlantis, but they were always pleasant, and in a way, comforting. I still likened myself to Thira, and Irini to Oia, and more often than not, I would wake up smiling.

The dragonfly necklace continued to worry me. Not the thought that it was hidden away by some doting collector, but that it was not being maintained in a fitting manner. To think of some aged aristocrat wearing it for a private dinner, the dragonfly necklace draped over skin splashed with astringent, then plastered in Estée Lauder foundation. Oh, and the horror of horrors, what if the necklace was then sprayed in a cloud of Chanel!

Then I had more debilitating what ifs. What if the wearer, being a little tipsy, had left it on a dressing table, only to be snatched by a drug-desperate thief? A villain with no notion of its value, a coke-brained, diamond-hunting desperado, who would snatch everything and toss what seemed worthless into the sea, or down a street drain. This thought made me actually want to vomit.

What if the owner died when the dragonfly necklace was left on the dressing table, and it ended up in some junk shop, car boot sale, or, God forbid, was melted down for the silver!

I *had* to find it.

\* \* \*

After meeting Harry in Crete, I returned to Santorini. The weeks turned into months, and the months flew by. Almost a year later, on the run-up to Irini's wedding, she Skyped to tell me she had secured a place for Tommy in the local residential home.

'I'm really sorry, Mam, I just can't cope any longer. He's not safe to leave on his own.' She went on to tell me he had run a bath and forgotten about it. 'The overflow was blocked, the bath ran over and it almost brought the living room ceiling down. Then he set the chip pan on fire because he fell asleep in front of the TV.' I could hear in her voice how difficult she was finding this decision.

'He's a danger to himself, and I'm worried about him every time I set out for work.'

'Irini, you've done the best you can. We're both grateful. Don't worry about it.'

'But I do. He hates the home, and now he's sulking. He hardly speaks when I go visit.'

'That's your father for you. It's not your fault. If anything, it's mine.' I took a breath. 'Would you like me to come over for a week or two?'

'To be honest, I could do with a couple of weeks on my own. It's been difficult, but Dad's all right now; he's taken care of twenty-four-seven. Anyway, it's not long to the wedding and you'll be over then. I'll book the guest room at the home, shall I? One week or two?'

'Two. I want to help as much as I can. What will you do with the house? Sell it?'

'No, I'll rent it out for a bit of extra income. I'm financially wiped out after moving Dad, and all the wedding deposits.'

'I wish I'd been there when you made your dress. I bet it's lovely. Will I get to see it before the wedding?'

'We'll see – if you behave yourself.' She laughed and I was uplifted by her happiness.

'I'm so pleased for you. I hope you're as happy as me and Tommy.'

'Oh, gawd! That sounds like a curse,' she said good-humouredly.

'We *were* very happy, Irini. You can't begin to imagine.'

'Until I came along?'

I sensed the conversation going the wrong way. 'No, don't say such things. We were happy beyond measure then. Anyway, where are you going for your honeymoon?' *Please say Santorini!*

'Italy. A two-destination package: Venice and Rome.'

'That sounds wonderful! I'm thrilled for you, darling.'

I closed my laptop and cried.

\* \* \*

At the site, the day was like any other, with a tinge of excitement in the air. We found more artefacts on the next level down and handed them straight over to the new museum. Some cooking implements had been uncovered, and all the time that ongoing suspense: just below the next brush stroke . . . just under the next centimetre of dirt . . . might lay the greatest artefact – a brooch, an earring, or a marble sculpture. Was this a lump of stone, or the top of an amazing statue of Zeus, Athena, or Poseidon? Was that light seam in the ground an old rodent tunnel, or a decomposed weapon?

The daily thrill of the dig was interrupted by one of the students.

'Bridget, there's a call for you in the shop!' she yelled.

Me? The shop? I'd never given the number out.

I hurried across the site. 'Hello, Bridget McGuire,' I said.

'Ah, hello, Mrs McGuire.' A woman's voice, nervous. 'I'm not sure if I have the right person. Um, sorry, but are you the head archaeologist?'

'I am. What can I do for you?'

'Um, it's difficult. Can we meet? It's important.'

'Sure. Come to the site any time – we're open until four o'clock.'

'No, I can't do that . . . I meant meet in Crete.'

'Crete! I'm not sure. Can you tell me what this is about?'

There was a long pause in which my skin started to tingle. *Crete?*

'Does 1990 B1 mean anything to you?' she whispered.

*Oh!* 'Don't tell me . . . Oh my God, not the dragonfly necklace?'

'Dragonfly necklace?' I heard a sharp intake of breath. 'Oh dear, is that yours too?'

'Wait, I'll come over right away. Who are you? Give me a number.'

'I don't want any trouble. I've had enough, really. I'm afraid. It's been terrible. I just want to give them back.'

'I swear on my daughter's life this won't go any further. You have no idea what this means to me. Where shall I meet you?'

341

She didn't answer straight away. 'I'm afraid,' she repeated.

'Look, have you got a pen? Take my mobile number and call me so I have yours. I'll be there first thing in the morning, on the first FastCat from Santorini. Please, meet me in the ticket-office café in the port. I'll be wearing all white, trousers and shirt. We can talk in the Ladies toilet if you are afraid. Please be there. Please!'

* * *

When I opened my eyes, it was morning. The light was still on, everything bathed in electric energy, unreal, and the air so warm I could hardly breathe. I showered quickly, dressed quickly, locked up, and rushed to the bus station. Did I need more money? Should I have gone to a cashpoint? Was there one at the port?

My fingers wouldn't keep still. I plucked at the knee of my linen pants and stared aimlessly out of the bus window. Who was the woman? I didn't even have a name, or an address. She had phoned my mobile, so at least I could call her if she didn't turn up – and that was my greatest fear. I realised she must have the jug, and that was what she had phoned about. I recognised the surprise in her voice when I mentioned the dragonfly necklace.

As soon as I had them in my possession, if indeed I got them back, I would phone Harry and tell him everything.

Then I would call Tommy. I nearly broke down right there in the bus just thinking about the moment when I would give him the news. The relief, this torturous trial that we had suffered for more than twenty years, over. We could return to the way we were. No more sticking knives in each other. Peace and harmony for the rest of our days. So many wasted years!

* * *

The FastCat seemed interminably slow, and the jostle of tourists unbearable as I disembarked. I raced along the cement quay, dodging holidaymakers and cars, suitcases and children, as I headed for the ticket office. Breathless with palpitations, I rushed into the café. Tables and chairs in the foyer, almost empty apart from discarded plastic beakers and crushed drink cans. In one corner, a few overweight men, smoking, huddled over tiny Greek coffees. A couple of backpackers reorganised the contents of their rucksacks on the floor. A family with three young children running wild, and the parents yelling: 'Get here now, or else!'

No woman on her own.

I bought a frappé. The caffeine hit made me even more jumpy. Despite the air-conditioning blasting away, perspiration prickled my brow. I stood and walked around, displaying my white-linen-ness, in case there was any doubt: *This is me, I'm here, waiting*. By the time half an hour had passed, I was angry. Really fucked-off angry. Me, who never swore, ever – I was fucked-off angry. This woman held it all. My peace, Tommy's peace, Irini's peace. My blessed release from over twenty years of torture was in her hands. She controlled my family's happiness for the rest of our lives.

I sat, stood, paced stiffly while listening to the sound of my own breathing. Doubt set in. Was there another ticket office, another café? Was the woman in that other place, about to leave, thinking I hadn't turned up? My heart thumped with the idea.

343

Needing space, I stepped outside and glared around like an aggressive kid in the playground: *Come on, approach me, you coward!* For a second the world seemed to stop, a photo snap of my surroundings, a frozen image of every car, every person. No sign of a lonely woman with a package.

The scene snapped into fast forward. Vehicles hurriedly parking, people dragging their suitcases, parents rounding up kids, backpackers studying maps. Still no woman on her own. It occurred to me she may be sitting in one of the parked cars, watching, seeing me hunched and glowering, giving off hostile vibes. I took a breath, relaxed my shoulders, and wiped the perspiration from my brow.

*I'm here. I'm a nice, kind person. Approachable. Come to me. Put an end to my misery. I'll help you do what's right.*

Then it was all too much. I leaned against a pillar, dropped my head in my hands and wept. So close. Why hadn't she come? Everything would have fallen into place and my wrongs righted.

'Bridget McGuire?'

I gasped, dropped my hands, and stared at the woman. Five feet tall at most. Late sixties. Bleached hair tightly permed and stiffly lacquered. Subtle, expensive perfume. Skin sun-wrinkled but expertly made-up. Professional French manicure. Pale blue eyes.

'Oh, thank God!' I whispered. 'I thought you weren't going to come.'

'Sorry, but I had to make sure you were alone. Will you get in my car?'

'Sure.' I sniffed, emotionally drained. Her new but cheap 4x4 was silver, with a booster-cushion on the driver's seat.

She drove into Heraklion, hugging the sandstone city wall until we came to the Chania Gate, which she drove through, and then parked near a towering, simple wooden cross. We got out of the car and walked over a grassed area towards a rectangle of enormous granite blocks, crudely hewn and pushed together. At one end, a cream marble slab was simply engraved with three lines of Greek letters. She raised a hand, indicating the inscribed tombstone.

'*I hope for nothing, I fear nothing, I am free,*' she quoted. 'Do you know the works of Nikos Kazantzakis?'

'I've read *Zorba the Greek*.'

'You should read *The Last Temptation of Christ*.'

I wondered why we were discussing books at a time like this. I couldn't keep my desperation out of my voice any longer. 'Why have you brought me here?'

'I want you to understand the mentality of Nikos Kazantzakis. If you did, you would have some sympathy for my husband, and perhaps a little forgiveness for what he did.'

'No, I don't mean here on this hill, I mean why have you brought me to Crete? Do you have the dragonfly necklace?'

She met my eyes and nodded.

My relief was so intense, I dropped onto my haunches, my back against the granite, and placed my hands over my face again. The struggle to hold my composure was a losing battle.

*Oh! Oh!*

She gave me a few minutes to recompose. 'I can see it means a lot to you.'

I wiped my eyes and pulled myself together. 'I made a terrible mistake many years ago and I've suffered for it ever since. Not just me. It caused a rift between my husband and I, and inadvertently my darling daughter too. If I can right the wrong that I did, then perhaps . . . I don't know, maybe . . . we can all come back together. Start to heal.'

We sat side by side on the granite. A sprig of vermilion bougainvillea wilted before the headstone, and the shadow of the cross fell in a dark stripe over our laps.

'I see,' she said after a thoughtful pause. Staring at the limp flowers, she said, 'My husband died two weeks ago.' She swallowed, frowned, her pain obvious. 'He was obsessed with ancient history – his heritage, he called it – and he collected things. It started with a small bronze goblet his grandfather dug up in the olive grove half a century ago. My husband traded up, and bought inherited bits from other Greeks who were desperate for money and had no idea of the value of some old pot or piece of bric-a-brac. Fishermen too, they were happy to exchange a barnacle-encrusted sculpture of marble or bronze, which tore their nets, for more hard cash than their catch would earn in a week.

'What started as an investment of a few thousand euros, ended up with a collection that I know is worth many millions. I found this hoard recently. He kept it locked away, a secret room, a mini museum for his eyes only. Now I'm trying to return the artefacts to their rightful places.'

'That's very noble of you, but why don't you simply hand them over to a museum?'

'He is . . . was . . . a very important person and, for the sake of his children and grandchildren, I don't want his name sullied. That's why I'm repatriating them myself. Anyway, my husband was a good man, but Minoan artefacts were his weakness, his temptation. Can I be assured they'll go straight to a museum?'

'I swear on my life.'

'That might be relevant, because there are other people after them. Dangerous people. Someone who was supplying my husband has threatened me.' She glanced around nervously. 'This man seems to think I'm dealing. I've been approached . . . At my age it's quite frightening. I think we're safe here, and I'll be glad to get rid of them.'

'Who is this person? Do you have a name?' I said, thinking of Harry. 'We need to catch these dealers.'

'No, I don't have a name. But my husband bought a few pieces from someone excavating a secret site near Agios Nikolaus, here on Crete.'

'Not the Sacred City of Istron?' I said quietly, thinking of my dreams.

She looked surprised and nodded.

'Please, tell me everything you know. I swear I will never involve you in anything,' I said encouragingly.

She jumped as some tourists approached. 'Not now. Let's go back.' She glanced around nervously again. 'This man, I don't know his real name but he calls himself Delta. Since my husband died, he has called me several times offering to buy my husband's collection. He says he wants to repatriate the artefacts, but I don't believe him. To be honest, I'm afraid of him.'

'I know somebody, a good man working for Interpol, he would take care of everything for you. His name's Harry Edwards. You can simply hand everything over to him. You haven't broken any laws, and you'd remain anonymous.' I pulled Harry's card from my wallet. 'Here, tell him I gave you his number. You'll be safe with him, I promise.'

Once we were in the car, the woman delved into her oversized Michael Kors and pulled out a carrier bag that seemed to be taped over a box. 'Here, hide them quickly. I'll take you back now and drop you. Airport or port?'

'Port,' I said, thinking of the security check at the airport.

An hour later, at the ferry, I scurried across the clanging metal boarding ramp, buffeted by the draught of articulated lorries rushed aboard by stevedores. Clearly, everyone was desperate to make the departure time. Despite billowing diesel fumes on the car deck, and the pushing and shoving of eager passengers, I relished being aboard the ship.

Almost light-headed with relief to have reached a safe haven, I took the escalator up to the air-conditioned lounge deck. This was the last boat of the day to Santorini – the slow ferry. Inside my tote was the package that I dared not open, not yet. I had to find a secure place and examine the contents in private.

# CHAPTER 32
## IRINI

*Crete, present day.*

BACK IN THE HOSPITAL ROOM, the doctor and nurse stood in the corner. I held my mother's hand and noticed its coolness. Dad sat opposite me and held her other hand. We both gazed at my mother's face, waiting for a sign.

'Mam, we're here by your bed. Me and Dad and Quinlan.' My father was too upset to speak and my heart broke for him.

Quinlan patted his back and said, 'Come on, Tommy. Bridget knows you love her. Just because you're a narky old bugger doesn't mean she doesn't love you. The woman's worshipped the ground you walked on from the moment she set eyes on you.'

Dad nodded, rummaged for his hankie and blew his nose. When he was done, I noticed my mother was breathing heavily, then a strange whisper escaped. My heart leaped, and I hoped, hoped, hoped the doctor was wrong. Would she recover?

'Mam, it's me, Irini. I want to tell you how much I love you. I understand everything now. I know you loved me, and I know what a sacrifice it was for you to make sure I was safe. I hope you can forgive me. I should have moved towards you when I was older instead of being so selfish and self-righteous.' I said it in a rush, a panic, sounding both phoney and disrespectful, but I couldn't think because my head was so full of hopes and wishes, and my heart was both exploding and mashed to bits.

'I want to tell you, Mammy. When I was in the convent, there was a nun – Sister Bridget – and she had auburn hair just like yours too. I imagined she was you, secretly looking out for me, making sure I was all right. I built up a fantasy in my little head. Wasn't that crazy? But you see, it meant I never forgot you, and always felt you were there near me. Sister Bridget loved me too, I felt it.'

Mam's lips hardly moved, but there was a soft sound whispering from her. Her face was completely still, yet I sensed that she smiled and I filled up with the saddest joy.

I leaned over and kissed her cheek. 'Can you hear me, Mam? I'm really sorry.'

Her eyes remained closed, but the sound came again. My throat was so painful I couldn't speak, but then I remembered she might only have a moment. I put my ear over her mouth to catch every syllable.

'Tell me, Mam, what is it?'

'Forgive . . . Love . . . Love . . .'

*Oh!*

'I love you too. So does Dad. He loves you so much he can't speak right now.'

'Alone?' The word hardly more than a breath.

'The doctor and nurse are here. Me and Dad and Quinlan will stay with you. Don't be afraid. We won't leave you. We love you, Mammy.'

'Secret . . .'

'What secret? Dad has told me everything. There's nothing to worry about. We'll get the dragonfly necklace and the jug back if we can, I promise you.'

'Secret. Game. Remember.' She pants softly between the words. 'Secret. Game. Remember.'

What was she saying? I didn't understand. 'What game, Mam? I don't understand.'

'Try. Remember. Love . . . love. Forgive. Love you, Tommy.'

My father found his voice. 'I love you too, darling girl,' he cried out.

Mam panted three times, and then she was gone.

*Gone!*

Just like that. She seemed to melt into the sheet and the monitor on the wall flatlined.

*No, not yet, not yet! There is so much I want to say. So many words queuing in my head. Don't go, Mammy . . . Please don't go!*

Dad lowered his head so it was against the back of her hand and started sobbing quietly.

'No . . . Oh no . . .' he whispered. 'My Bridget, my life.'

Now tears raced down my face. Poor Dad. Poor Quinlan.

*Oh, Mam!*

We stayed by her bed while the doctor did various tests, then he wrote on the clipboard at the bottom of her bed: *Time of death – 11.59 p.m.*

Dad wouldn't let go of my mother's hand.

# CHAPTER 33
## BRIDGET

*Crete, present day.*

MY JOURNEY IS ALMOST OVER. Would I have changed anything, knowing what I know now? Well, yes, but I don't know what. The people I love will put my body to rest in Santorini; and my mind, too, seems to have found peace at last. If I know my daughter, I believe she will find the dragonfly necklace before Tommy comes to join me in the afterlife, and he will feel a weight lifted from him when that happens.

Poor Tommy. His bitterness was simply because he blamed himself for the wrong I did.

I look down on my empty body. Irini, Tommy, and Quinlan are so terribly sad. They grieve for me and I ache for them. I hope they have learned from my mistakes. The lines between past, present, and future melt away, and my sadness for Irini lifts because suddenly I *know* she has great things ahead of her. She cries now, but her burden will ease with the joy and happiness of a wonderful life that awaits her.

My last few days of mortal toil were worth every moment. In this timeless, endless dimension, I feel a hand slip into mine, and I glance sideways. Thira is beside me. Her serenity overwhelms any anguish I may have experienced on my own.

She smiles softly. *Don't be afraid, sister. You are at peace now, and your people will travel the path of their destinies, holding the memory of you close in their hearts.*

I turn back to my family and recall the last few hours of my struggle to put things right.

# CHAPTER 34
## BRIDGET

*Santorini, one day before the accident.*

THE PORT OF HERAKLION had given me an uneasy feeling. I felt eyes on me, and malevolence warmed the air. Once on the ship, I rushed to the Ladies room and stayed inside a cubicle until I felt the ship leaving port. I planned to stay there for the entire trip, but soon found it impossible. Only two toilets, and no sooner had I opened my bag, someone was knocking urgently on the door. Unable to see who was there, I was too afraid to come out. With my nerves at snapping point, I listened to my neighbour as she vomited noisily. I could hear women chatting and realised the small Ladies had filled. Again, someone knocked urgently. I flushed the loo and rushed out.

I had to open my valuable package in private.

With the tote strap over my shoulder and the bag clutched fiercely under my arm, I went below decks and marched down narrow corridors of cabins, which made me feel trapped. Back on the passenger deck, I noticed a door marked *Mother and Baby*. Inside, I found a changing table, a nursing chair, and a toilet cubicle. Once inside the WC, I locked the door. Although I longed to splash cold water over my face, the urgency of the moment gripped me.

The carrier was taped around a large plastic sandwich box. Inside lay a pale-pink scarf printed with gold feathers. Barely breathing, I folded back the fabric. There it was. The little jug, swathed in bubble wrap. *Oh!*

Someone had come into the changing room. A baby cried. The mother there-there'd her infant.

I thought of Irini. Of everything I'd missed. Could I turn the clock back? No, but perhaps I could undo some damage.

I coughed, letting the stranger know I was there, unsure why; it seemed a courtesy. The ceramic jug filled my palm. I stared for a moment longer, then replaced the bubble wrap and returned it carefully into my tote.

If my heart would stop racing . . . if I could breathe . . . if the rest of my life was not suspended by the gossamer thread of the next few seconds. I lifted the next layer of scarf.

Sometimes, there are no words to describe a feeling. *Overawed* is at least succinct.

The necklace was attached to a cream velveteen display stand from a jeweller's window. My hands trembled. I almost touched it, wanting to confirm it was real. Then I withdrew my fingertips and placed them over my mouth.

I glanced around the cubicle, almost expecting to see Thira. According to the frescoes, the Goddess of the Marches actually wore that very same necklace four thousand years ago. There was the link that Tommy had hoped and prayed for. The proof that our Atlantis suspicions were finally a reality.

The necklace was smaller than I remembered, the string of filigree dragonflies more delicate, more beautiful.

I stared at it for a long time; a timeless time. This scrap of silver had caused so much pain to three people in my life. I had no notion if my dreams were pure fantasy, or really a vision of the past. If they were some kind of historical disclosure, then Thira's heart had shattered when she held this very necklace after Oia's death.

The thought bestowed such honour, that somehow the fates had chosen me as a vehicle by which Thira's story would come to light. The overwhelming idea made me whisper: 'Thank you'.

Although the concept was nothing of my own religion, it seemed holy . . . sacred.

I heard the woman leave. After several more minutes of self-indulgent nostalgia, I covered the necklace, replaced the jug, and then put the box back in my tote. Suddenly hungry and realising I hadn't eaten since the day before, I made a plan.

In the gift shop, I bought a notebook, pen, a packet of envelopes, and a book of stamps. Then I returned to the café deck, bought a tuna-mayo baguette, and found a quiet corner. I placed the tote behind my legs and slipped my foot through the handles for safety.

By the time I had finished writing, we were pulling into the caldera. I hurried to the gift shop, knowing it closed before docking, and popped my letter into the mailbox. I wished I'd had time to write another one.

* * *

Spiro waited on the quayside, but the edgy feeling that I was being watched stayed with me.

'Bridget, who you look for?' Spiro asked. 'Why you break your neck all the way up from the port?'

'I'm feeling spooked, Spiro. I thought someone was following me.'

'You want to come eat at my house?'

'You're too kind, but I'm very tired. I had a busy day in Crete and it's getting late.'

He dropped me at the top of the steps and I hurried down onto the patio. Every nerve tingled, every sense heightened by anxiety. I quickly hid the box before anyone could catch up to me and watch from one of the many rooftops that overlooked

355

our house. Once I had carefully concealed the box, I turned all the lights on, inside and out, and wrote a couple of cryptic clues as to the artefacts' hiding place, just in case.

Was I being melodramatic? With the box worth several million dollars on the black market, I didn't think so.

At eight o'clock in the morning, I planned to share the news with Aaron. To see the necklace first-hand would be one of the greatest moments of his archaeological life, and I could not deny him that thrill. Besides, I wanted him with me until I had handed it over. Then, at a more reasonable hour, remembering Ireland was two hours behind Greece, I would Skype Tommy and show him the necklace that he had only seen for a few minutes, twenty-nine years ago.

Once Tommy had received the good news and seen the necklace for himself, I planned to call the local newspaper to witness the moment I handed the artefacts to the director of the museum.

Had I forgotten anything? I didn't think so.

At five-thirty in the morning I made a coffee. For a second, I wondered if his dreams were as belligerent as his waking hours, and for no reason, the thought made me smile.

The house lights had blazed all night. Outside, everywhere was still, nobody about. I turned all the lights out and took my drink onto the patio. Dawn was breaking. I thought about Queen Thira. When I closed my eyes, I saw her wearing the dragonfly necklace and I felt her pleasure for me, how she was proud of my actions. I realised that in all my dreams, since the death of Oia, I had not seen the necklace.

A blade of silver separated the sea and sky on the horizon. Again, I was reminded of one of my dreams. Dawn over Atlantis. As light gathered around me, so did the joy in my heart. I heard the town stir and gradually wake. Soon, the world would know the relevance of this day. I had retrieved the dragonfly necklace!

I went over my plan.

I dared not take the artefacts to the site. I couldn't help worrying about the dealer that the widow was so afraid of. I wondered if he had followed me onto the ship. Or, if he saw me go aboard, he might have taken a flight to Santorini. He could be waiting for me anywhere. He could be watching me right now, though I doubted it. Even villains had to sleep. I was so close to putting everything right, I could not afford to take chances. Irini had said she would come to Santorini. And if anything happened to me she would have to come, so I left her a cryptic note to tell her where the necklace was hidden. I hoped she never needed to figure it out.

But it was better to play safe. Artefact dealers could be every bit as dangerous as drug dealers.

* * *

I got off my bicycle at the site entrance. My muscles ached, my mouth was dry, and every nerve was tense. I glanced over my shoulder at the sparse landscape that rolled down to the sea. I couldn't see or hear anyone. The gate was locked. Where could Aaron be? I let myself in and locked the gate behind me. Feeling light-headed due to lack of sleep, I stared around the site and listened hard. In the distance, church bells rang eight o'clock. Aaron should have arrived by now. I phoned him.

'Hi, Bridget! I'm on my way to get diesel for the generator. Do you need anything? I'll bring a couple of baguettes for lunch, if you like—'

I cut him off. 'I need to talk to you, Aaron. It's urgent. Please come back, soon as you can.'

If Aaron was surprised by my tone of voice, he didn't show it. He said he'd be there as soon as possible and hung up.

Calliope, who sold entrance tickets and ran the shop, arrived.

'Morning, Poppy!' I called, feeling a sense of security at the sound of my own voice.

'Good morning, Bridget!' She beamed and her statement lifted me further. This *was* a good morning, one of the best mornings of my life. So much would be put right on this day.

Nathan slouched in after Poppy, as he so often did, arriving on the local bus. His hoody was pulled down low, giving him the appearance of a monk.

'You all right, Nathan?' I asked.

He shook his head. 'Crap! Toothache – it's driving me nuts! Haven't slept a wink.' He slumped into a chair in the tea corner, then stood and paced. 'Aaargh! I want to pull it out myself!' He punched himself in the cheek.

'Shall I run him up to Grigoris? I can't see him getting much done as he is,' Poppy asked.

A couple of elderly Chinese tourists with professional cameras had followed Nathan into the site. I felt easier with the tourists about. 'Yes, take him. Try and get the next bus back, will you, Nathan? They're every hour.'

Another tourist arrived. Poppy sold them all tickets and then Nathan followed her to the car park.

'I'll be as quick as I can!' she called over her shoulder.

'Excuse me, miss,' the Chinese guy said politely. 'Where can we see the fresco of the River Festival?' He had Aaron's book in his hand.

My face flushed with embarrassment. 'I'm sorry, they're in the National Archaeological Museum in Athens.'

He spoke to his wife in Chinese, clipped, breathy words of frustration, then he turned back to me. 'Ah, so. We went to Athens and saw a few of the Santorini frescoes there, but they said the rest were here. We came all the way from China specially to see the frescoes of the town and the River Festival. We bought this from the internet.' He lifted the book.

'I'm so sorry. Some of the frescoes are in our prehistoric museum here. It's near the bus station in town.' They both looked utterly disappointed. 'I can show you where they were found, and if you come back tomorrow morning, the author will be happy to sign the book for you.'

Their faces lifted. 'Thank you!'

I led them down from the viewing gantry. 'Please don't touch anything. Some of the walls are still very unstable. We don't usually allow tourists down here.'

The other tourist, a dark-haired man, easily as big as Aaron, was dressed in jeans and an immaculate white T-shirt. He came to their side. Although simply dressed, he had an air of wealth about him, intensified by the heavy gold watch on his wrist, perhaps a Rolex. Black Ray-Bans hid his eyes. He nodded, but didn't speak.

We walked through the site. I pointed out the various areas described in Aaron's book and the Chinese couple were clearly excited. When we arrived at the triangular square, where Irini was born, I pointed to the wall.

'This is where the goddess fresco covered the wall. It seems that she ruled the island before the volcano erupted.'

The Chinese couple held the book open at that page and chatted excitedly to each other.

I took a pinch of crushed plaster dust from between the stones and sprinkled it between the pages of their book.

'Four-thousand-year-old stucco from the back of the fresco. A special souvenir for you.' I pointed at the necklace around the queen's neck. 'And talking of souvenirs, in the shop you can buy an exact copy of that dragonfly in the centre of the necklace. The archaeologist who wrote this book had copies made.'

'Thank you!' the man said, conversing with his wife excitedly, then he looked at his watch.

The large man, who had been listening to our conversation, lowered his glasses and stared into my eyes. A chill ran down my spine and the hairs on my arms rose.

'Where's the dragonfly necklace now?'

My blood turned to ice. He had found me. What the hell was delaying Aaron?

The Chinese couple bowed again, oblivious to the danger I sensed. 'Thank you, thank you. We will come back tomorrow.' They turned to head for the bus returning to town.

'Wait!' I didn't want to be left alone with the man. 'Wouldn't you like to see more? Let me accompany you to the shop.'

'We have a tight schedule. Now we will go to the museum in the town.' They hurried towards the exit, small, fast steps, the man cradling his book.

'The dragonfly necklace,' the large man said again, his voice deep and menacing. 'Where is it?'

I stood tall, calling on Thira to guide me as I tried to mask the nerves in my voice. 'I believe it's in a private collection, in Crete.'

'*I* believe you have it.'

'Me?' I blinked at him, feigning surprise.

*Where the hell was Aaron?!*

The stranger pushed his glasses up again, hiding his eyes. 'Don't play games with me, Bridget McGuire. I'll pay a fair price and take it off your hands.'

'You seem to be at an advantage, sir, knowing my name. What do they call you?' I was playing for time, hoping someone would return to the site – and soon!

'They call me Delta,' he said. 'But I'm sure you know that.'

My skin seemed to shrink over my body, fear thumping at my ribcage. I swallowed hard and stared boldly into his face. 'What would you call a fair price, Delta?'

'I need to see it first.'

'*If* I had the dragonfly necklace and handed it over to you, what would you do with it?'

'The necklace would be safe in another private collection, enjoyed by the owner rather than hidden away in some museum basement like so many of your frescoes.' He nodded towards the exit. 'You know very well those people who travelled halfway around the world are never going to see all the frescoes, don't you?' He huffed angrily. 'It's criminal that so many of the world's greatest treasures are taken away, never seen by the public again. Now don't mess with me. I know you're dealing, so you can stop the pretence and name your price.'

'How do you know? And how did you find me?' My heart hammered against my ribs.

'I saw you, yesterday.' He looked around again. 'A year ago, I came over to see if we could come to an arrangement, but you weren't here. How much do you want for the necklace?'

'I don't want money.'

'Then what do you want? Tell me.' The threatening tone left his voice and I relaxed a little.

'I might consider an exchange. What do you have from the Minoan era?' *Aaron, where are you?!*

'Bronze artefacts? Jewellery? Weapons? What's your speciality?' He folded his arms across his wide chest, his stance less aggressive.

361

Dare I try and gain something from this? 'Do you have anything from the Istron site?'

His brow furrowed and the slight twitch of his jaw told me I had hit a nerve.

'What do you know about the Istron site?' He glanced around, confirming we were still alone.

'I know enough. Take me there, I want to see it, then I'll consider selling you the necklace.' I spoke to my reflection in his sunglasses, glad he'd replaced them. I would not have had the nerve to bluff him out if I had to look into his eyes.

'You're lying. Nobody knows about the Sacred City; it's just a rumour between archaeologists.' He dropped his arms to his sides and bunched his fists. 'Now stop trying to fuck me over and get the necklace!'

Aaron's pick-up screeched to a halt outside. At last! Relief surged through my body. The stranger stepped behind a wall. I stuck my hand in the air and drew a breath to shout, but in that same moment I saw the man's shadow come alongside me, and pain spliced my head.

# CHAPTER 35
## IRINI

*Crete, present day.*

IT'S OVER. I didn't want to leave the hospital, to leave my mother. It seemed disloyal. As if the whole event of her death was reversible so long as I stayed close, in the vicinity of her spirit. I wanted to catch her life and throw it back at her so hard it fixed itself to her body and she could not let it go. The raising of Lazarus. They say 'life goes on', but no, it does not go on, not in the same way. Everything is changed, off-kilter, out of sync.

I stood in the hospital corridor, feeling cheated and empty, yet full of the deepest despair. My mother had gone and I sensed the greatest part of me had left the building too. I needed to catch myself and put myself back together. Yet at the same time, I felt she was near, with me. My mother. *Oh, Mam!*

Her last words came back to me. What did she mean: *secret, game, remember*?

Was her spirit watching as I walked towards the car park in the cool night air? Or perhaps she had already entered heaven. Perhaps there was no heaven and I clung to a fairy-tale. Misled by a lifetime of teachings from the church. Could it be that I am all that remains of my mother? I gained a little strength from that thought. I *am* part of Bridget McGuire, her flesh and blood. The deepest sadness dragged at the corners of my mouth and, much as I wanted to comfort my father, I could not speak.

I thought about her last words again. They didn't make sense.

Quinlan drove us back to the hotel that Angelo had arranged. We sat in the lounge, silent and miserable, each with a brandy that we didn't really want, alone apart from a smartly dressed man at the bar.

'Bridget wanted to be buried in Santorini,' Dad said. 'I know she made all the arrangements with the priest years ago. She bought a plot for us both. We'll sort out the funeral business tomorrow and she'll be buried the day after.'

How could he talk about her like that? I couldn't quite accept that she had died. I knew the facts, of course I did, but they didn't feel real.

'So soon?' I wanted to slow everything down. 'Can't we wait a few days?'

'It's about the only thing that's done on time in this country,' my father said gloomily.

'What do you think she meant: "secret, game, remember"? I can't stop thinking about it. When I was little, did we have a secret game?'

He was not listening.

'Dad, do you remember a secret game at all?'

He shook his head. 'Can't think . . .'

'Perhaps it wasn't a secret game,' Quinlan said. 'Could it be: keep it a secret. Remember the game. What was your favourite game when you were little, Irini?'

'Nothing special. Snakes and ladders, noughts and crosses. I used to play hide and seek too.'

We sat in silence until Dad spoke. 'There was a snake at the site once. Fell in a trench and couldn't get out. There are ladders there too. Can't think of anything relevant though.'

Quinlan went to the bar to pay for the drinks and returned with a puzzled look. 'Drinks were on the house, with the condolences of the hotel,' he said. 'Apparently that was the owner sitting at the bar.'

I blinked at the empty barstool. The owner. That was Angelo's brother, Damian? How did he know my mother had died? We hadn't had a chance to tell anyone yet.

* * *

The next morning, we had papers to sign at the hospital. Tired and defeated, I went to see my mother's specialist. Dad and Quinlan dealt with the hospital formalities. I feared this was the only chance I would get to talk to Mr Mavro.

'Please, take a seat.' Mr Mavro stood as I entered his consulting room, then indicated the chair opposite his desk.

'I wanted to thank you for the way you looked after my mother.'

He smiled sadly. 'It's my job. I'm sorry we couldn't do more for Mrs McGuire.'

'Also, there's something I wanted to ask you. I know this sound crazy, but I've searched the internet and I can't find the answer. You did say I could speak to you at any time.'

'I appreciate you looking it up, Irini. I wish all my patients did that. But you have me intrigued. What's your question?'

'I want to know if you can inherit a memory from, say, your mother, grandmother, or even further back. I mean, I've read about people who have said they were somewhere in a past life and describe it perfectly. Is it *possible* to inherit the memory of a place or an event in that way? Like I inherited my grandmother's red hair, or some people inherit a great artistic talent, or a singing voice, and so on?'

His head dropped to one side. 'Interesting question. One that's been discussed and argued over since the earliest medical writings. Pliny the Elder, Hippocrates, Darwin, and Sigmund Freud all discussed similar hypotheses. There are many theories, but in truth we don't really know. Why do you ask?'

'I wondered if my mother could have inherited the memory of an event from antiquity. It sounds crazy, I know, but she wrote things she could not have known, and with intense feeling too, as if she actually experienced them. I sensed these events were very real to her.'

Mr Mavro sat up and blinked at me. 'Have you ever thought you were psychic, experiencing your mother's thoughts like that?'

I almost laughed. 'No, not at all. I've never believed in that stuff.'

'Have you experienced any headaches lately?' His eyes narrowed slightly and his expression changed to a look of concern.

'Well, yes. I had a car accident on my first day here and the doctor said I suffered a little concussion, but nothing to be alarmed about.'

He turned my mother's notes over and wrote something on the back. 'When you get home, you must take this to your doctor,' he said, passing the notes over. 'You should be tested, to make sure you don't have the rogue gene. Now, your question. According to the latest research, there's a suggestion that memories *can* be passed down to later generations, through genetic switches. This means offspring may subconsciously inherit the memory of certain experiences of their ancestors. New studies show it's possible for some information to be inherited biologically, through chemical changes that occur in our DNA. So you may not be too far off the mark with your question. But from antiquity, you say?'

I nodded, relieved he had taken me seriously.

'I've never heard of anything like that, over such a time span. I can refer you to a specialist if it would put your mind at ease.'

I shrugged, thinking of my depleted funds. 'I'm not sure. Now that my mother's gone, there seems little point.'

\* \* \*

The next morning, my father, Quinlan, and I took the FastCat to Santorini. Everything about the island seemed disrespectfully vibrant and alive.

My mother's funeral was at three o'clock. Spiro picked us up from the port and then hurriedly helped arrange the front room to accommodate the coffin. I was weighed down by grief. At eleven-thirty the undertakers arrived at the *hyposkafa* with the casket. A stand was set in the front room, the casket lid removed and rested against the wall outside.

My poor mother lay under a blanket of white chrysanthemums, with only her hands and face showing. She looked so serene with her auburn hair shining and lips plump and moist. I had the impression she would wake with a smile and thought it ironic that I'd never seen her look so beautiful in life.

Female mourners, dressed in black, brought their own chairs and umbrellas, and sat around the patio perimeter. They talked quietly, crossing themselves often. Indoors, at one end of the room, stood a table covered in a white lace cloth. On it, flowers, candles, and pictures of the Holy Trinity surrounded an ornately framed photograph of my mother.

A stream of people arrived. Each one lit a candle at the shrine and stood it in the box of sand next to the table. The number of local people that came to pay their respects, and their display of emotion, moved me. Local men and women spoke softly to Dad and me, then they worked their way around the patio, exchanging condolences and hugging friends. There were no smiles, no celebration of life; the sombre occasion reflected all the misery of death.

At two o'clock, the casket was placed in a hearse. Mourners, led by my father and me, then Quinlan and Aaron, followed on foot. The austere pageant crawled through the town of Fira. Traders closed their doors and stood outside, heads bowed. Many left their shops and joined the procession.

The church bell tolled the funeral knell above the Catholic church. One flat and depressing 'dong' every ten seconds. Inside, garish icons with doleful eyes looked down on the pews and crammed aisles. The service bellowed into the streets from a loudspeaker on the church tower. In the fishing harbour below, fishermen stepped off their boats and stood beside piles of yellow nets on the quayside, hands clasped and heads lowered. Melancholy hung over the town.

Everyone knew Bridget McGuire the archaeologist, and everyone mourned her death.

I tried to concentrate on the service, but my mother's last words were still bothering me. They were important to her, or she would not have made the effort to say them.

*Secret. Game. Remember.*

After the service, we led a convoy of black Mercedes up the hillside towards the cemetery. The casket was closed and lowered into a white marble tomb. Mourners filed past, each one dropping a single white rose onto the coffin. The priest swung

368

and clanked his thurible, and plumes of sweet frankincense hung sickly in the air.

Overcome by tiredness, I leaned heavily against Aaron at the graveside. Quinlan was supporting my father.

'What will happen now?' I whispered as four burly men lifted the marble slab into place.

'Not much,' Aaron said. 'They'll close and seal the tomb, then say a few prayers.'

'Aaron, you know when I was little and my mother brought me to the site, do you remember what games I used to play?'

He frowned and shook his head. 'It's a long time ago. Let's see. Mostly you would draw or paint, but if you got restless one of us would play a board game with you. Sometimes Tommy would play noughts and crosses in the dust. You didn't understand the game, but Tommy would always shout: "You won! You won again, Irini!" when the last square was filled in. We could hear him all over the site and we would laugh too.'

I smiled, imagining the scene. Poor Dad. He was punishing himself now.

'Look, Irini, that's the guy that came looking for your mother.'

I spun around, staring in the direction he was pointing. 'What are you talking about?'

'When Bridget came back, a year ago, it was because he came to the site looking for her. I'm sure that's him.'

My heartbeat raced. 'Where? Which one?' I asked peering at the crowd that had come to the cemetery.

'No, over the road, behind the cars.' He glanced at me, then turned. 'Oh, he's gone.'

'So, somebody was looking for my mother? Is that what you phoned her about just before she left Dublin?'

He nodded. 'Bridget seemed eager to meet him.'

Who was he? Did he have something to do with my mother's accident? If only I'd seen where he'd disappeared to. I stood on my toes trying to spot him.

'Excuse me,' a young man said, distracting me. 'Are you Bridget's daughter?'

I nodded.

He held out a hand. 'I'm Nathan Scott. I just wanted to say that your mother was a marvellous person and I'm proud to have known her. She inspired me even before I met her, then I wittered on to her about archaeology all the way on a flight from Athens to Santorini, a year ago. I didn't know it was her. She must have thought I was nuts, but she was very kind. When I found out who she was, I could have died, really. Over the past twelve months, she taught me so much. It has been a great honour working for Bridget McGuire, I'll never forget her.'

A few simple words of condolence, yet they made me incredibly proud. Aaron slipped his arm around my shoulders and gave me a squeeze.

I swallowed hard and smiled at the young man. 'Thank you, Nathan, that means a lot to me,' I whispered, unable to hold back my tears any longer.

\*   \*   \*

A few days later I was back in Dublin. I returned to teaching and also to my old bar job at the Raglan Road in the evenings, to help clear my credit card debt. At seven o'clock on Saturday, I entered the pub and threw a cheery smile towards Brian, the landlord.

'Irini, you had a call from Crete just now. Angelo, he said – sounded foreign.'

*Angelo!* Oh, how often I had longed to be in his arms again. I could banish him from my bed, but not from my heart. My feelings for him were as strong as ever, and I hated myself for wanting him. There were moments when I found myself hoping, dreaming, and then getting angry with myself. Women have affairs with married men, they do, but could I? No, not under any circumstances. I couldn't do that to Sofia, or myself. Not after how Jason had hurt me. I had to leave Angelo in the past. I was destined to nurse my broken heart, hoping one day my scars would heal and I could move on.

'Any message?' I asked matter-of-factly as I started to bottle-up the fridge. My heart thumped as I lifted beers from the crate and shelved them in the chiller behind the bar.

'Nope.' Brian squinted sideways. 'He said he'd been trying to call you, but your phone was always turned off. Anyway, he's going to call again later.'

I wondered how Angelo had the pub's number. Fergus McFadden, who had taken to frequenting the Raglan Road since his return from Crete, winked at me and I suspected the old man had been up to mischief.

Although the bar kept me busy, I jumped like popcorn whenever the phone rang, but Angelo never called.

\* \* \*

That night, I tossed and turned in my bed.

Thoughts of Angelo kept me awake. I had to accept it was over, even though it had hardly begun. I tortured myself, hoping all sorts of things, but he was married and that was the end of it. I had made a mistake. Now it was time to leave the past where it belonged and move on.

I only wished my heart would listen to my head.

The next morning, I decided to accept any work Retro Emporio offered, not that I had any choice as the retainer had already gone towards Mam's hospital bill. Nevertheless, despite working for his company, I would cold-shoulder any romantic advances from Angelo.

On Sunday evening in the pub, the phone rang – louder, it seemed, than usual.

'Raglan Road public house, can I help you?' I said.

'Irini McGuire?'

'Angelo?' *The eyes, the voice, the smell of him, the weight of his body.*

*His wife, his son, his marriage.*

'Ah, you remember me then?'

I dampened my feelings and injected impatience into my voice. 'Yes, of course, but I'm at work . . . What can I do for you?'

'I am very sorry about your mother. I would have gone to Santorini for the funeral, but I had big problems with my family—'

'I know, Sofia told me,' I interrupted.

'Sofia? What is Sofia telling you?' The smile left his voice.

'She told me everything, Angelo.' *Tell me it's not true. Tell me that night meant as much to you as it did to me.*

'Everything?' Several seconds of silence, then: 'I have to see you. I'm in London and there's a flight to Dublin tonight.'

My heart sank. He didn't even try to deny it. I had clutched at a grain of hope when there was none.

'No, it's impossible,' I whispered.

'Why? Because of my family?'

'Yes, of course. Do you think it doesn't matter?'

'Irini, I have to see you, to explain.'

'There's nothing to explain. Go back to your family. Goodbye, Angelo.' I hung up, my hands shaking.

I sat on the stool and stared at the phone. It couldn't end like this, after so much – and so little.

I hurried into the Ladies, wanting to hide my misery. I had just splashed cold water onto my face when someone knocked on the door.

Brian called, 'Irini, your phone's ringing!'

I'd forgotten to turn it off for work. I hurried out, stupidly hoping it was Angelo.

'Hi, Irini, it's Paula. I've been trying to call you! I'll keep it short. I checked half-term, and we're working the weekend to accommodate you. I'll book your flight first thing. Call me tomorrow at five for the details. Make sure you save this mobile number. Oh, and yes, the publicity team loved the fashion shoot, and we all love your portfolio. Any questions?'

'No. Well . . .'

'Okay then. Talk tomorrow. *Ciao.*'

I stood there, blinking like an idiot.

'Well?' Brian said. 'Spit it out.'

Fergus came out of his corner and struggled onto a barstool to listen.

'They want me to fly off somewhere for a week and model for them.'

'Great.' Brian grinned. 'Looks like you've made it into the big time, at last.'

'I don't know if I can. What about my father, and the school, and the bar?'

'Don't worry. I can manage for a week, and so can Tommy.'

'What's a guy got to do to get a Campari and soda around here? Dance naked on the bar?' Quinlan's voice came from behind Fergus.

'What a 'orrible thought,' Fergus said.

'You all look happy. Good news?' Quinlan asked.

I poured his drink. 'They want me to model again, Quinlan. And Paula said they love the portfolio. I'd never have finished it without your support. I'm sure those fabric swatches of yours made all the difference. Thank you.'

Quinlan's mouth spread into a smile. 'Rubbish, lovey, you nailed the job, and the theatre isn't going to miss a few scraps of cloth. You're heading for the recognition you deserve and we're all thrilled for you, it's that simple.'

A small voice in my head asked if this latest development was all too good to be true.

*　*　*

After school, I hurried through town, delighted with an excuse to spend a little money on myself. I wished my mother was with me. Shopping with your mother must be one of those intimate, womanly things that both sides remember joyfully. The sudden burst of glorious autumn weather added to my excitement.

The sadness of my mother's death had given way to more pleasant memories, and quite often I imagined her at my side, sharing a moment or two. Yet on other occasions, grief would unexpectedly slap me hard and I would struggle not to break down. Dad also suffered and I tried to be with him whenever I could.

At five o'clock, I sat on a bench in Grafton Street and called Paula.

'Paula, it's Irini. How are you?'

'Ah, Irini.' She ignored the question. 'Have you got a pen? Take this down.'

I scrabbled in my bag. 'Okay, go ahead.'

'You fly six-thirty, Dublin to Athens, flight number BA556. Hand baggage only. I'll send the ticket to your phone. One of us will meet you at the other end. Don't forget your passport, some euros, and lightweight clothing. You're flying on to Crete and they're having a late heat-wave, so pack sun cream and glasses.'

I scribbled the details. 'Crete?'

'Yes. See you Saturday. *Ciao*.'

'*Ciao*,' I answered, then realised the ridiculousness of mimicking Paula.

I hurried from Next, to Dunnes, to Brown Thomas, bought a few bits, and a lovely turquoise evening dress with a matching rose strategically placed at my cleavage. In the fitting room, I'd imagined Angelo's admiring eyes on me. I wanted him to want me, but why was I torturing myself? It wasn't going to happen, I wouldn't allow it!

# CHAPTER 36
## IRINI

*Dublin, present day.*

AT FIVE, I RUSHED to the nursing home to see Dad. I told Matron about the modelling job at half-term, and she seemed pleased.

'It'll be good for the residents to have their own celebrity to talk about. Write everything that's happening on Facebook and post lots of pictures.'

'Of course I will. Thanks, Matron.'

In a day room that smelled of disinfectant and mothballs, I found my father dozing in front of the TV.

'Hi, Dad. How're you doing?' I had an urge to open a window.

He blinked slowly, then patted the chair next to him. 'Irini, we have to talk. I know you can't stay long, you're always in a hurry, but there are things I have to tell you.'

There was a strange, desolate look in his eyes. 'Shall we go and sit on the bench out front, get some fresh air?' I suggested.

'Give me a pull up then,' he said breathlessly. I remembered how well he was in Greece, despite the awful circumstances.

'How're you feeling, Dad?' I asked when we were settled in a sunny spot.

'I'm weary, Irini. Tired of life.' He rummaged in his jacket pocket and pulled out his inhaler. 'There's stuff I have to tell you. I promised Bridget.' He knuckled his eyes. 'I can't stand living without her. She was my life, even when we were apart, even when I was angry. I was always angry.' His head drooped and his hands hung limply over his knees. 'It all started before you were born, with my heart attack. Have you read all your mother's notebooks?'

I shook my head. 'It's been hectic since we came home. What with school, homework, and the bar, I haven't had a chance.' *And besides, I hadn't been ready.*

He went on to repeat the saga of the dragonfly necklace, clearly having no recollection of telling me when we were in Crete.

'You see, the dragonfly necklace is the only proof that the frescoes depicted actual events in the city that we excavated. It showed that the images on the walls were life portraits, not decoration. That's why it was so important.' He sighed. 'Your mother knew it too. I think it was the guilt she felt that caused her nightmares.'

'No, Dad. The tumour caused her to hallucinate – the specialist told me.'

He shook his head. 'Read the rest of her books. Some of her visions were random horror, I grant you, but most were connected to the demise of real people who lived in that ancient city. I truly believe that.'

I promised myself I would read the rest of my mother's books. 'Is there anything I can do for you, Dad?'

'If I had my health, I'd go and find the place she called the Sacred City of Istron, in Crete. That's where Bridget believed the migrants from Santorini settled.'

'Why don't we search Google Maps?'

'Eh? What's that then?'

'Satellite images of the earth. I'll bring my iPad tomorrow and we'll look together.'

His eyes lit up for the first time since the funeral. 'You really think you can find Istron? Your mother's laptop's in my room. I haven't used it since I came back; the battery might be flat.'

'If Istron exists, we'll find it for sure!' I felt his hope, his excitement, and it pleased me. Five minutes later we were back in the dayroom, his laptop plugged into the mains. I pulled up Google Earth, and searched for Crete. My father's face was a picture.

'I can't believe you haven't looked at this before, Dad.'

'Not my job. I was always in the dirt, digging and scraping, then proofreading your mother's articles.'

'Look, here's Crete, and there's Santorini.'

'Well, I'll be blowed!' His jaw dropped.

I couldn't resist having some fun. 'Let's see if we can find your house.' I zoomed in to Santorini. 'Let's get our bearings. Look, here's the bus station.'

He hunched forward. 'Must be early – only two buses out. Just gone seven, I'd say. I'll bet they're down at the main port waiting for the ferry.'

'Let's see, shall we? Yes, you're spot on. There they are.' I grinned at him, and he seemed uplifted. 'Let's look for your house.'

His sudden enthusiasm gave me great pleasure. I continued towards the caldera. 'Back to the bus station. Here's the prehistoric museum. There's the cathedral. Your house is a bit lower . . . Wait, there you are. Your patio and a bit of your roof!' His face was radiant and my happiness matched his astonishment. 'There's a shadow on the patio. Let's go right in. Yes, who would that be, Dad? There's someone at the table.'

'I don't believe it!' He gasped, pinched the bridge of his nose and gulped. 'That's my darling girl's chair,' he whispered. 'At that time in the morning, it could only be Bridget, writing in her latest *Book of Dreams*, or her Atlantis theory, or perhaps her next article.' He shook his head. 'You mean a satellite was watching her . . . taking pictures?'

I nodded, moved to see him so emotional. 'Wait a moment. I'll take a screenshot so you can keep the picture before it's updated. You can have it for your wallpaper, if you want.'

He glanced at the wall.

'On the laptop, I mean.' He nodded quickly as I saved the picture. 'Right, now let's zoom out and go to Crete.'

'Look at that! The Pillars of Hercules,' he whispered urgently, poking the image of Crete. 'Bridget, you might be right.'

He was talking to my mother, using the present tense. She was still with him all the time. My heart melted. 'Is that where Istron is, Dad?'

'No, no, east of Heraklion, a W-shaped landmass in the Bay of Mirabello, according to her dreams.'

I crept along the north coast, travelling east. 'There's an Istro on the map, could that be it?'

'Seems to fit the description. Can you zoom in there?' He sucked on his inhaler. 'God Almighty! Look, what's that there, on the barren peninsula? Looks like the tops of walls! I'll bet that whole area is . . . Oh, Bridget!' He hunched over, his face only inches from the screen. 'Zoom out. Let me see how Istron lies in respect to Santorini.' His words came fast now, excitement in every syllable. 'Would overloaded ships, depending on the wind, have landed here, considering the wind comes from the north-west?' He peered and grunted. 'I think so.'

I glanced at the clock.

'In the end, it's all my fault,' he said. 'If I hadn't had the heart attack, she wouldn't have sold the necklace to pay for my op, and she wouldn't have had the terrible nightmares caused by her guilt. Then we wouldn't have sent you away for your own safety.'

'No, Dad. Stop blaming yourself! The tumour caused the nightmares.' How many times did I have to tell him? Suddenly I realised he felt responsible for everything, and refused to forgive himself. My heart was breaking for him and I was so emotional I couldn't speak. The past seemed to be playing on a loop through his long, lonely hours in the home.

He sucked on his inhaler again. 'I have to try to get the dragonfly necklace back. I promised Bridget I would, but I don't know where to start. I've completely let her down and she didn't deserve that. Will you help me?'

'Do you remember what she said, just before . . .' I sighed, not wanting to say it.

He looked at me blankly. 'What did she say? I can't remember.'

'About a secret? My favourite game?'

He shook his head. 'She said she loved us, and she said "forgive". That's all I remember. I don't deserve her forgiveness, I really don't, Irini. I'm a hypocrite.' His eyes misted. 'Can you help me get the dragonfly necklace back?'

Of course I wanted to help him, but I hadn't a clue where to start. 'Look, I'm going to Crete on Saturday to do some modelling. I'll be there for a week, so I'll think about it while I'm away and see what I can find out. Who knows, I might even get to Istron. You see if you can come up with anything too. Try and figure out your phone, or use the laptop to search the web for information. Let's turn it into "The Santorini Project". Make notes of any ideas you get, and I'll do the same.'

He reached out and took my hand. 'We always loved you, Irini. You have to understand that.'

*　*　*

I dived into the Raglan Road at seven o'clock. 'Am I late, Brian? Sorry, sorry!'

'Calm down, Irini. You're right on time. What's wrong? You look flustered.'

'It's been a crazy day!' I threw my coat on the rack, slipped behind the bar, and started taking glasses out of the dishwasher. 'Dad made this mad promise to my mother, just before she died, and now he wants my help and I've no idea where to start.'

The bar was always quiet on a Monday night. Fergus sat in the corner with his Guinness. Siobhan from the post office and Molly from the Truly Irish gift shop played dominoes with their husbands, who both worked on the docks. Quinlan would be in shortly.

'Nice frock!' Brian said, his eyes travelling down my jersey harlequin dress to my short red boots.

'Do you think I should wear black ... you know, go into mourning for my mother?'

'Of course not. Bridget would have loved to see you in that.'

Everyone turned to face the bar. I lifted my hands. 'If anyone has any ideas on how I can help Dad, I'd love to hear them.'

They lifted their drinks and came over, taking up five of the six bar stools. I'd just started explaining when Quinlan arrived. I poured his Campari and continued to tell them everything.

'Sure to God that's a tragedy,' Molly said. 'You've made me go all weepy.'

'How on earth can I find the dragonfly necklace? I've no idea where to start.'

'Seems to me,' Molly's Billy said, 'you should start with Amazon. Buy this Aaron's book so you know exactly what you're looking for.'

'China,' Molly said. 'You need to go to China.'

'Don't be mad, Molly. I can't go to China, and anyway, what's that got to do with anything?'

'Your mother said artefacts are moved around the world with fakes and souvenirs. Go on the web and search "dragonfly jewellery". There'll be hundreds of pages of it, to be sure. When you find a copy of this necklace, you need to find out who ordered the original batch to be made. I'll bet it was copied from a photograph, and that photograph would be of the original. Yes, China's your best bet. That's where we get most of our stuff for the shop.'

'You mean they're not all made in Ireland?' I recalled the silver harp pendants, the map of Ireland tea towels, and the cute leprechaun garden ornaments. Molly scrunched her mouth to one side and gave me a *stupid* look that made everyone laugh.

Siobhan lifted a tablet from her bag and tapped a few keys. 'Thirty million, seven hundred results on dragonfly jewellery, to be exact.'

We all stared at her in silence until Quinlan spoke. 'No point in looking at anything until you've seen what the original looks like. Can you pull Aaron's book up and order it, Siobhan, and I'll give you the money?'

She nodded and tapped away. It took a few minutes as we didn't know the title of the book, or Aaron's full name.

'Here we are: *The Frescoes of Santorini* by Aaron Flint, twenty-five euro.'

Quinlan pulled a twenty and a five from his wallet and passed the notes over.

'You can have it sent to the shop, if you like,' Molly said. 'As you're all at work through the day.'

'Good idea,' I said. 'I'd like to take it with me to Greece on Saturday; see if I get a chance to go over to Santorini and talk to

Aaron. I could ask him to autograph the book and see what I can find out from him. It's mad, but I still don't know exactly how my mother's accident happened.'

* * *

Through the flight to Athens, I worried about Dad, money, and my reaction to Angelo. After passport control, I approached the lobby and saw Angelo straight ahead of me, staring anxiously into the stream of arrivals. He looked exactly the same as in Santorini, pristine white shirt, snug jeans, and those expensive shoes. My heart thumped and, for a moment, my feet refused to move.

Somebody bumped against my back. Travellers jostled left and right. Harsh airport noises faded and I seemed to be in a glass bubble with only Angelo's romantic words for company. Would he remember the things he said? I longed to fall into his arms, yet at the same time my anger and hurt made me wish I would never have to see him again.

Except now I was. I shouldn't have come.

'Hello, Angelo,' I said, meeting his gaze, then quickly looking away.

'Hello, Iris,' he replied and grinned.

'Stop it, don't call me that.' I turned away again, yet the moment confirmed: I loved this man and yet I almost hated him, too. Could I keep it a secret, even from him? Could I hold it inside me for the rest of my life?

'You're angry with me?' he said. 'Forgive me, I did try to call you many times, but the phone was always busy or turned off. I missed you, but now you're here . . .'

'No, Angelo, don't go any further.' I took a breath. 'I'm here for the work, nothing else.' I couldn't meet his eyes, so I concentrated on his mouth. Oh, that mouth, I could taste it, feel it against me in the most intimate embrace. I stared at the floor and feared I might blush.

Angelo slid a finger under my chin and lifted my face. 'I don't understand why you're angry. Come, we'll sit while you tell me everything. Can I take your bag?' He reached for the handle.

'No, I can manage perfectly well, thank you.'

'I was thinking of my shoes. Am I safe? Are you still a catastrophe?'

Despite my anxiety, I almost smiled, remembering our very first encounter.

'We have some time before the flight to Crete,' he said. 'Let's sit in the café.'

I was thinking how to handle Angelo. I didn't want to be unkind, but I had a moral obligation to keep my love hidden and discourage him from further advances. Perhaps then my feelings would fade.

'Irini, are you listening?' he said, as we sat at a Starbucks table. 'You look troubled. Perhaps the travelling upset you. Wait, I'll get you some water. I don't want you fainting again.' He seemed to recall every detail of our time together.

Angelo had gone before I could protest. He returned with a paper cup. 'Here, drink, it will make you feel better.' He grinned. 'I have never forgotten how much you like cold water.' He blew through pursed lips, shaking his fingers and rolling his eyes. 'Hot!'

I recalled that night, standing before him in my wet T-shirt. If I could turn the clock back, would I change anything?

He sat opposite me, took my hand and placed the water in it. I noticed the plaster cast had gone.

'Sorry, it's all the excitement, I guess. How's your arm?' Aware his hand still covered mine, I pulled away.

'It's okay.' He dragged his chair closer, placed his feet either side of my shoes.

'Please don't,' I said, shifting back.

'Irini, what's wrong? I've waited so long. Is there somebody else? It's better if you tell me.'

'There's nobody else.' I looked away.

'Then why? I thought—'

'It's better if you don't think. We made a mistake. Forget it. I have.' I spoke kindly, but struggled to stay on track. 'Excuse me, I need the Ladies.' Even as I looked at him I felt he belonged to me. If I was angry it would help, but all I had was remorse. How could I let go of that smile and frown that lingered in the back of my mind, lifting my spirit? What was its charm? Why had it captured my heart from the first moment I saw him at Heraklion airport?

Working together would be hell.

# CHAPTER 37
## IRINI

*Crete, present day.*

When I emerged into the fresh, herb-scented air outside the arrivals foyer, Paula breezed her way towards me. A line of taxi drivers seemed fascinated by the cut of her white pants.

'Irini, darling.' She kissed air on either side of my cheeks. 'Come on, I'm double-parked and the officer's given me two minutes, or I'll be for it.'

Paula had Angelo's 4x4. 'How was Angelo?' she asked as we buckled up.

'He's worried about his father, and disappointed that he's not coming to Crete with me, but apart from that he seemed okay.'

'They operate on Mr Rodakis tomorrow, something to do with his throat. Anyway, I'm glad Angelo isn't involved with this shoot.'

'Really? Why?'

'You'll find out soon enough.' She smiled at the windscreen.

We raced along the National Road towards Elounda and I cringed as we passed the garage where I literally ran into Angelo.

Crete, in autumn, had to be the most beautiful place on earth. Thanks to one unexpected night of thunderstorms and torrential rain, flowers grew everywhere, and the sea and sky were bluer than I imagined possible. Inland, high mountains rose steeply to challenge the sun. The island was so much greener and cleaner without the dust of summer. My thoughts returned to my mother. Would I get a free day to visit Santorini? I longed to be back in my parents' house.

At the hotel, I shared a suite with Tracy and Amanda. Although we could have done with two bathrooms, I got along well with my fellow models.

'Where's Sofia?' I asked the new make-up artist on my first day.

'She doesn't work when her son's home from school,' Joy said as she spread foundation over my face.

*Oh, Joy!* I was relieved.

\*   \*   \*

Our working day started before the tourists surfaced, then, between twelve and three in the afternoon we took a break. On the first day we were on the tiny island of Spinalonga, on the following morning, I posed on a brightly painted fishing boat, and on the third day, we spent four hours after sunrise on a luxurious sailing yacht, chartered out by the hotel. The swim-wear shoot would be on the hotel's beach, and the eveningwear at the pool cocktail bar.

The sun streaked my hair with strands of gold, and the fresh air and healthy food filled me with vitality. In my new bikini, shaded from the sun by a huge umbrella, I read my mother's notebooks. I preferred to keep my own company during our breaks. The promises I made my father worried me, and I searched for ideas on how to get the dragonfly necklace back.

Lying face down and looking at the pictures in Aaron's book, I tried to get sun cream between my shoulder blades. Someone took the bottle from my hand.

'Let me help,' Paula said, squirting lotion the length of my spine. 'Look, there's been a change of plan, Irini, and I'd like to discuss it over dinner. Meet me at eight in the dining room, will you?'

'Sure, happy to.' I rolled over and sat up, but she was already walking away.

I wondered what this was about.

At five to eight I entered the dining room. Paula already had a table before windows that looked over the darkening sea. To the left, colourful taverna lights twinkled along the promenade. Behind the village of Elounda, a row of wind turbines turned elegantly against the dusk sky.

'What an amazing view,' I said.

'Sure is. Let's order. I want to talk to you and I need an early night too.'

We both ordered the fish of the day, green salad, and sparkling water.

'We have a proposition for you, Irini,' Paula said, snapping the menu closed and narrowing her eyes at the waiter as he departed.

'We?'

'In confidence – I'm going into partnership with Angelo, in relation to Retro Emporio. There are some things I want to change.'

'That sounds exciting, but how would this involve me?'

'Bear with me for a moment,' she said. 'Have you ever modelled for anybody else?' I shook my head. 'That's what I hoped. You've done very well, considering.'

'Thanks . . .'

'You must be wondering what this is about.' She raised her eyebrows but didn't wait for a reply. 'I plan to bring out two new fashion lines with their own dedicated fragrances. One is a high-end mature range, which I'd like you to model. In fact, I want you as part of its branding.'

'Branding? I don't understand.'

'Yes, branding. You'll become part of our product; create emotional ties with our customers. They'll want the perfume and clothes because they want to mirror the image you'll put out. The problem is we need a mature model, but a fresh face, not botoxed, lip-plumped, and eyebrow-tattooed. Somebody "real". All the mature models in the business have worked many years, so finding a fresh face proved difficult. Then we came across you. Perfect.'

I frowned. 'I'm twenty-nine.'

She nodded. 'As we're aiming at the thirty-five-plus market, you tick all the boxes. Now, to get back to branding. Imagine George Clooney and I know you'll think of coffee, that smile, a certain vulnerability, richness, and humour – pleasant moments connected with the drink. That's successful branding. Effective advertising gives us a major edge in increasingly competitive markets.'

I stared at her. 'So . . . I'm sorry, are you offering me a job?'

She nodded. The food arrived.

'My God, I'm speechless.'

'Now there's a first. Irish *and* speechless,' she quipped, and we both laughed. 'If you agree, you'll be under contract to work for us alone. There'll be three months' hard work with the photographers and advertising. You'll do promotional trips, and you'll be well paid, more than double your teaching salary, plus expenses to start, with a review in six months.'

I couldn't believe what she was saying. This was a dream come true. Twice my salary? Then Angelo came to mind and I hesitated. 'I need time to think. Can I tell you tomorrow?'

'Of course. Meet me for lunch here immediately after the early shoot, okay?'

\* \* \*

The next day, after the hardest morning's work I had ever done, I sat at a table and watched Paula march into the restaurant. I couldn't help wondering what it felt like to have such small feet and wear towering stilettos.

'This is all so sudden, and the pay, well, it's wonderful,' I said.

'Irini, that's a base figure. You'll actually earn much more.'

'It's such a change . . .'

'We need a taster shoot, which we'll do tomorrow and Friday so that you can go back to Dublin for a fortnight and work your notice.'

Paula had an answer for everything and I didn't doubt she could knock me into shape. The woman could go through a combine harvester and still come out *Vogue*-ish.

'You say everything's set up. Where?' I asked.

'We need a minimalist location, rustic, rich, but earthy, to show off the reds and ochres of the collection, and the warm tones of the perfume. We are going to Nea Kameni. Do you know it?'

Hit by a jolt of excitement, I said, 'Isn't that Santorini – Burnt Island?' Perhaps I could see Aaron and get back on track with the dragonfly necklace . . .

'It is. So, what do you say?'

I grinned, nodding. 'When do I start?'

'Immediately. You'll be on a flight to Santorini this afternoon, and meet the team when we get there. We shoot for two days – one fashion, one perfume – then you have a day for yourself and a flight back to Dublin on Saturday evening.'

I thought about Angelo again and doubt set in. Then I forced myself to focus on Dad and the dragonfly necklace. With a free day, I would be able to visit the house and the site, and investigate.

'Right, I've things to do.' Paula stood. 'Pack your things, Irini, you're leaving for Santorini in an hour and a half.' Her phone rang. She glanced at the number, then at me. 'It's Angelo. I'm going to tell him what's happened. Keep quiet.' She put her phone on speaker.

'Hi Angelo. How's your father?'

'He's in theatre. Paula, there's a disaster. Something viral has wiped half the hard drives and, although the designers have backed up, they're clamouring for new computers in the office. When are you back in London?'

'Actually, we're almost finished here. I've managed to pull everything forward. I'm taking Irini to Santorini for a test shoot for the new range this afternoon. She's joining the company.'

There was a pause. 'Irini? Santorini? Okay, I'm coming over,' he said.

I shook my head.

Paula cut in. 'Rather you didn't, Angelo. Stay with your father for a few more days. I'll deal with this, thanks. See you back in the city, Monday. *Ciao*, baby.' She ended the call.

\* \* \*

Outside Santorini airport, I stood in the puddle of my own shadow as the sun blazed down. I hoped our taxi driver wouldn't be Spiro, but I had no need to worry. Paula's hire car waited. We whisked ourselves away to a beautiful private villa with a key-card entrance and a security guard outside. The view from the terrace was breathtaking, but no different from my parents' patio.

The meeting went on for an hour. Mostly about the logistics of moving equipment to the right places. The crew left and we continued with the photography team. They had a storyboard, and discussed lighting and make-up. I tried to concentrate but most of it was over my head.

'Any questions?' Paula asked.

'Will you need me this evening?' I asked. 'My mother's house is just up the road and there's a few things I'd like to collect.' I wondered if Paula remembered that she'd died.

Paula ran a pen down her list. 'We'll be finished here shortly. You can go but be back by seven, okay?' She pulled a clear plastic bag from her briefcase and handed it to me. 'Here, you'll need these.'

Inside, I found a black suede eye-mask, a pair of earplugs, a couple of razors, and a tube of shaving cream.

Paula continued. 'Just to remind you all, there's a wake-up call at four o'clock, and I want everyone on the quayside at four-thirty! No excuses. See you all in two hours for dinner.'

As I was leaving, Paula caught my arm. 'Use the razors and cream to remove *all* your body hair. Usually we wax, but there isn't time tomorrow.'

'All?' I blinked at her.

'Yes, even that bit. Every hair, unless you want someone checking your bikini-line on the beach.'

* * *

I called Aaron again and twenty minutes later I was beside him in the old pick-up, driving to the archaeological site.

'This is very good of you, Aaron. Thanks.'

'Sure, it's nothing. Glad to help, Irini.'

'Can you show me exactly where my mother had her accident?' I asked, when we arrived at the site.

'Of course. It's bothering you too then, whether it was an accident or not?'

'It's too horrible to think otherwise, isn't it? I just want to be sure, you know?'

He nodded. I followed him past the souvenir shop and through a maze of rubble walls until we came to the place where I was born. I stared at the blank wall.

'Where's it gone, the fresco?'

'Athens, I'm afraid. But you can see it in my book; I photographed all the frescoes before they took them away.'

I pulled his book from my bag. He opened it on the right page and handed it back. I stared at the image and took a breath. My mother's brutal nightmares painted up to look pretty. Pastel colours and swirling lines, pleasing to the eye – so distant from the pure terror Mam experienced in some of her dreams.

'The fresco appears quite new in print, considering. Wasn't it around four thousand years old?'

Aaron nodded. 'That's because of the procedure. It was strengthened and cleaned with resin compresses; the entire wall and pictorial layer were treated with barium hydrate.' I blinked at him. 'We have to do that before they take them away, to stabilise them.' His mouth turned down. 'The Greeks don't seem to realise that people don't come here because there's nothing interesting for the general public to see.' Anger buffeted his voice. 'This place could be a huge tourist attraction, and it would add so much to our coffers as archaeologists, but I'm banging my head against a thick wall. Even reproductions would be better than a blank space. Look how many people visit Knossos, which was pillaged and painted – this site is far superior.'

I remembered my mother's notes. 'Can you show me the last pieces you found?'

He smiled, his voice lifting with the pleasant memory. 'That was an exciting day. We stopped the cracks and detachments with lime putty, and then injected an epoxy resin mix into them to make the fresco strong. I'd been stalling for years, knowing what they'd do.'

'It all sounds very technical and, to be honest, I haven't a clue what you're talking about.'

He grinned. 'Sorry, I forget myself. When the frescoes were complete and stabilised, the powers-that-be decided they should be in Athens, along with the other main finds from here. The procedure for making them stronger takes a long time, but it's worth it of course. But to answer your question, the last pieces in the queen's fresco were mostly from the neck.' He took the book from me and pointed at the relevant picture.

I stared at the dragonfly necklace, clearly visible on the goddess. 'Where did my mother have her accident?'

He stepped to one side and placed his hand against a seven-foot rubble wall. 'Just here. This toppled and fell on her.'

I put my hands against it and pushed with all my might. It didn't budge.

Aaron smiled sadly. 'You won't move it, Irini. I re-built the whole thing myself.'

'So it was really unstable before?'

'Some of them are, that's why you see scaffolding about the place.' He picked up a scaffolding pole and came towards me.

'Are you sure it was an accident, Aaron?'

His eyes widened as he lifted the scaffold pole high above his head and put it to rest on top of the wall.

'Someone could trip over that. Students can be careless.' He turned to face me. 'I'm *almost* sure it was an accident. Why would anyone want to harm Bridget? I've thought about it long and hard.'

'You mean you had doubts?'

He shrugged. 'I just don't know. According to Poppy, we'd only had three visitors that morning: a man and an elderly Chinese couple. We don't keep records of who visits. They buy a three-euro ticket at the shop, come in, take pictures, and look around.'

'Were the police called? Did they check for footprints or anything like that?'

He shook his head. 'When we realised what had happened, we were in shock. I called an ambulance, and everyone helped to get the stones off her.' He lowered his eyes. 'She was in a mess, and to be honest, we thought she was dead already.' He swallowed hard and, staring at the ground, put his hand over his mouth for a moment.

'Sorry, Irini. It was awful. Bridget was like a mother to me.'

I remembered my father saying so. This time it didn't sting so much. 'She was very fond of you, Aaron. When she came back to Dublin, I know she missed you terribly.'

He looked into my eyes, and then turned away. 'One minute she was here. She waved at me when I pulled up outside, then I drove around to park my pick-up. When I returned . . . well . . .' He stared at the ground.

'It must have been awful for you.'

He nodded. 'I was a student when I first came here. My father in prison, my mother off with some bloke. I held a grudge against the world, but Bridget gently got me back together. She was a good woman, always looking out for people in need.'

I swelled with pride.

'Bridget and Tommy were excavation directors. Eventually they made me site manager, and once Tommy had retired to Dublin, your mother promoted me to excavation director too. A great honour. I had huge admiration for her. She struggled to get her qualifications long before these things could be done online.'

'So she did get her degree eventually? I never knew.'

'More than her degree, Irini. Doctor Bridget McGuire was very qualified, highly educated, and greatly admired for her work in archaeology.'

'Doctor Bridget McGuire,' I whispered.

'You know I was very fond of her? No, more than fond. The awful thing is, I keep asking myself: would it have happened if I had come straight back after she phoned?'

'How do you mean?'

'I was at the petrol station. She phoned, said she needed me right away, but I got delayed. The police came the next day and asked a few questions, but it seemed clear-cut.'

I nodded sadly and turned away. When I looked up again, I found myself staring at the bare wall that once supported the fresco. I lifted the book and pointed. 'I particularly like that necklace the goddess is wearing – the dragonfly one. It's lovely, isn't it?'

'Your mother was fascinated by it! I often found her standing just here, staring at the fresco. Come with me, I'll show you something.'

He led me up out of the site, towards the stone-built souvenir shop. Inside, there was a whole shelf of his books, framed photographs of various frescoes, and fake pots and urns.

'Come over to the counter,' he said.

Closer, I realised it was a display case and there, in the centre, was the dragonfly necklace. I stared at it. 'Oh my God, it's beautiful!'

'It's our bestseller ... unfortunately,' he said, glancing at the bookshelf. 'It's an exact copy of the central dragonfly in the fresco.'

'But how?'

'I drew it, and eventually got a company in Asia to make them for us. Wait a minute.' He took a stumpy key from his pocket and opened the cupboard under the counter. 'Here, look on it as a gift from Bridget.' He passed me a brown box, and when I opened it, there lay the exquisite dragonfly on a chain.

'Aaron, I don't know what to say. Thank you! I'll treasure it.' I touched the crucifix hanging from my neck and wondered if my mother had seen this replica of the dragonfly necklace. Perhaps she would have worn it once or twice, held it against her chest like some ancient talisman and made a wish. Reinvented the future.

Everything seemed so unfair. If I could change one thing, I wondered what it would be. Then I knew: I would go back to the beginning of time and zap that tumour gene. The thought reminded me: I must get myself checked out, and I would, the moment I got home.

'There is one thing that's bothering me,' Aaron said, breaking my thoughts. 'A few days before the accident, Bridget received a phone call here and was in such a state I had to take her home. The next morning, she went to Crete. No explanation. I told the police, but they didn't think it was relevant.'

'Do you think her accident, the trip, and the phone call were connected?'

He shrugged. 'I don't know, but it seems strange. I can't quite put my finger on what's bothering me . . . Just an uneasy feeling that perhaps they're linked.'

*　　*　　*

Back in town, I returned to the villa, Aaron's words going around in my mind.

I longed to visit the cemetery, to be close to my mother. However, after the five o'clock start and such a busy day, tiredness got the better of me. I settled in my room, intending to read the notebooks. Would I find more answers in there? But my eyes were tired and the words seemed to shimmer on the page. Soon, I made use of the mask and earplugs, and fell asleep.

*　　*　　*

Before sunrise, we boarded a minibus and raced down to the port. Paula, immaculate as always, hurried everyone aboard a chartered vessel. The wooden schooner's canvas sails were furled and we pitched and tossed with the engines at full speed across the caldera. Relieved to be on land again, I squeezed onto one of the overloaded quadbikes and then we raced to the location.

Burnt Island, the volcano that still smouldered, was black as coal with streaks of umber and rust-red. Fantastic rock formations scattered the landscape giving the impression of a Henry Moore sculpture park. Distorted towers of lava subtly changed, like dark reflections on water. Brittle, treacly-glass obelisks morphed into soft, liquorice-suede pillars, the gathering light tricking my eyes. As the sun rose, gentle, rounded profiles of wind-worn boulders huddled together to form dark, prehistoric monsters. The entire landscape seemed surreal, constantly shape-shifting, mesmerising.

At the site, Paula hurried me to the make-up tent. My eyes were blacked up and my lips exaggerated with scarlet matt crayon. On set, my surroundings buzzed with activity. There were two photographers, both of whom I had met the day before. The lead photographer, Simone, a French woman in her early sixties, dominated the shoot. Her back-up pro-tog was Andrew, a dark, thirtyish Londoner.

The clothes were incredible. Classic styles in rich, natural colours: cashmere, angora, heavy silk, and linen fabrics, in gold, cream, tan, and charcoal. We worked until eleven, had a break until three o'clock, then worked until six. By the end of an incredible day, we were all exhausted.

* * *

Another four o'clock start the next morning, but this time the shoot was on Santorini, in a remote area with cream, wind-sculptured cliffs. Below the bluffs, chunky black rocks and great clumps of delicate, white sea daffodils dotted a pale sandy beach. The flowers' exotic perfume was incredible and reminded me of why we were there. I couldn't imagine a more perfect location. The narrow beach led into a turquoise sea so clear I could see every pebble below the water.

Once again, I went straight into the make-up tent. Puzzled by a tall, clear polythene tube, like a portable shower, I asked, 'What's that?'

Joy, a gothic German woman you wouldn't want to mess with, told me.

'It's a spray-tan booth. Take your clothes off, put on the goggles, shower cap, and mask, and get inside.'

I glanced at the tent entrance.

'Don't worry, nobody will come in. Please hurry, we don't have much time.'

Paula came in and tied the door closed. 'Quick as you can, Irini. Chop-chop!'

'Twenty minutes, darlings!' Simone called in her terribly posh voice.

Suddenly, everything was urgent. I pulled my clothes off, but hesitated at my underwear.

'Come on, Irini, you haven't got anything that we haven't. Get your kit off!' Paula cried. 'It's cost over a grand to set this shoot up. We can't miss the morning light.'

*To hell with it!* I stripped and stepped into the tube. Joy sprayed every inch of me, apart from my face. I had to stand with my arms up and legs apart for five minutes while the tan dried, then I emerged, sun-bronzed and ready for make-up. Paula passed me a robe. My face and hair were dealt with by Joy, who, unlike Sofia, hardly spoke.

'Right, we're ready. Pop the flip-flops on and let's go,' Paula said.

'Wait, I haven't got the bikini on!'

'No bikini for this; we're advertising women's perfume. A woman and a personification of the perfume's all we need.'

Under the heavy make-up, I blanched. 'Paula, you don't expect me to pose naked?!'

'Yes, I do. Come on!'

'No . . . I mean, I can't! Not in front of all those people!'

'Irini, they've seen it all before; it's their job. Now come on! Here, use the umbrella to keep the sun off, I don't want you squinting.'

I followed her out, imagining dropping the robe in front of everyone. My heart thumped and I feared I would vomit with nerves. Everyone turned as I followed her to the foot of the cliff. Simone was ready, camera on tripod, remote in hand. Andrew stood behind her, his handheld Canon glued to his face. One of the crew, a woman in cut-offs and a bikini top, led me to a crevasse in the cliff face and then used a squeegee to erase our footprints in the sand.

'Okay, lose the robe, Irini,' Simone called.

All eyes were on me. Horrified, I stared at Simone. With a look of despair, she glanced at Paula.

Out of the corner of my eye, I saw one of the male crew rub his hands together and grin. I shook my head at the photographer and pointed at the offending guy, who repeated the gesture.

It was a *bastard Jason* moment, a *fuck the inequality and disrespect* second. Anger rose inside me and exploded, boosting my strength and determination to do this job to the best of my ability. I would not have my dreams destroyed by some spunky kid who thought he owned the women around him.

I turned to Simone and shouted, 'I'll not be the bar-banter and brag of that twat in trousers!' In a flash of anger, I pointed at the culprit and yelled, 'You! Get your kit off too! Every stitch! Let's have some real equality around here!'

The guy's grin fell and he paled. Now all eyes were on him.

Simone beamed and muttered, 'That's my girl. Go for it!' She turned to the offending guy and ordered, 'Yes, darling, get them off right now or you're fired!' And *she* rubbed her hands together and grinned.

Everyone froze, staring at the guy in his mid-twenties. He looked like he was about to throw up. 'No way! You're kidding me, right?'

Simone pointed at one of the other guys. 'You, drive him back to the accommodation, quickly as you can. He's fired. The rest of you men . . . boys – apart from Andrew, who's staying – walk that way.' She stuck her left arm out. 'Do not hesitate; do not look back. Keep going until you get to the beach taverna one kilometre away. Stay there until I phone! Got it? Disobey me, look back just once, and you'll not get another chance in this industry, *ever*. Believe me!'

They started walking, shoulders slumped, heads down. Simone lit a long pink cigarette and inhaled deeply, watching them for a minute. 'Wankers!' she muttered, and then stretched her neck and smiled.

'Right, let's get a move on, girls. Here's your chance to prove you can do their jobs! Irini, for God's sake drop the robe, be proud of your body, own it. If you really feel you can't do it, we'll all take our clothes off just to make you feel better, but I'm wearing my Tena pants, so that could be embarrassing.'

Everyone giggled.

'I just want to get the best possible shots, Irini,' Andrew said, lifting his camera. 'But I'll go if you feel uncomfortable with me here.'

I shook my head. It took me a while to relax enough to do the job but, eventually, I understood what Simone wanted and my confidence built.

# CHAPTER 38
## IRINI

*Santorini, present day.*

I LAY IN BED, relishing the luxury of a work-free day. Images of the week flicked through my head. Posing naked had changed me, made me stronger, proud of my body. Owning it, as Simone had said. Paula was right – if she had revealed what was expected at the start, blushing, respectable, religious-teacher me would have said: 'Naked?! No way!' This newfound inner strength bolstered my confidence. Now I could accomplish *anything* I put my mind to.

An hour later, impatient to get to my parents' house and eager to see if I could find something that made sense of my mother's dying words, I said my goodbyes.

Tourists were already flocking into town. I struggled up and down kerbs with my suitcase as the heat of the day intensified. Sweating and flustered, I reached the house, then realised I had forgotten the key! At the tin table, I fell into a chair and caught my breath, glancing at the pure, piercing blue sky. I recalled my mother's shadow, stretched across the patio when she sat in the same chair. Dad's astonishment as he stared at Google Earth made me smile.

With the intention of enjoying the view, I stared across the caldera, but recollections of Angelo and that night returned like a huge chasm to swallow me whole. I hugged myself, wishing with all my heart things had been different. That night, we were one person, lost in each other, a union of souls. Such a night would never happen again, but that part of him – could I call it a spark of eternal love? Whatever, it would always be with me, a precious interlude in the tragedy of my mother's death. I had no regrets.

My daydreaming reminded me of the spare key. Had Angelo replaced it, or left it inside? I used all my weight to tip the urn carefully, knowing I couldn't hold on if it tilted too far. With the front a couple of inches off the patio, I slid my foot under and flicked it sideways. The big old key and a small, startled gecko slid out. We blinked at each other, me feeling honoured to see this pretty creature.

The poor gecko was clearly petrified. I bent to scoop the little thing up and put it over the wall, realising that I would normally be too squeamish to do such a thing. The last few weeks had made me a stronger person. I could deal with new things and difficult situations because my timidity, like the robe, had fallen into the sand on a distant beach.

Taking a breath, I bent over the sandy-coloured lizard, but as I brought my hands together at its sides, the little gecko's tail shot off, startling me. I jumped and squealed. The tail leaped and spun with a life of its own. I couldn't take my eyes from it, my stomach rolling.

Horrified, I backed off until I hit the chair. What had I done? Why couldn't I have left the thing alone? The tail continued to flick and twitch and flip over. How could it?! Coming to my senses, I looked for the gecko and just caught sight of her on top of the wall. She glanced over her shoulder, then scurried out of sight.

My heart pounded as I tried to comprehend what I had seen. Had I witnessed a deliberate defence by the small creature? If so, it had certainly worked.

Inside the house, nothing had changed. I stood in the centre of the room, trying to catch the essence of Mam, imagining her life here. In the bedroom, the sheets were still tousled from my night with Angelo. I stripped the bed and banished the sheets and the echo of our lovemaking to the washing machine. Where would I find clean bedlinen? Under the bed, I discovered a suitcase stuffed with winter clothes and thought this was as good a time as any to sort things out. The task was never going to be easy.

Armed with a couple of rubbish sacks, I went through the clothes, separating them into give-away-able and trash.

Halfway through, I found the Oxo tin.

Suddenly, all the dots connected. Oxo – noughts and crosses! I eased off the lid. Perhaps she'd written a letter? Dad would be elated! This had to be what my mother was trying to say: *remember the game*.

Inside I found nothing of value, just bits of paper and knick-knacks. Nevertheless, perhaps there was something in the contents. One by one, I lifted them out: dice that probably came from a Christmas cracker, a small silver horseshoe from a wedding cake, plastic rosary beads, and a bingo ticket with one number circled in red. A couple of playing cards lay at the bottom of the box – an ace and a king. Under them, I found a carefully written letter, sent by me twenty years ago. It had faint watermarks on the paper. Were they my mother's tears? I held it to my cheek, the knot in my throat so hard and painful.

*Oh, Mam!*

The letter was, I supposed, normal for a nine-year-old. The weather in Dublin was fine, school was okay, Uncle Quinlan had taken me to the circus. I liked the clowns and ate a toffee apple.

405

I never said: *I miss you* or *when are you coming over?* Or *when can I come home?* No. Just: *Love from Irini.*

I sat on her bed and wept.

\* \* \*

A mug of strong, sweet tea got me back on track. I replaced everything and tucked the Oxo tin into my suitcase. Back in Dublin, I would have more time to study the contents.

After dealing with the gecko, the emotional tug of my mother's clothes, the letter, and the disappointment of the Oxo tin, I desperately needed a break. With my tote slung over my shoulder, I locked the door and set off for a walk across town.

\* \* \*

In the narrow streets of Fira, gift shops and eateries bustled with tourists. I continued to the cemetery. A bunch of wilted roses lay on Mam's tomb. I wondered who they were from. For a while, I sat there with a feeling I should do or say something, but after the events of the morning, I was quite drained of emotion. The other tombs were cluttered with silk flowers, ornately framed photographs, little oil lamps, and even toys. I pulled the necklace souvenir that Aaron had given me out of my tote.

'This belongs to you, Mam,' I whispered, and hung it over the simple marble cross that was inscribed with: *Bridget McGuire. Archaeologist. Rest in peace.* 'I feel terrible for not having more faith in you when it appears that you made the most painful sacrifice to keep me safe, Mam. Can you forgive me?' I felt unmoored, lost in a sea that had always been the sadness and disappointment of my childhood. Negative feelings had been real, solid, unchangeable, and in an odd way I was secure in them.

Now the ropes were cut and I had no anchor. Floating in the harbour of my mother's love, free to head for the solid ground of happiness. My tears were falling and I was not ashamed of them. I sniffed hard and swiped my eyes. 'I love you, Mam.'

On my way back to the house, I wondered what would become of my parents' home. I didn't want to sell it. Perhaps if Dad's health improved, I could bring him back for a holiday.

*　*　*

That evening, I hauled my case onto the patio and dragged the little table and two chairs inside, before I locked the house. When would I return? The week had been an adventure and I had gained a lot from it. I sat on the low wall and waited for Spiro, drinking in the view for the last time.

'Iris! Iris! Are you ready?' Spiro cried as he hurried down the steps. 'Here, I brought Bridget's mail. Her post-box is full; it's from before her accident.' He thrust a pile of mail at me and then started lugging my case up the steps while I shoved the correspondence into my tote.

On the way to the airport, I told him about the little gecko.

'Ah, he has a very smart ass, yes.' I giggled. 'While the crows and cats try to catch the jumping tail, the gecko is forgotten and he runs away. Is a good lesson to us, yes?'

'How do you mean?' I was still trying to stifle my laughter.

'You are holding much sadness. I throw something crazy before you, to flip and wriggle and make you laugh, and for a while, your sadness escapes, yes?'

*Oh, Spiro, you kind, kind man.*

*　*　*

I stared out of the plane's window at an evening cloudscape turned orange by the setting sun. When the seatbelt sign went out, I reached for my tote under the seat in front. I should go through the mail. There were another two electric bills, what looked like a couple of phone bills, three archaeological magazines, and a letter from Dad.

The kid behind me was kicking the seat, and my overweight neighbour hogged the armrest. The plane bumped and bucked, and the seatbelt sign lit up again. Three and a half hours to go.

I opened the letter first.

*Dearest Bridget,*

*Darling girl, I thought I had better write to you and let you know my new address. I've moved into the residential home. Irini couldn't cope with my weak bladder and forgetful head any longer. It's been difficult for her looking after me this past year. Poor thing, having us landed on her when she should have had the privacy she needed with her fiancé.*

*She tried her best, and I want to thank her and tell her how much I appreciate all that she does, but you know me, not great at telling my feelings, am I? I didn't want to go to the home, but it's for the best. Things came to a head when I forgot I'd put the chip pan on and fell asleep in front of the TV. I might well have burned the house down.*

*Perhaps I'm going senile in my old age. She doesn't deserve that dumped on her.*

*Irini tries hard, always juggling her time trying to fit everything in, and not having a moment to herself. I'm proud of her, but with the school, homework, her sewing, and the bar, she has hardly any time to look after me (or herself, for that matter).*

*I'm pleased to tell you her wedding is off! I never liked him, that Jason. Nevertheless, Irini is broken-hearted and that makes me very sad. But she was too good for him. Like any father, I only want the best for my little girl. On the good side, you will be pleased to know that you won't feel obliged to come back for a wedding.*

*I want to comfort her. It makes my heart ache to see her so sad, but like I said: I'm hopeless at finding the right words. Poor girl. I'm not sure there is a man on the planet good enough for her, but if there is, I'm hoping he will come along soon and I live to see that day.*

*You should write to her, Bridget. Please do. I know just the mention of her name breaks your heart, and you think it's better if she forgets you, but you're wrong. It would mean so much to her.*

*Write back, darling girl. To get a letter from you would be a ray of sunshine in this place of plastic teeth and old farts. There are things we should talk about.*

*I think about you all day, every day. As you know, you are always in my heart. I hope you are happy.*

*Tommy XXX*

I read the letter twice, deeply saddened and also surprised. I had no idea Dad was in contact with her before she died. Perhaps he wasn't and this was his first attempt at communication.

Next, I opened the magazines. They were American and I quickly found my mother's column. In the first monthly, she wrote how Interpol were pretty much the only official force that attempted to track antiquities and catch the villains. I moved on to the second magazine and saw the publication date was next week. It must have just arrived.

So shocked by what she had written, I read through it three times.

It gives me great pleasure to announce that one of the most important artefacts, looted from the archaeological site of Santorini, has been recovered and will shortly be on public view.

The dragonfly necklace, as seen worn by the Goddess of the Marches in the Santorini frescoes, and also a small jug, were stolen twenty-nine years ago. They were returned to me personally when the owner of an illegal collection of Minoan antiquities, in Crete, died recently. The man's wife did not realise the significance of her husband's treasures. When she had them valued, crucial information was discovered hidden inside the repair work on a reconstructed jug from the Santorini excavation.

The artefacts will shortly go on display in the Museum of Prehistoric Thira in Santorini, before being transported to the Thiran collection in the National Archaeological Museum of Athens, where a four-thousand-year-old fresco depicts the Goddess of the Marches wearing this very same dragonfly necklace.

This piece of ancient jewellery proves beyond doubt that the frescoes were actual portraits of life in the ancient city, and not just simple decoration. The eminent archaeologist, Dr Thomas McGuire, and his dedicated team have spent a lifetime attempting to prove that very thing. This artefact adds credence to Dr McGuire's theory.

The frescoes, including the goddess fresco showing the dragonfly necklace, are portrayed in an informative book: *The Frescoes of Santorini* by A Flint, a highly respected archaeologist who has worked at the Santorini site for thirty years. The book is available on Amazon and in all good bookstores.

I stared at the page, wanting to turn the plane around and see if the necklace was, in fact, in the museum. Surely Aaron would have known and said something? But then again, as far as I knew, Aaron didn't know that the dragonfly necklace actually existed. The modelling trip had been so sudden and hectic that I had not spent a lot of time with him, but he had my phone number. There was nothing I could do but wait until morning, then contact Aaron and the museum.

* * *

I arrived home in Dublin at midnight, but then remembered the two-hour difference and felt better realising it was only ten o'clock. A mug of tea and a microwaved burger filled a gap. After stuffing my clothes into the washing machine, I took a quick shower and fell into bed. I had school the next day, then Dad to visit. I was desperate for some food shopping, and needed to iron my clothes. Also, I had homework to mark, and longed to investigate the Oxo tin further.

Was my entire life destined to be one long rush of duty and domesticity?

* * *

Lunchtime the next day, I had playground duty. We were not supposed to use our phones, but I could not wait any longer. I called Aaron.

'Hi Aaron. I can't talk for long, but something has come up.'

'Is it about the article I've just read in *Archaeology Monthly*?'

'Yes. Have you seen these artefacts? Are they in the museum?'

411

'No, I checked first thing. I've been trying to call you all morning. I mean, I can't believe it. Does she mean the actual necklace in the fresco, the one I copied? Holy *shite*!'

I tried to keep my voice calm. 'Could you check the house? The spare key is under the urn.'

'Of course I will. This is remarkable!'

'Call me this evening if you find anything. My phone's off in lesson time,' I said.

'Okay. I can't tell you how excited I am, Irini. At last, a connection! Tommy must be ecstatic!'

\* \* \*

That evening at the home, I was bursting to tell my father the news.

'Dad, I hope you don't mind that I read this.' I handed him the letter. 'I wondered if there was a mention of something I should take care of while I was in Santorini. Such lovely, kind things you said.'

'I was trying to . . .' He sighed deeply. 'You have to understand, your mother and I, we didn't have a lot of use for chat. We talked about archaeology in depth, but apart from that we knew each other so well, like one person, really. It would be like talking to yourself, you know?'

He unfolded the letter on his thigh and smoothed it down gently, caressing it over and over with the palm of his hand, and I knew he was thinking of her.

'Like I said, without archaeology, your mother and I had little to say to each other in Ireland. Sometimes I know we just sounded like a couple of old grumps.' He looked into my eyes. 'I'm so glad she got the letter, Irini. It's really uplifted me.'

412

'I'm sure it made her very happy, Dad.' How could I tell him she had never received it? My lie was a gift that brought him a little peace.

He squeezed my hand and nodded.

'This magazine had just come, too. I think you might want to read the last article Mam wrote.'

He fished in his shirt pocket for his glasses while I opened the magazine on the relevant page.

After the first few lines he looked up, his eyes sparkling with excitement. 'You mean Bridget got the necklace back, Irini? She really got it back?' With a sharp intake of breath, he dropped his head into his hands. 'Holy God! What terrific news!'

'Listen, Dad, I read in one of her notebooks that the real reason she left us here, a year ago, was to try and trace the necklace. She had to get it back. It wasn't because she didn't love us, but because she loved us so much she wanted to put things right.'

He finished reading the article, then stared out of the window for a long time. 'Where is it now? Is it really in the museum?'

'I phoned Aaron, but he doesn't know anything, except that no, it wasn't given to the museum. He's just seen the magazine article and wondered if we had found the necklace when we were there for Mam's funeral. He's been in a quandary what to do. He's phoned me a few times but couldn't get through. I've been switched off a lot.'

'We should go back to Santorini. But you don't have the time, I don't have the energy, and neither of us have the money . . .' I could hear the desperation in his voice.

'Actually, I've got a new job.' I couldn't hold back a ridiculous grin. 'My finances are about to change.'

He looked into my face as I told him my news, blinking, amazed, as if he had just recognised somebody he hadn't seen for a long time. After a pause, he said, 'You look . . . I don't know . . .' He searched for the word I realised I had never heard him use before: *'Happy!'*

His downcast face cleared and shone with pleasure. Like wiping a steamed-up window, everything became obvious to me. I realised that all my life, I had mirrored my parents' misery, and in turn they had echoed mine. We had all lived in a downward spiral, so concerned about each other's unhappiness, we hadn't room for anything but misery. I felt myself on the brink of a new start. There must have been pleasure and joy in our lives before, and it was high time those emotions were brought out, dusted off, and proudly displayed on life's mantel, for all to see.

I flung my arms around him and gave him such a hug. 'I'm so excited, Dad!'

His wide smile brightened his face and shone from his eyes. I was reminded of the way my mother described him when he presented her with the dragonfly necklace in the notes I'd read.

I was also slightly shocked and uplifted to feel his happiness reflected mine.

'I wish your mother was here,' he said, but not with his usual misery. The delight remained. 'She'd be so happy for us.'

'What do you think she was trying to tell us, Dad? After reading the article, I'm sure it was about the necklace: *secret, game, remember.* I can't describe my excitement when I made this connection to the Oxo tin. I brought it back with me.' I paused for a moment. Thinking about my mother and that I would never see her again was still very painful, yet something had changed there too, though I couldn't quite analyse what

414

that was. 'You said I used to play noughts and crosses, when I was little. Can you remember anything else?'

'You loved playing that game, though you had no notion of what it was about. I always pretended you'd won.'

'After reading the article, I felt sure a clue lay in the Oxo tin, but they were just bits of paper, mementoes, and some plastic rosary beads.'

We sat in silence, me trying not to think about my heap of ironing, the stack of homework books, the woman who wanted to try on my wedding dress this evening, and time ticking by.

'She liked crosswords,' my father said, making me jump. 'Those cryptic ones. I could never fathom them myself. One of the expats would give her his *Sunday Express* so she could do the puzzles.'

I didn't see what that had to do with anything. 'I've told Aaron where the spare key is and asked him to search the house. I hope that's all right with you, Dad?'

'If I know Bridget, he won't find the artefacts. He needs to search for a clue. They'll be hidden, and we should be asking *why* she hid them? Why didn't she give them straight to the museum?'

It seemed my father's illness and old age had fallen away in an instant.

'Perhaps she didn't have time. She went on a day-return to Crete the day before the accident. I'm guessing that was the day she got the dragonfly necklace and the jug.' I took his hand. 'Imagine how happy she must have been to get them back.' There it was again, this positive emotion lifting me from the gloom of my mother's death and Angelo's betrayal. 'I'll bet she was longing to tell us. I can imagine her planning how to break the news once the treasures were safely in the museum. Wouldn't the museum have been closed by the time the last ferry returned?'

Tommy nodded. 'Closes at four, I think.'

'I guess she wrote the article on the ferry, or that evening, and posted it as soon as she could. I feel sure she's hidden the artefacts, but where?'

'I'll bet they're at the site. Didn't you say she went straight there the morning of the accident?'

'Yes. Aaron said she seemed agitated on the phone and wanted him to get back there as soon as he could. She was excited about something.'

Dad looked up to the ceiling and beamed. 'She would be excited. I'll bet she was wetting herself.'

His words seemed so out of character I laughed out loud. He turned to me, pulled his chin in, puzzled, then smiled again.

*Remember the game, remember the game.* The words went around in my head.

'Perhaps she wasn't talking about me when she said: "remember the game". Did she ever play any games herself – patience, bridge? There were a couple of playing cards in the tin.'

He looked at his hands and smiled. 'We would play pontoon for cents at Christmas, and in the old days, we gathered in the kafenio and played bingo with the other expats, but that was it, really. Bridget loved it, but I'm not a great one for social gatherings.'

I imagined my mother playing bingo and loving it, and Dad itching to get home. The vision made them seem so human, and I was grateful to my father for sharing the event with me.

Mam's death had drawn my father and I closer together, and I knew that would have pleased her. But the price of this new bonding was too great, and my heart ached with wishes that she was still alive. I pulled myself together and smiled at Dad.

'Mam phoned Aaron and said she had some important news that morning, but he was trying to get fuel for the generator before the jeep safaris made a queue at the petrol station. He found a tanker filling the pumps and it was almost an hour before he got back. By that time it was too late.'

Dad reached for my hand and gave it a squeeze. We sat in silence for a while, contemplating the past and remembering my mother.

*  *  *

At the kitchen table, I stared at my wedding dress, hanging from the top of the door. The woman hadn't turned up, and I had mixed feelings remembering all my pleasure making the gown. I wondered if I would ever marry. If so, I know I would wish in my heart that I had kept the dress.

To imagine walking out of the church into bright sunlight with the man of my dreams made me smile. Then, shocked, I realised it was a vision of Angelo I saw beside me, not Jason, or some yet-to-meet handsome lover. I dismissed the fantasy and concentrated on the Oxo box again.

The rosary beads – could they be a clue? My mother kept her faith right to the end of her life. At her funeral, the priest said she attended mass every Sunday. The bingo ticket made me smile. I could imagine my mother's fun and my father's restless-ness. Looking closer, I saw the number twenty-one circled in red ink. The playing cards, an ace and a king, didn't make any sense. I played solitaire on my phone sometimes, but that was it.

The clock over the mantel said six – eight o'clock in Greece. I phoned Aaron.

'Hi Aaron. It's Irini. I just wondered if you had a chance to search through my mother's things?'

'I'm here now, but no luck so far. I'll call you the moment I find anything.'

417

'Did you see any note? Did she write anything down at all? Even if it doesn't seem logical it might be important. I'm thinking of a cryptic clue of some sort.'

'Hang on, I'll have a look on the desk.' After a moment he said, 'No, just notes and references to the articles she wrote. Wait ... there's a shopping list. Nothing out of the ordinary: bread, soap powder, loo rolls.' Another pause. 'Something on the back in red pen ... *Irini, over twenty-one*. Does that make any sense?'

'Not really, though it seems an odd thing to write. Keep looking, Aaron. Please let me know the moment you find anything.'

*Irini, over twenty-one?* And twenty-one circled on the bingo ticket? From somewhere in the back of my mind, I recalled that a picture card and an ace also scored twenty-one. *Oh, Mam! What were you trying to tell me?* I grabbed Aaron's book, raced through the pages, found a map of the site. Each area was numbered, and although they went up to forty-five, there were some numbers missing and twenty-one was among them. I studied the photographs, each one numbered. Fig. 21 was a lidded urn already in the Athens museum, so that could be dismissed.

While ironing clothes for school, the words kept going over in my mind: *Irini, over twenty-one*. I couldn't think of any reason for my mother to write that, but felt sure it was relevant. She must have realised she was in danger while the antiquities were in her possession. I returned to the scraps and mementoes in the Oxo tin, even though I had studied them many times over the last few days. Still, nothing made sense.

The mother and father of all headaches descended on me, so I took a couple of aspirin, gave up my investigation, and went to bed.

# CHAPTER 39
## IRINI

*Dublin, present day.*

After school, I called in on Dad and then rushed to the Raglan Road. At seven-thirty, I found myself polishing glasses behind the bar. Brian and Quinlan were having an argument about whether television or bad education caused the falling theatre attendance. Brian banged his pint down to emphasise a point and slopped beer on the bar top.

'Would you look at that?' I said. 'You're a mucky devil, Brian.' I started to wipe up the mess when everything rushed away from me. The next thing I knew, I lay on the floor, a strange numbness about me.

'Move away! Give her some air,' Brian shouted as I opened my eyes. Quinlan, Siobhan, and Fergus's faces retreated from the confined space. They got me into a chair and put a glass of water in my hand.

'I don't know what came over me. Perhaps I caught a tummy bug in Greece,' I said.

'Are you feckin' mad?' Brian said, obviously worried. 'Coming in here when you're not well. You could have split your head open on one of those beer crates. Jaysus, Irini, what sort of eejit are you?'

Brian, kindness itself, never swore, and now to hear all this anger directed at me. I searched his eyes for forgiveness as he put his hand on my forehead. In a sickening moment, I remembered the tumour gene.

'Will I give the doctor a ring, Irini?' he said.

'No, Brian, I'm fine . . . It was just a bit of a faint. I'm sorry.'

Brian's voice softened. 'Don't be silly. Drink the water and I'll run you home in a minute. First thing tomorrow, you're off to the doctors. You don't know what you might have picked up, eating all that foreign muck.' He turned to Siobhan. 'Watch the bar while I get the car, will you?'

\* \* \*

In bed, I tossed and turned, fretting about the rogue gene, then stupidly got up and Googled the risks of brain surgery. Bleeding in the brain, blood clot, swelling of the brain, coma (oh God!), also impaired speech, loss of vision, poor coordination and memory problems. Sick with worry, I set off for Doctor Mahoney's, resigned to the fact I would need brain surgery. The only good thing to come from my mother's death was that I had been forewarned, and in consequence, would not suffer her fate.

In the small, cluttered surgery, I described my symptoms. He listened patiently while I told him about my mother's tumour, my car crash and the headaches that followed, and that this was the second time I had fainted in recent weeks. He shone a light in my eyes, listened to my heart and lungs, took my blood pressure, a blood sample, and then asked me to provide a urine sample.

I sat in the waiting room convinced that he would send me for an MRI right away. I needed time to adjust to the situation and my wait was pure agony. Ten minutes later, he called me in to hear his diagnosis. I sat in the chair opposite, chewing my lip.

'Tell me the worst, Doctor. How serious is it? To be honest, I'm scared to death but I can't go on worrying. Once I know the facts, I can start making decisions.'

'Irini, I must tell you, the gene you're fretting about is so rare, I'm sure you can put it out of your head, so to speak. Also, you don't appear to be suffering any concussion.'

'So why do I keep fainting? I've never done that before.'

'In Greece, it was probably a combination of things: heat, stress about your parents, overworked, not enough fluids.'

'But last night, none of those things applied.'

'No, that faint was caused by your hormones; perfectly normal when you're pregnant.' He smiled.

'Pregnant?!' Poleaxed by the word, I stared at him. 'But I can't be. It's not possible.' Shocked, then angry, I couldn't believe it. 'I only . . . just the one night . . . I . . . Oh, God, Doctor, what am I going to do?'

The smile left his face. 'What do you want to do, Irini?' He handed me a box of tissues. 'What about the father? He has a right to know.'

'No, I can't tell him.' I cringed, shame burning my face, even though I had known Doctor Mahoney all my life. 'You see, he's married with a child of his own. I didn't know at the time. They live in Greece. It's complicated.'

Doctor Mahoney nodded. 'It's best if you go home and have a good think, then come back and see me.'

I still couldn't quite take it in . . . Pregnant!

I left the surgery and walked aimlessly for some time, struggling to get my head around this new development. I sat on the banks of the Liffey, trying to decide what to do. The river, dark and morose on its eternal journey, seemed reluctant to lose itself to the insatiable appetite of the sea, reminding me of my mother and the Goddess of the Marches. It seemed I also had no other way to go.

To sacrifice your child, or to send your little girl away, or to terminate a pregnancy, were all soul-destroying events a woman should not have to experience.

Doctor Mahoney had explained my options and given me leaflets to read. I tried to go through them again but my sore eyes had trouble focusing. One thing he made very clear: it was my body, my decision, and nobody had the right to judge or influence me.

But the thing was, despite everything, I wanted to have Angelo's baby! Mad as it seemed after such a short time together, I knew I loved him. Oh, *how* I loved him. But we could never be together. What happiness could come from breaking up a young boy's family? Later, what would I tell my child? To live a lie would never work, I had learnt *that* heart-breaking lesson from my mother's life.

I had no choice but to terminate the pregnancy, and soon. I felt sick and scared at the thought, but I knew I couldn't pull apart a family, not after my own childhood experience. I returned straight to the surgery to make arrangements, before I changed my mind.

I'd hardly entered the doctor's waiting room when the heavy oak door opened and Dr Mahoney stuck his head out. 'Come away in, Irini.'

Sitting in the black plastic chair opposite him, I reached for the tissues, scrubbed the tears from my cheeks, and took a breath. 'There's no real choice, Doctor. I may burn in hell, but it's better than destroying a family because of my recklessness.'

'Take your time,' Dr Mahoney said. 'I can book you into the clinic on Monday evening. You're less than eight weeks, so it's early enough for you to have a medical abortion. It's very simple. A few pills and, in most cases, it's almost painless.

You have some time to think about it, so if you want to talk, just phone me.' He produced a business card and jotted his number down. 'This is the clinic's number, and here's my home phone. Call me any time if you want to talk it through. I'll help you all I can.'

* * *

I walked to Saint Stephen's Green and watched the children play on the swings. My tears were cried and my decision made; I simply needed a little time to harden myself before I could go home.

I walked past the Three Fates fountain, sure their accusing eyes followed me. On a park bench, I wrapped my heavy coat around myself, but I couldn't settle.

If only I could turn the clock back. If I'd grabbed my case at the airport and not met the handsome stranger, not wheeled chewing gum over his designer shoes. If I'd put my sunglasses on before driving out of the petrol station, where would I be now?

A woman about my own age pulled up and sat next to me, her baby peacefully asleep in a pushchair. I stared at it, trying to imagine . . .

'I wish the little bugger would sleep like that through the night. I'm absolutely knackered!' she said good-humouredly.

I don't know why I put my hand on my belly, and then had to bite hard on my lip.

'Ah, pregnant?' she asked.

I nodded and shrugged. 'I don't know what to do.'

She sighed. 'Gotcha. Difficult. Been there myself.'

'What? You mean . . . ?'

I wanted to search her face for answers, but she had already turned her attention back to the bundle in the pushchair. 'Had two terminations. Young, foolish, looking for love. Wasn't even sure who the father was. Had to go to England in those days – mad, really – but I never regretted it.' The baby stretched, fisted its eyes, and sucked on an imaginary teat. The woman smiled. 'Time to get him home – shovel food in one end and clean up the other. I haven't had a full night's sleep for six months. I'm a mess, my house is a mess, but I wouldn't swap the little sod for anything.' She pulled the baby's blanket a little higher and stood. 'Good luck to you!' she called over her shoulder before walking away.

Pacing the footpaths, I realised if I didn't deal with this right away, there was a chance I'd change my mind. I pulled my mobile out, called the clinic, and asked if they could fit me in right away.

\* \* \*

A protest was taking place outside the Well Woman Centre. I jostled my way through. The crowd of banner-waving anti-abortionists called out as I hurried up three stone steps and banged on the imposing mahogany door. I stared at the brass plaque. Yes, I had the right place.

A crackly voice reached me from a small speaker set in the doorframe. 'Who is it?'

'Irini McGuire,' I said into the mesh. 'I have an appointment.'

Behind me the noise grew. The mob had picked up my name. 'Irini McGuire, you can't go inside there and murder your baby,' a woman's voice yelled.

The thought that one of my pupils or their parents might see me there added to my distress.

A man's voice came from behind me. 'It's crying for your help, Irini. Don't you want to hold your baby in your arms? Don't murder it!'

'Murderer! Murderer! Murderer!'

I hammered the door. 'Let me in!' I gasped into the security microphone.

Glancing over my shoulder, a bobbing placard that bore the image of a foetus caught my eye. I pressed myself against the door, hoping to melt into it like one of those art sculptures.

'Don't kill the helpless innocent. It has a right to life, Irini,' another pro-lifer shouted.

'Murderer! Baby killer!'

A whirr and click, then the door catch released. I stumbled inside.

'It screams—' The door closed and I found myself in a high-ceilinged hallway.

By that time, I was a sobbing wreck. A uniformed nurse ushered me into a side room and placed a box of tissues in my lap. More tissues. Would there ever be an end to my tears?

'You're all right now. Just give me your name again.'

'Irini McGuire.' The words jerked out of me.

'Okay, Irini, you can relax now. Do you take milk and sugar in tea?'

I nodded, grabbing a fist of Kleenex. The nurse left and I heard her voice in the hallway. 'Maureen, call the station. Those people are getting out of hand again.'

The nurse returned with tea. I took a sip, scalding hot. The cup rattled on the saucer when I tried to put it down.

The nurse placed a hand on my shoulder. 'Don't let them get to you. Everything will be fine. When you leave, we'll let you out the back way.'

I looked down and imagined my belly distended with the plac-ard foetus curled up, warm, safe, alive. Visions tormented me: my baby's first cry; its first laugh; a wide-eyed, thumb-sucking face of contentment; first wobbly steps alone; school; puberty; romance; marriage; and grandchildren. The images picked up speed and raced through my head.

'I can't do it,' I said. 'I can't . . .'

'Listen, it's your body, and it's your choice. Don't let that lot outside upset you. You've made a hard decision and you need a moment to settle down. Look, I'll swap your appointment so you have time to relax. Think about it, okay?'

I nodded.

'I'll leave you be for a while. If you need anything, ask young Maureen at the desk.'

The hysteria ebbed. I took my cup into the hall for a top-up and saw Maureen.

'Are you feeling better? Help yourself to more tea.'

I imagined having my own teenage daughter, then thought of my own mother and how hard it must have been for her to give me up. I remembered her dreams: the tragic story of Queen Thira and her beautiful daughter, Oia.

'Actually, I think I'd like to get some fresh air. Clear my head. Perhaps you could show me the back way out?'

I returned to the park. The decision was too big for me to make on my own. I kept telling myself it wasn't actually a baby yet, more like a microscopic tadpole in its watery jar.

I had the bare bones of a plan. I would confess to Sofia, ask her forgiveness, and take it from there. I could imagine her nails raking down my cheek and her spittle in my face. If my plan crashed and burned, I still had time to go ahead with the abortion, but I would have caused more distress. Not exactly

426

a great idea. In fact, it was ludicrous, but I'd fallen out with God and couldn't concentrate on the problem for any length of time.

I could take a pill, a simple pill, to reverse this life inside me. No one would know. I wanted to take a pill and reverse my mother's death, shrink the tumour to nothing, banish her heartbreaking dreams and all they instigated. I didn't think I had ever felt as lonely as I did at that moment sitting on the park bench.

A woman, holding hands with two children, walked towards me. As they drew level, one of the little girls swung around.

'Good morning, Miss McGuire,' she sang, and I recognised Tiffany O'Leary, class know-it-all. She broke from her mother's hand, dashed towards me, and gave me an affectionate hug. 'Will you come to my party on Saturday, Miss McGuire? It's at McDonald's at three o'clock, miss. I'll be seven and we'll have balloons and everything.'

'Tiffany, come on!' her mother cried, grabbing the child's hand. Turning to me, she called, 'Sorry!' as she tugged her daughters away.

Tiffany swung around and waved.

*Oh God! I don't want an abortion!*

But logic told me it was the sensible thing to do. Have the termination and continue with my life like nothing had happened. Yet the conviction that I had to tell Angelo, and then make my decision, gathered strength. I could still return to the clinic on Monday. I tried to be rational. If Sofia and Angelo were sorting things out, and he tried to be a better husband, perhaps Sofia would agree to adopt the baby. After all, it was Angelo's child, and Michalis's half brother or sister, and Sofia did say she wanted another child, but couldn't.

But then I'd lose the modelling contract, the money, everyone's respect, and the school might not want an unmarried mother as religious teacher.

My plan was nuts. I walked past the travel agent's, turned, and went in.

'How soon could you get me to Crete?' I asked.

'When would you like to go?'

'Now?' I had no time to lose.

* * *

After a quick call to Paula while in the travel agent's, I learned that Sofia was still in Crete, and also the location of the Rodakis villa. Thirty minutes later, boarding pass in hand, I occupied a taxi speeding towards Dublin airport. Me and my impulses – this was a lunatic's plan.

The Cretan sun wasted itself on me. I took no pleasure from its warmth as it dipped towards the horizon. At the villa, I found Sofia looking well, surprised, but happy to see me. I got the impression she was lonely in her big house surrounded by perfectly manicured lawns. She wasn't sure of her husband's whereabouts, and clearly curious about why I was there. We walked through the French windows, towards their swimming pool.

Sitting under a gay umbrella halfway between the pool and the house, I watched her son, Michalis, dive-bomb into the water. A good-looking boy, a lot like his father. This was going to be difficult, and suddenly my strategy had no logic at all. So long as I kept my mouth shut, I could change my plan, return to Dublin, take the pill, and that would be an end to it.

Sofia broke my thoughts. 'Big energy,' she said. 'Is likes he never away from homes.' She looked into my face. 'Why you here, Irini?'

Michalis shouted in public-school English, 'Watch me, Aunty Irini! I can make the biggest splash ever.'

I forced a smile and nodded. 'I wanted to talk to you.'

'Is about husbands mine?' I caught a spark of fear in her eyes.

'I . . . Oh, Sofia. Sorry, I'm so stressed.'

'You wants lemonade?'

She seemed eager to end the conversation and get away from me.

I nodded and she went indoors. Michalis continued to show off. On returning, Sofia seemed embarrassed again. 'Irini, yous remember what I say of husbands mine?'

'Yes, of course.'

'Please, yous forgets now. He try hard to be goods to me. *I no want hims to leave.*'

Our eyes met, hers full of hope.

'See beautiful ring he gives.' She lifted her hand and wiggled her fingers, a diamond flashing in the sunlight. 'Bigger love he say has for me now. What I do? I tries to be good families for Michalis's sake.'

What was I doing? 'I understand, Sofia.' I gulped the drink.

'You like more lemon?'

'*Efharisto*,' I said, remembering the word.

She smiled, pleased I'd used Greek. I realised I liked her. How could I tell her I'd had a one-night stand with her husband, got pregnant, and wanted to offer the baby to her for adoption? It was all whizzing around in my head, as if I couldn't hold on to the idea long enough to say the words in a logical order. This was a stupid plan and I could hardly tolerate thinking about it.

I should go back home, take the damned pills, and that would be the end of it.

For a moment I was angry. How dare Angelo wreck my life, change everything without a thought? Leave me in this mess. But, like my relationship with my parents, I was responsible too. I must stop blaming.

Sofia returned with a jug of fresh juice, then shouted in Greek to Michalis. She turned to me. 'I tell him five minutes, then beds. Irini, you's look big troubled.'

I grabbed Sofia's hand and saw a startled expression spring to her face. 'Sofia, you see . . . I had . . . Just the once . . . I didn't . . .' I couldn't get the words out.

Her mobile rang on the small table between us – divine intervention? I doubted it.

Sofia pulled her hand away, picked up, and spoke loudly in Greek, her free hand gesticulating wildly, then she hung up and said, 'My husband's come. What you wants tell me, Irini?'

'What? He's here? Your husband?' I'd just got used to the idea of talking to Sofia on my own. Now what was I supposed to do?

'Yes, husband's here in ten minutes.'

Even if I left right now, I'd probably meet him at the gate or on the long driveway to the house. Anyway, I had to deal with this. There would *never* be a perfect time and I would never have the right words.

'Oh, lovely,' I said stupidly. 'Then I'll talk to you together. It's difficult, you see.' I wished I'd never come. Such a mad thing to do. What was the worst thing that could happen? I had two choices: to tell or not to tell.

Gravel crunched as a car pulled up at the front of the house. The drink in my hand shook so much I had to put it down. I stared ahead, over the pool, into infinity because I could not focus on anything. I heard the patio doors slide open behind me. In my mind's eye I could see Angelo standing there in his lovely shoes, and my heart melted. *I love you, I love you, I love you!*

*Don't cry. Whatever you do, Irini McGuire, do not cry.*

Michalis's face lit up. He leaped from the pool and ran towards us.

A voice came from behind me. 'Ah, we have a guest.'

I swung around.

# CHAPTER 40
## IRINI

*Crete, present day.*

A BIG, HANDSOME man stood before me, impeccably dressed and clean-shaven. He removed his Ray-Bans and our eyes met. Who was he? I had seen him before, somewhere.

Dripping wet, Michalis ran to his side.

'Watch the suit, son,' the stranger said.

Adoration shone from the boy's face.

'Eegh, Irini, you's meeting husband's mine before?' she asked and I saw a glint of fear in her eyes.

Confused, I shook my head. 'Your husband? No.' Her shoulders dropped. 'Sofia, I thought Angelo was your husband.' I stared from one to the other.

The man guffawed, reached out, and almost crushed my hand as he shook it. 'Damian Rodakis. A pleasure to meet you,' he said, his eyes flicking down, appraising my body.

'Angelo?' Sofia frowned. 'No, Damian is husbands mine, Angelo is brothers to Damian.'

'Brother? But in the trailer you said . . . I don't understand.' Then I remembered where I had seen him before. In the hotel lounge on the day Mam died. The man who paid for our drinks.

Damian put his arm around Sofia's shoulders and stood between her and Michalis, smirking at me, black eyes glinting. Although there was a certain malevolence about him, and despite the size and style difference, I could see a strong family resemblance to Angelo.

'No,' Sofia said again. 'Yous makes mistakes, I thinks, and I no speaks the goods English. Angelo looks out for me. Damian is husbands mine, fathers of Michalis.'

I stare at Sofia while rerunning snippets of conversation in the trailer. I don't know how I'd misunderstood but suddenly I had to leave. Dizzy with stress and confusion, I jumped to my feet and swung around. Instantly, blackness invaded my head from the corners of my eyes and everything rushed away again.

Vaguely aware of strong arms carrying me out of the sun, and words growled so low I couldn't interpret them, I sank into oblivion.

When consciousness filtered back, I opened my eyes and found myself prostrate in a beautiful bedroom with matching counterpane and curtains. Sofia knelt beside me, frantically patting the backs of my hands. I realised Damian had carried me indoors. I stared about, relieved he wasn't there.

'Sofia, tell me again, tell me.'

'What yous want? What I tell yous, Irini?'

*Oh, Angelo!*

I wanted to cry, to laugh, to sing with joy.

Sofia, alarmed by my hysterics, called out, 'Damian, *telephono* doctor.'

'No, I don't need a doctor. Please, Sofia, just to be absolutely clear, who is your husband?'

'Eegh, I tell yous, Damian is my husbands. I think yous know this. I talk of him many times.'

'Is Angelo married?'

433

She shook her head. 'You like him, yes? I sees this. I knows the look.'

Sofia was closing the guestroom shutters when Damian put his head around the door and spoke to her in Greek. Again, I saw the snake-eyed smile, then he said, 'Your friend will be fine resting by herself for an hour.' He turned to me. 'Won't you, dear? We have to go out.' Then he ushered Sofia from the room.

* * *

I must have drifted off to sleep – not surprising after all the recent stress and restless nights. I woke in the darkened room, confused for a moment, then I remembered the day. Such a stupid mistake. I slid my hand down to my belly. *I'm having Angelo's baby!* But would he ever want to see me again after the way I treated him? He had to, because above all else, I knew for sure that I loved him.

I slipped off the bed and opened the shutters. The sun had set and dusk spread its calming light over the landscape. Even the cicadas were silent.

Where had everyone gone? I opened the pine door the very second Angelo barged through it. We collided, rebounded, and then stood, shocked, staring at each other.

'I found you at last,' he said.

'I thought you were married to Sofia,' I blurted, unable to hold back.

His jaw dropped. 'I'm not married to anybody,' he stuttered. 'My mistake.'

He shook his head. 'You always make catastrophe.' His frowning smile felt like a balm to my wounds.

'I'm trying to change.' I slid into his arms. An embrace that I hoped would last a lifetime.

'You came all this way to find out, with no ruined shoes or broken bones?'

I nodded. 'I'm improving. How did you know I was here?'

'Paula called. I was in the hotel.'

I sat on the bed next to him and explained the mix-up. He held me, then kissed me tenderly, veering towards passion. Trembling, I pushed myself away, but still held his hands.

'Irini,' he said. 'I understand you want to go more slowly. You were upset about your mother; these things make us behave out of character. And me ... well, I could not resist you. I'm not made of clay. We can start again. What do you think?'

I wanted to apologise for doubting him but, before I could speak, Angelo pulled me to his chest. 'I'll never make you do anything you don't want, but I know that I love you.'

I couldn't speak for a moment and pulled away from him. 'There's something I have to tell you. I have a decision to make.'

He started to speak but I brushed my fingers over his lips and peered into the eyes that had haunted me for so many nights. I took a deep breath and struggled to tank my emotions.

'What's making you sad?' Angelo said. 'However bad it is, it can't change the way I feel about you. I want to help.'

'I'm not sad.' I took his face in my hands. 'And I don't need your help, Angelo – but your baby might.'

He froze, and for a horrible moment I was afraid. I heard a catch in his breath.

'What?' His eyes widened. He stared at me, then at my belly. His arm tightened around my waist, and with that simple action, my happiness soared.

I nodded. 'Yes, Angelo Rodakis, you're going to become a father. We're going to have a baby.'

*   *   *

That night, I stayed at the hotel with Angelo. At daybreak, he pulled open the wardrobe and threw my clothes – a floral skirt with a wide leather belt and a white T-shirt – onto the bed.

'Will you let me sleep another hour?' I begged, wanting him beside me.

'No, you are in Crete now – we start early and sleep at siesta. Come on, Irini.' He grinned, pulled my arm, and then flung back the sheet. 'Get dressed. I'm taking you away for a few hours before you go back. It's all arranged.'

I loved the way he fussed me.

In the car, he taught me some Greek words and laughed at my mistakes. We sped east along the coast, and when the road swept inland, he took a turn-off towards the sea. I watched bulldozers on a distant mountainside load enormous white rocks onto trucks. Bridal veils of dust were caught and lifted by the breeze. Huge vehicles – small in the distance, like amber, mechanical ants – worked methodically on the mountain's destruction. I wondered how long it would take for nature to heal the wound in the landscape.

'Gypsum,' Angelo said. 'You know gypsum? They take it from here.'

I didn't know gypsum but pondered the damage as we rounded a low hill and entered the village of Mochlos. The contrast was uplifting. A picturesque hamlet of whitewashed houses, surrounded by sea on three sides. Colourful window boxes on low balconies overflowed with exotic flowers, and huge crimson hibiscus nodded their heads in welcome. Narrow streets exploded

436

with red and orange geraniums, top-heavy lilies, and Michaelmas daisies, planted in a motley collection of household containers unworthy of such a magnificent display.

An enchantment lay over the village. The hamlet seemed to wait for us alone. Deserted roads ran onto a tiny quayside, where several fishing boats were having their annual lick of paint. I noticed most of the vessels had a blue and white almond-shaped eye, outlined in black, painted onto the prow.

'They're for good luck,' Angelo said. 'What do you do in Ireland for good luck?'

I thought for a moment. 'Old Fergus says "White Rabbits" on the first of the month.'

'Eh? You Irish are crazy. Does he catch many fish, your Fergus?'

'I think it would be completely honest to say no, none at all, in fact.' I laughed.

We sat alone at a small taverna on the edge of the sea, ate eggs on toast, and dropped bits of bread into the clear water. Small, silvery fish darted through undulating sea-grass, and I smiled to see them bump and jostle each other for a nibble at the crumbs. Angelo took my hand across the table.

'How are you both this morning?' he asked, his eyes flashing with pride.

'I don't think in my entire life I've ever been happier.'

Angelo seemed entranced. I caught my reflection in the taverna window. The sea breeze flirted with my hair. Long strands of curls lifted and swayed, dancing with the sunlight, the copper hue turning into a living flame.

He blinked and said, 'I have a surprise. Stay here, don't move. I'll be a few minutes.'

Five minutes passed, then ten. I started to worry. What if fate dealt me another cruel blow and Angelo never reappeared? My happiness had been so intense moments ago. It seemed indecent to feel so much pleasure. Now I realised that such joy came with the fear it could be lost at any moment.

I looked towards the car but saw no sign of him. A woman was busy laying tables and I was about to ask her if she knew where Angelo could have gone, when the sound of a chugging engine drew my attention. A red and blue *caïque* rounded the rocks and came bobbing towards the taverna. Angelo stood at the bow, waving. Trepidation forgotten, I returned his wave and suddenly wished my mother and father were sitting beside me.

He called, 'Catch the rope and loop it over a post, Irini.'

The wiry old skipper jumped ashore, tied up, and both men helped me aboard.

'This is Niko,' Angelo said. 'He'll take us to my special place.'

'*Kalimera,* Niko,' I said.

'Very good.' Angelo laughed.

Niko indicated for me to sit next to him at the stern. He untied the boat and we pulled away. The small craft hugged the rocky coastline. My old fear of water rose alarmingly. The wooden boat seemed small and flimsy in comparison to the vast sea. Niko placed my hands on the tiller and showed me how to steer.

'You put this right, the boat go left; you put this left, the boat go right. Okay, you *capitanos* now.' He got up and joined Angelo at the prow.

'Don't leave me,' I cried, terrified. They laughed and called, 'Left!' or, 'Right! Right!' The boat zigzagged wildly, much to the sailors' amusement. Eventually, I got the hang of it.

We pulled into a small cove surrounded by cliffs and bumped onto the shore. Angelo helped me out of the boat, and I was relieved to stand on the beach. He returned to the *caïque* for the picnic hamper and beach towels, and then pushed the boat into

438

deeper water. With much shouting and waving, Niko turned the small craft and left. The water settled, glass-like, reflecting tall, dark cliffs and the blue sky.

Angelo laid out the towels. I lifted my skirt and wiggled my toes in the water. When I turned, he was absolutely naked.

'Angelo!'

'What? Take off your clothes. No one can see us. There are no roads near here.'

It seemed silly to feel shy but, although we were lovers and I was having his baby, I had only actually been with him for a few days in total.

I remembered my new-found bravery, gleaned from the photo-shoot, pulled my clothes off and made a sprint for the shallows. Just as I reached the edge of the sea, he caught me and pulled me into the water. The gentle waves cooled my body. Angelo pulled me on, getting deeper and deeper, and suddenly I panicked.

'Don't! I can't swim!' I hit him, pushing him away, fright-ened, floundering, terrified I'd never make it back to the shore, images of the Liffey returning to cover my head and hold me under.

His fingers tightened on my wrist and he dragged me back, until we lost our balance and fell into water only inches deep.

'Sorry, I forgot you don't swim. But you mustn't be afraid when you're with me.'

He drew me on top of him and, in a sweet, exotic moment, the warm sun stroked my back as the sea lapped my shoulders and buttocks.

'Trust me, Irini McGuire,' he said. 'Relax against me. Breathe. Look, we are floating together.'

We were floating! I pressed my lips against his and we went under. I came up, spluttering and laughing, my eyes screwed against the sun, my fear shrinking. The water hardly reached my knees.

'I'll make you sorry for that!' Angelo hit the water with the side of his hand, sending great slices to shower over me.

I dashed for the dry sand and wrapped myself in a beach towel. 'Can I open the hamper?'

'When you're with me, you can do anything.' He lay beside me, played with my hair, his breath stroking my skin.

'I think I'm in love with you,' I whispered.

'Good job,' he said. 'With a baby on the way.' He paused, his face showing his pleasure. 'I can't tell you how happy I am. I love you too.'

We made love while the sea caressed the shore and a skylark trilled its joyous flight above us.

Afterwards, we hardly spoke, communicating by looks and touch alone. Back in the sea, tender in mood, we washed the sand off each other.

'I'm hungry,' I called, heading for the hamper again.

We fed each other tiny vine-leaf parcels with succulent, herb-flavoured rice inside, and dipped plump asparagus into thick yoghurt; we sucked each other's fingers and kissed the olive oil from each other's lips. Once again, we became hungry for love.

After, I hugged my knees and watched Angelo sleep. I wished time could stand still.

The sun moved around and slid behind the cliff. We faced the sea, aware that the mountain's shadow crept slowly towards us. It touched our sun-warmed shoulders with a cold awakening, like a nightclub bouncer insisting we'd had enough pleasure, now it was time to leave.

'Don't look so sad; we'll return,' Angelo said as we pulled on our clothes. 'Look, here comes Niko.'

As the *caïque* approached, Angelo stood behind me, his arms about my waist.

We loaded the craft and shunted through boisterous waves towards the village. I clung to Angelo.

Niko shouted down the boat: 'I catch a big fish today. You come to my house and eat now.' He wore a wraparound grin that exposed a row of tobacco-stained teeth.

Angelo made excuses in Greek. I knew he wanted to be alone with me for as long as possible.

'I told him we have an appointment,' he explained.

'And do we?' I asked, feeling safer in the middle of the boat with his arms around me.

'I think we can look at the new hotel my brother is building at Istron. We will drive past on our way back and nobody works on a Sunday. But only if you're not tired.'

*Istron?!*

* * *

Angelo turned off the village road through Istron. He drove towards the sea and parked under a tamarisk tree on the deserted shore. A short walk along the water's edge led us to a tiny white church with a blue-domed roof, which marked the end of the beach.

Behind the chapel stood a stone well and beyond this, a rugged promontory of land poked out through the waves like a gnarled finger. On this peninsula, a narrow track zigzagged up between slanting, wind-worn vegetation. Low-growing juniper trees perfumed the air, and the only sound was the clatter of smooth pebbles rolled by gentle waves.

'This is Rodakis land,' Angelo said. 'Sofia's dowry.'

'Dowry?'

'Yes, when Damian married Sofia, her family gave it to our family. This is the way with Cretan families.'

I glanced across the bay, trying to orient myself with the Google map I had studied with Dad.

'We'll go this way, like the goats,' Angelo said. 'Walk behind me and be careful for the small trees.' He pointed at the scrubby vegetation.

'Bushes,' I said.

'They have spikes. Even goats don't like them.'

The needle-sharp spines on knee-high shrubs snatched at my skirt. Twice I was yanked back to untangle fabric from long thorns. In the process, my shoulder bag slipped and fell into the dust. Exasperated, I gathered my skirt around my thighs and threw the bag strap over my head.

Angelo turned to see what was slowing me and his face broke into a grin. I looked down. The bag strap divided my breasts in the thin white T-shirt.

'Very nice!' He walked backwards, his eyes glued to my chest.

'Cheeky,' I said.

'You make me crazy.'

'Angelo, be careful . . .'

'Ouch!' The vicious spikes drove into his calves and he leaped towards me in a wild dance of lunacy.

I clapped a hand over my mouth to smother the laughter.

He ran at me, mock anger on his face. 'You laugh? I'll teach you a lesson, Iris!' He caught me in his arms.

My joy was so intense, I felt that if he kissed me at that moment I'd become a victim of spontaneous combustion.

'Go!' I pointed towards the brow of the promontory. 'And mind the thorns.'

He called over his shoulder, 'You're a wicked woman, Irini McGuire. I can see you are going to give me great trouble.'

Minutes later, we stood on the crest of the rocky peninsula. Halfway down the slope, the ground levelled and a row of mechanical workhorses waited for Monday. Beyond the bull-dozers, cranes and mixers, the skeleton of a concrete building loomed from a massive puddle of grey cement dust.

'Come.' He held out his hand. We stepped onto a wide, pleated track made by heavy machinery.

'I can't believe you're so excited. It looks awful.' I stared at the dull columns and twisted iron building-rods.

'You don't see it. Look, here are the best rooms; each suite has an infinity pool pointing out to sea. The next rooms are above and further back, with smaller pools on the roof of the first floor.'

I adored his child-like enthusiasm, and how proud he was to brag about the achievements of his father and brother.

Angelo gazed at the ugly, half-built hotel. 'I've seen the plans – it will be one of the best hotels in Europe.'

Overcome by tiredness, I sat on the footplate of a cement mixer, while he strutted around the embryonic building. I closed my eyes. The sun warmed my face, blanked my mind, and I dozed.

I didn't realise my head had slipped in relaxation until it fell forward and woke me with a jolt.

Angelo caught my startled expression. 'Are you okay? Forgive me, you are tired. Come, I'll make you some coffee in the work-ers' place and show you the plans, then we'll go home.'

Bless him; didn't he look after me so well? I didn't like coffee and wasn't interested in the plans, but never mind.

'Any chance of a cup of tea, do you think, Angelo?'

'I'm sure there'll be a can in the fridge.'

'Tea in a can? You're joking? You're not right in the head, you Greeks.' At the high mesh gates, I asked, 'What is this place?'

'I'm not sure, probably the engineer's office.' Angelo introduced himself to the security guard, who led us inside and unlocked the wooden building, which had trestle tables against all four walls.

'I don't understand,' Angelo said, scratching his beard.

One table supported several containers of fine white powder and many brushes. The end of the worktop was spattered with white plaster and displayed a jigsaw of broken pots.

'Antiquities,' he murmured. 'What the hell's Damian up to?'

I glanced at the broken urns. 'You mean there are antiquities here and Damian's digging them out, like my parents? Isn't that good?'

'No, Irini, it's not good. It's against the law. You can't build on an archaeological site. And what's Damian doing with the artefacts? I know him; he doesn't care for such things. He only cares about money. He will be selling them. Three people work here. Look – three chairs, three mugs on the nails.'

My pulse raced. My mother and the dragonfly necklace! If Damian was finding and dealing, then he would know other people in the business. I moved towards a dusty chair across the room but stumbled as I went over.

Angelo caught me. 'Careful!' We both looked to see what caused the trip and saw a loop of rope threaded through the floorboards. 'What's that? Looks like a door in the floor.' He slid both hands into the rope handle and pulled. It lifted a few inches. 'Too heavy; I'll get help.'

He stuck his head outside and shouted. The guard appeared and they had a conversation in Greek.

'What did he say?' I asked.

'He knows nothing about what's down there. His job is making sure nobody comes inside the fence, that's all.'

The men hauled up the wooden pallet. Angelo escorted the guard to the door and let the lock click into place when he had gone, then he kneeled and stuck his head inside the hole.

'There's a light switch and a ladder. I'm going down.'

'Not without me, you're not. This is exciting stuff!'

'No, it's too dangerous. Stay here.'

'Bullshit! Wait for me.'

He disappeared down the hole and I followed.

We held hands and stood, speechless, at the bottom of the ladder. Again, I wished my mother was with me. The space, lit by a bare bulb, was as big as the building above. Walls of stone block bore the chisel marks of some ancient tool. In the dim light, Angelo said he thought we were inside a Minoan building, but he flicked another light switch, and all was revealed. We stood in shocked silence.

# CHAPTER 41
## IRINI

*Crete, present day.*

IN THE SUBTERRANEAN archaeology site, Angelo and I stared at a quadrangle surrounded by buildings with streets running off.

I gasped. The feeling of *déjà vu* had me reeling. I had been here before!

'Unbelievable,' Angelo murmured, his voice awed. 'You know what this is? Damian is excavating! Those dolphins carved into the lintels are identical to the Santorini site.'

I gripped his arm. '*Yes*, Angelo, I *do* know what this is.' I could hardly get the words out for excitement. '*This* is the Sacred City of Istron!'

He swung his attention back to me, shock clear on his face, then he shook his head. 'No, Irini, that's only a legend . . . What makes you think—'

'You are wrong! Listen to me, Angelo. This is it; I have no doubt. I would stake my life on it! The Sacred City of Istron. Wow! My mother had visions of this place; she knew it was here. She saw the people led by the great Queen Thira. She was with them when the tsunami hit. Thira loved these people so much she sacrificed her own daughter to try and save them.'

I saw the shock on Angelo's face. Shaking my head, I realised it would take too long to explain. At that moment, I understood everything. Rightly or wrongly, my mother believed – feared – I was a reincarnation of Oia and I was bound to join Thira in the

Elysian Fields after death. That was why she tried to keep me safe by sending me away.

I closed my eyes, my mind reaching out through the dark ether, heading for a prick of light that was my mother's soul. As I approached, bathed in a kind of holy light, I was filled with love and I knew my mother was with me.

*It's here, Mam. We found the Sacred City of Istron! You were right all the time. Can you see it with my eyes? I'm rejoicing for you and I'm so completely honoured to be your daughter.*

I felt my mother's protective arms slide around my body and her presence engulf me with such intensity that I gladly submitted to her embrace.

'Oh, Mam,' I whispered. 'I'm really, really proud of you . . . And I miss you so much.' A sob jerked my chest, unlocking an emotional door and letting my imprisoned grief run free. Tears fell from my closed eyes and all the heartache trapped inside me for so long poured out.

As my tears abated, I felt lighter in body and mind. The relief of letting go had given me the freedom to move on, although I knew her memory and her love would always be in my heart.

'Better?' Angelo whispered as he released me from his arms.

I nodded and wiped my eyes. 'Sorry, I'm a catastrophe.'

He inspected his shirtfront. 'Mm, but you are getting better, I think. No mascara.'

'Oh, Angelo, I do so wish Dad was here to see this. Please get your phone out; let's take as many photographs as possible. My father will tell you the truth about this place, but he needs pictures. You're looking at a Minoan city built by the people who came from Santorini not long before the island erupted.' I lowered my voice. 'They were the people of Atlantis.'

'Atlantis?!'

'Yes, but keep that to yourself or you'll have every grave robber from here to the North Pole digging up the site. The tsunami that was caused by the volcano's eruption wiped out most of the Minoan civilisation. I can't believe this! What an enormous discovery. Let's explore.'

We walked into the widest street, where Angelo flicked another light switch. The buildings had walls more than half a metre thick. New steel beams, like lengths of railway track, supported the earth above. Through the doorway of the first building we saw picks, shovels and jackhammers, and further along, a mini digger with 'Bobcat' painted on the side.

'I don't understand,' Angelo said. 'Why's all this so far underground?'

'When the volcano on Santorini erupted, thousands of years ago, the towns on Crete's north coast were buried or pushed into the sea. But you know this, don't you?'

Angelo nodded. 'No one's quite sure what happened because hardly anyone survived. Anyway, the few that did had no way of recording the event. As you said, historians think a giant tsunami crashed into Crete, flattening everything on the coast. The wave continued inland until it met the mountains, destroying settlements and drowning the Minoan population.'

I nodded sadly, yet the excitement I felt for my parents bubbled inside me. 'Exactly, then the volcano collapsed in on itself and the opposite happened.'

Angelo took my hand and we walked together, our raised phones flashed with each picture. 'The hollow mountain dropped into its magma chamber and the Aegean Sea followed it. Imagine the force, Irini? Tsunami waters tearing back to the gaping vortex. Think about this: when the tidal wave was sucked out of the Istron valley, it would have stripped all the soil and loose rocks from the foothills and deposited them over this area. Slurry and rubble must have covered the place. So now, after all this time, trees and bushes have grown, hiding everything.'

'I feel so sad for the unmourned people that perished right here. It's difficult to imagine, but my mother saw the actual event in her dreams. She saw their fear, felt their panic and their pain, again and again. Night after night. What a terrible thing to live with.'

Angelo stopped walking and lowered his phone. 'So here we are, you and I, nearly four thousand years later, beneath the Cretan earth.' He wrapped his arms around me again. 'It's an incredible moment, isn't it?'

I nodded. 'My mother was convinced this place existed. I'll bet there's another floor below this one. Perhaps we're actually standing on the great treasure warehouses of Atlantis.' I had to place my hand over my mouth to stifle another sob. 'And somewhere here, in this place, lay the bones of the great Queen Thira, Goddess of the Marches and Supreme Ruler of Atlantis.'

'After all that you've told me, I wonder if the spirit of the Goddess of the Marches roamed the earth, searching for a woman to reveal the story behind the demise of her people.' He said it so matter-of-factly, this preposterous idea that I had never dared voice for fear of being ridiculed.

'Perhaps she chose my mother,' I suggested quietly, feeling the weight of my sadness. 'Do you think that's crazy?'

Angelo frowned for a moment. 'Or perhaps she chose you. If you believe in God, then you believe there is a spirit world of some sort, yes?' I nodded. 'So how can we know what goes on there? We guess, but that's all it is – guessing. Then we choose to believe whatever appeals to us the most. Isn't that what religion is?'

He made me smile, this Greek man of mine. Although he admitted he didn't really know anything, he was sympathetic to my mother's dreams and illusions, and that drew me closer to him.

'These houses had two or even three floors,' he said. 'Look, halfway up, you see the holes? Tree trunks slotted into the stones, reaching across to the opposite walls. Remember the site at Santorini? The same building techniques took place here.'

I knew because Aaron had explained to me already. 'You know a lot, Angelo.'

'I'm interested in archaeology. Most Greeks are. That's why your parents were so admired.'

Hand in hand, we turned into the main square and took a smaller path.

'It's a little creepy,' I said, sticking close. 'So quiet. I wonder where they . . . you know, died.'

'They'll be dust now, unless they were encased in mud and the bodies mummified.'

A shiver ran through me. We found wheelbarrows, more tools, and sealed wooden crates. Angelo took a shovel, eased the blade under a timber lid, and swung on the handle. Nails squealed and then, with a sudden pop, the lid flew off and Angelo went sprawling into the dirt.

I shouldn't have laughed.

He got to his feet and peered into the crate, pulling away empty sacks. 'I think it's bronze.' He examined the goblets, plates, and bowls of dark metal. 'This is serious. These things belong in a museum. My brother will sell the lot if he has his way.'

450

'How could he do this and not be found out? I mean, how many men would have been needed to dig this out? Where is all the soil? How did they get the Bobcat and forklift down here?'

'There must be another way in. Let's look around, if you're okay, and then I'll talk to my father. I'm sure he doesn't know about this.'

'It's getting late, Angelo, and I've a plane to catch. Let's separate, investigate, and compare our findings on the way back to Elounda.'

'You're sure you're okay? Be careful, and don't touch anything, Irini.'

I rolled my eyes good-humouredly. 'I'm not a baby. I'll be fine.'

We parted. I sidestepped my way around the work tools and found another narrow street leading off to the right. I had enough illumination from the main passage to make out several rooms. Gaping doorways, like open mouths, revealed interiors half full of earth. In this area, planks and posts of new wood supported the roof, and the resinous smell of pine filled my nostrils. At the end of the light, the floor rose with soft, loose earth underfoot, and I was forced to stoop.

I became accustomed to the gloom and was drawn into the last room, which seemed clear of dirt. On the far side I could make out large bulbous shapes, like Ali Baba baskets. Curious to know what was inside them, I slipped my phone into my bag and went to investigate, feeling around with my foot for a step.

Angelo called, 'Irini, are you all right?'

Distracted, I tripped on a plank that slid away as I went to step on it. Lurching forward, I realised too late the board covered a hole. Everything happened so fast. I tumbled into the black

451

space like Alice down the rabbit hole, terrified of what awaited me at the end of the drop. My shoulder crashed against the side as I failed to grasp something to break the fall.

My scream echoed through empty corridors, until I hit the bottom of the dry well with a crash that knocked the air out of me. Excruciating pain tore through my ribs and shoulder. Winded, it took a few moments before I got my breath.

'Help!' I called.

The horror in Angelo's voice was clear. He yelled my name repeatedly. His shouts came closer and then they faded. I tried to move, then let out an agonised howl. Instantly, he was above me.

'Irini, where are you?'

'I'm down here. Be careful, there's a hole.'

'Are you okay?'

'No, my shoulder.' I imagined the bones jagged and splintered. The pain was terrible. Worried about my pregnancy, I slid a hand over my belly and abdomen, but didn't feel any tenderness there. 'Oh, thank God,' I whispered. 'You stay safe in there, baby.'

'Wait, I'll get some light. Don't move,' Angelo said.

I didn't want him to go.

He shouted, 'I'm pulling down the electric wire with lights.'

I strained to listen and heard popping cable clips as he ripped the crude lighting system out of the main passageway.

'I'm coming back,' he yelled.

The illumination became brighter, and then a black, fiendish shadow leaped and danced on the ceiling high above the hole. I feared the devil himself had come for me – stupid, really.

'I'm here.' He blinded me with light. 'I'll lower the cable.'

The bulbs arrived, spinning and swaying. I fended the glare with my hand and saw Angelo three or four metres above me.

'Don't worry, I *will* get you out. I'm going to get a ladder.'

The pain in my shoulder increased as his footsteps faded. Time stood still in the silence, and heat from the bulbs warmed the stagnant air. I tried to look about, but the slightest movement of my head sent horrific pain through me.

Angelo clattered and cursed as he manoeuvred a crude ladder over the hole. Clods of earth fell around me.

'I'm coming down to get you.' He started to lower the ladder, but the bottom rung jammed firmly in the soft earth above.

'*Malaka!* It's stuck. Wait, I'll just . . .'

I could see him trying to jerk it free. The top caught the roof beam. He swung a hefty piece of timber at the side of the ladder to dislodge it.

Then the nightmare escalated.

A groan came from the shoring beam above. It twisted slowly, like warm toffee, and everything shifted – slightly, at first, then gathering force, until the tremble became a rumble and the rumble became a quake.

I saw Angelo's features warp with horror. A hailstorm of earth fell and covered most of my body. I swung my good arm over my face to protect it and pushed my chin to my chest.

With a deafening roar, the beam crashed down like a snapped matchstick and jammed in the wall of the well before it reached me. The sides of the sinkhole started to collapse. Soil, rocks, and planks rained down. The broken beam slipped lower and jammed across the hole just inches above me. It supported a crushing amount of rubble that continued to fall and closed the entrance of my tomb. The beam sagged and slipped under the strain, and then the bulbs went out.

I tried to drag myself from the covering of earth and curl against a rocky part of the wall. A moment of complete silence was broken by a distant groan and then the sickening sound of splintering wood.

The rock wall behind me moved away, and in the dark I lost all orientation. I heard planks above rupture. Everything roared into freefall, including me. Loose dirt travelled with me as I was propelled down a steep incline in the pitch black. I felt sure I was about to die.

\* \* \*

I remembered the chaos. Everything had stopped; even time itself seemed to be on hold.

The silence and blackness were so absolute, I wondered if I was dead. Then, I realised I was lying horizontally, my head clear of dirt. I could move it a little, but a great weight pinned the rest of me down and, because of it, I could hardly breathe. I had dirt in my mouth, and when I coughed, a stabbing pain pierced my ribs. I pulled my left arm out of the soil, but every movement caused more pain down my right arm.

I reached out, felt cold, smooth rock near my head, and followed its contour. It arched over me and seemed to have protected my head and shoulders from the avalanche. Disturbed dirt fell into my wide, unseeing eyes. The rock had saved my life, or what might be left of it.

How long would the air last? With my good arm, I pushed soil away from my body.

'Angelo?' I called, wincing.

Complete silence.

Breathing became difficult, and when I brushed the dirt from my face I found it slimy with sweat. I managed to clear the soil as far as my hips, but stones and small rocks pinned my legs down.

454

'Angelo, where are you?' He could be right next to me for all I could see.

I had to immobilise my injured arm before I attempted to sit up. After pushing more dirt away, I felt for the metal buckle of my belt. My hand rested on my belly for a moment. 'Be safe in there,' I whispered. 'We'll get out of this somehow.'

I pulled on the leather belt and twisted onto my back. Terrible pain seemed to suck the marrow from my bones, but thoughts of the baby renewed my determination. The struggle to get the belt behind me was exhausting. I paused, sweat and dust stinging my eyes.

Eventually, I brought the buckle to rest on my ribcage and managed to slot the end through it. Difficult with only a couple of inches to work with, but I got it through and pulled tight to pin my arm to my side.

*Relax,* I told myself. *Lie still and take slow, steady breaths.* After a while, the shoulder eased a little.

'Thank God,' I whispered, more out of habit than sincerity, yet the words gave me some strength.

'Angelo,' I called again. Still nothing.

I struggled into a sitting position and was reminded of the overhanging rock when my head cracked against it.

One by one, I rolled away rocks and pushed at the loose soil. My legs were uncovered to the knees when I touched the leather strap of my shoulder bag. I scrabbled between the rocks. Sharp pain speared my fingers as nails broke to the quick.

I hauled on the strap. Each pull sent excruciating pain up my right arm but my bag inched through the rubble until I dragged it free.

I fumbled inside, discovered my make-up bag, perfume, wallet, and then the hard plastic of the mobile. I drew my hand around it, hoping the phone hadn't been crushed into terminal switch-off. If only I had some light. If I'd bought the smart phone sooner, I'd be more familiar with it, but it was no good wishing now. My fingertips recognised the screen and the charging socket at the bottom, so I had it the right way up. I tried to remember the buttons, but it must have been the bang on the head or shortage of oxygen, because I couldn't concentrate. I had hardly used the phone since I'd bought it.

'Angelo! Where are you?' I listened for a whimper or groan but heard nothing, so I returned my attention to the phone.

Something was wrong. I could hear my own breathing, rapid and shallow as it was.

*You're having a panic attack. Calm down!*

Dirt fell on my face. Horrified to think another avalanche might be on the verge of crashing down, I gave up on trying to fathom out the phone. Tiredness and fear destroyed my confidence. I knew I had to go ahead and press a button. If I flattened the battery in the process of figuring it out – tough. Anyway, I probably wouldn't get any signal.

The glowing light from the phone was the most beautiful thing in the world. I shone it around at arm's length. I wasn't in a cavern, but in the corner of some kind of room. Ahead, I could see an ancient block wall and a doorway filled with rubble. To my left and right, there were marble columns snapped into short lengths and loosely scattered. Approximately a metre and a half above me, a huge slab of smooth, pale marble was supported by broken columns on either side. Angelo was not lying unconscious nearby, as I'd feared. I was alone. He must still be up top, getting help. I wouldn't consider anything else.

The rocks over my legs were the tail end of the landslide that had swept me here, but the light from the phone faded and, once again, I was plunged into darkness.

What if the battery died? Then the light came on again. I screwed my eyes to focus on the screen and, to my disappointment, saw there was no signal.

Too late, I heard the rumble and hardly saw the rock before it ricocheted off my temple.

# CHAPTER 42
## IRINI

*Crete, present day.*

Irini's insentient mind, suspended in total silence, experienced what she would later label as a weird hallucination. Most of the time, she had always accepted that there was a God, perhaps not the creator of heaven and earth, but possibly.

She usually translated her own inner strength as God's support and took comfort from the guiding principles that her religion gave her, such as: 'love thy neighbour as thyself'. Irini believed, without doubt, that all gods should concentrate on setting such a strategy for humans instead of counting heads in the battle for supremacy.

Now she felt the presence of a celestial entity and realised that she was in the company of a powerful deity – a goddess, for want of a better word – the mother of earth, water, birth, and nature.

The spirit took shape before her in the form of a woman in a long and heavy robe of blue and yellow, embroidered with delicate crocus flowers. Her blue-black hair was coiled and waxed elaborately about her head, and the neckline of the garment was cut below her breasts in a simple display of womanhood. She wore a necklace of silver dragonflies, with the wings touching to make a circle around her neck.

Irini knew this was Queen Thira. The woman did not speak, but as she gazed into Irini's eyes her hands rose to her nape and touched the dragonfly necklace. Irini heard the deity's words inside her head, echoing strangely without true resonance.

*You have a purpose: daughter, wife, mother.*

'Who are you?' Irini whispered, her voice hardly more than a thought in a breeze.

*I am the Goddess of the Marches. I am everyone and no one, and you are my daughter. Your destiny is written and you shall fulfil it, affecting all those around you and setting the path for those who are yet unborn.*

'I don't understand.'

*When your mortal time on this earth is complete, you will understand everything.*

The goddess smiled and the silver dragonflies quivered, broke apart, and changed into living creatures of dazzling beauty, flitting and darting in the darkness.

*I'm dreaming this,* Irini thought. *I must be, there's no logical explanation. Perhaps it's all a dream and I am in my bed, asleep.* She tried to follow the dragonflies, but one by one they disappeared. When she returned her gaze to the Goddess of the Marches, she too had vanished, but Bridget now stood in her place.

At the sight of her mother, all Irini's pain and fear were driven from her mind.

*Don't give up, Irini. Your daughter depends on your strength right now. My darling Irini. I know you'll make a wonderful mother. Learn from my mistakes. Don't forget me.*

\* \* \*

Consciousness returned. Alone in the dark, I found myself shivering and afraid. My shoulder and head hurt so badly I felt the pain seep into every part of my body. Time and space became

459

nothing but wretched despair. My own life seemed suspended as I withdrew into myself, blanking every thought, just waiting for someone to find me.

* * *

I heard them. Distant clattering, and then voices. A narrow shaft of light blinded me.

'Irini, can you hear us?'

Angelo's voice . . . He's safe!

'I'm here, Angelo! Help me!'

* * *

In a hospital bed in Agios Nikolaos, I learned that Angelo had called all the emergency services. A beam had knocked him unconscious for a short time. He was slightly concussed and bruised but insisted on helping to find me. They reached me through a wall of rubble. Four hours after the initial collapse, I lay in Angelo's arms.

We spent the night in a hospital room, where my bruised ribs and shoulder, dislocated but not broken, were dealt with. The doctor reassured us that our baby was unharmed.

I told Angelo everything: about the dragonfly necklace, and how important it was for me to get it back.

He confessed that his brother was a compulsive gambler. 'Most weekends he goes to the casino on the island of Rhodes. I guess dealing antiquities feeds his habit.'

We were leaving the hospital when Angelo said, 'I've been thinking, it wasn't Damian who got the dragonfly necklace from this Splotskey, he would have been too young then. But I'm

460

guessing he knows the collector who bought it. If we handle this carefully, we still might be able to trace the dragonfly necklace.'

'I don't see how. Why don't we just tell the police everything?'

'Look, Damian will most likely go to prison, or at least have a huge fine to deal with for excavating the site. I'm in a difficult situation – he's my brother. Besides that, your mother would be discredited. Imagine how the archaeology world will react if they discover she sold some antiquities.'

'But she didn't . . . it wasn't like that at all.'

'Do you think the press will care why she did it? The name of Bridget McGuire would be damned around the world of archaeology.'

'So you think we should . . . what?'

'Let the police deal with Damian. Meanwhile, we could try to find out who buys antiquities from him.'

'How come he's allowed to build on an archaeological site?'

'He isn't, it is forbidden, Irini, but if you know people, and you hand over enough cash, you can get a building licence, or an illegal building made legal, almost anywhere in Greece.' He scowled and stuck his jaw out, then his face softened. 'Don't think too badly of us. We live in a corrupt society, and sometimes it's the only way to get things done. Most of us would prefer it if everyone kept to the rules, but that is, how you say, the wishful thinking.'

\* \* \*

I used the hotel shampoo on my hair, in the shower. The bathroom door swung open, startling me.

'Your phone is ringing,' Angelo said, holding it out. I stepped onto the bathmat, answered the call, and recognised Paula's voice.

461

'Hi, Irini. Sorry this is short notice, but we need you in the London office tomorrow afternoon. Can you get yourself a flight? I'm up to my eyes here.'

'Yes, I guess so.'

'Good. Keep all your receipts and we'll organise an expense account when you get here. Let me know your arrival details and I'll get someone to pick you up at the airport.'

I glanced up to see Angelo leaning against the bathroom wall, his arms folded. He grinned, rolled his eyes, and then watched the shampoo suds slide down my body. I couldn't resist doing a little shoulder shimmy, but then winced with pain and almost dropped the phone.

'Irini! Are you there?!' Paula cried.

'Yes, sorry, I'm in the shower. I'll do my best to be there by noon.'

'Good, see you then. *Ciao.*'

I turned to Angelo, who was still grinning. 'That was Paula. I have to be in London tomorrow afternoon.'

'Then you must stay with me. I have an apartment in the city, above our office. Anyway, I want to go through the portfolio with you.' He started unbuttoning his white shirt.

I stepped back into the shower with a smile on my face. 'You mean *my* portfolio?'

He bit his lip, eyes narrowing as he slid his jeans zip down. I turned my back on him, anticipating his touch under the streaming water.

\* \* \*

Our flight from Crete to London was a journey of discovery. Angelo and I talked incessantly, exchanging parts of our lives, ambitions and dreams. Despite his family's wealth, I learned Angelo was a self-made man. We enthused about fabric, style, drape, cut, and buttons with the excitement of children in a sweetshop.

On the subject of our baby, there were long silences filled with joy and hand holding. Neither of us had experience of a baby in the family. Angelo had been twenty and living in London when his nephew, Michalis, was born. We gazed into each other's eyes, smiling as we imagined how it would be. I thought about my mother's notebooks, how thrilled she was to be pregnant, and how she loved me.

I wanted to share my joy with her so badly.

'You look a little sad . . . tell me,' Angelo said, breaking my thoughts.

I smiled, but inside I was weeping for my mother, all that I'd lost, and how it could have been. 'Oh, I was just thinking about Mam. I wish . . . you know?'

'Yes, I do know. I was six when my mother died.' He swallowed hard and stared out of the window for a moment. 'I'll tell you about it one day, but not now. They are always with us, Irini. I was so afraid I would forget her, I started drawing simple pictures of her and the things she did. But I never forgot. She is as real today as she was all those years ago. Only the pain has faded. At the moment, you feel as though it never will, don't you?'

I nodded.

'True love never dies,' he said simply. 'Anyway, those drawings led me to take up photography when I got older, and that's my other passion!'

I was so uplifted by his words, I wanted to kiss him right there in the plane. 'Would you be looking for a model, for your photography then?' I quipped.

'Ah, the fees are too expensive, but I have a cunning plan to marry one.' Then Angelo's grin fell and his questioning eyes met mine. 'While we're in London, I'd like to buy you a ring.'

Caught by surprise, I stared at him and, after a breathless moment, I chose my words carefully.

'Angelo . . . working for you has changed me. I'm no longer the person you got to know in Crete.'

His smile fell, replaced by a slightly worried look.

'I'm stronger now, more determined, self-confident, thanks to the modelling,' I said. 'So, *I* want to ask *you* something.'

He nodded, although his frown deepened. 'Anything.'

'Will you marry me, darling?' I said, already knowing the answer. His grin and the relief on his face made me laugh out loud. 'But will you wait until after our baby's born, because I *have* to get into my wedding dress.' It felt strange, old-fashioned, calling him darling, yet I couldn't find another loving word that fit so well, and from the smile in his eyes, I guessed he liked it. I was reminded of my father – he always called my mother 'darling girl' – and I found myself smiling too.

I thought of Dad all alone in the home and couldn't remember the last time I'd spoken to him. 'I must call my father the moment we land, darling.' He nodded. 'And I have to tell Paula I'm pregnant as soon as possible. I don't want her planning this advertising campaign thinking I'll be working for your company. I'm disappointed that I won't be the model she wants. It's been an amazing experience, but I have to face facts.'

'I'll speak to her.'

'Actually, I'd rather deal with it myself. It's very kind of you and all, but I don't want any favours, Angelo.'

\* \* \*

The following Monday morning, I sat in the boardroom of Retro Emporio.

'So you see, Paula, I thought it best if I told you as soon as I could. There's no problem to rip up the contract and take your money back.' I'd eaten every flavour of humble pie.

Paula, and James who was head of publicity, and their photographers Nick, Simone, and Andrew, exchanged stern glances.

'Would you leave the room for a moment, Irini?' Paula asked.

'Sure.' I left them to decide my fate and sat in the corridor, my mouth clamped shut and so dry I could hardly swallow. I placed my hands on my belly and thought about the baby inside. She would grow into my beautiful daughter. Yet how did I know I was having a girl? A broken dream, intuition, something in the back of my mind that I could not put my finger on . . .

I didn't want to lose my job. I loved it, and felt terrible about letting everyone down, especially after the Santorini shoot. However, there seemed no option.

The office door opened and Nick stuck his head out. 'Irini, come in, please.'

I approached my chair and held on to it while my heart sounded a drum roll. It had all been wonderful. The modelling had brought me to Angelo and I was having his baby. The job had made me good money for a short time, not that I'd had a chance to spend much, and now I would have to give it back. But my life had changed dramatically with the adventure. I had matured, experienced how different some people's lives are. I understood the pressure of Paula's job, the dedication of Simone, and the risk they had taken by employing me. I had lost my shyness, the cursed blush, and learned to be confident in my body.

'Sit down, Irini,' Paula said.

I took a breath to compose myself and then turned to my boss. 'Paula, may I say something before you sentence me?'

She nodded.

'I just want to thank everyone, especially Nick for teaching me so much on that first shoot, and also Simone for her incredible patience on the beach. I'm sorry for letting you all down.' That was enough. A lump in my throat told me perhaps I hadn't hardened as much as I'd thought.

The room was silent for a moment, everyone exchanged glances, then Paula spoke. 'We've considered everything, and have a few questions.'

'Anything. Anything at all.' I stared at the tabletop, not wanting to meet their eyes.

'Irini.' Paula pushed paper and pen over. 'We want to know the date you expect the baby, when you'll be unable to work, and any special requirements you might have.'

I looked up. Was I dreaming? 'I don't understand. You mean I'm not sacked?'

Paula rolled her eyes. 'The fact is, Irini, I told you we were bringing out *two* ranges for the mature woman of thirty to fifty. There is a huge gap in the market – nobody designs maternity wear for this group, even though the age of pregnant women has increased dramatically. This new breed of mothers-to-be, executives and businesswomen, want to look good and dress in high end fashion. We plan to ensure they can continue to do that while they're pregnant. We're actually delighted.'

Shocked, I stared around the table. Not only was I still a model with my money worries over, but also pregnant myself. Everyone was happy.

'We'll reschedule your work to fit the confinement,' Paula said. 'But if you'll sign a new contract, allowing us to follow

your pregnancy, you'll be highly rewarded for the extra publicity. How many people know?'

'My doctor of course, and Angelo. That's all.'

'Angelo . . . You told Angelo before you told me?!' Clearly
Paula was taken aback and annoyed.

'Well, yes, sorry, but you see, he's the father.'

Jaws dropped and there was a moment of stunned silence
before Paula resumed, businesslike as ever.

'Right, well . . . we must keep this out of the press for another
month while we prepare the campaign.'

'So, mum's the word?' I quipped.

'Exactly.' She reached out and took the pen from me. '
Actually, we could do this later. Be in my office in an hour.'
She stood. 'Come, I'll see you out. Oh, and congratulations,
by the way.'

* * *

The next Friday evening I was back in Dublin, loving the tranquillity of my little house. My father seemed to have found a new
lease of life in the home. I had taken all our photographs from
Istron on a memory stick, and he was busy analysing them and
writing a paper for the Archaeological Society. I spared him the
details of my accident, nor did I mention it was Angelo's brother
who had opened the illegal dig.

The fact that Damian may have been responsible for my
mother's death still twisted in my gut. After a lot of soul searching, I agreed with Angelo. If my father got to hear our suspicions,
it might well kill him too. Damian was locked up, awaiting trial
in Crete. He would be punished severely without the need to
discredit my parents' good name.

I was in the process of a good old spring clean when the phone rang.

'Hi, Irini,' Aaron said. 'How's the homeland treating you?'

'Hi. Life's good, Aaron. Lovely to hear from you.'

'Ah, you might not think so when you hear my news, but don't shoot the messenger, right?'

'Oh no! What's wrong?' A feeling of trepidation rose in my chest.

He sighed into the phone. 'We've been burgled. Your house was broken into, and also the site. Nothing seems to have been taken. Well, not at the site, anyway. They didn't even bother to open the till.'

'Bugger! Poor you. Is the house in a mess?'

'Yep, they really turned it over. The police seem to think they were searching for something. There was nothing of value to steal, so God knows what the bastards were looking for. You might want to come over. I've put a new lock on, but it's an absolute tip inside.'

I had just ended the call when Angelo phoned.

'Any news about the artefacts?' Angelo said, after asking me how we were, and me standing there with the phone in my hand, grinning like a lovesick eejit.

'Unfortunately, both the house and the archaeological site have been broken into. I have to go over as soon as I can. Aaron said they trashed the house, and I suspect they were searching for the necklace. Will you come with me? Can you spare the time?'

'I'll call Paula. We can go tomorrow morning, yes?'

'Great. I was a bit nervous about going on my own. Aaron's had a new lock fitted. They smashed the old one, so I need to call him and get the key.'

\* \* \*

468

The next afternoon, Aaron met us at the airport and drove us to the house.

'Sorry about the chaos, guys. I haven't had a chance to clean it up at all. Whoever did it, well, they seemed intent on searching every centimetre of the house.' He unlocked the door and stood back.

I stood in the doorway and stared at the mess. 'My God, look at the state of the place! Thanks, Aaron, I know you did your best. Great that you got a new lock fitted and called the police. Did they come up with anything?'

'No, except that they were sure it wasn't a local.' He lifted the tin table and two chairs out of the room and placed them in their usual spot on the patio. 'If you need anything else, let me know, okay?'

'Actually, I wanted to ask you something. I've been looking at your book. Why isn't there an area twenty-one at the site? I couldn't find one on the map.'

'Twenty-one?' He scratched his head, frowning for a moment. 'Ah, there is, but it's only a small store room.'

'Can we investigate this afternoon?'

'Sure. I'm back in town later so I'll pick you up. What's going on?'

'We're not sure, Aaron. I'm still trying to solve a puzzle, a clue my mother left, something to do with the number twenty-one. I'll explain everything this afternoon,' I said. 'First, we need to get this place cleaned up.'

\* \* \*

The house *was* a mess. Everything strewn about. But apart from the smashed door lock, nothing was damaged.

'How would the police know it wasn't somebody local?' I asked Angelo as we started picking up the debris.

'A local would have searched for the key of the door outside first. There aren't many places on the patio to look, but it seems they didn't bother.'

It hit me like a thump in the chest. 'That's it! Bingo! The bingo ticket! Twenty-one, the key of the door!'

Angelo stared blankly. 'I don't understand?'

I pressed my hand on my thudding heart. 'What was she telling me?' There was a bingo ticket in the Oxo tin with a red circle around twenty-one. There were two playing cards, an ace and a king – twenty-one. *Over twenty-one*, Mam wrote in red on the back of her shopping list.

I recalled my twenty-first birthday. Sausage rolls and crisps in the pub, my friends singing: '*She's twenty-one today! Twenty-one today! She's got the key of the door, never been twenty-one before.*' My mother was telling me . . . yes, that's it! *Over* the key of the door!'

Angelo glanced at the new lock.

'The spare key, Angelo! The key of the door, it was under the urn. Now I remember – there was soil on the patio when I first arrived at the house. Aaron thought it was cats. He stuck souvlaki sticks in the pot to keep them from using it as a toilet. My mother had arrived back from Crete in the evening. She must have known the danger she was in so long as the artefacts were in her possession, so she hid them and left me those clues, just in case.'

We stared at each other for a moment, then rushed outside.

The terracotta urn stood waist-high. We pulled out the sticks and the dried-up geranium, and then we tilted it over until the urn rested on its side.

470

Angelo slipped his posh shoes off and put them safely to one side, then got on his knees. 'Let's hope you are right, and also that there is not too much cat kaka in here.' He thrust his hands into the soil and scooped it out.

About one third of the way in, he stopped and got to his feet. 'Nothing yet. I just need to straighten my back for a moment.'

'Move over,' I cried impatiently, dropping to my knees. I delved into the urn. The soil was dry and warm. After a couple more scoops I felt something solid. 'I have it!' Holding my breath, I eased the object out, but it was only a rock and I tossed it aside.

'They put stones in the bottom to make the pot stable, and for the drainage,' Angelo said.

The artefacts had to be in the pot. I plunged in again, scooping out more dirt and stones, and then my fingers touched plastic. I got a grip and retrieved a sizable lunch box.

'This has to be it!' Suddenly afraid, I glanced around. My mother had been killed for this, now I was sure of it. We were in danger.

'Angelo! Oh hell, do you think we're being watched?' I whispered. 'I've got a strong feeling . . .' A horrible thought struck me. 'And they knew the house was empty, that's why they broke in. So whoever it was must have been watching the place . . . I'm afraid.'

Angelo dropped to his knees beside me so our heads were together. 'I'll call the police and explain. You call Aaron, and Spiro, and tell them to come. Say it's urgent, an emergency, to get here right away. The more people on the patio, the better.'

We both pulled our phones out and, still bending over the pot, we surreptitiously made our calls.

'Push it back in,' Angelo said. 'Let's pretend there's nothing here.'

I did, then we pushed soil back in too and stood the urn up.

'Come here,' Angelo said, taking me into his arms.

I peered over his shoulder. 'There's a guy with a camera hanging over the wall on the street above,' I whispered. 'And a couple sitting on the roof to our left.'

'Kiss me,' he said, turning me so that he could look around. 'The ones on the roof seem to be watching us.'

'You've got soil in your beard.' I brushed it away and kissed him, but my heart wasn't in it. 'I'm scared, Angelo.'

'Me too.'

'I wish someone would come.'

'Iris! Iris! What's the problem?'

'Oh gawd! It's Spiro. Look, the people on the roof are standing.'

'Spiro's better than nobody,' Angelo said. He spoke to Spiro in Greek, then turned to me. 'The guy with the camera is coming down the steps. If there's trouble, lock yourself in the house and call the police again.'

I looked up and saw Aaron racing past the stranger, who stopped.

'Irini, are you all right? What's happening?'

Much to his surprise, I flung my arms around his neck and whispered in his ear: 'I think we've found the dragonfly necklace, but we're being watched.'

'Holy God! The actual dragonfly necklace? The one Bridget wrote about in the magazine?'

'Yes. Act normal. We don't know if they're armed. We've called the police, but we didn't want to wait for them on our own,' I said.

'Listen,' Angelo said. 'If they come onto the patio, grab them, take them by surprise. It's them or us.'

The guy with the camera came down a couple of steps and stopped to take photos of the caldera, although I felt sure we were in the pictures too. Then I heard a siren in the street above. The cameraman seemed to hesitate. A moment later, two policemen hurried down the steps. They caught up with the cameraman and a great deal of shouting and arm-waving went on. The two policemen followed the man onto the patio and, at the same time, the couple that were on the roof appeared on the patio too.

Before anyone had a chance to speak, Angelo cried, 'Now!' and grabbed the cameraman by surprise, twisting his arm up behind his back.

Aaron threw himself at the other man, who fell to the floor and was quickly pinned down by the sixteen-stone archaeologist. Spiro grabbed the woman around the waist and hung on with his life, despite her yelling and walloping him viciously around the head. Everyone was shouting and struggling, while the two policemen tried to intervene.

Then, in the midst of the chaos, a gun went off and everyone froze.

'Stop!' one of the police officers cried, lowering the pistol he had just fired into the air. He applied the safety lock and holstered his weapon. 'Now, everyone, calm down!' He turned to Aaron. 'Let him up – he's with us.' Then he turned to Angelo. 'You too. Let him go.'

'What about me?' Spiro gasped, struggling to keep a hold of the woman.

The policemen seemed to hesitate, exchanged a glance, then one said, 'Yes, let her go, she works for the police as well.'

Clearly not used to such vigorous activity, Spiro almost fell to the ground once he had released the woman. He staggered to the wall and sat, swiping the sweat from his face. I had backed into the corner under the bougainvillea, but now that I realised we had misjudged the situation, I ventured out. The gunshot had attracted a small crowd that gathered in the street, and even the jeweller had come out to see what was happening.

'Now, let's all calm down and find out what's going on here. Who called the police?' the taller of the two policemen said.

Angelo lifted a finger. 'We realised we were being watched and felt threatened.'

The cameraman spoke in Greek and then turned to me. 'You are Irini McGuire, yes?'

'Yes, my mother—'

'We know all about your mother. That's why we're watching the house.'

'Right . . .' The truth of the situation dawned on me. 'I guess we've messed that up. Sorry, but we think we've found the artefacts that the thieves were after. I think it's these same thieves that may have been involved in my mother's death. We were afraid . . .'

The policemen exchanged a glance again, before the shorter one said, 'Where are they, these artefacts?'

I hesitated. 'I have to play it safe. I can't tell you unless someone is here from the archaeological museum.'

'Madam, there are nine people here – one is an archaeologist and five are with the police. We are all on the same side. What's your problem?'

'It's what my mother would have wanted. I suspect that protecting these things cost Bridget McGuire her life.'

The two policemen swapped a few words with the plain-clothed officers and seemed to come to an agreement. Then one spoke to Spiro. 'Go and get the director of the museum right away. Tell her it's urgent.'

474

Angelo put his arm around my shoulders while we waited. I felt sick. What if we were wrong and there was nothing of value in the Tupperware? We should have checked.

Ten minutes passed before a suited woman accompanied Spiro onto the patio. I trembled with tension, and a certain amount of fear too. The crowd of tourists grew, phones raised; we were tomorrow's Facebook fodder.

Angelo made a quick explanation to the director, then introduced me. She reached out and shook my hand. 'Your mother was a marvellous woman, greatly admired for her work. We owe her a lot.'

Angelo asked the cameraman if he would video what was about to happen. He agreed. The tourists also had their phones raised.

'Come on then,' Angelo said to me. 'Let's see if we're right.'

'Wait! I have to Skype Dad. He has to see this.'

'I'll do it,' Aaron said, and for once, my father answered straight away. 'An important moment for you, Tommy. We think Bridget got the necklace back. We're just going to find out, but Irini wants to share the event with you.' He held the phone up.

We tipped the urn onto its side and I pulled out the sandwich box. I could hardly breathe. Nobody spoke as we placed it on the tin table.

'Go on then, do it for your mother,' Angelo said.

*Oh!*

'Are you ready, Dad?' I said to the phone. Everything welled up inside me as I eased the lid off.

There was a pale pink scarf of soft wool inside. I carefully unfolded it and gasped as the small sandy-coloured jug, decorated with swallows and lilies, came into view. I put my hands over my mouth and struggled to stay in control. Then I handed the jug to the director.

'If I am not mistaken, you'll find that my mother hid some information in the repair work.'

I folded back another layer of fabric and there it was, the dragonfly necklace.

I slid the box from underneath the scarf, so the necklace lay flat on the table. The cameraman moved in. I stared at the delicate, filigree insects, four thousand years old, worn by Queen Thira, supreme ruler of this island. Whether it was Atlantis or not no longer mattered. This was the sacred jewellery of the Goddess of the Marches, as seen in the famous frescoes of Santorini. A fact that could not be disputed.

Thira had given it to her daughter, and my mother had passed it on to me.

The necklace had saved my father's life, but cost my mother hers. It had separated my parents, and brought them together again; and inadvertently, it had brought Angelo to me.

'Thank you, Mam,' I whispered as tears filled my eyes.

# CHAPTER 43
## BRIDGET

*Present day.*

I HAVE LEFT BEHIND nothing but the fingerprint of who I was and what I did, and my undying love in the hearts of my husband and daughter. Has my existence changed their lives, or anyone else's, for the better? I don't know. I hope so. Only time will tell.

In this spiritual world, I have glimpses into the future. I don't see everything, but my greatest questions are answered. I know that Tommy will have another heart attack and join me in this afterlife, but not before ten years have passed. First, he will hold his granddaughter, and I feel his intense pleasure from that experience. He has always shared his love with me, and for that I am honoured. His happiness is also mine.

Irini was destined to find the dragonfly necklace, but will she marry Angelo? I feel I should know, yet that revelation is kept from me. I watch and wait and hope. Thira discloses nothing in this ethereal suspension that is not like earthly time. There are moments when we are one, Thira and I, and Oia is with us too, a melding of spirits. And my darling mother, and dear Uncle Peter, and Pa – all of us together in one essence, like water in a slow-running river.

I have no explanation for these things except that these are the spirits of people who filled my heart on earth, and I am shown snippets of the future, glimpses of things that are important to me. I understand that Nathan Scott, the young student archaeologist, will go on to discover great things. He will remember me and, for some strange reason, try a little harder because he met me that day on the plane. Nathan will also decipher the terracotta pot that I found impossible. The same terracotta pot that caught Oia's lifeblood before it was poured over the altar of Poseidon; the pot that cut the umbilical cord between Irini and I.

Many years will pass before the truth about Atlantis comes to light, and knowing this, we all smile to ourselves. I wonder if Plato is here in this spiritual domain, and Solon, and all those who kept the mystical story alive in the minds of men for thousands of years. With that idea, I wonder if Mary and her son Jesus are here, and Moses and Eve, Allah, Buddha, and Shiva. They are just names given by humans. In the spirit world, I am surrounded by goodness, and love, and nothing else matters.

Mortals die, that is the inevitability of things, but their love is eternal. While I am above and beyond physical feeling, I sense the truth of this fact all around me. After death, all that remains from each of us is a spiritual embodiment of all the love we have given and received.

# EPILOGUE
## BRIDGET

*Santorini, present day.*

MY GRANDDAUGHTER, ANGELINA BRIDGET, came into the world just before midnight on Easter Saturday. Like me, Irini went into rapid labour and gave birth to her daughter in the *hyposkafa* with Angelo at her side, and Tommy and Quinlan waiting nervously on the patio.

Hundreds of church bells rang out to welcome Easter. The midwife arrived when it was all over, and after checking baby Angelina, and Irini, she announced both were fine. As the midwife left, Greek people filled the streets, their faces glowing from the flickering light of their holy candles. They walked back from the cathedral, carefully guarding the flame that would bring peace, love, and prosperity into their family homes.

'She's so perfect,' Irini whispered, holding her baby. 'I wish Mam could see her.'

Angelo nodded, took his baby daughter into the warm night air, and lifted her towards the star-spangled sky.

'Your granddaughter, Bridget McGuire!' he called out, just as a shooting star fired an arc across the heavens.

If you enjoyed *Secrets of Santorini*,
you'll love Patricia Wilson's
other novels . . .

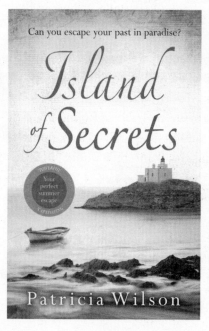

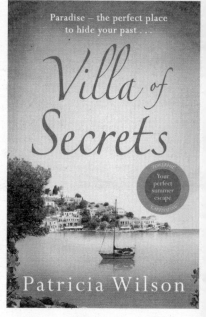

# ACKNOWLEDGMENTS

THANKS TO MY EDITORS, Sarah Bauer, Joanne Gledhill and Katie Lumsden. Also, thanks to the entire team headed by Kate Parkin at Bonnier, particularly Margaret Stead and Eli Dryden for their tireless support. Also thanks to Natalie Braine and Laura Palomares, and to my amazing agent, Tina Betts.

Many people helped me to write *Secrets of Santorini*, and I would particularly like to thank: Patricia Mustafa Kelmet, who inspired me to write about the love that is left behind. Also, Helen Rendell, Diana Urrego, Shosh Mutal, Joan Lee and Barbara Stroud, for their tireless help and support. Christos Gastouniotis at DataSync for rescuing me from various laptop emergencies. Mal Wright, accountant extraordinaire. Andrew Dawson for his great legal advice. Caroline Ashford at IAS Medical. Dublin author Eamon O'Leary, and historian George Cafcakis. Dr Barbara J. Hayden, archaeologist at Istron, Crete, Dr Nanno Marinatos for her remarkable book, *Art and Religion in Thera*, a must if you visit the Santorini archaeological site of Akrotiri.

I must stress that, although a dragonfly necklace is depicted in the fresco of the queen-goddess of Akrotiri, this novel is a story of pure fiction.

# THE STORY BEHIND THE STORY

*SECRETS OF SANTORINI* began thirty years ago when I started planning for early retirement. In 1989 cheap last-minute flights were listed on TV. So, one cold February morning when a return ticket to Rhodes came up for £20, I leapt at the chance. Shortly after, I was flying at 35,000 feet somewhere over Europe when the pilot announced that due to high winds in Rhodes, we would have to land in Crete. I instantly fell in love with the place.

The following year I signed on the dotted line to become the proud owner of a lovely little stone house with nineteen olive trees in the garden. The property was close to the beach at Istron, near Agios Nikolaos. The olive harvest had finished and there was I with loaded trees, only a few days before my return to the UK. I had no knowledge of what to do. An elderly neighbour called, bearing a welcoming plate of hot cheese pies that would have easily fed a family of six. With much arm waving, she told me to pick the olives or I would have trouble with the trees next year. Her family and friends arrived, all eager to help.

Two days later, George, the taxi driver, took us to the last open olive mill in the area. With no regard for siesta time, he banged on the door of a local priest and asked him to deal with our crop. The priest unlocked his mill, started the olive press, then fed us raki, olives, and fresh bread while we waited. Word spread and the villagers woke from siesta and filled the little factory. Some brought dishes of Cretan food. A young man turned up with a lyra and played fast music. Elderly women skipped in a circle. We were grinned at, and patted on our aching shoulders. When we emerged into a star-spangled night, I knew I would always remember those big-hearted people from the village of Prina.

With only one day left before leaving for England, my husband and I hurriedly gathered fallen twigs and leaves to burn before they attracted the infamous olive fly. My new rake caught a broken piece of pottery. Mysterious symbols surrounded the inside of the terracotta dish. I wanted to investigate, but with packing to do, I brushed away the loose soil and left it in the house until my return. From a pencil rubbing of the markings, I learned a little about the pottery from an American archaeologist who was excavating at Istron. Eventually, I fashioned a copy of the base from cold-clay and handed the original to the Museum. My curiosity and interest in archaeology was aroused. Back home, I came across a stack of ancient history books about Greece. I bought the books, and with the pottery still on my mind, read them many times. The facts ignited my imagination. I *had* to visit Santorini, and when I did, the bare bones of this novel took shape.